NOTES FROM THE SUPERHORSE STABLE

Nigel Jarrett

Published by Saron Publishers in 2022

ISBN-13: paperback: 978-1-913297-30-5
e-book: 978-1-913297-31-2

Cover design by Matt Jarrett

Saron Publishers
Pwllmeyrick House
Mamhilad
Mon
NP4 8RG

saronpublishers.co.uk
info@saronpublishers.co.uk
Follow us on Facebook and Twitter

For Tommy, Polly, Bradley and Hugo

Also by Nigel Jarrett

Funderland
Slowly Burning
Miners at the Quarry Pool
The Day's Portion
Who Killed Emil Kreisler?
A Gloucester Trilogy

Consider the cattle, grazing as they pass you by. They do not know what is meant by yesterday or today; they leap about, eat, rest, digest, leap about again, and so from morn till night and from day to day are fettered to the moment and its pleasure or displeasure, and thus are neither melancholy nor bored.

Nietzsche, *Untimely Meditations*

I expect you've seen the footage: elephants
finding the bones of one of their own kind
dropped by the wayside, picked clean by scavengers
and the sun, then untidily left there,
decide to do something about it.

Christopher Reid, from *A Scattering*

While I am confessing debts, let me mention John Napier, who created the tough, bright masks of horsedom; Andy Phillips, who lit them superbly; and, above all, Claude Chagrin, who animated them: she created, with the help of six human actors, a stable of Superhorses to stalk through the mind.

Peter Shaffer, on the first performances of his play *Equus*

On the bounce: A camera set up by Dora Nightingale captured nocturnal trampolining by one of two fox cubs that pay regular visits to her garden in Worthing, West Sussex.
The Guardian, Saturday 11 May 2019

Oakwood Lodge

Forest of Dean

Gloucestershire

On Digression

Look upon it as a walk. We don't ramble head down without taking in the view. It's always there, unchanging, and not part of our relentless forward motion ...
Luigi Amedeo, Duke of Abruzzi – first to climb Mount St Elias in the Rwenzori Mountains

'But I digress...'

How often do we hear speakers say that as an apology for not having stuck to the point? The path from which they stray may be so obstacle-strewn that their detours have little need of excuse. In other cases and to make their speeches or lectures compelling, they may require examples, themselves of necessity calling a temporary halt to the procession of facts and arguments. Then again, the story they are telling - and it could well be a story, a fiction - may rely on incident and anecdote as elements in its construction which do not and cannot be called up chronologically.

An example is provided by the animal behaviourist Dr Konrad Lorenz, who ended his career giving talks that consisted almost entirely of recollections brought forth in no particular order but illustrative of a kaleidoscopic life of observation and experiment. So much of our time is undirected. One supposes that Dr Lorenz first steered his interest in zoology towards co-operative instincts among higher vertebrates, then simply applied it to one group of them or another. There's a story, no doubt apocryphal, that in his dotage he began work on evidence of hierarchies in single-cell organisms - creations of social order under the microscope - and that his findings had been suppressed by colleagues wishing to preserve a hitherto distinguished contribution to knowledge. In short, the esteemed doctor had grown batty. There had been talk of his rashly substituting the microscope for binoculars. But there must have been episodes in his life which he could have related in successive stages - A leading to B leading to C etc - until it concluded. But his career as a whole, apart from, say, his moral development, or his growing professional reputation, or a worthy and extended campaign to bring about some universally desired result, must have seemed in its later stages to have been formed from happenings remembered in no logical manner. Having discovered how geese act in consort, he turns his attention to sparrows and the way they form teams to exploit food sources at the feet of tourists in East Africa. He notes how they see off larger competitors while feigning (his word) a native timidity. Asked to give an account of himself, Konrad Lorenz would have been just like the rest of us in expecting his auditors to take on trust a lot of what he said; but being a scientist, he would no doubt happily have adduced evidence and testimony in support.

The story embedded in the lengthy jottings I make here could be summarised thus: a chance, albeit willed, discovery; a shock; a sinister entanglement; a ...well, I don't wish to give too much away at this point; suffice to say that as well as delineating the main path, I want to take in the surrounding landscape, not as something for the reader to enjoy while resting (I follow a reasonably short and direct route) but as essential information and context and if only to offer proof of what might be considered debatable. Of course, landscape can always be made appealing: the view of the serpentine River Wye from Symonds Yat Rock near here, for instance, the serpent well into a relaxed slither and its course through the greenery almost, but not quite, straight.

I haven't mentioned Dr Lorenz at random. A year ago, a member of staff here suggested it might be a good idea for visitors to donate books for the use of residents. Although it's usually a mixed bag - Rick Stein fish recipes, an introduction to Egyptology and the ancient pyramids (which my partner Julie borrowed before I could read it), the autobiography of David Essex - we now and then find something unusual such as Burton's *The Anatomy of Melancholy*. I snaffled that in the hope of making some personal use of it. But I should have known it would be more dense and wide-ranging, less focused, than I might have expected. The next one I liberated from the dross was *Man Meets Dog* by Lorenz. It was a 1949 first edition with a dedication in violet ink dated 1950: 'To Kathleen on your 21st birthday. From Uncle Ken and Aunty Joyce.' Maybe Kathleen had just graduated in Natural Sciences and her uncle and aunt, having missed out on a university education, were demonstrating their inspired sympathy as well as their delight. It was an interesting volume though I later sold it on eBay for £40 (it would have been far more if Ken or Joyce hadn't defaced it). My action was a clear abuse of the donation scheme. I sometimes think the punishment is to have Lorenz and the animal kingdom follow me about till the end of my time, like a flock of his honking geese. (Early on, and soon to be related, I had an intimate encounter with a horse, or a simulacrum of one.)

Now I re-read these notes, but curiously not while I was writing them, it seems that a touring menagerie had begun accompanying me, one or other of its occupants decamping now and then to distract my attention as though wanting a part in any which way that events led me; the least I can do is acknowledge them, if only to give them a significance that they, being sensate but unable to reflect, could not possibly have sought. Maybe not denying them entry is part atonement for removing from the rows of garbage on our shelves such books as might edify our residents in their dimming twilights.

But I, too, digress.

Not everything in the stories we tell about ourselves falls neatly in place. Dead people we refer to cannot speak - in any case, the dead 'couldn't care less', as Julie used to say, and even the living must remain victims of the impracticality of offering them a platform at every turn. There's also the possibility the teller of the tale, despite pulling in extraneous testimony and descriptions of the 'landscape' from every quarter, is in fact constructing an ornate veil to be drawn at the end across the truth. The reader abides; the storyteller decides. That's how it is.

Anyway, this is not so much a story - though there's a story in it - more a rattle-bag of scribbles on my PC as and when I could remember anything. Some recollections might be out of harmony; it often happens when the main whoosh of your memories flood-floats on a time frame. There may even be inconsistencies and repetition. It's a bit like an old-fashioned notebook: written for something to do or as an inexplicable matter of urgency, corrected and chaotic, and now and then abandoned. ('Flood-floats' is an expression I stole from Julie.) Make of it what you will. There'll be more questions than there are answers to them and episodes more important to me (well, I am the author) than to the reader. There'll be much seeing through a glass darkly and no knowledge of, let alone wish for, the end of time. Not for me, at least. By then, it'll be too late, if it isn't already. Oh – and there'll be a fair amount of walking, and brewing of tea.

Duckface, Brexit, Showing and Telling

I don’t know what to call these opening remarks. 'Author's Notes' is too stuffy, 'Introduction' too dull. So I'll leave them to stand beneath a couple of expressions taken at random from new words which have slipped into the Oxford English Dictionary: 'silent killers', my come-and-go partner Julie called them. I'm telling you that. So here I am showing it: 'I hate these commonplace neologisms,' she once said. 'It's death to the language. They creep up behind and infect it.' (Not a lot of difference.) I didn't agree with her. We disagreed all the time, as I hope to show as well as tell. Nothing wrong with telling, she would have said: it's what she did.

As with many other new words, we know what a blog is but find it difficult to come up with a definition. Jottings, diary, random thoughts, observations, recollections: it's all of those; except that a blog shines its own light into the face of the blogger as though it were celebrating some kind of Eureka! moment, when in fact the words and sentences are often as ordinary as those written with pen on paper. It's narcissism, the bloggers' image reflected back at them in words.

The OED regularly allows expressions like 'blog' and 'duckface' into the fold. There follow sniffy newspaper articles and letters from readers complaining about how the language is being debased. I wasn't absolutely sure what 'neologism' meant before Julie told me. Then 'blog' was rounded up and trooped in to be immortalised with 'iPad', 'Skype', and 'snafu'. According to the OED, then, a blog is 'a regularly updated website or web page, typically one run by an individual or small group, that is written in an informal or conversational style'.

I think it's more than that: a blog is written for others to read, unlike a diary entry which is private, at least while the diarists are alive; and often in a strange way *after* they've died.

Julie being Julie, a blog was all and none of these, sometimes ultra-private, sometimes meandering, sometimes unintelligible with James Joyce-like disdain for punctuation (in normal circumstances we might have discussed that). The heart was hidden away and protected or, at other times, worn on the sleeve. It was also for her eyes only and was thus a digital notebook, an on-screen journal, which she just happened to call a blog. She blogged properly on her website but that was something different, rational thoughts on books, authors and publishing. But her private 'blog', her diary, was often scatty. (I wonder if 'scatty' is in the OED.) I was shocked to find, for example, that she confided to her blog the detailed intimacies we shared in the early days of our relationship. I've put an example of that in. Other, less intimate familiarities were to be found there too; I like to think that these were missives-to-self which in pre-computer days would have been sent as love letters. Love has been one of hi-tech's casualties.

Then there were the entries in which she seethed about this and that. It's a wonder she wasn't an activist of some sort. I can just see her with a balaclava over her head and a pair of wire-cutters, approaching via torchlight a fenced-off vivisection facility (she would have hated 'facility'), where monkeys sit apprehensively in cages after hours, wondering what that continuous background buzz is, what that off-and-on red light is in the top right hand corner of the room; and awaiting dawn at a high window and, unknown to them, probably the oncoming electrode and scalpel. But one of my reasons for including some of her private blog posts arises from doubts I have about the direction of her anger; indeed, whether it had any direction at all. I think it might have arisen within her, unbidden and wayward, only the sight of a passing 'cause' releasing it, again without prompting. I think that was the case when . . . well, you'll see what I mean.

There are all sorts on her laptop. I took it - stole it - before she had a chance not to bequeath it to me which I think she might have. But who knows? No one objected. Now I search her Documents in order to reproduce something she'd written which will help give her some solidity; for as sure as eggs, anything I say about her will be challenged or repudiated by friends who are probably no more capable of doing her justice than I am: I imagine a series of testimonies, all biased, all giving one side of Julie's story and even when lumped together, scarcely adding up to anything rounded. Even my choice of her blogs will be construed as prejudiced. But it's not. Take my word for it. It's the best I can do.

And there'll be other inclusions, each intended to say something or add something to what I have to relate. Such as what follows in a few paragraphs: a piece in memory of Mr Robert Berridge, an Aussie domiciled in the UK, a former bookie and for a short time one of our residents here. Only later did I realise it was from an online encyclopaedia and that Bob had written the entry himself or so he claimed. Unlike most of the others here, he possessed a laptop and a tablet and had stories to tell (though his mobile phone was one of the early foldover sort); or rather, he was willing to tell them. What he didn't know about the geegees wasn't worth knowing. His notes on a sporting mystery might be thought to stall my tale before it's begun, but I include it at this point because he's the latest person to leave us and he is clear in my memory, therefore still so present as to be almost alive. I think, from what he told me at various times, that his love of racehorses as majestic creatures in themselves overshadowed his interest in them as bloodstock and sources of cash. His occupation had depended on them but his real interest came from somewhere else, some centre capable of inspiring awe. It's always best to look at people like that, divorced from the titles and predicates that nominally define them. He once told me that, as a child, he'd been taken to see an albino carthorse, a stallion, 'all pink and white'. Lifted by the armpits to the top of the stable door, he'd come upon an impossible scene, like a ship in a bottle, as the horse stood statue-like at an angle and seemed to make its confined space glow, its head almost brushing the ceiling, one back leg cocked and pale eyelashes flickering. 'And the smell, the horse stench, was overpowering,' he said, adding something about 'the dangler in its case, soft as a chammy' and primed like the barrel of a cannon. Anyway, and least of all Robert Berridge, we are not each one of us inspired every waking moment to commit something to print in the hope of having it published for posterity. If I headline his piece with a word he might not have approved of, it's only because I'm being cynical and realistic where he never wished to believe the worst. And we are not all like Julie, a writer of novels who'd just begun to develop a minor reputation before disaster struck, as she would never have described it.

She and I were close in another way, though. She was a writer; I'm an actor. We met while I was playing the lead horse in Peter Shaffer's play *Equus*. So what am I doing fetching and carrying and lifting and playing the fool in a remote Gloucestershire nursing home?

Well, first let's give Mr Robert Berridge his six hundred words of fame, not that they haven't already been read by ten million surfers - and I don't mean the seaside crowd riding the waves. I read it because Bob had written it; and every writer needs a reader.

(My personal disaster arrived via the jaws of a pig, which is why I'm here, doing things mostly non-theatrical. Explanations in a bit.)

Horsemeat

Shergar's first run as a two-year-old was a win in a field of 23 by just over two lengths in the Kris Plate and he set a course record at Newbury. In his only other run - the William Hill Futurity Stakes (now the Racing Post Trophy) at Doncaster, won by Beldale Flutter - he was second, losing by the same two-and-a-half-length margin by which he had won his first race.

His three-year-old debut race was the Guardian Classic Trial at Sandown Park in 1981. Racing correspondent Richard Baerlein, after watching the colt win by ten lengths, famously advised race-goers that 'at 8-1, Shergar for the Derby, now is the time to bet like men'.

After winning the Chester Vase by 12 lengths, Shergar started odds-on favourite at Epsom, ridden by 19-year-old jockey Walter Swinburn, also entering his first Derby. Swinburn recalled that early in the race, Shergar 'found his own pace and lobbed along as the leaders went off at a million miles an hour, with me just putting my hands down on his withers and letting him travel at his own speed'. Shergar pulled to the front early and went further clear, so far that John Matthias on runner-up Glint Of Gold thought he had won: 'I told myself I'd achieved my life's ambition. Only then did I discover there was another horse on the horizon.'

Shergar's next race was in the Irish Derby, ridden by Lester Piggott. The apparent ease with which Shergar passed the rest of the runners, winning by four lengths, caused TV commentator Peter O'Sullevan to exclaim: 'He's only in an exercise canter!' The horse became a national hero in Ireland.

Seeking to exploit Shergar's value at its peak, the Aga Khan sold 34 shares in the horse for £250,000 each, keeping six for himself, producing a valuation of £10 million, then a record for a stallion standing at stud in Europe. Among the buyers were bloodstock millionaire John Magnier and Shergar's vet Stan Cosgrove.

Shergar also won the King George VI and Queen Elizabeth Stakes at Ascot by four lengths. After that came his only failure as a three-year-old when the colt apparently failed to stay the extended fourteen furlongs and finished fourth in the St Leger Stakes at Doncaster. Swinburn was sending out distress signals with two furlongs to go and Shergar finished behind Cut Above, a horse he'd beaten in the Irish Derby. Lester Piggott's view was that 'he must have been over the top by then' but, whatever the explanation, Shergar's racing career was over. He had six wins for £436,000 in prize money.

Shergar produced 35 foals from his single season at stud, the best turning out to be the 1986 Irish St Leger winner Authaal. The syndicate was able to charge a stud fee of £50,000-£80,000 for Shergar and if his offspring did well on the track, that fee would have doubled. But, despite the thoroughbred's value, the Ballymany Stud was poorly protected and a criminal gang intent on stealing him had little difficulty in gaining access. The theft was the first of its kind in Ireland.

In February 1983, one week before the start of Shergar's second season at stud - with up to 55 mares - a horse trailer arrived at the stud buildings at 8:30pm. Inside his house, Shergar's groom James Fitzgerald thought he heard a car in the yard. He listened, heard nothing more and forgot about it. At 8:40pm, there was a knock at the door. Fitzgerald's son Bernard answered it. The caller was dressed in a Garda (police) uniform with a balaclava. He asked for James Fitzgerald and knocked Bernard to the floor as he turned away. James Fitzgerald came out of the sitting room to see his son lying prostrate. Three men pushed their way into the house and held the family at gunpoint in the kitchen. According to Fitzgerald, the thieves were exceptionally calm and well organised and referred to each other as 'Cresswell'.

The intruders signalled for him to put his coat on and two of them took him outside. Fitzgerald was taken to the stud buildings and led the thieves to Shergar's stall. Fitzgerald was forced to help the thieves load Shergar into a double horse box which had been drawn up to the stall. Fitzgerald said the gang numbered at least six men. Shergar was then towed away and Fitzgerald was forced into another vehicle and driven around for some three hours before being thrown out of the car seven miles from the stud, having been given a password the thieves would use in negotiations.

The subsequent investigation of the kidnapping has been called 'a caricature of police bungling'. The immediate investigation was hampered by a piece of planning by the gang which had selected the same day as the biggest horse sales in the country when horseboxes had passed along every road in Ireland. Leading the investigation into the theft was trilby-wearing Chief Superintendent Jim 'Spud' Murphy, who was the subject of much media coverage. His detection techniques were unconventional and a variety of clairvoyants, psychics and diviners were called in to help. During one interview, Mr Murphy told reporters: 'A clue: that is what we haven't got.'

While the police searched farms in the Republic of Ireland, the gang members set about seeking a ransom. Initially they requested negotiations with three racing journalists: John Oaksey and Derek Thompson, both working for ITV, and Peter Campling, working for *The Sun* newspaper. The day after the theft, Thompson took a call at 1:15am from someone claiming to be one of the thieves. He was dispatched to negotiate in the full glare of the media circus that descended on Ireland. He managed to get the press off his tracks and spent his time in the house of a racehorse trainer called Jeremy Maxwell, taking various calls from the criminals. All he got were demands for a payment of £40,000. On Thursday morning, he received a call telling him that the horse 'had an accident' and was dead.

Away from the TV cameras, the real thieves had got in touch with the Aga Khan's Paris office, not realising that he only had a minority share in the horse's ownership. On discovering that Shergar had multiple owners, the gang agreed to provide evidence that he was still alive. Cosgrove, Shergar's vet, was deputised to collect the evidence which was to be left at a hotel reception. However, a conspicuous Special Branch presence warned off the gang.

The criminals made a further call threatening to kill Shergar and the Aga Khan's negotiators. Eventually, however, a photograph of the horse's face next to a newspaper was sent to the police but the owners were still not satisfied. The gang never realised that the syndicate had no intention of paying because they wanted to deter future thefts.

Four days after the abduction, the thieves made their last call. The syndicate issued a statement blaming the Provisional IRA for the crime.

The thieves have yet to be brought to justice. Several theories as to their identity and motives have been put forward. But the fate of Shergar is still not known, though most in the racing fraternity believe he no longer lives.

*

Well, I expect Shergar's dead by now, whatever the cause. Julie would probably have thought that Bob's encyclopaedia piece had been edited or even re-written and that he'd never have used an expression like 'media circus'.

But let's go back a while, to something I kept on my mobile answerphone and transcribed for these notes.

Julie and Francis

J: It's not working out, is it?
F: What do you mean?
J: Us, of course. You've no commitment, Francis. It's not as though your bloody career is going anywhere.
F: Yours is, I suppose. Well, I know it is. Every time I ring, your mobile's off. You know what they say about writers? They're loners.
J: We have to be loners.
F: Yeah. But not every fucking minute of the day.
J: That's unfair. And don't use that sort of language with me.
F: OK then. Every other frigging minute.
J: You're being stupid.
F: Am I?
J: I consciously devote time to you, Francis. But I think you have a problem with women. That's why every time we go out somewhere, your male friends are never far away. They're like a supporting cast. Mostly of the 'rude mechanical' type.
F: That's not my fault. I don't arrange it. So precisely what is this problem I have?
J: I don't know. It's just that your mind doesn't want to engage. It hovers. Maybe it's me. Maybe I'm not the right kind of woman for you. Who's that actress you were seeing? Mona something?
F: Actor. What about her? You know who she is.
J: Moaning Mona. Maybe she's more your type.

F: Mona Strange is the past.

J: (*Sniggers*). Mona Strange. Excuse me while I stifle a titter. You seem very sure of that. It wouldn't surprise me if she made another appearance. What did you say about her? That she was selfie-obsessed? That was quite good.

F: It was a joke. She takes - took - a lot of selfies. They bored me in the end.

J: And, if I remember, some dubious stuff as well, of a politically incorrect nature.

F: Like I said, Mona's a memory.

J: It sounds like the title of a song.

F: What do you want from me, Julie? As if I didn't know.

J: And what's that supposed to mean?

F: It's this 'warmth' thing again, isn't it?

J: Well, the warmest I've seen you, Francis, is the first time we met when you were playing that horse in *Equus*.

F: That was graft, sweat. I was working hard, giving everything in a cause.

J: Oh, yes. The art of theatre. But that's interesting. Because you've never done that for us.

F: It turned you on, though - me sweating in white Lycra. That's what you said.

J: We were abed. People say anything in extremity.

F: Lovers, you mean.

J: No, I don't mean. It's never come to that. Love is not love which alters when it alteration finds. Men - a quick shag and we're yours.

F: Don't use that language with me. Are you quoting?

J: Shakespeare. As an actor I'd have thought you'd know the Bard by heart. But then, you're not exactly rolling in roles.

F: Do you know something? I hate that I have to do all the running.

J: What?

F: You know what. Like cloven-hoofed brutes of the field. She submits, he makes the beast with two backs. Why don't you do the bestial thing, for a change? I'm not always up for it.
J: Jesus!
F: Look, I don't know what I want from this relationship.
J: Well, you should by now.
F: I don't know what you want either because, quite frankly, I can't make you out. You seem to inhabit your own province. I don't intend to be downstairs ironing while you are upstairs writing.
J: I love the way actors describe themselves as 'resting'. Unemployed, not wanted on stage, is what they mean. You seem to spend a lot of time between productions. The part of a horse with no lines to speak. Or should that be 'whinny'? And what's this latest thing about your family tree? More time spent not looking for a job.
F: Don't be ridiculous.
J: What have you found out? Nothing.
F: Well, that's where you're wrong.
J: Do tell.
F: I've re-discovered a distant relative; on the South Coast.
J: Is he grateful for your intercession?
F: What? I don't think he's all that well.
J: Really? Look, tell me about it some other time. I've got to go.
F: Is that a loaded sentence?
J: If you want it to be.
F: You're so bloody exasperating.
J: You too.
F: Likes repel.
J: They certainly do.
F: So you want me to change so that you can stay the same. Opposites attract.

J: Well, I'm not changing; not in the way you want.
F: That's it then. To be honest, it hasn't been a great thrill.
J: Bollocks to you, Francis. Why don't you try pantomime? With your CV, you'd fly through an audition and have a choice of back or front of the horse costume.
F: Bollocks to you too - and yours, however few they may be.

Therapy

The male side of a family is more interesting because it's about men seeking work in a variety of places and often making something of themselves. That's not a chauvinistic statement. More's the pity that women have never been in a position to do the same. Men may have been equally liable to find themselves in dead-end jobs close to home but the physical search for work, the activity, leads many of them to find careers or make names for themselves. Parish records and the National Census register distaff Taylors as housewives or servants. The categories of service do not make their work any less menial. But the male Taylors - what genealogists call the 'spear' side - pop up in surprising roles and locations. As well as millworkers and labourers, I've discovered a suffragan bishop and a Royal Navy ship's master. Yet the more these opened up in the distant past, the more I was shamed into admitting scant knowledge of the present. Opportunities to do different things have made us more selfish and non-reproductive so that even the few relatives we have are unknown to us. Thus it was that I homed in on my father's distant cousin, Harold Taylor.

Harold lived in Goring-on-Sea near Worthing, which is near Brighton. It's the way Harold himself put it. He called that part of the coast 'my seaside trail'. I think he imagined travelling eastwards along it on some kind of miniature toy train with carriages and rubber wheels, the whole thing painted brightly for tourists and day-trippers.

If there was one, he probably had. I can just see him sharing a carriage with a couple and their child, smiling and rocking back and forth and listening out for the bell that signals the next stop or warns pedestrians that it's bearing down on them. He couldn't have looked more out of place, especially a childless older man on his own in the almost certain company of kids; but in another sense, it was a familiar ride. He was brought up in Cumbria and used to be a coalminer in South Wales so he's even more of an oddity than most of them are; not that anyone would guess, especially in flaunting Brighton and district, where most things are slightly peculiar. That promenade toy train, though, would have reminded him of a past life. Harold Taylor. He was not a well man.

So here I am, Julie-less in the English countryside. More about her absence later.

I've done a fair bit as a thespian since that run in *Equus,* including the usual voice-overs and a few mute appearances as an extra. But hardly anything since I came here as a temp. I've done a few stints as a theatre stage manager.

The problem is, that pig - actually a sow confused by a phantom pregnancy - buried its teeth in my left thigh while I was on location for a TV documentary. My 'resting' is therefore literal and serious.

But I was flattered when one of the management here, knowing from my interview that I was in what she called 'showbusiness', suggested that I might entertain. It's a captive audience, both its attentiveness and its boredom induced by pharmaceuticals (I sometimes do the Medicine Run in the company van). From its comatose or over-excited circle has arisen a fan base of roughly ten. Their most enthusiastic member was Mrs Jean Grimaldi who pre-deceased Bob Berridge by a few weeks and who I sometimes felt was here under false pretences, so lively was her dance towards the blue yonder. There was life in her yet.

Mrs Grimaldi was most impressed with my Prospero speech. Well, they all were. Being an actor, that's what I've elected to do in this place when I'm not telling stories of life on the boards and I don't have many of them, at least not ones that involve famous members of the profession. Even my admirers with short memories or little memory at all are beginning to think that I've told them the one about Peter O'Toole at least twice before. Maybe I have. Needless to point out, it's not an anecdote of which the estimable Mr O'Toole would have liked to be reminded. (Bob told me that O'Toole had owned a couple of racehorses.) I'll say no more. But it was better than my story: that of an only child who read too much of the wrong thing, flunked English after two years at Lancaster before going to drama college, and turned his flunking into a kind of superiority about the subject amid suggestions that it had been the university which had failed him and not he the university, insofar as it could be bothered one way or the other. I was now an actor: they didn't require antecedents for that.

It was Mrs Grimaldi, once our self-appointed resident 'fixer', who remembered me not from any playbill but from some early appearances in *Emmerdale*. I obviously made an impression on her because none of the others recognised me as a TV actor and all without exception had to take her word for it that I had also performed on the stage. Prospero has never been one of my roles; in fact, I'm not much of a Shakespearian, having appeared only in touring versions of *As You Like It* as Le Beau, the courtier attending upon Frederick - *Good sir, I do in friendship counsel you to leave this place* - and *Twelfth Night*, as Fabian, servant to Olivia - *She did show favour to the youth in your sight only to exasperate you, to awake your dormouse valour...*

Dormouse. Mmm...

I normally avoid the worthy activities here like a renegade. But to be honest, I think my acting days may be over; at least, I'm not seeking work and I've ditched my useless agent, though I suspect I wasn't one of her brightest talents. For a while, I was with an agency which emailed me jobs I might have been interested in. It was always a different e-mailer - with the impersonal touch, as I liked to describe it. What we actors did to keep sane! I don't mind being asked to provide relief from tedium here, though it's additional to my normal caring duties.

One story I like to tell, (not in what the management call 'a structured setting'), is about the time while on location that I was bitten by that pig; actually, as I said, a sow defending non-existent piglets, so the on-site vet told me. The wound was stitched up and I soon forgot about the incident, but for a year I've been experiencing severe pain in the region of the bite and X-rays have revealed deep-seated lesions whose late re-awakening is giving me grief. It's worse than that: I can't walk without pain - I try not to show it - and some prognoses warn of latent tumours. My resting phase may yet turn out to be permanent. At the interview, I almost told them about my black dog, half-expecting them to remind me that no pets were allowed (though there are signs of minor relaxations to this rule) and, *ipso facto*, not ready for someone able to characterise depression with a metaphor. I wouldn't have exaggerated my case but I thought the condition might have been helpful in dealing with those here who are continuously afflicted. Old age is bad enough, let alone aggravated by delayed lack of self-esteem. 'Winston Churchill?' I might have hinted. 'Ah,' they would have said, remembering that the great man was not mentally without problems and perhaps reminding me, later on, that the kind of art he produced in paintings of accumulating crap was just the thing to make people here believe that along the path to the abyss were places where they might be entertainingly waylaid.

But I don't paint and I wouldn't 'do' classes if I were a resident. My second-floor room - part of the servants' quarters when this was a decaying country pile - looks out on a sea of forests in which I know there are pleasant family walks and picnic sites as well as burnt-out cars and occasional, if rare, body finds. The wildlife, if one could get away from signs of human visitation, must be overwhelming. Few realise that the red kites have arrived from breeding programmes farther inland. At least, no one I've told had known. It used to be buzzards with their plaintive, infantile cries which circled in the distance above the trees but they now share aerial manoeuvres with the kites. Who knows what hidden tearing of flesh has gone into such co-existence? I hear that farmers in Oxfordshire want to cull the newcomers, which have been filmed descending on their fields in coppery flocks, reportedly at times swooping on new-born lambs and taking them away. Likely stories!

Anyway, on my afternoons off, silence, as they say, reigns except for the far-off mewling of the buzzard. Its bleakness can set me off so I usually do some volunteering. I used to take Mrs Grimaldi and her 'orders' into town and follow her with her shopping list around Sainsbury's. (Actually she took me, in her death-defying Toyota.)

'You should get paid extra for this,' she said, peering at rows of chocolate biscuits over her specs. 'Why don't I put in a word?'

I leaned on the trolley, staring down at its nibbly bits and pieces. 'Good god, no,' I said. 'Don't you dare.' Mrs

Grimaldi made me think I was in charge of a small, performing whippet. Any moment I expected her to drop on all fours from the almost upright position she maintained and trot away.

When we returned, I followed behind her in the community suite with the shopping-bag as she handed out the purchases, as though giving to beggars. She herself then flopped into her armchair exhausted, joining the comatose and forgetting about her recent concern for my financial well-being. I mean *really* forgetting about it: you can always tell.

Upstairs in my room I wonder whether my life is a stuttering conclusion, destined to carry on at this place until the ending which brooks no further delay. It depends, I suppose, on the old leg - and whether or not there are still parts to be played and if I'm even interested in taking them on.

The story I can't share is the one I tell in the following pages, prompted, I suppose, by that angry sow's lunge at me, like a violent reminder of a presence to which we normally pay little heed. It can't be told here, because most information communicated in this establishment is forgotten as soon as received, a condition which in some circumstances might be considered a blessing if it did not irritate those of us sustained by life's complexity and the need for someone to listen, understand and, above all, sympathise; and if it didn't now and again raise a smile that was genuine, yet blank and uncomprehending.

Whatever. Writing it has filled my rest days and blocked out not a few thunderstorms on my weekends off. Where people in my story speak, it's only me remembering the gist of what they said. After all, I am an actor. And I make notes. I've even thought of writing a play, maybe based on my time here as chivvying companion to the end-of-lifers.

Flicking through my scribblings the other day, I came across the following tale of a bird. Its relevance to my story will be made clear in time. The modern novel, as Julie once told me in order to defend her avant-garde take on things, requires its readers to wait around and admire scenery they would normally have missed in their headlong pursuit of an ending. 'Demented page-turners,' she called them, 'unable to put a book down.' She meant unable to put a book down and think about what has been written and read. I agreed with her. In the matter of narrative, of story-telling, we were *flaneurs*, idlers, explorers of the byway and the margins while we left the main road for a moment, knowing that we would have to return and head into the wind towards that flickering beacon. Digressions.

Norm

When my father died, I inherited the family's pet budgerigar. His death enabled my mother to express her hatred of it. I was the end of the line, the last remaining dispenser of birdseed and dried, light-as-balsa cuttlefish. He was called Norman and he could say his name. He could also swear. 'Uckoff, uckoff' was the result of my father's attempt to spice his repertoire. He was one of us. We called him Norman Taylor.

My father - and my mother by innocent extension - would tell visitors that Norman was actually saying something else and that if you said, 'What's that noise?' he'd reply, 'A cough, a cough.'

Such a gloss indicated my father's slyness, cowardice and subterfuge. Only in my mother's absence and mine, and for long periods, could Norman have been taught foul language. I remember the day he first came out with the expression. 'What's that thing saying?' my mother asked, above the tinny duelling of her knitting-needles. 'God knows,' my father said, smirking.

'Fuck off' remained 'a cough', much to my father's delight. When one of my new friends stood like an idiot before the cage asking, 'What's that noise?' my father would throw me a wicked glance as Norman responded on cue, his head bobbing. I just shrugged my shoulders non-committedly and turned away.

I hated that; hated the way my father had put one over on my mother who had come from a chapel-going, nonswearing family, unlike him. I've never been to chapel and I often swear (but only rarely, if at all, in these notes), so in him I might have expected to discover an enlightened ally but he was a disappointment on that score to the extent that I looked upon my mother, despite her meekness and propriety, as the more virtuous. His behaiour seemed cruel, a sort of thoughtless animal act, animals having no proper feeling, no qualms about anything except their own comfort and survival. And I hated the way he wanted me to join him in a conspiracy to deceive.

Even the way Norman had been caged for years seemed to me base. Not even my mother, tricked and never let in on my father's joke, was blameless. They'd bought powder-blue Norman at the market and locked him up for life.

Only when you think about it, the captivity, do you entertain the idea of freedom and how wild animals have no sense of being free, only of being not-free, of being contained and mysteriously agitated, though of course they have no sense of mystery either. And having committed the act, gone down to the animal's level, so to speak, you yourself are trapped, for there was no way releasing Norman would result in anything but his swift and certain death, predators always homing in on bright plumage.

Then I heard about the escaped parakeets that had begun breeding in trees and bushes beside the Thames and I thought of how they were now among us, having got even as it were, and how the celebration of their thoughtless creature instincts was simply a reflection of our own desire to get what we wanted at all costs. Keeping a bird in a cage was the failure to clothe our animal cunning, our selfishness, in what we thought was kindness and kinship.

I didn't have Norman for long. I'd got to calling him Norm. For a few seconds before you discover a budgie flat out and dead at the bottom of its cage, hidden below the silly pelmet (a bit of floral curtain material in our case), it appears as though the occupant has flown ethereally through the thin bars that had kept it confined. It's a sort of religious feeling, a soul travel experience.

I felt foolish but I took Norm into some woodland, dug a hole, and buried him. If I'd put him out with the rubbish, wrapped in a newspaper, it wouldn't have made any odds. I mean, there is a difference between a dead bird and a dead parent. But perhaps not that much. When they're dead, they're dead. And gone. Both of them. I felt he deserved a burial, if only for his plumage, which had given pleasure, a curious sort of peacock pleasure associated without his knowing it, of being conscious of it.

*

While Julie and I were deliberately incommunicado, I learned a bit about Harold, though not as much as I did about the techniques of genealogy. As I've suggested, they told me that some discoverees in the family tree were suspicious of hearing from unknown relatives in case they wanted money. There was this image of an importunate seeker after knowledge at the base of the trunk and his reluctant quarry squatting in a high branch and trying to make himself camouflaged and as small as possible. I didn't mind. No venture, no gain.

Julie and I had little contact following that break-up on the phone. Then I happened to catch sight of her across the street and went over to say hello. She appeared almost pleased to see me. It was odd. We went for coffee. The following week, we met for coffee again and arranged to go to the cinema. There was a film we both wanted to see. We discussed it like two delegates at an Arts Council seminar. During the film, we shared a bumper carton of popcorn with our knees up; once, we both dipped in at the same time and our hands touched. We looked at each other and laughed.

It was a boring film, an art house thing. When it was at its most uninteresting, I wondered why Julie had not just greeted me, chatted briefly and continued on her way. Had she been ruminating on whether or not Mona Strange had re-appeared and decided on the pavement to discover if it was too late to pre-empt her? She didn't mention Mona's name. Mona Strange, she of the ample form. Actually Mona at that time was as far away from contacting me as I could imagine.

There was a long and inexplicable scene in the film - it was about an Albert Schweitzer-like figure with a 'we are all equal in the sight of god' take on tending to the sick in the jungle, including everything from face-painted natives on the perimeter of his clearing, their broken arms in crude slings made out of leaves, to a pink fairy armadillo permanently curled up in a supreme act of animal introversion. For what seemed an eternity, the camera roved along the forest floor and travelled up and down trees - family trees, in fact - looking for its occupants: snakes, grimacing monkeys, beetles rolling little boulders of shit; well, bigger than themselves. Julie was engrossed, popcorn held in suspension before her open mouth; whereas I'd reversed genders and was observing that if I'd approached her in order to step in before someone else made overtures, it would be a recognisable act, the male seeing off other males who were sniffing around his quarry. Julie was always different. I used to wonder if she was by nature (though not by act) bisexual, or asexual even.

By then, I'd contacted Harold and been south to visit him. He didn't say much about himself. We'd talked mainly about things that popped up before us on a stroll along the seashore. We saw kittiwakes and went to investigate a group of people encircling a dead porpoise left by the outgoing tide; it had dried out and the stench was terrible.

He confirmed facts I had only half understood. Born in Old Westmorland, he'd moved to South Wales as a twenty-year-old to work as a coalminer. Then he'd moved back on retirement with his Welsh wife who died just after their arrival in Appleby. Infected by some sort of wanderlust, he moved to Sussex, a place he'd never been to before. It was all fascinating, like an eternal and aimless migration. Nowt as interesting as folk. That said, he hadn't been talkative, though before I left and like someone who didn't wish their shyness to be taken for suspicion or a want of interest and feeling, he invited me down again.

Julie and I didn't talk about the bitterness of our break-up on the phone. I could see all my arguments and all hers evaporating, their disappearance fuelled by an unspoken determination to begin afresh. I asked her if she'd like to visit Harold with me and stay overnight; that's if it were OK with him, as I was sure it would be. She was enthusiastic but I thought it strange that she asked me for his phone number. I gave it to her, not enquiring why in case it started something unpleasant or that would lead to unpleasantness. Harold looked forward to both of us arriving but in the end, that first time, Julie didn't come; she said her mother was unwell.

When I got to Harold's place, he told me something else: that he'd 'survived' cancer and was taking tablets for related conditions. He was seventy-two, thirty years older than me. It had been prostate cancer and he'd had radiotherapy. It sounded odd to me, that word, suggesting a regime of listening to omnibus editions of *The Archers* for two months. I smiled, which must have looked unfortunate, but I didn't make a joke and I don't think it registered with him. Before I went to bed, a good while before him, he told me he'd had a call from Julie. He must have noticed my raised eyebrows but he just said how nice she sounded and how disappointed she'd been not to be able to visit. Next time, he said. I didn't know whether these were his words or hers.

Lying on the bed in Harold's spare room, I heard him in the kitchen. He dropped something metallic, a colander perhaps, as it spun a while on the tiled floor before he silenced it with his foot. Then I heard him climbing the stairs, humming to himself. He was asleep before I was. Throughout the night, he groaned; it could have been in pain or at some untoward event in a dream. I imagined it happening without anyone, like me, to hear and to contemplate action. I looked across at the other side of the bed. Julie should have been in it, and I choked at its emptiness. I wanted her properly back, and I felt she wanted me back too. But I still wasn't sure.

Taylor, Harold of that Ilk

We often don't realise a new direction has opened up until we are well on the way to a destination and sometimes not until we've reached it. Nor do we know till later that things are starting to come together or that some calamity will change everything.

A week or two after the last visit, I phoned Harold again. I enquired about his health and what he'd been up to. His voice was slurred and he sounded more tired than usual.

The garbled voice was new. Harold didn't drink, though for weeks he'd been taking that daily slingshot of pills for one thing and another.

'I can hear them on the go,' he joked. 'Lots of marbles jangling inside.'

He always referred to being able to hear but one of the things he'd told me when we first met was that he was 'a bit deaf'. Under-statement.

I used to wonder if his medical people ever got together to assess the combined effect of all the stuff they individually prescribed for him. He didn't think so. Perhaps they believed that if they chucked everything they could at him, they might achieve something positive by default.

Anyway, he apologised for having to end my call because he was 'knackered'.

'I'll see you in a few weeks then,' I'd said.

He signed off with a 'Mm. OK. Thanks for ringing.'

I sensed a new phase, another slip on what I hoped wasn't an inevitable descent. But these things were difficult to predict. He'd been like it once before and had then rallied to a place far beyond the point of his relapse.

I rang Julie.

Whenever I spoke to her, Julie always asked about Harold first. I didn't call her after that previous alarm. It would have been too involving, a sign that we weren't as estranged as we both thought, as we both needed to confirm. He was my relative, however distant and long separated.

My family history research wasn't serious; more a hobby while I was between parts. I'd watched a TV programme about some celebrity or other who was investigating her background and the results had been surprising - tragic and tearful even.

I thought it sad that we all might be unaware of something in our lives that was capable of moving us to tears. I was curious, that's all.

'Are you OK?' I asked.

'Yes.'

'Are you sure?'

'What? Of course I'm sure. About Harold. You should go and see him sooner than that. If you're worried.'

She hadn't usually offered unsolicited advice.

'Oh,' I replied. 'But I am worried. There was something in his voice.'

'Well, you should. Why don't I go with you this time?'

As a query, it was barely rhetorical. How could I refuse? How couldn't I refuse?

We talked about the usual things, that familiar litany requiring only updates.

I sometimes thought we were heading somewhere in those dutiful conversations - back to an abandoned intimacy perhaps. Being a chap, I assumed this was an exclusively female thing, a strategy. We do sometimes pick up enlightening things, we blokes.

Then I ditched the idea because it wasn't supported by consistent or even insistent behaviour. Julie'd been nothing if not honest and open. I knew she was always right about everything and that I was too often wrong or self-interested, which amounts to the same thing. But that was before things took unexpected turns.

It wasn't that we never talked about these differences, this schism: it was the recognition of them that had driven us apart.

'About Harold,' I said finally and to make the point. 'I think I'll go on my own again. Next weekend maybe. I'll phone him.'

'Remember me to him, then.'

*

Some 'resting' actors write books; some make snow globes; others train their memories. I joined the *Ancestry* website. That night I spent hours there, idly surfing. Herded on to a page of National Census returns with their neighbours was the family of Lydia and Arthur John Lawrence and their son David Herbert, with his brothers and sisters, all neatly catalogued in copperplate at their address in Eastwood, Nottinghamshire. Unknown to me, it foreshadowed something in which Harold was already interested. Harold the burrower.

Climbing the Tree

My family connections are not complicated. In fact, their very lack of complication would make an outsider wonder how I'd managed to see so little of Harold in the seven decades he'd been alive. Unless, of course, all families are the same. Here I'm tempted to paraphrase the opening sentence of *Anna Karenina,* about all unhappy families being unhappy in their own way. Julie once tried it for the final draft of a story, only to be dissuaded by her editor. He thought it too smart by half, I suppose.

Our family, or that part of it which concerns me, is uncomplicated in its own way. It explains relationships but not their consequences: why, for instance, a widower with three young children should re-marry less than a year after his wife's death. It would seem an obvious move for someone hard-pressed to function as a parent discharging responsibilities. But no one can prepare for the shifting assumption of attitudes; not that the likelihood of disapproval will alter what people are determined to do in their own interests and the interests of others. Forgive me if I suggest instinct, a carnal need so cruelly cut off.

No one talks about cousins once removed or great uncles and aunts. Although close in bloodline terms, they are often socially remote. My cousins once removed and great aunts and uncles are defined not in relation to me but to my parents whose cousins and aunts and uncles they are. I might see an uncle once every couple of months; a great uncle usually by accident or at a funeral or some anniversary or other, lurking in the background as though already half-embraced by the past - or unless they themselves have died in a place awkward to reach for the two hours of a funeral. My uncles and aunts, when not trying to ingratiate, are superior or patronising as though acting *in loco parentis* and with the authority such a connection might justify to them. So imagine how farther removed a great uncle might consider himself, perhaps so far gone towards his own demise that any real interest in me would be long past, while cousins once removed could be, and in my case are, virtual strangers, a few of whom I've not seen or spoken to for twenty years. Harold might as well have not existed for all the likelihood of my ever making contact with him. The branch to which he clings, like a Capuchin monkey cornered by a gang of marauding chimps, has sprouted thus:

My father's name was Luke. His father (my grandfather Arthur) had a brother, John, who married Ruth. John and Ruth, my great uncle and great aunt, had three children: David, Mary and Rachel, my father's cousins. When the children were aged six, four and two, respectively, great Aunt Ruth died of ovarian cancer. Within nine months, great Uncle John had re-married, his bride being Kath. Harold was their only child, my father's half cousin; Childe Harold, as Julie jokingly called him. Very literary. Harold had been married to Marjorie who'd died of a stroke.

To go back one more generation, my paternal great-grandfather (Jack) was a carpenter. His brother Matthew was killed by a sniper in the Great War while on sentry duty after surviving the Battle of Loos.

Both my mother and my father had brothers and sisters, some of whom had children, my cousins. But I never see much of them. That's families for you. (I remember Bob Berridge drawing Shergar's lineage for me with a shaky hand and from memory; it was like any family tree, its uninteresting - or non-achieving - members falling away into obscurity as soon as noted. That's most of us, I suppose; though perhaps not most racehorses.)

All our family have been late starters when it comes to producing offspring, my mother and father being no exceptions. Towards the end, I had little contact with my dad, the man who'd taught our budgie to swear. I suppose if I too leave marriage and parenthood too late, there might be repercussions. Anyway, Harold obviously knew of me when I contacted him ('Oh, aye - Luke's boy'). I'd had some vague idea of where he'd gone after his wife died so it was easy to locate him. Whether or not he wished to be located by someone who wanted answers, even someone in the family, remained debatable for a while. There was some suggestion that we'd met once or twice at family gatherings when I was a kid. I didn't recall.

Flying South

Miserable weather meant the trip from Manchester to the South Coast took longer than usual. At a crowded service station halfway along the M40, I sat for half an hour thinking about Harold.

No-one I came to know called him Harry. Harold was a dignified name for a dignified man, a gentleman - a gentle man. Julie and I agreed on that when she too had got to know him. Harold Taylor was dignified. Maybe his dignity, his old-fashioned bearing as some would call it, had been the example we'd needed to repair our fracture, Julie's and mine.

I rubbed a circle into the restaurant's steamed-up window and watched the multitudes coming and going on their oblivious journeys. In the best and worst of senses, we're all living our own unobserved lives.

Then, as if to confound the thought and because the restaurant was busy, a little girl and her grandparents - we make quick reasonable assumptions - approached and asked if they could join me at my table. I nodded and smiled.

The girl was clutching a pink-and-white toy elephant and could just about haul herself and her fluffy companion on to a chair. The grandfather pulled up a third chair so that both adults could sit either side of her.

She stared at me uncertainly, making me feel uncomfortable, this being the age in which every lone male in the proximity of a child is a perceived threat. In my experience, no stranger ever offered sweets to a kid and no kid ever had to decline in obedience to a parent's warning. These days every parent thinks the worst of a stranger and has the half-worried quizzical look that goes with suspicion. Not a nice world. It was the grandmother who broke the silence.

'We're on our way to the Cotswold Wildlife Park,' she said. 'But we had to stop for you-know-what. A young one never misses a chance to top up.'

The 'you-know-what' would have confused me if the grandfather's nod of resignation and embarrassment hadn't reminded me of Harold and what he called his 'night journeys'.

'There's meerkats,' the girl said, wriggling into an eating position.

'They didn't have meerkats in my day,' said the grandfather. 'Nor them other things. What are they called?'

'Marmosets,' his wife said.

The child looked at me. 'You can go in with them,' she explained, waiting for my reaction. 'They won't bite.'

It sounded like an invitation from an innocent or, depending on the books you'd read, an innocent with a dark knowledge she was determined to keep to herself for the time being, prior to entrapment. In the presence of doting guardians, a child can have a fearsome quality. I imagined myself storing these thoughts for when I next talked to Julie. We'd once discussed marriage - well, partnership - and kids as part of apprehending a hazy future together. The haze never really cleared. Discussions of the future seemed already to be picking at the compactness of the moment, its joyous lingering intensity, in the same way that the girl opposite was now pinching fur from her degrading elephant. I think we were both clinging to those moments, even if they were now memories. I was, anyway. The girl's unwanted attention was speeding the elephant's decline. I recognised that, too, as having resonance.

'Did you get that at a Wildlife Park?' I asked.

With a puzzled expression, the girl appealed to both grandparents as if I'd asked her about a scratch on the back of her hand. The grandfather pointed to the toy.

'Mummy bought it,' she said.

I felt I should have known that and she did too. I got up and said I hoped they'd enjoy their day out.

'Oh, it's not a day out,' the grandfather said cryptically, again as if I should have understood or had known and forgotten.

We let the mystery lie uncovered and I made for the exit. When I looked back at them, the girl was waving to me, the man and woman lowering their faces to their plates like the feeding animals they would soon be staring at. The elephant had fallen to the floor.

Before leaving, I rang Harold. 'I'm sort of halfway. With a following wind, will be with you in about three hours. Are you all right?'

He still sounded washed out. He said he'd have 'a bit of tea' ready and to ring him when I was closer.

I texted Julie with the same message. Whenever we were doing anything that involved long journeys, we used to keep in touch. Why was I doing it again? I didn't know about her but I used to do it because I thought that, when travelling, we were at our most vulnerable. It wasn't just about physical pile-ups and derailments; it was about possibilities and disappointments. She texted back: *OKx.* I had the feeling that she was busy and that her reply was unthinking, half-automatic, the lower case 'x' a keyboard slip, like sending an embarrassing emoji at the end of a message to your bank manager.

I began thinking about the youngster and her grandparents. There'd been something about them that wasn't quite right. Was she their great-grand-daughter? It was possible these days, with early marriages or hasty marriages or no marriage at all combining with longer-living older generations. The couple had looked about to be out of their depth. Perhaps their son or daughter had re-married someone younger with an equally younger child - 'baggage', as it was glibly called, the child as unwanted in a perfect world and therefore doomed to be an adulterated blessing. For all I knew, the three could already be dead, sprawled across the motorway short of their Wildlife Park turning and covered by blankets, the scene festooned by flashing blue lights. I hoped not. I hoped there was no mystery and that, far from not being right, their world was perfect and their blessings unadulterated.

By the time I reached the M25, the sun was dipping. I wondered if autumn had officially arrived. I accelerated; after a while I was soon speeding towards the coast.

Vulpes

Harold was waiting for me on the huge paved area with which the previous occupants of his house had obliterated the front garden. The building faced due south. It was only a twenty-minute walk to the sea. The sunsets were amazing and prolonged. I'd somehow forgotten that, what with everything else happening. His car, now rarely if ever used, was mouldering in a shelter under a tarpaulin.

Standing there shielding his eyes, he seemed unaware that his surviving physical attributes looked odd without the ones that had gone forever. Height without bulk.

I'd always thought miners were short and squat for obvious reasons. His arms bore tell-tale flecks, like blue parasites asleep under the skin, waiting to wriggle to somewhere more deadly. He probably had been forced to bend a little to get at those obstinate seams, though not on his knees much and not always armed with a weighty pick. As he'd obviously avoided any kind of lung disease, I thought his enduring strength and stamina would see him through. But some illnesses creep past the best of defences. None of us is immune. We just hope and, if we're as devout as Harold Taylor, pray for good health or deliverance from infirmity. Julie probably thought it wasn't as simple as that, though we'd never got round to discussing Harold in much detail. But he'd taken to her. He told me as much, gently chiding us both for the split. Like his life as a working man in Wales, Harold's existence was simple - basic, as he put it. He grew beautiful dahlias. He was also a very good amateur artist.

'How do you feel?' I asked.

'Tired. Always tired these days. I'm not going to be much of an entertainer. Anyway, I've been keeping something from you. Cup of tea?'

I was intrigued.

'Yes,' I said. 'I'll just put this case upstairs. Usual room?'

He nodded and went into the kitchen.

The kettle was quietly roaring to boiling point when I came down. Harold was in the front room, sitting in his armchair. I flopped into the settee opposite, facing a new flat-screen TV.

'I should have told you before now,' he said. 'It's just that, well, I've got problems down below again.'

He sounded like a ship's captain faced with a mutiny in the boiler-room. But I knew what he meant. The grandfather at the motorway services probably knew too.

'Down below?'

'The cancer. It's been on the move.'

The statement was almost designed to make you feel awkward, uncertain about the right thing to say. I didn't want to say I was sorry, though I was.

'How long? I mean, how long have you known?'

'A few weeks?'

He made it sound like a question to which I might have a more comforting answer. I wouldn't have known what a comforting answer was. He'd kept the news from me till then.

'Why didn't you say?'

'I was going to. Just waiting for the right moment, I suppose. When I knew what was what.'

'Do you know now?'

'Oh yes,' he said. 'I start chemo in a couple of weeks.'

He hadn't told me that, either.

I'd quickly appreciated that the background I was interested in, and wanted him to recall, was as nothing compared with his recent happenings. A late chapter of his life had become crammed with incident and was accelerating towards some still-vague outcome. It had left the years that had gone before standing and deprived of their interest. Little cancerous growths had been found on his prostate before we'd made contact and he'd gone for radium treatment. That much, and only that, I knew. I assumed the pills he took were related to something ongoing. I didn't want him to sit down and re-live those years or go into detail about them in a letter. There'd only been one missive anyway since I'd discovered him and that was more of a scribbled note with a few photographs included. He appeared to me to be fit for his age, a survivor.

He looked at me like someone who'd been told about chemo but had been too embarrassed to ask exactly what it was. Something told me that in fact he knew all about it.

'What then?'

'Monitoring. Checking that it's not opened up a new face.'

He smiled at his coalmining metaphor. I told him that a new face must have been good news underground.

'Aye, well, you weren't always chasing coal. You could be working two seams at the same time, three maybe.'

We said nothing to each other for a few seconds as I translated this daft workaday example into medical reality.

'What do they call it?'

'Secondaries,' he said, firmly.

I could tell he knew everything, what the likely outcomes might be.

'I don't know what to say.'

'Nor do I,' he said and laughed.

'Your voice was a bit slurred. On the phone last time.'

'Different medication, see. Not so much jangling but priorities. And painkillers. I'm doing a lot of sleeping. Do you fancy a walk after we've eaten? It's not much. A bit of cake and stuff. Oh, aye, and an apricot tart made by a new friend of mine.'

His Northern accent was snagged with flecks of Welsh. I'm used to picking up such things and half-heartedly storing them away.

He returned to the kitchen and re-boiled the kettle. The tart was good. With Harold's favourite evaporated milk, it was even better.

'Are you sure you're up to walking?' I asked.

'Of course I am!'

'And who's your culinary friend?' I inquired, pointing to the remains of the tart, which had been neatly pricked and decorated in a dish with pictures of apricots on the side - an apricot tart dish no less.

'Ethel. I'll tell you later. There's something else too.'

I expected more bad news. He rose from the table and went to the sideboard, returning with two or three photographs. He handed them to me without saying anything.

'Take a look at that,' he said. 'More cake?'

I shook my head. They were pictures of his garden. In one, an adult fox was sprawled across the middle of the lawn while three cubs rolled about and played nearby. In the other, a fox was asleep inside Harold's blue covered gazebo just beyond the kitchen window.

'There's a den at the bottom,' he said. 'Among the brambles. If they weren't so cheeky, you wouldn't know they were there.'

'Are they there now?'

'Probably. You don't always know. The council's trying to get rid of them but the harder they try, the more foxes there seem to be. I think they've given up or are hoping the things'll go away. It's ever so strange. The most I've counted out there at one time is seven.'

'Seven foxes!'

Harold wouldn't have appreciated the observation that his worshipful God had engineered this nature-study scene in his backyard to remind him of what was happening to his insides. The thought reminded me that I'd have to go to church with him on Sunday, when I could inwardly rant at the malevolence of it all or at least the indifference. He knew I didn't believe but he never minded. I knew the hymns. That had impressed him the last time. When my voice rose above the throng, he'd stopped singing, turned to me and grinned, possibly seeing me as conversion material. My singing voice was passable. Having tracked him down in the first place, it seemed only right that he should know as much about me as I wanted to learn about him. Julie was more of a non-believer than I was and, I suppose, a better person. That was something for Harold to think about. Or any other churchgoer, for that matter.

I'd missed Julie. I think, or hoped, that she'd missed me. Knowing that we could soon drift so far apart that each of us would be scarcely a memory for the other, I felt in danger of losing something precious and that action was needed to forestall things and that I should be wherever she was and not sitting in a house lost in the South Coast's sprawl, waiting to walk one of its sun-flooded strands as a means of consolation.

I went upstairs to unpack and get ready. Harold and his Welsh wife had returned to 'Old Westmorland', as he used to describe it. It was Cumbria now. Within three years, Marjorie was dead. A few years later, he upped and came south. It always seemed to me a long way to travel for a widower's retirement. But I remembered he'd told me that miners loved the seaside. Each summer, convoys of them, whole pits and their families, would descend on the South Wales coast for their two-weeks' holiday. That was in older times. I think miners started travelling abroad as soon as they could afford it, just to show they didn't lack imagination. He was enjoying, or trying to enjoy, living in a place that he'd chosen without her having a say in it. Perhaps it was the first time it had happened. I can only report what he used to tell me. In my room upstairs, there were plenty of photos of them doing just that at Llandudno, Blackpool, the Llŷn Peninsula, the Northumbrian coast, always with unforced smiles for the camera. Perhaps he thought the foxes had followed him from a place where they were ritually killed, a place he knew as a boy, to where they could be the subject of proper astonishment. He'd taken part in the killing as surely as he'd stood in his kitchen window watching what they did when they were not being hounded. Annoyance never needed a huge place in his heart. Somehow, I didn't think the foxes bothered him. I couldn't wait to see them.

*

When I said Harold was a very good amateur painter, I was possibly doing him a disservice. He'd been included in a book called *Seeing The Light: The Coalminer-Artists of Britain.* There were a couple of his pictures on the walls but not many: I think he was slightly embarrassed by them, by the unbridgeable gap he'd noticed between the enthusiasm of the amateur - his own - and the rigour of the professional. That he was aware of the gap said a lot about him. There was just one picture by him in the book, a louring Welsh mining cottage interior which he said belonged to a generation before his but whose likeness he vaguely remembered as a farmer's child in the Westmorland hills; he meant a different lifestyle but a common deprivation and abode. He'd said something about work, coalmining, being all about 'bringing the outside loos inside'. Someone had bought the painting, a private purchase, and he didn't know what had happened to it. All he had was the book and its quarter-page illustration, with a hundred words of biography in small print beneath it (I'd bought a copy on eBay). The author's appeal for pictures through the National Union of Mineworkers had resulted in a cataract of submissions. I told him he'd survived the cataract but he had no sense of fame, however transitory. About thirty of the artists had been featured at length. Harold didn't know any of them. Few of the book's paintings, even the prominent ones, were about anything other than mining and the mining community. Harold still painted and sketched but art was not an obsession. The activity seemed to belong to his past.

*

That night, I'd been asleep for little more than an hour when a commotion outside woke me. Car doors banged shut and children's voices could be heard, then tired adult ones in loud exasperation above them.

The noise was coming from the front so I got up and peeped through the curtains. I could see maybe four or five young kids running in and out of the front door of the house next to Harold's and a man carrying things from the car boot. I'd never noticed them before.

I looked at my watch; it was just past midnight.

There were so many lights on in the house that its front lawn and half of Harold's huge patio glowed. I'd never heard such a racket.

But after a short while, the door was slammed shut and everything went quiet. I could still hear what sounded like a score of voices inside the house but they were muffled.

I got back into bed. My room, having briefly reversed from darkness to twilight, returned to the black and stillness of night. I saw the double orange flash and heard the click of the car being locked from inside the house. Then total silence, as if the house's occupants had all succumbed to sleep at the same time.

I must have fallen asleep straightaway too because I couldn't remember lying awake and wondering who those people were. Harold had told me that a single man had once lived there, a widower like himself but a bit younger. This person had obviously gone. The couple on the other side of him kept to themselves, he'd informed me.

Wesley, Aurora & the Crazy Gang

'Who are the people next door?' I asked Harold at breakfast. 'The family with all the kids?'

'Oh, them,' he said. 'Did they wake you up?'

'They came back late from somewhere.'

'I know. I heard them vaguely. All the lights were on. The kids are known around here as the Crazy Gang. Well, that's what Joe and Phyllis next door, on the other side, call them.'

'Do they give you trouble?'

'Only in a manner of speaking.'

Joe and Phyllis were the ones to Harold's left. The Crazy Gang had five members, four boys and a girl, the youngest, with not much more than eighteen months between each one so that if they'd appeared together or in a line, they would have been tiered. Not that they stayed still long enough to be regimented. I observed all this later. Four boys in a row. What are the chances of that happening? And then the girl. I wondered if a girl was what her parents had been praying for or was just the fifth child, whose gender was just a change - a change as good as a rest from a gang of scab-kneed mudlarks.

'What do you mean by "in a manner of speaking"?'

'They get a bit out of control. But they're all right, quite well spoken. They're always ringing my doorbell to tell me something or ask me a question. Once, they brought me a homing pigeon in a shoebox. They said it was injured but it wasn't; it was just tired, resting. I explained what the metal ring was around its leg. I didn't tell them that, if it had been injured and badly, I would have wrung its neck. I said I'd try to find out where it was from, give it half an hour and then let it go. They didn't seem to mind. I don't think their parents knew they even had it. They said they found it outside my place in the road, walking towards my entrance into which it turned, so perhaps they thought I was the one to show it to. I said I'd call them when it was ready to fly but they forgot about it and went out for the day. So I let it go myself. It didn't need any encouragement.'

'What happened to the other chap, the one who lived there before?'

'Trevor? Oh, he moved on. It was his fence that buckled up or rather he was there when it buckled. It was a funny thing but we could only see each other where the fence had started to collapse so that's where we used to talk. I never went over to his place. I invited him here a couple of times but he never came. When I first arrived, Joe and Phyllis had me around for an evening meal. But I haven't been there since. I thought it might have been something I said. Their fence is pretty solid as you can see. The thing about Trevor was that he didn't seem to notice that our fence needed mending. Well, it was his fence, his responsibility to fix it. I didn't tell him though I was getting around to it when he just upped and left.'

After we'd tidied the kitchen, I went upstairs to dress and use the bathroom which was at the back of the house across the landing. It must have been about ten o' clock. I could hear the kids next door playing in the garden. Through a slightly open window, the fence with its wavy S-bend like some fairground ride was visible. It could have passed for a piece of modern design, a shared sculpture. The garden was all worn grass, with a swing, a slide and a trampoline. The gang members were scattered. One was standing on the base of the kink in the fence, bouncing up and down as though testing it; two others were on the trampoline, surrounded by safety netting that reminded me of a cage. As I withdrew, a woman's voice shouted something. I looked and saw her hanging out of an upstairs window and waving towards the back of Harold's plot. Emerging from the brambles down there was the girl, who appeared to return and squeeze through some other gap in the fence at the very end of the garden and re-appear in her own. Five minutes later and back in my bedroom, I saw a fourth boy walking out of Harold's place with a football under his arm.

I mentioned all this to Harold as we prepared to go out.

'Typical,' he said. 'Kids the world over. D'yer know what she's called, the mother?'

'No.'

He stumbled over the name. 'It's Auro...Aurory. Aurora.'

'Aurora. Where does that come from?'

He smiled and shook his head. But I guessed. A child of late Sixties parents, begetting a wild bunch.

I opened the front door for him.

'She's older than he is,' he said.

'The husband?'

'Aye. Wes, she calls him, mostly at the top of her voice.'

I can't imagine how or why but as we were getting into my car, the boys had assembled on their driveway to watch us depart, one with the football still under his arm. But not in ascending order of height. They looked uncharacteristically disciplined. Perhaps it was me they'd noticed, a stranger come to disturb their feral wanderings, and they'd closed ranks, becalmed.

We drove off down the service lane that separated Harold's road from the busy main one. As we passed the boys' house, they waved and we waved back. In their doorway was a young man smoking a cigarette. He looked like a throwback, a greasy Teddy Boy from the Fifties, thin and nicotine-stained and wearing skinny jeans and tattoos. Harold saw me craning to look at him.

'Wes,' he said. 'Wesley.'

'By the way, there's a gap in your fence at the bottom of the garden.'

'Aye, I know. It's where the foxes go in and out.'

He hadn't noticed Wesley signalling to me with the envelope I'd left him containing my contact details. I'd dropped one through Joe and Phyllis's letterbox as well. I couldn't think of any circumstances in which either of them, either of his next-door neighbours, would let him know what I'd done. We'd recognise ourselves as conspirators in the cause of Harold's well-being as people do when their better natures are called forth. I saw him as being surrounded by a ring of good will.

Joe and Phyllis

It was a while before I got to know their surname - Lewis. I'd gone around there to re-introduce myself, as I'd only done so before over the garden fence and while they were on their way out. They'd acknowledged receipt of my note. Apart from a five-minute chat once when they were about to go somewhere in their car, we'd only ever exchanged pleasantries. Harold had now told them he'd got cancer, something I hadn't mentioned directly in my note to them. I'd already had a word with Wesley and Aurora. But I didn't want anyone on either side overstepping the mark in the way of being helpful. This was before we realised how large his friend Ethel, the maker of apricot tarts, loomed on the scene.

Joe and Phyllis Lewis. I wondered if Phyllis, agreeing to marry Joe, knew that, in taking his name, her full name would have a strange euphony - Phyllis Lewis. Luckily her middle name wasn't Clarice or Lois or both. Having started on family history and arrived at Harold, who had detained me and still did, I'd got into the habit of tracking people down on the periphery. Phyllis's second name was Margaret. Joe was Joseph Hubert Verdun Lewis.

The first thing that struck me about the Lewis house was the huge print of Landseer's *The Monarch of the Glen* over their fireplace in the sitting-room. 'Impressive,' I said. They were proud of it as if it were the original which I believed was a monster canvas on display somewhere in Scotland. Joe explained that the animal in the picture had twelve points on its antlers, which made it a 'royal' stag, not a 'monarch'; eighteen were required for a stag to be called a 'monarch'. He explained it in the way some men have of making useless information sound important, even urgent, and imparting it with no reference to what their women might think.

I gave them further details of my relationship to Harold and explained the potential seriousness of his condition.

Phyllis said, 'My brother died of prostate.'

'More people die with it than of it,' Joe countered.

'You are always up in the night, aren't you, Joe?'

'It's my age. (This said to me, like an apology). You can't get this far without having something.'

Looking at them both, I guessed that she had got as far as he had, at least.

'He's on medication.' She sat forward, having introduced a new topic.

'I'm on this,' he said, reaching for a blistered foil of tablets from among others on a shelf in a wicker bowl. 'And this.' He strained to retrieve and shake a green bottle of pills. 'I swear by Prostaid.'

'And Saw palmetta,' Phyllis added.

'Saw *palmetto*.' He looked at me with a grin as he corrected her, a man emphasising the error of his little woman and expecting me to be complicit in his victory. Phyllis really was little. I imagined her as once being taller and bulkier, her annual decrease in height and size going unnoticed by Joe. 'Of course, these are not strictly medication. These are what's called herbal remedies; medication is what the doctor gives you to take. When I asked the doctor if he minded me taking these others as well, he said he didn't. I don't know what's in them. I don't think anybody knows.'

'He'll be having treatment,' I said.

They looked bewildered for a second, then twigged.

'Tell you the truth, we don't bother with Harold much,' Phyllis said.

'He's never bothered us at all,' her husband added. 'He's absolutely no bother.'

'You always talk to him over the fence, Joe.'

'Yes.' He pondered this, waiting but failing to amplify his affirmative. 'Of course, we always hold parcels for him - if he's out.'

'I don't think he goes out much,' I said.

'No,' said Phyllis. 'Course, you couldn't leave anything valuable with the other side.'

'Wesley and Aurora,' I said, imagining they were hearing the names for the first time.

'Those kids run riot,' Joe explained.

'Tell him about the fence, Joe.'

'It's all about lowering the tone and I don't mind admitting it,' Joe said. 'The fence between them and Harold's was down, had been for a long time. Trevor's fault, the bloke who sold to Wesley and Aurora. Good fences make good neighbours. It looked terrible from up top.' I assumed he was referring to the back bedroom windows.

'Harold should have done something about it,' Phyllis said.

'Fact is, we had words. See, Francis, if you allow next door to rule the roost, it's as if they take you over. Some nights, even when Harold was in, we used to see those kids playing in his garden and jumping up and down on the fence. They made it worse, that Wesley and, er, Arora. It should have been out of bounds, Harold's garden, but they extended theirs into his. It was as if he'd given in and couldn't care less. And we were next in line if you think of everything going bad in our direction. I offered to help him fix it but he said OK and that's the last we heard.'

'Then there's the foxes,' Phyllis said, tut-tutting as she smoothed her dress over her knees.

'I told him to get rid of them, get the council or someone round, ' Joe said. 'For his benefit, mind. Foxes are vermin. And squirrels. But in a way, I don't think he minded much. The kids as well. Perhaps he'd lost interest. You must do with cancer.'

Phyllis elaborated: 'Yes. Poor Harold. Wild things coming in from next door and wild things at the bottom of his garden.'

Joe stared at her with a hint of distaste as if she'd upstaged him by saying something profound.

'It affected her nerves.' He looked at her again. 'Didn't it, Phyll?'

'I was on diazepam,' Phyllis said, affecting a little tremor as if the condition were returning at the mere mention.

'Didn't bother me much,' Joe said. 'We just felt sorry for him. And now this.'

'He used to be a coalminer,' I said.

'Never in this world,' Phyllis said. I was amazed that they didn't know.

'A coalminer.' The way Joe said it, matter-of-factly, staring into space, could have meant that he knew or that it had come as a surprise to him, but not so much of a surprise as it had been for Phyllis. 'A coalminer.' His repetition, likewise, sounded both philosophical (he knew) and incredulous (he'd just found out).

I'd already noted the prizewinning order of the Lewises' back garden: beyond a small striped lawn, scarcely meriting the attentions of a mower, was bounty designed to be harvested in waves. In one square, there were enough cabbages to feed the street. The same with lettuce, runner beans, onions. I wondered if they'd offered Harold any of their superfluous crops. I'd have to ask him. Out front, instead of Harold's pavioured flatness in which weeds were trying to invade, the Lewises had planted shrubs and multi-coloured borders, having erected their own white-painted trellis next to Harold's unpainted flimsier one and encouraged clematis to weave its way through the gaps and, it must be said, into Harold's side, giving it when in flower a gratuitous decoration, a gift. Their fence was holding up his and in that unsolicited support and the tentative sharing of blossom, I found something pathetically British, neither kindness nor selfishness but an odd amalgam of the two and both unremarked. They'd obviously had conversion work done inside. It was the same house as Harold's but it aspired to something higher, a central edifice in a plot repelling borders and vulpine incursions. (I got 'vulpine incursions' from Julie. She used such terms unselfconsciously, and Harold would glance at me when she did, assuming - and he was right - that they weren't ready to fall from my lips or his. I liked that; it bound me to him in a way I hadn't expected. Any common ground would do.)

I got up to go. It was getting dark. I also gave them Julie's contact details and confirmed they still had mine, explaining who Julie was. I think I called her my friend. Joe folded the slip of paper and placed it behind a brass ornament on the mantelpiece. When Phyllis put the lights on, a strip lamp I hadn't particularly noticed went on above the painting, like the start of a film, a documentary about the Highlands. They both came to the front door and said goodnight. I heard the door being locked behind me. Looking over my shoulder, I could see the stag behind their still-open Venetian blinds, like something that had taken over inside the house. Then the blinds closed too, seemingly of their own volition.

'What did you think of their stag?' Harold asked when I got back, as though referring to a real animal grazing on the Lewises' midget back lawn. Before I could reply, he said, 'Not a bad painting, but referring to something else.' Harold had depths, reflecting those he'd once plumbed.

I wondered what he meant. Referring to what? Something, probably, that neither Joe nor Phyllis divined.

Surfing the net before I turned in, I found the encyclopaedia entry for the painting. According to the information, it was not eighteen points the monarch's antlers required but sixteen.

The Denton

Harold had a passport photo of Ethel in his wallet. Ethel Chrimes. He showed it to me. She'd obviously had a few of them done. Its informality reflected friendship being bullied by acquaintance.

We were walking towards Worthing on the esplanade that led to the pier. Everyone seemed to be using it - cyclists, skateboarders, joggers, strollers like us. It was a cakewalk. The sun was blinding and behind us but it wasn't hot. A blonde woman wearing sunglasses under a see-through plastic parasol glided past, out of a dream. She could have been a Brighton eccentric on the way home from a party.

Harold stopped and handed me the picture. 'Not bad for one of those photo booths,' he said.

It wasn't, though I wondered why he didn't have a better print, something more professional or a passable amateur snapshot. Ethel looked younger than him, ten years at least. She also looked as though squeezing herself into a photo booth had created a discomfiture she would have preferred to forgo but at the same time one she was prepared to endure with grace. One wouldn't have been surprised, even on the evidence of a crude image, to have been told that she was indomitable. Perhaps it was because she'd been requested not to smile but, knowing the injunction to be null and void, had been forced into unnecessary compromise. She was wearing a pearl necklace and something similar but less resplendent beneath it, which I realised was a scar.

We continued walking.

'So where did you meet?'

'The book club. Have I told you about that?'

He had. He then obviously remembered that he had.

'The book of the month was some short stories by D H Lawrence. There was one about the father, a miner. I was interested in that and the others were interested in me because of my coalmining. They asked me if I recognised the background. I said it was almost a generation before my time, but that, yes, I could understand what was going on. There are no pits down here. Well, Kent was the nearest.'

I told him I'd found the Lawrences on *Ancestry*.

'So what *was* going on?'

He answered as though he hadn't heard me.

'It's not always a book that's just been published - the one we choose, I mean. It can be a classic.'

Then he explained.

'Something between the father and the mother, D H Lawrence's parents. She had high hopes of the boy, you see. I think the father probably did too but the mother must have been affected by the father's presence. When you've been digging for coal all day, you must feel you've done your duty by everyone.' He smiled at me, knowing the supposition hadn't applied to him as his marriage had been childless. 'I thought of inviting her for lunch tomorrow. Perhaps we can go out.'

'Why not?'

'In fact, I have invited her.'

For some reason, possibly a stirring sense of adventure, he'd got out of farming as a young man in the Eden valley and gone south to Wales. It must have been some trip for a lad his age. I thought farming, the outdoor life, would have been preferable to working underground. Obviously, there were gaps to be filled. Whether he would be forthcoming enough to provide the information I needed remained to be seen. He'd been reasonably open up till then; in fact, I sometimes felt like a returning prodigal.

We were approaching the Denton Lounge. He'd told me about it but this was the first time we'd been there. The Denton was a cavernous tearoom at the entrance to the pier. Harold said it was famous. Like so many other things in the Brighton area, as I was later to discover, it had a warmth that seemed to arise from its clientele as much as from the sunbeams piercing its high windows. It was also a warmth that resulted from the friction between a more gracious past and an encroaching seediness, though perhaps in the light of what the whole area exuded, 'seediness' was the wrong word. There was certainly something about the place that spoke of elegance holding out against the erosion of a lesser quality in which the multitude was complicit. Out of the throng now and then would emerge a raddled ghost from this past, no longer anchored for a while to a stronghold preserved and sustained through the strength of claims on a notion of style and solidity. Or so I thought. That was something else I had to come to terms with: the idea that Harold might not think like I did or put things the way I did. But it was obvious that I'd already begun to under-estimate him.

First, we rounded the Denton and walked a little way along the pier, stopping to lean on the rail and watch a group of men down below showing off in dinghies with powerful outboard motors. They would accelerate, score foamy figures-of-eight on the sea's surface and then quieten the engines. Their persistent calligraphy was not so much a sight as a sound, like chainsaws taken to an unyielding tree trunk, so that the pier seemed to be under threat. Then I spotted four swimmers slowly stroking to where the men were making the water boil. They were elderly and wearing bathing caps. One was a woman. I pointed them out to Harold. He just smiled.

'Watch,' he said.

The twirling dinghy sailors did not stop their antics but, realising the swimmers were deliberately heading their way, shifted their focus gradually towards the end of the pier, though not fast enough to give the semblance of a retreat. The swimmers drew closer, refusing to veer off their intended line. One of the sailors, his craft slowed to a swan's paddle, penned them in with a lightly drawn circle and then roared off with the others, disappearing beyond the ironwork, at which point the swimmers began treading water and floating outstretched on their backs, their mission completed. Harold chuckled and said something odd or said it in an odd and unexpected way.

'That's what I call colourful,' he said. 'Wanting to go as far as you can into the danger zone without getting hurt - or maybe getting hurt. And at their age. They're all doing it down here. I think that's why they call it a colourful place.'

I must have looked bemused because he laughed, reached up to put his hand on my shoulder and headed us off in the direction of the Denton. 'I'm ready for a cuppa,' he said.

We seated ourselves at one of the Denton's big shiny-topped tables. It was an hour before closing so the place was thinly populated with stragglers like us. Someone drew a curtain to shield themselves from the sun, now beginning its vertical drop into the channel but still seething with yellow brilliance. I'd never seen sunsets so unhampered. There was nothing to interrupt them and cast diverting shadows. It was a solo performance with only the sea's surface as a prop, ever glistering, ever threatening to steal the scene.

The first time I met Harold, it was as if I were being re-united with an old trusting friend. As a result, it took a while for us to exchange information on my first visits to his home and by phone. I didn't want to interrogate him and he showed little detailed interest in me. I got used to that. We knew the basic stuff. The rest would follow when it was ready to be dislodged from the coal seam of memory. He was more interested in me and Julie, an arrangement that had come undone, than anything about my past that could help him to offer meaningful advice - that's if he wanted to. For my part, I couldn't fail to be interested in his illness, concerned about him. Neither of us knew how far we could go in these well-intentioned manoeuvres and that slowed things down even more.

It was no surprise, therefore, when he further ruffled the present by telling me more about Ethel Chrimes. Just before he did, a waiter re-opened the curtains after the customers who'd drawn them had left. The re-introduced sunshine was obliterated momentarily by a woman dressed in a fur coat and a hat with a feather sticking out of it and it seemed as though Ethel, of whose general appearance I had no idea except for that official-looking and unsmiling photograph, had materialised in grand silhouette at Harold's mention of her name, one of the painted host about to return to her notion of the past but for a brief moment stopping to consider us as we sat there like the colluding personification of old times and new.

I looked across at Harold. His face was awash in sunshine and his eyes were closed. A smile on his face.

'Lovely, isn't it?' he said.

I made some affirmative sound.

'These foxes, do they stop you going into the garden?'

'Good heavens, no! But when I'm in the garden pottering about, they're never there. At least they don't come out.'

'Aren't they vermin? Joe thinks so.'

'I suppose they are. In the country they are. Squirrels are vermin.'

I'd forgotten that he knew about the country. He seemed to be parroting Phyllis and Joe.

'You need to be careful with them, I should think.'

'Well, I wouldn't go out and join them if they were around. They'd probably run off anyway. I prefer to watch them through the window. That's how I took the photos. I knew a postman who was bitten by a squirrel - it ran down a telegraph pole and went for his leg. Walked with a limp after that, on his rounds. Everybody knew about it, about why he delivered letters with a limp.'

Squirrels and pigs – vicious beasts.

'On my way down, I met a little girl who was taking her grandparents into a cage of wild animals. At a wildlife park.'

'Oh, aye. I've read about that.'

'Marmosets, apparently. I don't think I know what a marmoset looks like.'

'No, I mean it was in the papers, some zoo or other. Someone got bitten, so they stopped it. They're like pretty monkeys. Slow-moving, with long tails.'

'I hope they know. She'll be disappointed.'

'She'll get over it. They always do.'

Coming from a childless widower, this sounded odd but it reminded me of something Julie once said about knowledge and experience: that it was essentially personal and imaginative. You could think your way into other people's lives and feel as they do. It was the sort of thing she was always saying. I repeat, Julie was a writer. She also had an old-fashioned video camera.

Messages

There's something about the home of a widower that speaks rather obviously of a woman's absence.

For a start, there's the smell. It's not actually unpleasant and emanates mostly from the kitchen but it's the sort of thing a woman - at least, my mother - wouldn't abide. It's compounded by other things that would not be tolerated if a woman were around to prevent them, such as the washing-machine processes - basket of items ready to be washed, basket of items ready to be ironed, basket of whiffy items drying out - which seem to be eternally in a loop and left for all to see, the odd drying sock having failed to keep up with the group. I noticed it all as soon as we returned.

We had more tea, watched some television and talked a bit more about cancer. Harold wondered if his might be connected to having been a coal miner. I thought not. But what did I know?

Then he asked me if I minded his turning in early. He looked tired. I wasn't bothered. I let the TV witter away quietly before switching it off. I was planning to show him my iPad but decided to leave it to the next day.

I sent a text to Julie. In the circumstances I thought she'd appreciate some kind of update about Harold. *It's the prostate cancer again,* I said. *He seems OK but a bit knackered. Will be in touch. By the bye, there are foxes in his garden. X*

When it was dark, I went into the back room, a sort of semi-conservatory, making sure not to turn on the lights. There was no sign of fox life. I sat on a small settee and kept vigil for an hour.

Nothing happened at first but I became transfixed by the way the surrounding street lights and other illumination - a full moon was up - gave a gloaming appearance to the garden and an atmosphere of expectancy. It was an empty stage on which you knew something was bound to happen sooner or later, if only you had the patience to wait. No foxes but bats and their flickering tracery; a stealthy cat; a procession of crows like raucous partygoers against the moonlit sky. Support acts without the headliners.

I couldn't think of anything in any detail. It just seemed sad that I might be losing Harold not long after I'd found him. It was almost as sad as acknowledging that it was OK to text or email Julie, the messages always brief, but not always to phone her directly. It was the difference between maintaining a distance and dramatically shortening it. He might survive, of course. But age was against him. He too told me that 'loads' of men had prostate cancer but few died of it: they died *with* it, and with lots of other things. In his case, that didn't seem much of a consolation. It was something else Joe knew.

Back in the kitchen, I started clearing up without too much noise. I tried to make it seem as though I were being helpful rather than critical.

One of the things about me that irritated Julie was my tendency to clear up after her, especially before we turned in. 'Leave it,' she'd say. Then, when I didn't, 'For god's sake, frigging well leave it!' It wasn't that she felt it to be her responsibility, rather that I were making some comment about her standards of tidiness. The edge in her voice indicated that, as a pair, we were moving towards some kind of landmark.

But I loved her dishevelled appearance, a semi-bohemian thing that I always thought was meant to undermine her indestructible beauty. It never worked. We'd stayed together mostly at her place. I'd made no impression on it. She'd published two novels and worked as a freelance journalist. There were not enough royalties from the books for her - us - to live on. I was an actor, mostly unemployed; she a scribe always waiting for payments. It wasn't promising. When I think of all this, it's no wonder to me that we couldn't make a go of things. But the qualities that initially attracted us to each other were still reachable. I guess it was why we were still in touch in a meaningful way, both of us recognising the difference between laughable eccentricity and dependable virtue. But always at a distance, its length a recognition of lives still separate, not yet ready to renew proximity. I don't know what she thought my qualities were. A third novel was with a publisher, awaiting imminent rejection or approval.

I picked up my mobile. There was a reply to my message. It said: *God, that's awful. Give him my love. Tell him I'd like to see him. Has he given up on me? I hope not. Weather awful here. Look. Foxes? Christ Xx*

I realised that I hadn't remembered her to him as she'd asked before I left. She'd uploaded a picture of an electric storm in which two bolts of fork lightning lit up a townscape. It was beautifully composed, almost artistic. With phones and pads, we are all photographers now. She'd taken it but there wasn't enough detail for me to recognise it as the place where she lived. But she assured me it was. I had an image of her and her neighbours battening themselves down. Somewhere in the distance, those symmetrical pincers of lightning would have struck something, a couple of trees perhaps, which would have stood for a moment in the plant kingdom equivalent of shock amidst steam and hissing and momentary fire but witnessed by no one. It would be something to see, wouldn't it - a massive bough ripped off, the point of rupture glowing white in the storm, the sap on the boil?

I was going to reply to Julie that we could use her video camera but I thought better of it. Harold's foxes video-ed. We could film it on our mobiles and have it on YouTube in seconds.

As I lay on the settee, waiting to grow tired enough to sleep, I heard a regular rumbling noise coming from above. I went to the foot of the stairs. It was Harold snoring. I was reminded of a wild animal betraying its presence to a more-alert predator.

But Harold's raider was already inside the gates, helping itself. The only consolation, actually no consolation at all, was that it would die with him, its insatiable greed walling it in week by inevitable week. Unless, of course, something could be sent down the line to kill it, to release it.

On Julie's digital photo, there was a white smudge against a street light. A passing seagull, probably, screeching above the heavenly pandemonium.

Underground

'I've got a pretty good idea,' Harold was saying at breakfast the next morning. 'I mean, they've gone through it with me.'

We were talking about chemotherapy, my questions sounding not like someone trying to discover if the other person were fully in possession of the facts but building up his own database with the help of an unreliable informant. We could all find out about cancer if only we wanted to know in the first place. One in three will get it but we are never that one. *Ergo*, we're not interested. Luck be a lady...

I told him I didn't mind if he wanted to go to church. It was a mile away. I'd even go with him if he could stand my singing and my silence during the Lord's Prayer. He laughed at that, said he'd intended to give it a miss as I was down visiting. But if I insisted, we could both go.

'Your singing's not bad,' he said, and stared for a few seconds into the distance. I knew he wasn't reflecting on the accuracy of his estimate. He was doing it all the time - saying something, then appearing as though he might have regretted it or wondering if it could be misconstrued.

I watched his miner's hands tapping and peeling a boiled egg. His face wore a look of resigned satisfaction with the hint of a smile. I wondered if he experienced that glow of life said to brighten an individual who knows he's not long for this world. Julie wouldn't have liked the expression 'not long for this world'. Well, I know it's a euphemism but I sometimes think roundabout ways of describing things are often a means of avoiding intemperate or provocative bluntness. In any case, if you know you're going to die there's little point in admitting that your 'passing' is imminent. That's for others to say out of a sense of decorum and no one is about to pick them up on it. We could all do with pastel shades now and again as a change from primary colours. Personally, I'd be quite happy when the time comes, to think I was about to 'pass away' and I certainly wouldn't mind others referring to my death as such. Apart from anything else, and like 'not long for this world', it would involve a human recognition that there's something outside ourselves that will remain when we have gone: something we pass out of, something that no longer has need of us. I wondered if there would ever be a time when I could have a discussion with Harold along those lines. It's foxes that die. Foxes don't 'depart this mortal coil'. But people do leave a gap and the gap is filled by someone else, as well as the memory of the one who has left.

'I've booked a table at The Town House in Arundel,' Harold said, just before I was about to mention Ethel Chrimes. 'For one-thirty. It's just that they do a lot of veggie stuff.'

'You're not vegetarian.'

'No, but Ethel is. Swears by it. Goes in for that herbal medicine as well.'

'Oh.'

I wanted to ask him if Ethel were more companion than friend. It happens with widowers. I remembered a book I'd just read, *A Summons To Memphis*, by Peter Taylor, an American writer. Julie'd put me on to it. In the book, the narrator tells how his father, an elderly widower of means, has announced that he's decided to re-marry. The news is given long-distance to the narrator by his sisters who are concerned at the turn of events for reasons that are obvious but difficult to articulate or admit. But my imagination was running off again, as it had done since I'd met Harold and realised that he wasn't going to sit down and give me his life story in any immediate detail. I supposed news of the cancer would postpone it for even longer. On the other hand, it might encourage him to open up, the loss of inhibition and all that. We started talking about something of which neither one of us knew much.

'It's never been an issue with me,' I said. 'But I can understand how it exercises some people. I mean, killing animals for food seems to me to be a lot different from killing them for pleasure but I suppose it amounts to the same thing. Thou shalt not kill animals - should that be a commandment?'

'We had a few pit ponies when I was younger,' he said. 'They were coming to an end. I saw a couple drop dead in the shafts. They must have pulled thousands of tons of coal in their lifetime. Those that survived, they used to pension off. I volunteered for the detail once. Well, you got attached to them and you wanted to see them released into the fields. There was a place that took them on, out in the country. They went mad in the sun at first, then they were quiet, like as if they realised there was nothing to get excited about. Why should they get excited? They'd spent their whole time having the life wrenched out of them. Sometimes they resented it, lashed out with both hind legs. They must have got to the stage where they didn't expect good things to last. Not as though they weren't fed and watered and looked after, mind.'

He could have been talking about coalminers themselves, about a life difficult to ease in any appreciable way. Perhaps he was also reassuring me that underground there was none of the magnified enmity to be found among factions in a community whose rivalries are overridden by common and universal suffering - no tendency to be more cruel to horses because they were no better than yourself. I suggested this might have been the case.

'Well, if you hadn't looked after them, they'd have made your work harder,' I said.

'Aye, that was the case for some. But not for yours truly.'

He looked at me wryly, as if a lifelong churchgoer would by definition be above anything so demeaning.

'So there could have been mistreatment?'

'There was bad treatment, beatings. A sackable offence. I never saw it. But you knew when a pony was being abused. You could hear it.' He stared ahead of him. 'We were all being abused in a way of speaking.'

I wanted to say this was exactly the point I was trying to make, but I thought better of it. I poured myself another cup of tea and examined the bookcase below the TV. It was a self-educated Christian man's repository, a small piece of furniture rammed with essential texts - a dictionary, the Bible, an English hymnal, biographies of Keir Hardie and Aneurin Bevan, a compendium of *Classics for the Working Man*, some Orwell, some Mark Twain, a *Best of Picture Post* lying horizontally between vertical tomes and the shelf above. All worthy stuff, as a cynical friend of mine might have put it. And the odd art tome - Van Gogh, Michelangelo, Jeffrey Camp's *Draw: How to Master the Art.* It evoked a few images - the talented and curious prole, the Workers Educational Association. I smiled. So it was true. But the books seemed glued together. I never saw them in any other positions on the shelf. But maybe their time in that household had come and gone or would never now arrive.

'You haven't told me much about Ethel,' I said.

'No, I haven't.'

I waited for an elaboration. None was forthcoming.

'So it'll be a surprise.'

'Aye. Something like that.'

There was a hint of a smile and an impish glance in my direction.

'I suppose it couldn't have been more than ten minutes,' he said.

'What?'

'Them ponies going mad in the hay, in the sunshine.'

'It must have been a sight.'

'It was that, all right. I wish I'd had a camera, or pencil and paper.'

It was then that my phone started ringing upstairs. I waited for him to tell me. But I realised he couldn't hear it. It didn't ring for long. I knew who it was. Later, I picked up a voice message: *'Hi. It's me. How is he?'* Julie's ethereal voice asked. *'How is it going?'*

I texted a reply. If she came down to see Harold, perhaps it might be worth her bringing the video-camera after all. Before it went out of date. It wouldn't be obsolete for Harold, at that time owning neither a mobile nor a PC.

Now Thank We All Our God

Walking with Harold through the tunnel of yews at St Bartholomew's Church, I wondered if my bright red weatherproof jacket were out of place.

The thought first occurred to me when we were getting ready for morning service after breakfast. He was dressed smartly in a dark suit and grey herring-bone overcoat. But I didn't say anything and he didn't look sideways at me as I put the jacket on.

As if to counteract his sober attire, he'd chosen a relatively garish necktie: bright blue with abstract Paisley curlicues in red, the sort of thing artists might go for as recognition of a lively side to their personalities and with that necessary dash of flair, a conscious thing. His shoes were buffed to an explosive shine, sort of military. My suede boots wore a watermark hemline which made sidestepping of the yews' scattered red berries seem a joke.

He reminded me that they were deadly poisonous.

'That's why they're red,' he explained. 'To put grazers off. Red for danger. They call 'em arils.'

I wondered if, also as an artist, he was making an unspoken connection between the red cups and the brightness of my jacket. It was the sort of kinship writers also identified, as I knew from Julie.

I was reminded of Julie when we were waiting in the vestibule for the people in front to move along. One of the posters on the noticeboard was headlined, *Conscience Is*

A Man's Best Compass, apparently a quote from a letter by Vincent van Gogh to his brother, Theo. In her two novels to date, Julie had placed a quotation at the front.

I didn't read the rest of the poster closely but the gist was that we should all get together to guide our fellow beings in the direction of God, who was represented by a large emblazoned white star. Next to it and just as prominent was a flyer for the RNIB, showing a picture of a black Labrador in a Day-glo jacket.

Our wait wasn't the result of a long queue. Once inside and seated, and as the service was about to begin, we turned out to be about a tenth of the congregation. It was like an assembly not long before visited by the plague. I wondered why everyone didn't sit more closely together, at the front. Perhaps the quaint diaspora was meant to give an illusion of full attendance reduced by unavoidable absentees. On a leaflet I picked up inside the door, it said St Bartholomew's served a parish of over seven thousand - a 'rainbow' parish. It read like the supreme example of optimism. Compasses had probably sent many of them in another direction wearing jackets like mine, fit for another purpose.

The first hymn was *Jesu, Lover of My Soul*, to a tune I didn't recognise but everyone else did, including Harold. Being slightly deaf, he was the first to start singing, and he did so in a passable tenor, if a little uncertain of pitch.

Not to be outdone, I skipped the first verse, mumbled my way through the second and by the third was able to accompany him in what sounded to me like a duet, its volume above and beyond everyone else's effort.

The vicar, perched in his raised pulpit like a ministering angel, smiled our way while still singing himself. He probably appreciated effort by the few as a consolation for the dwindling of the many.

An unfamiliar tune, like an unfamiliar text, was for me just something to be learned - the hymn-sheet as playscript. At college, I'd been taught to sing and dance. You never knew when they might be required on stage.

As we sat down, I was aware of something moving in the high timbered roof. It was a bird. I couldn't tell what sort. The swifts and house-martins would soon be ready to migrate, at least in my part of the world. Probably a sparrow. At the beginning of the first prayer, one newly minted by the vicar whose heavenward stare and contorted features suggested he was concentrating on remembering it, the sound of intermittent birdsong floated down.

My head bowed, I could see that Harold's eyes were closed. As the Lord's Prayer was intoned, and with my eyes remaining open but head still lowered, I uttered only the words and phrases that weren't morally loaded – 'father'; 'this day'; 'daily bread'; 'for ever and ever'. I was taking advantage of his growing deafness.

Looking up as the sermon began, I saw the bird flying agitatedly but in slow silent circles. A counter-attraction, full of the inexplicable and awesome, it was more interesting than the sermon which was probably trying to subsume it. Like religion, I thought, its expression of freedom was a fantasy, a demonstration of joy in a confined space.

Harold was an active member of the church and obviously well-liked. Afterwards, all the other worshippers stopped to talk to us. We chatted to the vicar whose razor that morning had missed some stout grey bristles at the corner of his mouth, and his wedding-ring was almost hidden by enveloping flesh. As we made our way towards the yew canopy and their sinister red traps, he called out, 'Oh, Harold, Thanks for doing the crystals. We're going to have to keep an eye on that.'

I watched Harold turn and wave.

'What did he say?' I asked.

'Oh, after Men's Fellowship last week, I re-filled the Crystalkil boxes. You know - the little boxes with poison stuff in them to get rid of the mice. Did you see one under the pew?'

'A mouse? I saw a bird in the rafters. I was looking up - towards Heaven.'

'No, a box. I've got a pack of them at home. I'll show you. They're flat and you pull them into shape, like one of them Toblerones. The crystals are locked up in the vestry.'

I thought of saying something about all god's creatures but stopped myself. How many men do you need to create a Fellowship at St Bart's?

Then, for some weird reason, I had this image of Ethel Chrimes administering one of her homeopathic remedies: the minutest amount of poison that cured you out of sheer devilry because it hadn't reached a level that could kill.

'It's not dangerous,' he assured me. 'As long as you wear gloves.'

I was shocked; I thought he was referring to the Ethel of my thoughts. He toed a few of the arils which rolled away to rest among confetti trodden into a drab mosaic. 'Not like them.' He made sure he hadn't spoiled his shoeshine.

'Bird?' he queried. 'I didn't see it.'

'Have you caught any - you know, mice?'

'Can't tell. They're taking the stuff. They go away and die somewhere else.'

It sounded like an allusion to his own life's journey.

He hadn't seen the bird. And he certainly wouldn't have heard it.

Ethel

When Ethel Chrimes entered The Town House, she might have been the embodiment of that Denton spectre, come to confirm what she'd noticed already in passing. That the previous appearance - a featureless silhouette momentarily effacing the sun - had been acknowledged only by me seemed to make it personal and I felt that even now she was present solely on my account. At any rate, I had a faint idea of what it must be like to be haunted.

Harold stood in greeting and was about to introduce me when she anticipated him.

'You must be Francis,' she said. 'I've heard so much about you.'

This surprised me because my conversations with Harold had so far been mostly one-way: I asked questions and he slipped me bits of information about himself. I certainly knew more about him than he did about me but I put that down to the caution of someone who'd placed himself at the disposal of a more-or-less complete stranger, possibly against his better judgement.

I was about to say I hoped that all she'd been told about me was complimentary when I checked myself. It was the kind of familiar remark you made to someone younger or with a sense of humour you'd assumed from the company they kept. So I said nothing except that I was pleased to meet her.

'I suppose that Harold's told you about you-know-what.'

The object of her supposition looked at me from behind his menu and raised his eyebrows.

'Yes,' I said.

'Well, we have to do something,' she said. 'Now, what are we all having to eat?'

She chose an Italian dish from the vegetarian options and I was surprised to see Harold do the same. By 'we', I wondered, did she mean us?

'We've been talking about meat,' he told her, referring to our exchange at breakfast. 'Francis here is all in favour.'

I think it was the first time he'd uttered my name since I'd first contacted him and he said it as though it betokened something unfamiliar he wasn't sure of. I wasn't exactly 'all' in favour.

For a few seconds, I thought I might have to defend myself. But Ethel was not ready for an argument.

'That's all right,' she said. 'I don't mind.'

Somehow I knew she did. Maybe it was her schoolteacher bearing, an impression of being in charge after a lifetime of diplomacy and negotiation in which she had always had the last word; and a certainty of opinion stemming from never having been seriously contradicted.

'Ethel was a lecturer,' he explained, as though he'd read my thoughts and wished to make the slightest of corrections in order that I might nevertheless wish to alter my view. I realised we were all an educated lot, Julie included, in one way or another. At least, I have three 'A' levels and an acting diploma, if not much else. And Harold could paint.

'Domestic Science,' she added. 'Except they call it something different these days. It was a long time ago. Well, twelve years. Anyway, it was Domestic Science when I started.'

'Food Technology,' I said. 'My partner's young brother is studying it.'

'That's right,' she said. 'When am I going to meet your partner? Julia, isn't it?'

'Julie,' I corrected.

So Harold had told her. Perhaps he decided to let me tell Ethel that Julie was my former partner, although even I couldn't bring myself to call her that. In any case, the precise nature of our estrangement was something I didn't expect him to fully grasp. I thought I knew him well enough to know that attempting to do so would have been insensitive. Irrationally, I looked upon Harold and Ethel and people of their generation as strangers to sexual skirmishing. They had become elderly and it was only then that their problems were beginning, in Harold's case - and Ethel's if she faced them - to be dealt with virtually alone. They were physical difficulties, unlike the emotional ones Julie and I were confronting. I suddenly saw my relationship with Harold as an intervention which might help him deal more effectively with what lay ahead. I decided to volunteer some facts.

'Actually, Julie and I had more or less broken up though we remain friends - best friends,' I said.

'I'm sorry to hear that,' Ethel said. 'These things happen and we get over them.'

There was something peremptory but unconvincing about her tone, as if she'd had a similar experience but had mistaken forgetting for a determination to forget. It was that teacher image again, the need to assert an authority she exercised by definition. I felt emboldened to confound it.

'Well, it's not exactly a *fait accompli* and, at the moment at least, there's nothing to get over,' I said. 'Though there are matters to attend to.'

I hoped she wouldn't follow through and ask me what those matters were. In any case, the arrival of our food interrupted the exchange - some kind of green vegetable risotto for them and venison for me.

'Looks good,' said Harold, eyeing my more substantial plateful. Theirs were buried in the central depression of a bowl with a ridiculously wide lip.

Blood began flowing from the heart of my meat into the surrounding *jus*. I could see that Ethel noticed the difference between our modes of attack: she and Harold daintily with just a fork, me aggressively with a fork and steak knife.

'And there you have it,' she said. 'Culling to keep the deer population down or farming herds for commercial slaughter. It doesn't matter what your reason for being a vegetarian is, the advantage is in the renunciation. We would all be better off, animals and eaters.' She looked at me and smiled. 'I hope you don't mind me being controversial.'

I sensed a challenge. 'You mean it's healthier.'

'But of course. Isn't it, Harold?'

There was a hesitation in his reply that spoke of wishing to say the right thing in her presence. 'I'm willing to give it a try, anyhow.'

She seemed eager to explain this willingness and its possible source in prevarication. We continued eating in silence, observing what was going on around us. She said:

'I've told Harold I have my doubts about the course of treatment he's about to undergo. It's not that I think he shouldn't start it but there are other methods. Acupuncture, for instance.'

'Acupuncture?' I must have sounded faintly incredulous, though I managed not to grin or splutter. Acupuncture and cancer sounded like a David and

Goliath thing before the outcome. She might have thought the same but her imagination had rushed ahead to the unexpected victory.

At that moment, and when we were only halfway through the meal, there was a thud at the bay window behind us and a couple with a teenage girl sitting there rose to their feet and looked out. 'It's a blackbird,' I could hear the girl say. 'Look!' One of the waiters joined them and stared into the bushes. 'I'll see to it,' he said, and left the room. Seconds later, he was outside cradling the bird which we could see struggling in his cupped hands, a wing hanging limply and the yellow beak agape in shock. He held it up for all of us to see, touching the tip of its tongue, then walked off as the three sat down again and resumed eating. After a few minutes, he returned and explained something to the couple and the girl, but we couldn't hear that. The girl looked our way, directly at me, I thought, but I couldn't be sure. I wondered how that marmoset adventure had gone or if Harold had been right about the newspaper report and the motorway trio I'd met had been disappointed. I mentioned seeing the sparrow flying in the fastnesses of the church roof, saying that episode and now this one reminded me of something from Hitchcock's *The Birds*. Neither of them commented. It occurred to me that they'd never heard of the film or had never seen it.

'Broken wing, I expect,' Harold said, referring to the blackbird with a former country boy's nonchalance. 'Best put it out of its misery.'

I half-expected Ethel to counter with something about animal rescue, makeshift splints, recovery, rehabilitation and eventual release, but she'd not lost her train of thought.

'We should see how it goes and if it goes badly, then we should give something else a chance. You'd be up for that, wouldn't you, Harold?'

She said it rhetorically, expecting nothing but agreement.

Harold, it seemed to me, was floundering behind an over-zealous advocacy of his case. An idea had been put to him, possibly over tea and biscuits at a meeting of the Book Club, and like most males of the species, he was postponing a decision. 'Male of the species' was another expression Julie would not have used nor did she think that males of whatever species always blundered in while hunting and gathering of one kind or another. Often, but not always. Like that blackbird. Ochre beak, raven plumage - it was a male all right, heading for disaster.

Ethel had that annoying habit of admitting you to her company and just as formally abandoning you by raising subjects with others present that pointedly excluded anything you might know or be interested in. It was worse than rude: it was deliberate. More so as they'd finished their rice dishes while I was still carving my meat. Once, while talking to Harold about some kind of building work soon to be carried out on her property - I got the gist - I saw her glance my way, first at my plate, then at me with a look of mild disgust barely moderated by impatience.

I finished my food, placing my knife and fork together at twenty past the hour, an indication to the waitress (so I'd read) that she should clear my part of the table. I thought Ethel, as a former Domsky lecturer, might have recognised the signal from her study of etiquette, surely a branch of her specialist subject. But she didn't notice and nor did the waitress, because she passed our table twice before I leant backwards to draw her attention to my readiness. So much for an admittedly tame desire to impress.

Suddenly Ethel asked, 'How old are you, Francis?'

'Forty-two,' I replied, losing the opportunity to make some youthful counterpart to those jokes about age being no one's business but your own.

'Still young enough to have no idea what's to come,' she said.

It sounded like a reproof, as though I should be blamed for not being older and wiser.

'What's to come is still unsure,' was my theatrical retort.

'Shakespeare,' Harold said. Harold was full of surprises.

Facing him but turning to look at me, Ethel doubly dismissed my upstart knowingness and Harold's piercing example of having been improved by the Book Club. 'With Harold's help, I've mapped everything out,' she said. 'We've agreed that it's important. The prognosis is not good.'

She turned to Harold for a confirmation no one had denied, least of all him. 'What I mean is, there'll be procedures and there'll be results. The results we'll have to act upon. These days, the medical profession is ruled by the drug companies. They'll prescribe anything in order to be seen to be doing something. They never stop to think that what they are doing might be totally the wrong thing.'

She leaned towards me. 'At forty-two, Francis, you have not started going down. It's about outcomes and there's no time to dither. Now - dessert.'

I could barely suppress a snigger, apart from the fact that her final two words sounded like an order for me to leave the restaurant. At forty-something, I could safely say I'd gone down many times and been gone down upon come to that, though not often enough as I'd explained to Julie. Harold hadn't seen the joke. I began to notice the subtleties of a generation gap, in which severity was countered by levity and the old sometimes claimed a spurious authority based on their age. Older and wiser. Harold wasn't saying much. Perhaps he wasn't sure about his Shakespeare reference and believed that we knew he was wrong. The old say outrageous things as a result of having lost contact - with society, the world, changes in habit and direction. Oakwood Lodge told me that. Unless you were tolerant, they could be a pain. The trouble with tolerance is it leaves no indication among those being tolerated of how different and how strongly you, people in general, now felt about things. And yet, like Harold, the old are indeed on the way out, closer to the exit than the young wish to imagine. But I had the feeling that Ethel Chrimes was not of their company and could be kept alive with the help of stem-ginger infusions. This made her in my eyes both a joke and an enemy of reason; but she had her own way of reasoning.

Emboldened, I said: 'Mapped out. What do you mean by "mapped out"?'

Harold decided this was a point of entry. 'They've given me a calendar, a sort of timetable. I haven't shown you yet. It's got the times of treatment on it and the rough dates when I have to see the specialist.'

'The oncologist,' Ethel interrupted. As if neither of us knew. Actually, I didn't or had forgotten.

'It's a bit, how shall I say, presumptuous,' Ethel commented. We agreed about that.

It was only then, because diners at adjacent tables were sometimes looking our way, that I realised how raised above the confidential Ethel's voice had become. By contrast, Harold's was almost a whisper.

'We'll have to see how it goes,' he said. 'Doctor's orders.'

At this, Ethel uttered what I can only describe as a tiny animal sound, a cross between a bark, a sigh and a squeal as she cast about for the waitress's attention. Leaning back in her chair, you could see that she was the largest person in the room. She and Harold together resembled the henpecked husband and the heaving-bosomed wife of an old-fashioned seaside postcard except that our conversation had over-ridden any visual comedy.

Harold scanned the menu and declined. Ethel also said she didn't want anything more; not, I felt, because she was no longer hungry but out of kinship. Still beyond whatever accommodation they'd agreed on, I ordered Peach Melba and ate it quickly as they both watched.

That was the impression I got anyway. It wasn't an examination or an expression of impatience. I made some remark to the effect that it was almost as good as her apricot tart, but she smiled and turned away from me to stare at Harold who himself was looking towards the window where the blackbird had been stopped in mid-course. She broke this uninterrupted line between our table and the window by searching for something in her handbag while it was on her lap and while Harold was still meditating on bird-brained flight. She found it and passed it to me, not furtively but equally not waiting for Harold to turn his attention to us again. It was an illustrated card that may have belonged to a pack and on it was a picture of some exotic trees shaped like giant umbrellas. Underneath the picture in a flowing script was what I took to be their botanical name - *Didymopanay morototoni.*

'It may be the answer to our prayers,' she said, loud enough for Harold to hear and intended to retrieve his interest. She took the card from me and held it up for him to see before returning it to me.

'Oh yes,' he said. 'The Brazilian wonder cure.' I wasn't sure whether there was a hint of sarcasm in his voice or if he was pretending that he'd told me about it and was offering a reminder.

'Extract of the leaves, stems and roots of this tree was used by the ancients, and is still used by jungle-dwellers, to treat pain,' Ethel said. 'Medical research has investigated its properties and it is now being given to cancer patients in America with remarkable results. The compound manufactured from these extracts is called Metaferon. Demand for it and testimonials from satisfied sufferers attest to its success in treatment.'

She sounded like a drug company rep given a spiel to learn; 'Metaferon' sounded as though it were dignifying something beyond the pale of orthodox medicine. As she spoke, Harold listened to her, his arm leaning on the table.

I didn't know what to say. Why, if Harold believed it was worth trying, would there be any point in cautioning him? But surely she was not thinking of it as an alternative to the treatment he'd planned on his calendar. I felt brave enough to raise the point.

'We're going with the specialists to start with,' he said, his stern expression as he faced Ethel seeming to indicate that he would do as he saw fit, whatever hopes were being raised by her from another source. But it was the 'we' that struck me as odd, as if the opening of hostilities to fight his illness was to be a joint effort. It wasn't the royal 'we'.

I could see that Harold wasn't keen to talk about his problems in public. He must also have recognised my isolation at the table, my non-involvement in the conversation except as someone who might raise his companion's ire. So he changed the subject and seemed pleased to have done so on my account.

He told us a story about blackbirds. About how as a boy he'd discovered a nest of fledglings which had unaccountably died one by one and how he'd realised too late that the parent had abandoned the nest or been killed.

'If I'd been a few years older, I could have done something about it,' he said.

It was a story of no apparent consequence but that's what made it poignant. It was an illustration of helplessness founded on ignorance and immaturity. I could see he knew that. I also understood there was no sentiment, no extrapolation: the featherless orphans weren't mirrored in an image of bereft human urchins being looked after by relatives.

It was only then that I realised how little contact Harold seemed to have with his relatives. Maybe they were not all that close. He said they knew about his illness. But their absence from these notes will be conspicuous. They were never with him when Julie and I were.

Chanctonbury Ring

Outside the restaurant, Ethel didn't talk much more about Harold or his condition, nor did Harold say a lot about her on the drive back to his place. We talked mainly about our family connection, then about the places we mentioned while doing so - Wales, Cumbria, Lancashire.

Harold praised my hymn-singing. Ethel attended some kind of congregation but we didn't raise the subject of belief. I got the impression that Ethel Chrimes regarded herself as a possible saviour so would have no truck with any exclusive kind of redemption.

She'd caught a bus to get to the restaurant because her car was 'out of commission'. We gave her a lift back to her house in Rustington but we didn't go in. She hoped she'd see me again. The house looked neglected somehow, the front garden in particular: a half-rotten window frame, an unkempt border, weeds in control, net curtains hammocked across the window rather than taut. She didn't ask me to return the card. In the drive - barely a drive, more a patio outside the front door - stood a Nissan Micra that looked as though it had just taken part in a rally.

It was mid-afternoon and still a fine day when we got back. We were hardly inside the front door when Harold suggested we visit Chanctonbury Ring, a local hilltop arbour said to have been built by the Romans. I thought it would be too long a walk but the idea was to drive to a spot from which the actual landmark could be approached without too much exertion. I noticed that, unlike the day before, he seemed far less tired. I guessed this was how the cancer visited: today arriving with the intention of staying a while, tomorrow a drive-by wave. Illness is always in control, dictating the terms of its lodging.

We drove up to a grassy pull-in and parked next to three other cars. The famous ring of trees - actually an oval - was half a mile ahead. I expected to see more people out walking. Some, I supposed, would have set out from a point down below and, anyway, all would have dispersed over the Downs. On a worn path beyond a stile, I could see a straggle of walkers making its way to the top. It seemed like a pilgrimage, which is what I chose to think it was, the pilgrims by their small number pursuing the memory of some obscure or forgotten saint. Bartholomew perhaps, whoever he was. Saint Bart. Harold had found reserves of energy and strode along as if he'd been out and about for two hours. It would have a tough time, this cancerous enemy within, against the stamina that a lifetime in the pit had embedded in his constitution. I knew about the rings of trees that capped the hills as far as you could see but I asked him about them anyway, often a strategy inviting disbelief at my lack of knowledge. (For some reason, I'd answered 'No' when he'd asked me if I knew the work of Josef Herman, the Polish artist who'd worked in the Welsh coalmining village of Ystradgynlais and almost deified its blackened sons of toil. I 'knew of' Herman, but that was different; my negative had been intended to get him to talk, which he had.)

We walked the ring, or oval, and he told me he'd sketched and painted it when he first arrived on the coast. He gave me more information about his family and his life as a married man. He said it had been a happy if childless marriage, as if that were sufficient and required no detail, the happiness continuous and unsullied, though he knew and I knew that no couple could make such a statement, a boast, with impunity. Halfway around, a strange rasping noise came from nowhere, suddenly growing louder, and out of the clouds appeared a microlight, huge-winged like a pterodactyl and almost skimming our heads, close enough anyway for us to see the pilot looking our way and waving.

The mist was closing in as we descended. Harold had a habit of walking one or two paces in front, so that, for a while, I was staring at his back and noticing the comical way his slightly overlong coat made his legs appear shorter than they actually were; though being squat and hunched around the shoulders, he was the typical miner, built for pick-axing and shovelling in a confined space. I imagined him or his forebears walking like that to the pit entrance and then continuing his heavy tread another few miles to the coalface. Most of his working life underground had been in deep pits, reached in a plunging metal cage with as many of his mates as could be packed in, arms by their sides, but for a couple of years as a young man he'd worked in an adit mine, entered from the flanks of the mountain and involving a tram ride before a virtually blind trek downhill. 'A mile there and a mile back,' he'd told me, without needing to amplify what that had meant day in, day out: the exhaustion and deprivation and, for many successive days in winter, never seeing the light. One of his paintings showed a miner in a tin bath in front of a coal fire a generation before him, being scrubbed and sluiced down with a bucket of steaming water by his wife and beyond the window, a summer scene devoid of reminders of his workplace, though his immediate landscape would have included enough of them, also depicted in another painting, which seemed to have been executed with the dust he'd breathed in and which, in the first, floated as scum on the bath water.

The mist, wafting in from the sea and having crept up on the Ring beyond us, now followed us down, leaving it proud and drenched in sunlight and without a single human presence as far as I could tell. Harold sensed that I'd stopped to look back and he halted too, not joining me in dwelling on the scene above but perhaps seeking in my expression something that reflected his own deeply-lodged reaction to heights and depths, leaving the first to enter the second, the path growing indistinct, the visibility more obscure, the destination never guaranteeing a return. Maybe it was his mythical or heroic status but whenever I was with Harold, I was always conscious of his background as a coalminer. During the 1980s miners' strike, I think everyone secretly knew that the miners were right, that their cause was just – a strike in 1972 had been successful - even when they were knocking policemen's helmets off and dropping rocks from motorway bridges on to the cars of unsuspecting scabs. But my father never thought so. 'Who in his right mind would want that sort of life, burrowing like an animal and then waving banners in the streets as though you were going down there out of a sense of duty to society? It's up to us to decide who our heroes should be or even what heroism is. Charging a German machine-gun post - now that's heroic.' My father was a big supporter of Margaret Thatcher and her Falklands adventure. Civilian militancy never impressed him; a foul-mouthed budgerigar always did.

We started downhill again. At one point the mist was so thick that Harold almost disappeared from view. He'd once done a lot of disappearing acts, every day. By the time we'd driven halfway back, the sun was shining. It hadn't gone away of course, for those who hadn't momentarily been enveloped, the ones walking the esplanades in bright light. Before we arrived back at his place, he'd started nodding off.

Byron's Otter

On the Sunday evening, when I was thinking about driving home the next day, Harold looked terrible. I don't think it was the walk because we'd hardly stretched ourselves. No, the walk had done him good. We were watching *Antiques Roadshow* after we'd had tea - Harold wasn't a 'dinner' man - when he groaned. I could tell it was real pain from the lack of self-consciousness with which its momentary stab was endured and his terrible look of helplessness and fear with that naked hint of the hard-done-by.

I don't know why I remember it in particular, apart from its oddity, but someone had brought to the TV show a stuffed otter that had once belonged to Lord Byron. Harold had remarked on how lifelike it appeared, even allowing for the slightly mangy coat. But with its yellow teeth bared, I thought it seemed to have snarled down the years. The taxidermist had positioned it in alert mode looking up and it struck me that this was how the animal had frozen as death closed in. In his reaction to the pain, Harold had bent forwards in his armchair and looked up at an angle in the same way, over my shoulder and beyond as if towards some vague aerial threat.

The otter came under the heading of Miscellanea. The expert valued it at £140 but told the owner she could multiply that by at least twenty-five because of the literary association. Three grand for a mad poet's pox-eaten otter full of straw! I didn't mention it to Harold but I wasn't sure if Byron had just owned the stuffed animal or had owned the live animal and had had it stuffed when it died. The programme didn't explain.

'Are you all right?' I asked.

He didn't answer my stupid question but walked across to the settee and lay on it with his feet up and a cushion behind his head.

'I'll be fine in a minute,' he said. 'Just need to let it pass.'

I assumed from his use of 'it' that this was not the first time he'd been reined in by anguish with no one on hand to help or sympathise.

'I'll wash up,' I said, getting to my feet and rounding up empty beakers and plates.

'There's no need.'

It sounded like the admission of a man who'd given up hope. But he probably meant I was reducing the number of domestic tasks that kept him occupied, the basket of ironing/washing notwithstanding. I went ahead anyway.

As I stood at the kitchen sink, tea-towel in hand and looking out at the garden, I saw in the brambles at the bottom, face-on, the head of a fox, like a drawing in a kid's picture book. I was about to shout and tell him when he appeared behind me, apparently recovered, and jumped in before I could say anything.

'You were going to tell me about your next role,' he said. Because it was unusual, vaguely glamorous, I'd obviously told him about my career, such as it was.

'Oh, that.' I pointed towards the fox-face and he nodded. As he did so, it vanished.

'Aye. Television, wasn't it?'

'*Coronation Street* - again. Only a walk-on part. Well, walk-off really. I'm standing there with a couple of others in the background, chatting, and then I wave and leave. If you blinked, you wouldn't notice. You probably wouldn't notice anyway. I'm wearing a black leather jacket.'

This confused him, as it referred to a scene already filmed but not broadcast. I explained this. He asked when it was going to appear. I told him about a fortnight.

'You'll let me know.'

'Of course. I also have an audition coming up for a TV documentary about the Middle Ages.'

He didn't appear to hear that last bit or perhaps thought of it as the sort of unremarkable and inexplicable thing an actor like me did.

'They won't come back,' he said, wistfully, staring out of the window. 'The foxes, I mean. I don't think we scare them. They're probably not looking at us anyway. They've already seen me up here and this area is a place they now keep their eye on, just in case. Like that otter, something will come for them one day, when they're only half expecting it.'

He stepped forward so that he was a stride in front of me and kept staring, as if not wishing to be proven wrong about something that was now so familiar as to be almost commonplace. From his face, I could tell that the jolt of pain had weakened him.

'Are you sure you're all right?'

He turned to me and forced a smile.

'Why? Are you afraid I'll drop in the shafts? I'll be fine.'

'I can stay. There's nothing on the diary.'

'Can you be heard? Are you having an argument? Everyone on *EastEnders* is having a shouting match about something.'

I couldn't tell whether he'd forgotten what I'd told him or was making a general comment about 'soaps' and their constant, viewer-grabbing tribulations. Perhaps he preferred southern bluster to northern obstinacy now that he was an honorary Southerner himself.

'Oh, that. Not really. You just talk about anything you like, so long as it looks as though you're engaged in a real conversation. Which you are most of the time. It's easy once you're used to it. Most of us talk about the rest of the cast. Or just move our lips if we're feeling bored.'

It wasn't the first time I told him something about myself that seemed so trivial and unimportant compared with the life he'd led, the contribution he'd made to society. Sometimes I imagined that he felt this too and could scarcely conceal his justifiable lack of interest. Again, it was the way he'd avert his gaze to something else in the room, which I imagined might be the shade of his wife whom he could see and connect with and I never would.

I converted his present pain into the pain of a whole life and compared it with mine. No comparison, really. The luxury of boredom against an existence shoved daily towards fatigue. My pain was the emotional sort - uncertainty in life and love, both of which I could do something about if I wanted. Well, and a bit more.

'Look, I think I'll stay another day if it's no bother, just to make sure you're all right.'

'I'll be fine. But stay if you want. I can always call Ethel.'

I took that to mean he'd called Ethel before. I was glad there was somebody he could contact. From my front bedroom window on a previous occasion, I'd seen the young couple two doors down next to the Lewises leave early in the morning in two separate cars and return late. On weekends, they made a similar getaway and arrival on mountain-bikes, a misnomer in those parts though perhaps they headed for the Downs. Anyway, they always came back covered in mud. Discussing his neighbours with him in terms of the help and assistance they might be able to give would be the first step towards me taking responsibility for him or at least indicating that I was prepared to be more than a materialised distant relative with lots of questions. Hadn't I left notes with both next-doors? His other relatives didn't seem to be bothered.

'I'll stay then.'

He smiled and did a thumbs-up, not out of delight, I thought, but as relief that I'd resolved a personal dilemma. People preoccupied with the sudden and uncontrollable misbehaviour of their own bodies must often tread the line of least resistance.

He volunteered some information about his travels and why he'd gone south to work as a coalminer. Yorkshire would have been closer. He'd been restless, he said, and tenant-farming was just a way of life for his family. There was no future in it, no prospects. I wondered what future there'd been in mining; a guaranteed job with better pay, I guessed. Not for the first time did my clever mentality find something he said funny - the idea that there was a future in mining; a future *for* mining, yes and possibly, but no advancement beyond at first the twice-daily footslogging.

'You was just keeping yourself alive up there,' he said. 'Not going without food and drink, mind, but not changing. Like an animal - you know, not thinking about how your life might be different.'

'But what about mining, burrowing down there in the dark?'

He laughed and confirmed. 'Ah well, you was getting paid more.'

'And then there was painting.'

'Painting?' It was if he'd forgotten about his paragraph of recognition in that book or had immediately thought of the word in the sense of undercoating a door and not been able to correct himself with the same speed.

I pointed to the picture on the wall. 'You know...'

'Oh, aye. Well, that was just a hobby. No chance of doing it full time.'

As on other occasions, I waited in vain for him to elaborate. If I'd come from a similar background or had been a manual worker like himself, he might have been more open. I had to struggle with the 'kindred spirit' thing. It seemed almost sarcastic to say that I and Julie belonged to the blood-and-sweat brigade just like himself, or that, parroting my father, few of us worked out of a sense of vocation like nurses and doctors, and not all of them. I could have told him how labour-intensive a part in Michael Frayn's *Noises Off* was or how a novel was still being written when others had finished or not yet started their eight-hour day. We hadn't yet talked about the miners' strike and the closure of collieries. I guessed he would have been sympathetic. But just raising it would have seemed akin to talking about his own troubles and where they were inevitably leading. The death of mining and the death of a miner. His illness, like toothache, was all-consuming when he could feel it inside him, doing its worst.

'I need to contact Julie,' I said. 'Won't be a minute.'

I disappeared upstairs, partly to relieve him of having to continue a conversation that looked open-ended.

Julie

Julie was born Julie Williams but her publisher had changed her name to Julie Redmayne. She was told that Julie Williams made her sound too much like a housewife. Having fumed inwardly, she went along with the suggestion, convincing herself that she might have done the same. 'Redmayne' was one of the publisher's suggestions and she'd chosen it. I always think the name was intended to reflect a certain kind of personality - free and fiery, windblown. Actually, Julie had very short platinum-blonde hair, bristling at the nape. She used to knock around with a woman called Bronwen which was amusing because Bronwen was as tall as Julie was short.

At that time, I text-ed her more than I phoned her directly. It was a means of keeping our distance. We were both wondering where the relationship was headed but we were leaving the options open. I probably thought Harold and his problems were a subject on which we might both have a view. Not letting her know what was happening might have caused friction. We were trying to avoid too much of that, even if our paths, unknown to us, were maybe ever diverging. I liked to think that sharing concern for Harold was something we would have done as friends. But male-female friends who are also former lovers – lovers? - enjoy a different kind of friendship, one receding from an intense core rather than moving towards it again, though you never knew; it could be cyclical. It's a journey that can lose its significance as it increases its momentum. Beyond a point of unlikely return, any kind of regular contact would not be considered.

'Hi,' I said. 'It's me. Are you OK?'

'I'm fine. How's Harold?'

'That's why I'm ringing. He's none too well. We've done a fair bit but he's knackered. I got a bit worried about him earlier on so I've decided to stay an extra day, maybe two or three. I've got nothing on.'

I didn't expect the unintentional double meaning of the last sentence to register with her, though no response to it at all might have been deliberate. Mona Strange would have picked it up straightaway. One never knows about things like that. Saying the right thing or not saying the wrong thing and who did more of it in our time together was something we'd often discussed. Anyway, there was no reaction of the kind.

'Can you manage?'

'Of course I can manage.'

That was probably if unconsciously harsh, a way of re-defining our positions if re-definition was necessary. So much is at stake in statements like that, so much that's precarious.

'I could come down. I'm stuck at the moment. I need a break.'

'Well, why *don't* you come down?'

The emphasis almost suggested that something was stopping her or something would have stopped her if I'd invited her in the normal way. I let it go. There's only so much one can do in these emotional manoeuvres to say what you mean. That was probably the wrong thing.

'All right. If you want me to. I'll get an early train. You'll have to pick me up at the station. Littlehampton.'

That she knew the stop meant, I assumed, some sort of pre-considered contingency, maybe part of an idea that somehow she could get to see Harold while I was with him. I would also have to take her back, not that I said so because she'd failed to. She had no car; it had been sold as part of setting herself up as a full-time writer. I decided to wait and see what she intended doing. She might have other plans, might even be calling in to see Harold and me on the way to something more important and already planned. Without a car, one quickly becomes an expert on public transport. She said she'd ring about train times the next morning. I told her in detail about St Bartholomew's and Chanctonbury Ring and our lunch out but not about Ethel Chrimes.

'Oh, by the way. Don't forget the video-camera if you've still got it.'

'Why not? I could shoot the foxes properly. Are they still there?'

She giggled after mention of the foxes. It was ages since I'd heard her snigger. We'd had fun times in the early days.

'Yes,' I said. 'They're not going anywhere. Not yet.'

After signing off in terms of incipient endearment, I realised I hadn't asked Harold if he minded Julie popping in, maybe staying. I somehow knew he wouldn't. We'd pay our way. When I went downstairs to ask, my question seemed to make him feel better and my bravado was totally the result of excitement. I so wanted Julie to be with me. I allowed myself that silent confession, knowing that to admit it in front of her would be a mistake, the display of weakness. I didn't even believe that a church-goer like Harold, a man who also wore blue-and-red Paisley ties, would object to Julie and me sleeping together. I assumed he'd think nothing of it, just as I supposed that the prospect of sharing a bedroom with Julie after so many months had nothing to do with any tangled consequences.

'I'll come with you,' he said. 'To the station.'

Taking My Word

It's only fair to say at this point that Julie is no longer with us; a couple of the others as well. Dear departed. As I've noted, the way one lapses into these euphemisms says something about humanity, I suppose, or the larger chunk of it - about its need for a sense of respect and awe in a time of cynicism and plain-speaking. I'm certain it's how Harold would put it. Anyway, Julie is dead. She's passed on. Before her time, as they also say. Julie has departed this life. But there's more to tell about the living Julie.

So I ought to explain the opening of that phone conversation I had with her: *Are you OK? Yes. Are you sure? Yes, of course I'm sure.*

Julie was unstable. I never discovered its exact source, but her instability required constant medical treatment. Pills mostly but also visits to a psychiatrist as and when. She was a chronic case. The doctors said it was a form of social anxiety disorder, of depression, though I rarely found her dejected; sometimes feeling low, yes, like the rest of us, but never abyss-deep. She did shun wider company. I assume there were seemingly hopeless episodes like that when she was on her own. Never was a personal problem more personal. But when she wasn't outwardly sick, her appearance was normal and her demeanour reliable.

I met her first backstage after a performance of *Equus*. She was there with Bronwen. She said very little and what she did say was snappy and combative. Mostly she sighed heavily whenever any one of my mates said something mildly controversial. It wasn't long after we started seeing each other that she told me about her illness. She never appeared to be ill; a little brusque and always pale-looking maybe, but hardly ever reporting sick or confined to bed. Not that a writer had much need to contact anyone about such matters - unlike an actor, in big or minor roles. (An understudy for Lear once told me he got up early each day during the run and waited for the phone to ring while rehearsing Lear's big speeches, his other part, the Duke of Cornwall, I believe, remaining secure.)

Julie made me wonder about mental illness. She seemed - there's no better word - 'normal', like everyone else. I came to realise that her tormentor which 'had a mind but no proper body and was mad about that' was internal and so long as it didn't 'escape', was under control. I learned a lot from her about it but there came a time when she considered my knowledge complete and from then on, it was something I had to deal with, as she did; it was shared ownership, an unspoken pact. That involved not making allowances. I did make them - who wouldn't? - but tried not to show it. The worst consequence of that was being thought unfeeling or uncaring whether I made allowances or didn't. I cared a lot - believe me. She said caring was the practical expression of love, ever spreading outwards as its core intensified and the spread taking everything with it to the margins, like the incoming tide. I had to work that out. I think she meant that things she cared about, including people, went away from her but the anxiety of it ended up inside. That included people who were once close but were now relegated. We never had mutual friends. The nearest she ever came to confessing that she needed support was when she said, 'I'm the centre of everything, Francis. But the centre is where I'm most uncomfortable.' I once joked that my occasional depression, not diagnosed and therefore far from being up-and-down 'bi-polar', came in a poor second to her disability. She had a small circle of friends - don't we all? - but questions, especially about her writing, were mostly deflected; to avoid criticism, I supposed, but there could have been other reasons.

The first time I sensed there was something wrong was when she gave me the manuscript of *Piersfield* to read. It was her first book and about the working relationship of two men who had managed to co-exist for years in an atmosphere of barely suppressed envy and bitterness, both one-sided. Things come to a head. I enjoyed the book. Well written and thoroughly researched, it had a coalmining background, which, I was later to realise, would obviously interest Harold. I had a few queries about details. For example, one minor character was described at the start as 'pale and bronchial' but towards the end as 'a true working-man in all his physical rectitude' - but my main reservation concerned the two protagonists themselves and how the one could have possibly survived the demeaning spitefulness of the other; indeed, why he chose to do so. I recall saying something flippant about sado-masochism but it was a mistake to joke with Julie at an inappropriate time. That was another of the early warning signals: the disappearance of a sense of humour as though it had never existed or was something foreign. But her scenario didn't ring true.

She accepted the detailed criticism but it would be an understatement to say that she balked at the other. In fact, she physically attacked me in a way that made the expression 'storming the defences' fully justify its uncompromising force. She pummelled my chest with her fists in comical fashion (except that some aberrant clawing scratched my cheeks), and then threw a small saucepan at my head, causing a boxer-style cut above my eye that needed five stitches. She often went in for chest-pummelling, in anger or frustration. Like that flawed fictional character but taking a few seconds rather than a dozen chapters to alter shape, she'd changed - from weakling to violent aggressor. What worried me most was not the outburst or the injury or even her stomping out into the night - it was raining heavily - but her long-delayed contrition and her lack of an apology. All typical reactions, I later understood, but never easy to manage.

When we got together again at my suggestion, she was evidently still in the middle of self-laceration. It was disturbing to watch, as though normal human emotions were clashing and coming out deformed. I knew there was no point in arguing and she never gave me the opportunity to forgive her. It's difficult to forgive someone who hasn't said they are sorry. If apologising meant tacitly blaming what had happened on her 'problem', then she apologised. Funnily enough, she never referred to it as that; scarcely referred to it at all. But in declaring herself, she won me over. It was I who apologised. Hers was a weird form of regret too, based on something to which all attention was unavailing. Only then, or from then on, did I understand how impossible it was to deal with actions that were at the same time vindictive and uncontrollable. In such a partnership, there would always be two victims, unlike the one she'd written about in the book. I suppose we stayed together long enough to find out if the impossible were nothing of the kind.

For my part, the guilt of having abandoned a sufferer would always be over-riding if not ever-present. Before I decided to visit Harold, Julie and I were in each other's thoughts, though not frequently in physical contact. I was always looking for ways of drawing her in, bringing her back.

She never changed the gist of her story. She must have thought publication vindicated her. One had to be so careful. I didn't risk any more scenes by suggesting that the book possessed qualities that transcended its faults, which it did, or that any perceived misgivings vanished once a book came out. Hers attracted middling reviews, none of which picked up on my criticism. Julie must have noticed that. But she never mentioned it. Sadly I put this down to her inner turmoil, not to politeness or diplomacy, the reactions of the sane; and I use that word not flippantly or in error but with a vexatious heart.

It's more important to speak honestly than ill of the dead. They can't answer for themselves or take offence. But neither can the living when one decides to say anything about them. I'm sure Harold wouldn't have minded my paraphrasing our conversations. In any case, I feel more like an observer in these pages, hiding behind a window on the memory and describing movements that return to me ever more clearly. Sounds, words, sentences once uttered die on the breath and on the breeze. What we remember of them are their defining character, those intimacies of love, those calls of the wild, those gasps and whispers that for others keep us in our place and at a safe distance or attract us to them. Julie may not have asked for my forgiveness, though it was typical of her, and of people with her illness, to have described the state that might have preceded it: 'God, I behaved like an animal.'

Goings-on At Piersfield

'Should I have read them?' Harold asked me as we reached the shoreline and the road turned at a right angle on its way to where the River Arun rolled into the sea. The first fallen leaves were collecting in the gutters.

I'd told him about Julie's two novels, *Piersfield* and *Doing The Tango*. The first had been mentioned before because it impinged on what he'd done for a living but he'd either forgotten it or it had momentarily slipped his mind.

'I don't think so. You probably wouldn't have read about them in the papers. Publishing is a bit dog-eat-dog. It's often a case of who you know when it comes to publicity. There was a story about her in her local paper. And some reviews.'

He contemplated this, perhaps recognising the modicum of fame he'd also known and the total obscurity that followed it. I was always conscious of not speaking to him on his own terms. It was the British class system at work, I suppose.

'I'll get Ethel to put them on the Book Club list. Well, the first one anyway. If we like an author, we usually read other books by them. What's it about again, that *Percefield,* apart from coalmining, like you said?'

'*Piersfield.*'

I told him about Julie's few years as a reporter on a weekly paper, an old-fashioned publication soon bought by a bigger group, and how the book was based on her experience there. To be more precise, it was based on the odd way the paper was run almost fifty years before her time and - this was the fiction, a transposing of place - how the two eccentrics in charge had been out of their depth when a coalmining disaster - at Eight Bells Colliery - had occurred on their doorstep. I told him that the name of the colliery had been made up but the disaster was based on a real one, in Wales, even before he was hewing coal and the two newspapermen had arrived at the paper together.

'Oh, aye. I remember you saying. Long time ago. I know about the Welsh one. Terrible business.' Well, he would.

When does cancer begin its reconnaissance and where does it go first to make a nuisance of itself? The brain, the memory? He wasn't saying much when we first met him. Julie thought he might be suspicious of our arrival. No subject Julie and I raised with him got much of an airing.

We were sitting on a platform bench at Littlehampton station, waiting for Julie's train. The early-morning commuter rush was over. He was telling me about the history of the town and the rest of that strung-out coast towards Brighton and the Channel ports. In a lull, he bent forwards and peered down the line.

'What's the other one about?' he asked, not looking at me. '*The Tango.*'

'Oh, the second book. *Doing The Tango.* Completely different. It's about two people, a man and a woman, a young man and woman, and the break-up of their relationship. You know - it takes two to tango?'

He turned and looked at me but said nothing. It was - how can I put this? - a look of wisdom and superiority, more than that of an older experienced person eyeing a younger callow one with a hint of disdain. There was knowingness and a streak of sympathy in it and an unspoken invitation to be candid in front of someone who would listen and be understanding. Without his uttering a word, I'd suddenly learned more about him.

All he said before we heard the train approaching was, 'Redmayne. Julie Redmayne. I'll have to write it down. I've got to write down lots of things these days.' That was new.

Julie's first book had been set in South Wales because she'd been Googling 'famous mining disasters' for an incident to hang her story on and Senghenydd had popped up. So she transposed her weekly paper to it, not that the history of the one she'd worked on was probably any different from the invented one. Being self-critical, she did think that her lack of coalmining knowledge had contributed to what she felt were the novel's faults. Her two main characters - the editor and his deputy - were rivals because the deputy was older and had a reputation as a minor poet of the 1930s, thus making his boss jealous. Without going into it too deeply, I should say that the deaths in the book's underground explosion resulted in demonstrations, riots and a notorious court case at which the two were required to give conflicting evidence of what they'd witnessed. The book tells how, later in life, the editor, now embittered and cantankerous, was living at a home for retired journalists - Piersfield Grange - while his deputy, the subject of renewed interest in his literary work of long ago, continued to visit him before a fire breaks out, the editor dies and the deputy is lauded even further for his part in a heroic rescue attempt. The publisher had got someone to say that the book was 'a minor classic in the making'. It was printed on the back cover. I thought, and still think, that *Piersfield* hovers around a moral dimension it refuses or is not convincing enough to enter. It has nothing to do with Julie's ignorance of the background; but personal experience of that can never be enough to engage the bigger issues.

Julie walked towards us, beaming. I got up to greet her. She was dragging a small trolley suitcase and carrying a large shoulder bag, and she was wearing a black belted woollen coat-cum-jacket with a pair of what Harold's generation called 'slacks'. Instead of smart shoes which would have completed the outfit, she wore a pair of white trainers. Oh, and a black beret was perched Army-fashion on that severely cropped head. That was new to me and quite fetching. She looked thinner than when I'd last seen her. She was never overweight.

I gave her a peck on both cheeks and said: 'Harold insisted on coming to meet you.'

She wanted to give him a kiss but he held out his hand and she reverted to shaking it. I don't think he noticed her smooth change of body movement. Writing, she once told me, was an act of 'becoming' - one 'became' another person, or what another person was, in order to understand them and not to seem different. Like acting, really. She was different, of course, as I was, though I liked to think she and I were more or less similar. In one of our rows, I'd accused her of deception, saying that her so-called 'becoming' was a means to an end which the other person was unaware of and that she was therefore taking advantage of another's innocence. She'd said simply and dismissively: 'Well, the thought's always there.' Was our similarity the reason why we'd separated? We hadn't been together long enough to discover if our differences were stronger than what appeared to unite us. It might have been worth staying together again to find out. I don't believe either of us wanted to be estranged. I was thinking about all this while Julie questioned Harold about his illness as we walked to the car. I was behind them, wheeling her suitcase and trying to listen in. Like a lot of other things about her and me, one rehearsed them without knowing if circumstances might allow us to talk about them sensibly. To my cost, I'd probably reached the stage of telling her that *Piersfield* was seriously flawed. I wondered if members of the Book Club might spot it. It was at this point, too, trailing the pair of them four steps behind like a flunkey, that I first heard mentioned the name of Charles Lovell Darling, another eccentric minor writer with whom she was to become slightly obsessed. I saw Julie lean towards Harold and shout the name in his ear, he clearly having failed to pick it up in conversation as the wind gusted. Her voice had an edge to it as though she were impatient or intolerant of his deafness. 'CHARLES LOVELL DARLING!' Harold nodded half-apologetically but in part to acknowledge that he understood but the name must have been as foreign to him as it was to me. At first, I heard what she said as 'CHARLES LOVELL, DARLING!' She couldn't possibly have reached that stage of endearment with Harold, though I already knew that some of the things she did and said were surprising, shocking even. Part of the reason why we'd split up was to do with my fear that this was behaviour I would never understand. Harold insisted on sitting in the back of the car. As Julie leaned across to continue talking to him, I noticed how deserted were the streets we passed through and how momentarily traffic-free was the road we were driving down, the one that, for a quarter-mile, hugged the promenade and was sprinkled with sand, just like snow after a flurry. It was as though the vast sky and flat sea to our right had witnessed some cosmic event to which it had happily been party and now lay forever neutral and motionless, perhaps even polluted. Julie, either down-to-earth or fearing the unknown, might have commented: 'It must be Monday.'

That night, in bed, I asked her who Charles Lovell Darling was.

'Oh, him. A Victorian oddity. A magazine has asked me for something about him. He ended up in Dieppe. I might have to go there. Fancy a trip?'

'Why not?'

I might have expected her to tell me that she'd mentioned him and her project to Harold. It was typical of her that she had said nothing to me about Darling and her project or her discussion with Harold - that's if it had been a discussion. Some things you share, some you don't; the non-sharing of things you might have expected to be told about was something I could never understand where Julie was concerned. I know it was late and she was tired, but she didn't expand on who Darling was or why she was interested in him, nor did I expect her to. Sometimes, if I enquired, she took umbrage.

The Guttural Muse

'I've got loads of them,' Harold was telling Julie as I emerged from the kitchen with three mugs of tea on a tray. He'd just come downstairs and was showing her the collapsible mousetraps. On the low table in front of them were three cardboard arrow-tips, the compressed traps. He picked one up, pinched two tabs either side and pulled it concertina-fashion into a six-inch triangular box, open at one end.

'How many do you get through?' Julie asked.

'Oh, about a dozen a month at present,' he said. 'Once they've taken all the bait, you can't re-fill. Somehow, they seem to know what the thing's for, though it's curiosity that gets them inside, feeling safe. That's the idea. So I have to go around collecting up all the old ones. Down on my hands and knees with some of them.'

The image reminded me of a Pentecostal gathering, with worshippers looking for their god among the pews.

Julie looked up at me and smiled. Perhaps she pictured Harold doing what he'd done many years before, on all fours in the dark - well, as dark as his secretive places remained under St Bart's sombre lighting. Or perhaps she was indicating that here was another thing he wouldn't be doing for much longer.

'Are church mice really poor?' I wondered. 'I mean, there can't be much to eat in there.'

'You'd be surprised,' he said. 'People drop stuff. The thing is, they're there because they're always looking.

Ravenous. Did you ever hear tell that the call of a seagull is a cry of hunger?'

I rapidly shook my head, as though half-disbelieving. I loved the 'hear tell' expression, the sort of thing a sceptical mind might utter. But sometimes at night, in the spare bedroom at the front, I could hear gulls way off. I thought of that smudge on Julie's storm photo.

'Well, it is, apparently.'

He glanced at Julie for signs of any mutually-supportive doubt shared with me but there was none. She looked tired, especially around the eyes. I used to wonder how much of a financial struggle full-time writing might become. Not asking a former partner about any perceived difficulties they might be experiencing after a break-up was one of the crueller forms of maintaining a distance, a separate life. Her lack of interest in what I might or might not be doing on the boards or on the telly was possibly her way of accomplishing the same thing. I hoped she thought that because, if so, there was a chance of us both returning from our self-conscious redoubts fairly easily. I at any rate was still at the point where I thought our separation was unnatural. But we'd need to do something fast and we'd have to want to do it. Wanting was the thing time was wearing away, quicker than the sea tides were gnawing at the rocks.

While they were talking, I decided to assume further occupation of the bedroom by taking Julie's things upstairs. There was a third, box-style room I'd never entered. Its door was always half open and I could see the end of a bed and an uncarpeted floor. But I ignored it and took Julie's luggage across the landing into mine. The suitcase barely required its trolley mechanism and the extendable handle wasn't working properly anyway. It reminded me so much of Julie - compact, neat, nothing extraneous, inefficiencies concealed and not mattering. In the shoulder bag, I could see the video-camera case. She'd remembered. Not remembering things like that was a bad sign in our circumstances; it was thoughtless. Things you felt should matter simply didn't; you said something but realised later it hadn't registered because the other person had suppressed the means of receiving, often deliberately. While thinking these thoughts, I was staring at Julie's stuff and realising that in a way she'd brought everything with her. I mean in the sense that she'd left no one behind. At least, I didn't think she had. Maybe she'd arrived to tell me something conclusive about us, that this visit was nothing to do with any re-engagement but part of a new travelling life in which we as a pair had been left behind but could be re-visited without complication, this being the idea's first practical test. It was then, looking through the window at the wider world in which such a journey, if it existed, was taking place without us, I turned and noticed an extra pair of bath towels at the bottom of the bed. Harold had put them there while I was in the kitchen. It wasn't the gesture or its moral assumptions that struck me first but the roughness of the material, the laundered product of someone who knew little about fabric-conditioning and probably cared less; they resembled towels he might have taken himself to the pithead baths. But for both reasons I found it touching. Back out on the landing, I could hear a familiar story being told downstairs punctuated by the same anxious, inadequate words of consolation. The same as mine. I thought, there's Harold and there's us, the two of us, and the idea of Julie and me making reparation in this irreparable house moved me, even though it was selfish.

I'd told Harold my car was at his disposal so that afternoon he thought Julie might like to visit a few places in the area. First, we went to St Barts for him to lay a few more traps; then to Chichester where we saw in the cathedral the Arundel Tomb and its side-by-side effigies that had inspired Philip Larkin's famous poem.

We returned to Littlehampton where there was just time to walk to West Beach, a favourite of Harold's. We crossed the river at a point where it had not yet gathered pace to rush at the sea and walked south to the pebbled strand. The sun had shone up to that time but was now setting behind swirls of grey cloud. We stood there looking out at an immensity, undisturbed apart from the herring gulls at the sea's edge fighting over scraps. It was growing colder.

As we turned to re-trace our steps, Julie linked arms with Harold and started telling him about me or about some of the things, laughable things, that she and I had done together. Harold's broad grin as she touched on situations he must have recognised as a former husband seemed to rejuvenate him. I heard the name 'Eight Bells Colliery' mentioned.

He responded to Julie in a different way from how he reacted to me. With Larkin still on my mind in a place that smelled of the sea and the river, I thought of the poem by Seamus Heaney about the slimy tench and how, when it brushed against other fish, it healed their troubles. What was happening beside me was what he'd meant, though the tench is a freshwater fish and that was an illimitable place dissolving all, like the old Channel pacifying the Arun at its brackish point of no return.

Again, they got ahead of me as I stopped to look at the place where, so Harold had told me, a village of unsightly houseboats had been removed, leaving mudbanks spiked with boat skeletons and dabbed with prints of gulls' feet. The timber remains too, I assumed, would be rotted and eventually washed away.

Catching up, I could hear Harold telling Julie things he'd not told me and in a different, almost jocular, voice. Was this what remission meant - a slide into the fresher waters of old and a pleasant enough billow downstream, however temporary the good feeling, however inevitable the destination? She was telling him and I am telling she was telling. That's how it is in a notebook.

Stake-out

Some vague sense of decorum that night insisted that Julie and I should turn in before Harold so I half-feigned tiredness and she followed suit. We both recognised something histrionic in the gesture and Harold probably did too. We both said 'Goodnight' and went upstairs, leaving him with the end-of-day formalities of the host; not that there was much to do. I let Julie use the bathroom first with her rough-woven bath towel which she held up for me to see. I indicated that I'd already noticed. When she came back, I took my turn.

It was the first time we'd shared a bed since we parted, though because the split had been undramatic, no issue was involved, certainly not the idea of the bedroom as a venue for continuing hostility. I thought of it rather conventionally as a test. Her pyjamas were new - thick Winceyettes that seemed to match Harold's towels - instead of the nightie I remembered or more often than not just her pants or, in summer, nothing. When I returned and slid into bed, I simply wanted to go straight to sleep but I knew it would be impossible without some kind of statement of intent, however tacit. For a few minutes, we lay there like Larkin's prone statues at Chichester, staring at the ceiling. Harold hadn't entered the duvet age so we were covered by white sheets, blankets and a pink satin bedspread. It took a while to get warm, especially as the radiator under the windowsill had switched itself off.

'I've got goose pimples,' Julie whispered.

'You and me both.'

A silence followed in which we could hear Harold in the kitchen. Maybe we each thought the reason for saying nothing was our interest in what Harold was doing. The inside of the room slowly revealed itself. We both needed to say something or signal our intention to nod off. Doing nothing, just lying there two feet apart, seemed a risky undertaking.

'What do you think - about Harold?'

'I think there's nothing much we can do,' I said. 'Apart from letting him know we're there to help.'

'We?'

'Well, me.'

'You live two hundred miles away. What can you do?'

She was right. I hadn't worked anything out. I was a distant relative in at least two senses. Is a cousin once removed distant? I'd arrived on the scene late, though, in fact if not in practice, I was closer than either he or I had yet to acknowledge - not properly anyway, in terms of what the realisation would actually mean. I didn't really know if he liked me.

'There's someone else,' I mumbled.

'What?'

'He has a lady friend. A bit spooky, to tell the truth. She's called Ethel - Ethel Chrimes. The three of us had lunch together. It was a bit confrontational in a probing sort of way. She knew you and I were - used to be - an item.'

I mentioned the Goring Book Club and the slightly unkempt house in Rustington. I said nothing about alternative medicine.

'He's lucky to have her. Someone, at any rate. Someone close by.'

Another silence. All had gone quiet downstairs. I wondered at that point if any suggestion of intimacy was being postponed because one or both of us might misinterpret intentions. It would have to be formal, mechanical even, simple self-gratification. We could both deal with that. But I for one didn't want to be seen to be making a pathetic attempt at reunion. Nor, I guessed, did Julie. How to say or do something guaranteed to meet with approval. That would be the first stage of reparations, if there were to be any.

'Harold's going to suggest that they read and discuss your book.'

'Which one?'

'The first.'

'Ah. I've finished the third.'

I knew about that one but we rarely discussed her work-in-progress. I also knew its title - *American Smooth* - and that it was a sequel to her second.

I was about to suggest that everyone was dancing in one way or another, some of us leading others a dance, when there was a quiet knock at the door. I opened it to see Harold standing back out of old-fashioned chivalry.

'Sorry to bother you but they're there,' he said meekly. 'The foxes. Five of the buggers.' Bugger – the churchgoer's concession to raw speech.

*

Julie had swung out of bed and was taking the video-camera out of its case. It looked ancient. I grabbed my mobile.

'We can film them,' I said to Harold but he was already halfway down the stairs.

It was freezing in the conservatory. When we got there, the foxes had disappeared. The garden was bathed in moonlight. On the rickety fence sat a ginger tom, waiting, like us, for something to happen, its pendulous tail swinging slowly back and forth. Julie looked at me. I knew what she was thinking. It was a stage out there and we were the audience, watching expectantly in the darkness. It was our joint territory, she the inventor of scenes and characters, I their embodiment. And then they appeared one by one to make it live. There was enough light for Julie to keep filming. Harold stood in front of us, stooping slightly under the vestige of old burdens and their replacement with new ones but also with some kind of eternal curiosity and delight.

'Would you believe it?' he said, as the ginger tom, unmoved, followed the comings and goings. 'Who'd ever have credited it?'

It turned out to be a short, anarchic act. No fights, even in fun, just aimless wandering with heavy brush tails drawing lines in the dew, the formal occupation of territory. And then, also one by one, they returned to their den among the brambles. It sounds ridiculous but I thought the last to leave sat for a few seconds and stared at us over his or her shoulder. Stared at something anyway and with pride of possession. Or fear. I suppose it was what kept them going and accounted for their bravado.

'That was amazing,' Julie said.

'Did you get it?' asked Harold.

'Oh yes. I'll plug it into the TV tomorrow. We can watch it on the big screen.'

Harold still had a cassette-player but I wasn't sure if it would work with his new TV. I'd also filmed the scene with my mobile.

'Well, you two go on up,' he said. 'I won't be long.'

In bed again at ten minutes to midnight, we heard Harold climbing the stairs and flushing the lavatory. We saw the landing light go out. A couple of minutes later the telephone rang. Harold's phone was at maximum volume. There was initially no response and I wondered if he'd heard it. I don't think he had a bedroom extension. I was about to go and take the call myself or alert him, when the landing light went on again. We heard him go downstairs, pick up the phone and answer it. Its persistence had overcome his impairment. It was evidently someone he knew and the conversation soon became one-sided. We both lay there, trying to pick up the gist of the exchange. But it was impossible. Apart from 'Yes', 'No' and 'I'll see', Harold did all the listening, and it was as though we were listening with him. I guessed who it was and Julie did too. But we mentioned no name. Julie said something about late-night phone calls always bringing either bad or assertive news and when not bad, it was not unexpected. That Harold decided to respond, even though he'd gone to bed, suggested it was not the first time the phone had rung at an odd hour or that he'd dutifully roused himself to take the call. He was on the line for about ten minutes. Then the laboured climb again, the light switched off, a door closing quietly.

'Why *American Smooth*?' I asked.

'One of the characters goes to the States.'

'Oh, right. OK. I'm going to sleep now.'

'Me too.'

We exchanged Goodnights then turned in opposite directions. For a few minutes, I listened out for what I thought I might recognise as a fox's bark, like a dog's but somehow coming from somewhere remote. I think Julie was asleep before me. The faint glide of traffic, the day's roar, had almost petered out.

*

Here I'm going to insert the first extract from Julie's laptop. Appropriately, I believe, it's about the first time we met, from her viewpoint. I'm a bit player, though accurately depicted. This is the work of an observant writer. It gives some indication, too, of her writing style: forthright, witty, detailed, liable to run off into the wild. Bronwen's there, the friend I never got to know. Sometimes she seemed to go to places with Julie as a kind of companion, an inert physical presence, perhaps there for reasons of safety, a chaperone. Everyone looked taller than Julie, not least me, and Bronwen was even loftier than I was. They looked like a Northern comedy turn, Julie as Hylda Baker and Bronwen as her stooge. Friend or not, Bronwen does not escape Julie's sarcasm. Nor, in other parts of her notes and in incidents I've retailed, do I.

One of the interesting things about Julie's recollection is its effacement of my fellow actors, the other five who wore more or less the same horse suits as mine in the performance of *Equus*. We were all jostling in the corridor where Julie first saw me and where I walked off to take a phone call - from Mona Strange as it happens. There's no mention of the others, the rest of the mythical herd. She only had eyes for me, as Barbara Cartland might have put it. The 'pack of males' reference is her first sighting of my rude mechanicals. The Shakespeare is an actors' pub, though not exclusively. She can obviously swear, to her own satisfaction at least.

On that Night of the Foxes, except for a minor disturbance, she slept like a child, sucking her thumb.

There'll be a couple of other extracts later on, plus something else from her computer's Documents. They break up my story but they are the only means I have of giving Julie a voice, the one that has a bearing on our relationship. In fracturing my narrative, they also reflect how we could not really accommodate each other without things going awry, or the threat of it.

From Julie's Laptop - 1

To the Flagship Theatre with Bronwen for a performance of *Equus*. A touring company, not half bad. Shaffer's drama violently Greek, its central appalling event - the blinding of six horses by a teenager armed with a spike - already a matter of record before curtain-up. Passion, violence, sex, religion, etc, etc. A shocker, I suppose. Not B's bag, as she would say, but she knows the Assistant Director and has arranged to go backstage with me afterwards to meet him. Much taken with the horseman/Nugget character, a male clad in white Spandex with a horse mask on his head. The moment when the boy mounts Nugget reminded me of a Marini sculpture, the groin contact sexual, coital. Is this play about whether or not normality is desirable? The 'normal' life dull, without feeling; the abnormal (Shaffer's 'disturbed' teenager) skywards ecstatic in the St Theresa sense, mouth open wide, the life transcending its poverty? B's AD late twenties but with a waxed moustache and wearing a waistcoat with garish leafy motifs. The trouble with theatrical types is that they're always playing parts. (That dullard in Alan Bennett's *The History Boys*, who says history is just one bloody thing after another.) Feigning ignorance of Assistant Directorship, I ask the AD what he does. He tells me in that way men have of not suspecting that you could possibly be feigning ignorance. Although small, he's taller than I am - just. Beside B, I could almost pass for her daughter. B is always trying to minimise her height, and sometimes looks like someone with a prematurely curved spine. And, as I'd never say if I were her daughter, I keep reminding her to stand up straight, on the grounds that that's what my mother used to say. She, B, wishes she weren't so towering (her word). Nonsense, I tell her. She'd like to be midway between me and her. Normal, I say. Normal is boring, as we'd just witnessed. Had we? I was thinking about all this while the AD was rambling on. I caught the gist of what he was saying - something about looking after things during rehearsals when the director had to be elsewhere doing jobs that sounded as if they ought to have been delegated by the director to the AD while the director himself was in his proper place - among the cast, directing. AD utters the word 'creatives' and I cringe, visibly and audibly. B notices and gives me a nudge. I assumed she wasn't upbraiding me for my reaction but directing me to the horseman/Nugget actor who had appeared a few yards away in a badly-lit corridor and was on his mobile to someone while still in his white clingsuit and with his horse mask under his arm. I could see that he was handsomely shaped. He combs his shock of soaking black hair with the fingers of his left hand. No wedding ring (why do I notice things like that? Bloody Mills & Boon). He places his left foot on the bench where he's standing and lowers the horse mask to rest gently beside it. It's not a realistic horse's head but a formalised one, the equine anguish unmistakable. The way this actor's just-groomed hair falls forward again makes me smile. Suddenly he laughs out loud. I notice that there are no sweat patches; under the arms, in the crotch region, down the rolling hill of his back - nowhere - and guess that the Spandex material is breathable, like the

Gortex walking-jacket I have on. He turns to face us, still talking into his phone, as if we've hailed him or waved to him but then he takes a few slow steps down the corridor in the opposite direction towards more privacy, the side of his head a lurid neon glow. I ask AD if he thinks the horseman/Nugget character is hard to play, somehow knowing that, in having to impress B rather than me, he can indulge me in order to gain B's further approval. Must ask B if she is seeking said approval; AD not bad looking in a dandified, thespian way; if she is, must remind her to remain stretched to her full height because that way she can employ physical attribute against conversational one if, as is likely, she grows over-impressed and speechless and daunted by a garrulous date. Suddenly think of short-arsed men in relationships with tall, elegant women; wonder about the logistics of congress, think of the Gerard Manley Hopkins line from *Binsey Poplars*, 'whose airy cages quelled, quelled or quenched in leaves the leaping sun'. Imagine AD quelled inside the cage constructed from B's arms and legs. 'Would you like to meet him?' AD asks me. 'Well,' B says. 'Yes,' I say, cutting her off. We troop down corridor following, I imagine, an ectoplasmic stream of mobile neon, AD leading, B in the middle, and me bringing up rear - 'bringing up rear': where does that come from? As I pass the discarded horse mask, I stop and pick it up, surprised to find that it's as light as balsa and has a Velcro strap. I wondered what would happen if the Velcro stopped working in the middle of a performance (that forest of little plastic hooks often gets clogged with fluff; always wanted to see it with a magnifying glass). Anything untoward can happen to us at any time. I lift it to my face. It smells faintly of something pleasant on the verge of unpleasantness, the nightly squirt of some

Meadowflower spray just about holding out against what's nauseating, what's normal, in the exudations and exhalations of men. I don't think he wanted to meet anyone, least of all anyone chaperoned in by the dull popinjay of an AD. He still had his suit on as if not wanting to lose it just yet, like me not wanting to wash after being kissed on the hand by Erasure's Vince Clarke at the Locarno in Liverpool in 1994. That's not quite true: he'd begun to roll it down then left it, so that it resembled an off-the-shoulder number. The wall mirror in front of his dressing-table was framed by bare light-bulbs (one blown), as we non-theatrical types assume they have been since the beginning of actorly time. The Flagship used to be a music hall. On the worktop, next to what looked like the bits and bobs of a woman's make-up kit, was a thick glass ashtray. A half-smoked cigarette was balanced on the edge of it, streaming Coleridge's smoke phantoms.

'This is Francis Taylor,' the AD said.

There was a three-second silence, in which the name waited for recognition. None came but one sensed it would one day. On the dressing-table, a caller flashed and vibrated a message to Francis Taylor's mobile. I could just about make out the name MONA in capitals on the screen. He ignored it, picked up the cigarette, placed it in the corner of his mouth and prepared to squint against the sting of its smoke. 'Did you enjoy the play?' he asked no one in particular. I, being the one who'd wanted to meet him, felt obliged to answer. 'You were awesome,' I said. (Jesus, why do I come out with things like that in the company of blokes? Why do we all? Is it the fear of failure in what we suspect might be the start of something, not wanting to make a bad impression at the opening gate?) I wondered who Mona was. Girlfriend? Sister? Francis and Mona. I gave him my name: Julie Redmayne. Julie and Francis. Not my real one. Not a lie, more an untruth. I blame my publisher, a woman in all other respects blameless; in fact, the woman who has enabled me to become what I've always wanted to be. B wasn't saying much. She must have thought we'd landed on too low a rung of the *dramatis personae*. I don't think AD was of a mind to climb it: meeting the cast wasn't part of the arrangement. In any case, there was something sparking between me and Francis Taylor like a flint being repeatedly scuffed to create a flame. (For fuck's sake, come on; I can surely do better than 'sparking'.) On the back of his chair was a pair of moleskin trousers with braces hanging from them, trousers with a fashionably high waist that looked somehow old-fashioned. I'd seen pictures in the catalogues I scour for female models of below-average female height. I don't know how B copes; makes her own vestments, maybe; some of them look as if they've been run up as the midnight oil burns. I know she's a knitter, her gaudy products denoting lack of taste rather than bravado. Multicoloured scarves mainly, far too long; on me, I look like a defenceless creature being squeezed to death by an anaconda. I notice that in the horseman/Nugget's nether region there's a bulge that has shifted slightly. Reminds me of a ballet dancer. Is the thing that holds in the equipment loose or part of the costume? I imagine myself asking these things and being given mock-embarrassed male answers. When I get home, I Google Francis Taylor. He has an agent. There is a contact address and an 'if you want to contact Francis directly' email address. I type in the latter and thank him for receiving us. I tell him who I am and give him the title of my first book. Have to spell Piersfield for him. Go to bed late. Much jouncing.

*

Saw F again, at the Shakespeare. As usual with potentially interesting blokes on these occasions, he was with a pack of males. How else to describe them? They bay and cackle and shuffle themselves into ever-changing peck orders. With F, I could at least have a conversation (if only about the dermatological risks of wearing a rubber suit for too long on stage) that didn't involve anyone else so that I could ask, 'What are you doing next?' without his immediately turning to the others and asking them the same question but reflexively, 'What am I doing next, lads?' in the certain hope that they'd say something about him intended to impress or belittle me, such as 'We couldn't possibly answer that in polite company'; and then the follow-up, *le suivi audacieux*, directed unblinkingly at me on the lines of 'Are you polite company, er...?', so that the gallant (we live in hope) F might ask me my name again - that's if he'd forgotten it (likely) - and then turn to them and tell them, whereupon another, picking up a female scent, could chip in with, 'None of the Julies I know is polite', whence they could bind us, me and F, in an act of tacit inclusivity. I cast about; other Shakespeare females in the group of feathered hens beyond all hope. F & I talk a bit about *Equus* and he says, before that, he understudied Lucky in *Waiting For Godot* at Paine's Plough. (Does WFG have understudies who are not to be found elsewhere in the cast? Did he have to turn up every night of the run and stick around to the end?) Seemed genuine enough as he supplied dates. Asked him if all Lucky had to do was drool about the stage with a rope around his neck. Had to be careful not to suggest that this was meant to signal to him that I knew what WFG was and what happened in it; in other words, that for a woman I was not getting above myself. 'Do the qua, qua speech,' I say (Lucky's party piece; if it sounded like an order, I was lost, if lost was something I wanted to avoid because pushy distaffs are, in that sort of company, mere flirts for whom leaning imperatives are things to be confronted & subdued.) 'What's the quack, quack speech?' the male beside F asks, evidently a non-actor and more interested in how F was progressing with me than the conversation he was involved in but mishearing me deep in the Shakespeare's boozy din. 'It's a speech in a play I was in,' F said, endearingly failing to correct himself (actors need all the work they can get). He did not face his questioner when replying, instead looking at me with what I suppose was a genuine hope that I would not correct either. Detaching himself as best he could from the group, he began Lucky's incoherent address. I hadn't meant to embarrass or test him, so I held up my hand, Indian greeting-style (palm outwards) for him to stop. Which he did. 'Was it a tirade?' I asked him, knowing Lucky was an angry, put-upon character, a slave in fact, an animal. 'I suppose so,' he said. Quack, Quack spins around and asks me what I do. 'She's a writer,' B says. B is always trying to be my spokeswoman. Then have to explain what I've written, what I'm working on, etc., etc. B also finishes my stories, steals my punchlines. I've threatened to put her in one of my books if she persists. B shadowy & embittered figure (the fiction, I mean). F nice judge of what is and isn't appropriate at first (second) meeting. We always have to make that judgement - what's worse: being too interested or not interested enough, and if not enough, then wondering if it's a strategy that plays with our desire to impart more about ourselves; and if being too forward ('She's forward,' my mother used to say of me) if it's a ploy to overwhelm or influence. Crow's feet appear at corners of F's eyes when he smiles, like imprints of old age foretold and biding their time. How old - early forties? I tell him about *Piersfield*; he tells me something vague about family history. 'Genealogy,' I say, and regret it. He nods but I know there's a difference. Maybe he thinks that pointing it out might make him sound superior. So much is about not knowing, so little about knowing and doing right by the knowledge. We shall meet again - seriously. B is looking round for a taller man. City v United on big barside screen. Why are Manchester pubs so effing huge? The pack congregates, the stay-where-you-are women cluck and preen and prattle.

Home. 1,000 words. Bangladesh sweatshop collapses. Jimmy Savile (SoVILE) gets medal for being worst celeb groper ever - shouldn't that be 'best'? Google WFG, Paine's Plough; no understudies mentioned. Spandex can give you dermatitis and yeast infections. Romp with candystriped rhythm stick. F not at other end with crow feet smile and rolled-down wetsuit. Nothing so fucking predictable.

Unloved ones

That Ginger Tom watching the goings-on in Harold's back garden reminded me that when Julie and I first got together, we each had a cat. It was about five years before. I'm honestly not sure of the date. Julie would know it exactly and be able to call it to mind without thinking, not as something with which to start a gender skirmish - though she'd be justified in doing so - but as part of the constructive attributes of a woman. Male forgetfulness is destructive because it erodes memory, the thing that buttresses the present and one's hopes for the future. Without a past, there can be no sense of direction or improvement and no estimate of what has been meaningful. Out of little details, women compose a clear picture of what it is to lose something; men look over their shoulders and see an edifice crumbling or already razed through their carelessness and neglect. 'You just don't care!' was Julie's most frequent admonishment whenever we had a row. We men are relentlessly barging on, breaking free of anchorages and not caring.

I'd inherited the cat when my father died. My mother still had Norman but for some reason didn't want the 'hassle' of cat and budgie together. Not long after, she didn't want the hassle of Norm either, but I didn't have them both together for long. They'd had the cat about three years. One of my father's friends had rescued it as a kitten from a gang of kids who were throwing it in the air and trying to catch it. Some of the offending youngsters were almost untamed, like the Crazy Gang. The friend had seen the kitten, a furry rag, drop straight to the ground a couple of times as the kids declined to break its fall. My father said he'd look after it. Following some initial skittishness, probably not natural play as it would turn out, the cat settled down for my father to take a strange, objective interest in its welfare. He called it Kitty and I always wondered if this was a lack of imagination or interest, or a benign form of the cruelty from which it had been retrieved, a kind of deprecating estimate of what he knew or soon discovered would be a one-sided relationship. I believe he took umbrage at the animal's independence, interpreting it personally. On one visit, I suggested that it didn't look too well and my father, rather dismissively, commented that it had been 'like it for days', as though it could please itself whether it recovered or not. It did recover and proceeded to please itself as before. I won't go into details but I believe that, on one or two occasions, my father treated it badly. My mother wouldn't have known - subversion again. Perhaps it was a class thing: my father's class kept things quiet, minding their own business, whereas the cruel kids' class did things in the open - literally so on that occasion witnessed by my father's friend - and not out of bravado.

Anyway, I took Kitty over. I saw the transfer as a second rescue and my father's attitude as outmoded. (He once suggested that, being essentially wild, Kitty should be able to fend for herself with his desultory help. He did have her neutered - but I wondered how he treated her when I wasn't there to disabuse him of such baseless severity.) She was no trouble, though by that time, I guess she'd cultivated some kind of animal stoicism. She spent a lot of time sitting and sleeping. I was living in a ground-floor flat and I took Kitty there a few days after my father died. I also took her basket and a half-empty box of cat biscuits. There were no tins of meat, unopened or half-eaten, suggesting that he - they - really had been cavalier in the feeding routines, but I couldn't complain as he'd not been taking food very much himself in the weeks leading up to his death; short of sitting with him while he ate, there was no way of ensuring he was getting enough. His death was sudden. That's how I described it in the notice I wrote for the newspaper's obituaries page: 'Suddenly, on January 15, at his home in...' I meant 'unexpected'. Someone rising eighty could hardly claim to have much longer to go. There weren't a great many at the funeral. I read a monologue - 'We are an abstemious family...' - from *Dear Octopus*, a play he'd seen an amateur drama society perform but I wasn't fussy about.

The decision to keep Kitty in the family, as it were, may have heralded future trouble for me and Julie. When I told her about it, not thinking she would be anything other than sympathetic, she asked me if it was really a good idea in the light of our intention to move in together and knowing that she had a cat of her own, an emasculated tortoiseshell male called Ringo. I wouldn't have put it as strongly as 'intention'; we'd talked about it in positive terms which left the matter undecided. That's how I remembered it. I never thought Kitty had much of a personality but Ringo was almost human and he fascinated me, especially the way he made a low voice-box sound as if in greeting each time he was let into the flat. He also had a habit of staring at you while apparently asleep, whereas Kitty always had her eyes innocently closed. His most weird performance was to nudge his plastic food dish a few feet from where it had been put down for him and before he began eating; it was an act of independence way beyond a cat's customary repertoire of contempt. But the two didn't get on once I'd begun living with Julie. Kitty grew irritable and always seemed traumatised; she couldn't relax, which is what a cat mostly does when it's not doing panther impressions. The vet prescribed some kind of feline Valium. It didn't work. When she began crapping inside the flat, refusing to use her litter-tray, the vet told us it would be doing her a favour to have her put to sleep, a mixture, Julie said, of the idiomatic and the euphemistic that meant he couldn't place us socially. She probably wrote it down. So that's what we decided. We both took her to the surgery and I held her while the needle went in. No sooner had it been removed and the vet had placed his stethoscope over her heart than I knew Kitty was dead: it wasn't that she went limp or cold but that her eyes suddenly became unseeing. It was peaceful and violent at the same time - sly, almost sinister. We took up the vet's offer to have her cremated but we didn't want the ashes in a copperised urn or burial in some trendy pet cemetery. When we got back to the flat, Ringo was sitting in the window, looking out at us. For a moment I hated him, saw him as usurper. I felt ridiculous and the feeling was short-lived. But for much longer, I had to stop myself blaming Julie. Try as I might, I couldn't get rid of the idea that she was refusing to apologise for her part in what had happened. I didn't expect an apology but I was aware of its absence, the refusal to make it. I said and intimated nothing of this. Only later did I believe in its status as a seed of destruction, one that would grow and spit poison in the darkness and begin its evil dividing and ultimate rule.

I don't think anyone involved in these episodes - me, Julie, my father, his friend, my mother, the vicious kids, the vet - actually loved the cats in the sense of being 'animal-lovers'. Certainly not the kids, though even they might have been visited by remorse, a sort of love deferred. It was a while after that Julie and I parted. Two months before we did, Ringo was run over and I knew things were going wrong when I refused to show Julie much compassion. She was upset and I commiserated. But it's easy to show commiseration and not mean it. It's as easy as just accepting that, cats being the sort of creatures they are, accidents will happen now and then. Like an apology, it can be cheap. After all, I'm an actor.

*

I'd lain awake thinking about all this but was asleep when I heard Julie whispering in my ear. She was standing between me and the window.

'There's a woman out there,' she said. 'On the other side of the road. She's looking this way.'

'What time is it? A woman? What sort of woman?'

'I don't know. Nearly two fifteen. I thought I heard something out the front.'

I got up and parted the curtains. The outside was bathed in tangerine light. There was little traffic. I could see no one.

'You must have imagined it.'

'I don't think so.'

There was a time when my statement would have been taken as an insult, a comment on what she did for a living. Now, her reply had an element of self-doubt; she didn't take it personally but got back into bed. I lingered at the window to make sure there were no intruders.

'Probably some night hawk, some oddball,' I said. 'This place is full of them. Someone looking for love.'

But she didn't hear me or she chose not to answer. It wasn't meant to be a loaded remark. We both slept deeply until gone nine o' clock when Harold knocked at the door to ask if we wanted a cup of tea.

Googling

We told Harold not to bother with tea and said we'd be down in fifteen minutes.

It took no time to Google Ethel Chrimes on my laptop. Her name was highlighted in bold on the website of something called the *West Sussex Convention of Soul Travel Experiences*. I just searched her name and there she was, sitting at a table during one of its meetings and looking across at the photographer, just as I remembered her at the restaurant. She wasn't smiling as much as acknowledging recognition. She looked almost regal, in a 'Queen Mother' kind of way.

Julie was used to me being on the internet early in the morning. Despite having an agent, it was a way of finding work if you knew who to contact. As she stood there towelling her hair, her dressing-gown fell open. There had been a time when I would have stepped towards her, slipped my hands around her damp, naked waist and pulled her close, and there was a time when she would have responded. But part of our unspoken arrangement in the weeks before we split up was that such a thing could no longer happen. This mutual reserve would have to be broken before any renewal became possible. She too seemed to be thinking about that. But the fallout from separation was the feeling that any first move in such a direction would be interpreted as giving in where once it had been thought of as presumptuous or aggressive.

There needed to be new rules and we hadn't even spoken about them.

'What's a spirit-wrestler?' I asked.

'A what?'

'I've got something here about Soul Travel.'

'Soul Travel? Well, blow me,' Julie said, in a not very Julie-like way.

'Pardon?'

'That's what Charles Lovell Darling believed in. I think he invented it. Soul essence.'

'Invented? Soul essence?'

'No. Expounded it as a belief. Established the movement. He was the founder.'

She was right. I scrolled down the page. Just a paragraph. The entry was almost dismissive in its brevity. Soon, I was never to divine what Julie knew about anything, or whether she'd be willing to confide, especially concerning matters relating to me and Harold. She really was in a region of her own. During all that time with him, coincidences happened in our lives - some recorded in these notes - and I began to think that Julie or Ethel, or both, were responsible, or were people towards whom the lines resulting in destiny's conjunctions were headed and more likely to meet. But maybe all that was groundless, on a level with my sighting of an uninterested ghost in Warwickshire, about which more later.

After breakfast, we managed to connect the video-recorder to the TV and watched the foxes again. Something had gone wrong with the shooting, as now and again the animals and the garden looked ghostly, like a scene filmed in ultra-violet light. Then the shoot ended in a splutter of jagged lines, as though from some kind of interference. I'd got some mobile footage.

Harold had been watching in silence from the living-room door, a mug of tea in his hand. Then, again without saying anything, he returned to the kitchen. When everything had been cleared away, we sat round the table, wondering what the day's plans might be. I'd brought the laptop down with me and had pushed it to one side.

'Can you look up anything on that?' he asked.

'Of course,' I said. 'I was going to show you how it works, anyway. You should get a computer.'

'What - now?'

'Why not?' Julie asked.

'I want to find out about something,' Harold said, staring at the laptop apprehensively as though it might be some kind of Pandora's Box.

'What in particular?' I asked him.

He hesitated, then reached across to the sideboard and picked up a scrap of paper with three words scribbled on it: *amyotrophic lateral sclerosis.*

'It sounds medical,' I said and passed the name to Julie.

'I think I know what this is,' she said. 'It's something to do with paralysis - how it passes from one part of the body to another like ink being blotted up.'

As she spoke, I tapped in the words. She was partly right. I recognised the more common name - *motor neurone disease.*

'It's a condition that attacks the nerve cells which control muscle movement.' I looked up from the screen and added, 'An American baseball player called Lou Gehrig contracted it first. It's what that scientist Stephen Hawking's got, the one in the wheelchair.'

Because I'd memorised this and was looking at Harold when I said it, he must have thought it was information I already knew.

'I wish I'd had an education,' he said. 'Like you two.'

'I just read it here,' I protested, turning the screen in his direction.

Julie chipped in: 'Why do you want to know?'

She returned the piece of paper to him and for a few seconds he stared at it, mouthing its words. Then he said: 'They've found a cure.'

Julie and I turned to each other. 'I don't think so,' she said. 'How do you know?'

'Ethel told me. My friend Ethel.'

His eyes sought mine. He wouldn't have known I'd told Julie about his lady friend. He hadn't mentioned Ethel to her himself, I was sure. He continued to stare at the words and I felt he had just found the courage to let Ethel Chrimes find her way into the conversation after a deliberate lapse. Although he hadn't said anything, I believed he wanted to apologise to me for her provocative tone at the restaurant. I wasn't about to mention the West Sussex Soul Travel Convention or the mysterious woman Julie may or may not have seen across the road. I didn't want to accept that she'd seen anyone, still less that, if she had, it had been Ethel Chrimes.

Harold sat up and placed his hands palms down on the table. 'She says it's cured other things as well.'

Julie and I said: 'Such as?' simultaneously.

'I don't know. AIDS.'

There was no interrogative lifting of the voice at the end of the word which might have invited us to wonder if such a thing were feasible, though it was uttered without commitment in the sense of our being free to entertain doubt.

For a moment and for the first time, Julie and I must have crossed the boundary into Harold's zone of ignorance. Faced with the probability of his death by disease, we'd been behaving like people to whom the word 'inevitable' had been proscribed. It was the region of miracles, of outcomes hoped for against hope, beyond reason. By taking one step at a time, we could view the destination as eternally deferred. I knew of an actor colleague who'd died of AIDS. That I didn't know if these days it could be cured or its ravages postponed was merely another example of ignoring something in the hope that it might go away. I'd been playing Rosencrantz in Stoppard's play when Julie and I began fighting to get out of our relationship - it's never a question of just walking away - and she told me that, in her view, assuming a part was a retreat from the self as much as an embrace of another's elation and turmoil. There was no way we were going to leave Harold to suffer alone. Not now that we'd descended on him two-pronged. Perhaps it was late in the day to find out anything more about his background. He might think such enquiries pointless. That could be why I'd made no further headway. Convincing him that I was really there to bind us to our common past and not to accompany him on a walk to the future we could now predict would require animal cunning. Strange expression. What's the difference between animal cunning and human cunning? The first is never pondered, the second never left to chance; the first is pure, the second is corrupted by guilt and the prospect of remorse. I was pretty good as Rosencrantz. It was a short run by a new company, now wound up. The Ham 'n' High critic said I'd been 'hungry' for the playwright's words. But the phone didn't ring. In those early days, we looked forward to a decent meal. Sometimes still do.

I needed to find out exactly what Harold was facing in the way of NHS treatment. Having been admitted to our company, Ethel was 'banished to another room' while we discussed it. Changing the subject was one way of pretending she was no longer there. Julie must have sensed this too. We hadn't entirely lost what had bound us so completely.

'While this is still on, I'll look up urban foxes,' she said, rapidly typing the words.

She invited Harold to sit beside her.

'So you really think I should get one of these,' he said.

Julie didn't answer. He took that as a Yes. Even in daylight, their faces were illuminated as some bright website flashed before them. I could hear an excited commentary, some YouTube amateur and her friends video-ing foxes as Julie had done. I got up and stood behind. These foxes were in the street at night, trying to plunder wheelie bins. Someone in the background, barely audible, could be heard saying, 'Foxes cunning? Cheeky little bastards, if you ask me.' And someone else, 'I'd shoot the fuckers; no problem.' Why did I know it would be impossible to have a rational argument with these people, these citizens of the worldwide web?

Looking at the deserted street and the foxes running wild, doing as they pleased, I was reminded of a future from which we flawed humans had been removed. I think the video-ing hangers-on had gained that impression as well, for they had fallen silent or had left the scene while the person in charge of the camera continued to record. The only sound was a distant car alarm. The clip had so far been viewed 2,967 times. We've never had so much to look at and consider, yet we have never been so easily bored. In the recesses we have abandoned, the night prowlers run amok.

From my position at the rear and staring down at the top of Harold's head, I casually asked, 'How does Ethel think motor neurone disease can be cured?' I knew the answer.

Without hesitating or turning round to face me, he said, 'Metaferon, of course. They think it can cure cancer as well.' Speaking to Julie, he added, 'You should meet Ethel. I'll give her a ring.' He must have realised that mentioning her earlier might have meant nothing.

'Metaferon?' Julie said. 'What on earth's Metaferon?'

'Metaferon,' I repeated, at the door to the conservatory.

'Metaferon,' Harold confirmed, again without facing me. He spelled it out. It was a way of closing the conversation.

Julie's face adopted a schoolgirl's puzzled expression. Later that night in the bedroom, I explained.

But first, I strolled to the bottom of the garden. There was no sign of foxes. I supposed they were asleep, huddled together. Little point in disturbing them to see if they were actually at home. It was their victory over me, over us. They were here to stay, like children in their den. There was nothing we could do about them. Sometimes they were up and about, sometimes not.

While we were upstairs, Harold phoned Ethel. We were to call in for tea and biscuits.

Flowers of the Amazon

Harold shouted up from the bottom of the stairs: 'I'm just popping to the shop for a few things. I won't be long. It's not far.'

From the window, I watched him leave the house and walk diagonally across his brick-covered driveway. He was wearing an old man's cap and over his smart day clothes an overcoat. But he did not have a retired miner's stoop or a faltering gait. There were thirty-odd years between us and other gulfs, the sort you couldn't observe visually. This being Britain, I'd found my family-history research continually revolving around class. Harold did not belong to the 'educated' class, though his paintings were not primitive or naïve. I would never have told him but they were the work of someone whose talents had been stifled and had then escaped into an area of desperation in which he had evidently tried to paint like professionals or like famous artists whose work he had got to know, presumably to his own satisfaction. Actually, they weren't half bad. There was nothing childlike or innocent about them, no uncomplicated, fully-fledged vision. But I think it was their subject-matter rather than their artistic merit which had caught the attention in that trawl for miners who could do things, surprising things, other than hack at coal. All my ancestors were uneducated people of the land, mostly labourers or farmers. No actors or writers. You can never talk about these things without embarrassment but the points of contact are limited and since we live our lives by the hopefully limitless extension of what we have in common, there are places we can never visit together.

Julie's first book explored such a schism, though in an odd and unexpected way. Her weekly newspaper editor in *Piersfield* was of the old school, his assistant - actually the newspaper's accountant - 'a Varsity man' with, as I say, a reputation as a minor poet. The story moves towards a conceit in which the assistant happens to find himself at a miners' demonstration following the mine owner's conviction for lack of safety procedures underground which had led indirectly to an explosion and loss of life. The miners end up in court, accused of inciting a riot, and their fate depends upon conflicting evidence, including from the editor, who was also at the pithead gathering, and his assistant, also a trained shorthand note-taker, who heard something different shouted, different from what the editor said he'd heard. The assistant's evidence is accepted and the ringleaders are jailed. The whole scenario belonged to the previous generation.

Julie was rummaging in her bag.

'Did you bring the book?' I asked.

She smiled at me, reached for it and held it aloft.

'Brilliant. He'll like that. The gesture, I mean. I've told him about it. He's suggesting that his reading group takes it on and discusses it.'

I like the end of the book best. The editor falls ill and is transferred to a home for retired journalists. After several years in which he rebuffs the assistant on his weekly visits, the home catches fire. This happens while the assistant is being driven there. The editor dies but the assistant, despite his age, helps rescue some of the residents. A story is written about him in the national newspapers, someone recognises him as a forgotten poet and his modest fame is resurrected, his work of twenty years before re-valued for a new generation. It's a story about tables being turned, but it's also more than that, maybe about the triumph of art and the imagination over the claims of social status and local reputation. But to make the case, she'd had to get the assistant, an office-bound non-journalist, to a news event at which he had no place. That's what Julie didn't like - my pointing out what was a strained device, a conceit. She went mad and I have the scars to prove it.

Anyway, I was glad she'd remembered to bring the book. When Harold returned, we chatted some more about our shared history and Julie talked to him with authority about his art work and picture-making in general. Writers of novels always seem to know a lot about other subjects in the creativity line. We had a light lunch, took a walk along the salt-tangy beach at Goring and then we got back and prepared to drive to Ethel's.

On our way there, we turned off the main road, carried on for a bit down a tree-guarded avenue and then took a left into the long cul-de-sac towards Ethel's place. I was driving slowly, the better to imagine Harold's walk towards it from the nearby bus-stop. He didn't seem to use his car much. I guessed it was by then a familiar route for him. I had this image of her enticing him out to her place more and more until he was...well, I wasn't sure what. At that stage, I was probably being a bit fanciful. But I'd taken against Ethel Chrimes as my ancestors up North might have put it.

There'd been no way she was going to invite us in when I'd dropped her off after our lunch at The Town House. She'd insisted that I should not trouble myself about getting out of the car and performing some act of unnecessary politeness. Her thanks and farewells were said before she'd got out. Then it had been straight to her door without even a wave.

Now it could almost have been recently abandoned or vacated. A threadbare lawn was fingering its way into the cracks of a cement path and to the right, a fence separating the house from an allotment site had tumbled into serpentine shape like Harold's and was badly in need of paint, like the house's window-frames.

I noticed a movement of the closed curtains upstairs. She'd been waiting for us. I didn't mention this to the others who appeared not to have noticed. Ethel was the sort of woman whose little, discrete actions told you a lot about her. That's what I thought, anyway. Another person in similar circumstances would have been doing something else before the arrival of guests who would then interrupt them pleasantly. I felt that Ethel had long completed her preparations, such as they were, and had hidden herself at the window, consumed by who knew what thoughts.

'So here you are,' she said, opening the door to us. It was a statement of fact that barely concealed an admonishment. We weren't late or anything.

Instead of leading the way into whatever part of the house she wished us to make for, she stopped in the hallway and fixed her gaze on Julie who was between me and Harold.

'You must be Francis's other half,' she said before reproving herself. 'Stupid me. Of course you are. Who else could you be?'

There was always something sinister about a lot of what Ethel said, even at the pleasantry level. And a chill ran through me when she said, to no one in particular, 'Sorry about the windows. They need painting. And that wooden fence - someone is supposed to be seeing to it, but like everything else, we have to live in hope.'

I expected the inside of the house to be dark, musty and crowded with ornaments, but it was not so much airy and free of clutter as temporary-looking, a living-space occupied for the time being by someone whose investment was not in material things but in something spiritual, something for which objects had become a meaningless distraction. But maybe that was self-fulfilling prophecy, considering what we suspected after that brief discovery about 'Soul Travel' and our further researches, such as they were.

She showed us into a middle room between the front and back. It was bare apart from a carpet and some cheap-looking furniture. On a sideboard was a miniature version of a bell-jar covering a posy of pink-tinted china flowers, the sort of thing you sometimes saw on old graves in lieu of real flowers or as a reason for their appearance, through poverty, to be forever postponed. Above a fireplace was a framed print of *The Last Supper*, with an inscription from the New Testament.

Considering that Harold was a friend of hers, it seemed odd that he should remain seated and not enter the kitchen where Ethel could be heard rustling crockery - odd, too, that Ethel herself had not uttered a friendly word of welcome or even asked us if we wanted tea straightaway or announced when it would be ready.

Julie just sat there, looking around. Not that there was much to see. Once, she smiled at me and raised her eyebrows, as if to comment on what a rum scenario we'd become part of. I guessed, however, that for Julie, this was the kind of new experience on which writers thrived; so, for the time being at any rate, her smile could be explained as the end point of a rush of excitement, a quiet thrill. She was on the outside, fearlessly observing, whereas I already felt on the borders of entrapment. After that restaurant exchange with Ethel, I was also prepared to resist it.

'Here we are,' the woman herself declared as she entered the room holding aloft a tray of tea things. 'Harold - why don't you take off your coat?'

I wondered if this were a sarcastic remark prompted by the sight of mine and Julie's jackets on the backs of our chairs. We'd made ourselves at home in lieu of a formal request to do so. Most people don't mind. Then again, it sounded like the prelude to something, an event unable to proceed while Harold was dressed like a man who did not intend staying long. Why did I know that he would dutifully obey Ethel without saying anything and leave the room to deposit his coat in a place familiar to him but off limits to me and Julie?

Our tea was almost cold. She'd added milk and sugar without asking if we took either. Harold, who liked his tea hot and strong, was handed it in a thick mug, in contrast to our cups and saucers. It was steaming. There were eight biscuits arranged in a rough crescent – two each. All the time she was sorting the cups and plates, Ethel was watching Julie. Ethel ate nothing.

'And what do you think?' she asked, as though this were a resumption of our lunch at The Town House and she'd suddenly noticed there was a fourth at table.

'About what?' Julie answered, as abruptly as the question had been sudden, apropos of nothing she could have guessed.

'About poor Harold here, of course, and how we are going to rescue him from the clutches of the medical profession.'

'Now, hang on,' Harold said, leaning forwards. But she was ready for him.

'Just a moment. Let the young lady have her say.'

For once, Julie was speechless but finally managed to rally to Harold's side.

'Well, it's surely a matter for the patient, isn't it?'

When Ethel seemed not to respond to this, or pretended she hadn't heard, Julie continued. 'You're talking about Metaferon, I assume. Harold's told us. As I understand it, the drug is still on trial.'

'Over here,' Ethel said. 'But the Americans are far advanced. They've shown it works. We're always bringing up the rear.'

At this point, Julie began to giggle, making the impression worse by trying to stifle her merriment. 'Sorry,' she said. 'That just reminded me of something funny.'

She didn't explain and Ethel seemed not to want an explanation. But I'd learned that these idiomatic expressions always amused Julie, especially when she could remember something from way back that poked fun of them. We just wondered about their origins. This one was a childhood recollection of a seaside postcard on which a matriarch with a big bum was being hoisted by the butt of her one-piece from the sea at the end of a pier and the guy doing the lifting had turned to tell a breathless colleague belatedly running up to help, 'Thomson, you're always bringing up the rear!'

I thought this might have further soured what had begun as an awkward meeting, but instead, Ethel smiled and asked Julie about her first two books. As they chatted away, Harold poked me and started fanning himself with a serviette to indicate how a little local difficulty had been narrowly avoided. He must have found my expression neutral. I didn't know what to make of the Harold-Ethel arrangement at that moment. He seemed to have her sized up but at the same time to be unduly under her influence.

In slightly charged atmospheres such as that so-called 'tea' with Ethel, my mind wanders, though I'm aware of everything that's going on. It's a defensive ploy, superglued to my spinning twin helix of genes. If Julie were still alive to give an opinion, she'd describe what follows as a conceit (she never got back at me rationally for my criticism of her first book). I noticed on the inside of the sash window that looked out on to Ethel's back yard - there was no garden as such - a fat, jewel-like bluebottle. It was darting about on the glass as if trying to escape, because every few seconds, it would buzz away from the surface and launch itself at it again, like that blackbird at the restaurant. We all must have heard the buzzing, except for Harold, ever oblivious to low-volume sound. An insect, gorged on the luxuries of summer in and about a home and eager to flee the captivity enforced by newly-closed windows, little knew that outside, it would soon perish. It was animal instinct confounded by animal ignorance. I noticed the fly's upwards trek towards the tree growing at the bottom of the garden behind Ethel's property and overhanging it. My eyes became accustomed to the tree as the fly slipped out of focus, giving way to a leafy network of branches - well, some leaves were beginning to fall. They seemed to face each other, fly and leaves, as if part of a process momentarily held up but nonetheless inevitable. As I looked, one of the leaves detached itself and floated out of sight. It was then that Ethel disturbed my reverie with mention of *Didymopanay morototoni*, the Brazilian wonder-plant. As I say, everything being said was audible to me but mention of the 'umbrella tree', as I'd come to refer to it, reached my ears at normal volume as if Ethel had shouted it to attract my attention. She hadn't, of course.

'What was that?' I heard Julie ask.

Ethel turned to her and scowled, like a teacher would before a bright but inattentive child. 'Metabolites. To be strictly accurate, secondary metabolites. They normally defend the plant...'

'Didy-what's-its-name?' I interrupted, to show I was trying to keep up.

'Yes. Secondary metabolites protect plants like *Didymopanay* from the attentions of grazing animals. But in small doses, the accidents of ingestion, they have been shown to be beneficial.'

It appeared we were talking about the bark and fallen leaves of *Didymopanay.*

'How?' Julie asked.

'By suppressing the pathogens that can impair the animal's health,' Ethel intoned, her gaze directed at Harold who at that point was picking sandwich crumbs from the front of his pullover. I couldn't help smiling.

Ethel continued: 'In animals, the grazers, it alleviates stress and fear. Metaferon is derived from the essence of these metabolites and is being used successfully to treat a wide variety of conditions.'

I asked Ethel if she had a computer.

'No, she hasn't,' Harold answered. 'Neither of us has.'

This was odd considering the Soul Travel Collective was on the internet. So I pictured Ethel at Rustington Library, if there was such a place, logging on with her membership number and taking notes, adding to the site's information. What she was spouting sounded like the sort of thing you could find on the web.

'But it's not just the medicine,' Ethel said, cryptically.

'No?' said Julie.

'No. One has to have faith - belief that the medicine will work. And we can help each other, sometimes just by linking hands in silence.'

I looked at Julie. Ah, I thought - *Soul Travel.* I wondered if Harold had been inducted yet. He hadn't said anything. At that point, I believe he still thought of himself as approaching an unmoving horizon, rather than having become aware of the horizon starting to advance towards him. Ethel's unconventional remedies were still part of a future he hoped was some way off, perhaps never to be apprehended, one way or another.

'What do you think, Harold?' Julie asked.

With a barely concealed glance at Ethel, he said: 'I suppose I'll try anything when the time comes.'

He seemed pathetic then, more than ever in need of rescuing from the influence of this daft bat who'd befriended him at the Reading Club. So much for literature. Perhaps it did attract unstable types. I didn't want to think of Julie as unstable - just quick-tempered maybe, or lacking in self-control. It was then that Ethel returned to an earlier statement.

'Tell me - what was funny about the expression 'bringing up the rear'?'

'Oh, nothing,' Julie said. 'To do with one of those saucy seaside postcards.'

'I see,' Ethel said, pulling the hem of her dress down to cover her knees in a risible accompaniment to the mention of sauciness. 'Sadly, cancer isn't funny.'

It should have been a banal statement of the obvious but it somehow held the prospect of determined intervention. It was then that I willed Harold, a man of few words, to say something, anything. But he'd taken my place as daydreamer, staring beyond Ethel at the window-framed tree opposite, which would soon be merging into dusk. Had Ethel deliberately not switched on the light? There was an hour left of our visit in which Ethel expressed more interest in Julie and me and my relationship to Harold, but it wasn't healthy curiosity, reciprocated by volunteered information about herself; it was more akin to alignment and positioning. Although Julie talked about her third book, I could see Ethel wasn't listening, wasn't interested. Watching but not listening. Harold had begun to nod off. We seemed to resemble souls, waiting for the perfect element for travel. I suppose it was pure fancy, but I seemed to sense that Ethel's left hand was being raised and, momentarily hovering, prepared for a surreptitious excursion to the left where my own was waiting to meet it.

Serfdom

The audition I told Harold about was for a TV documentary on village life in the Middle Ages. I went for the head of a household working tenanted land and I got the part. I had a wife, an aged parent and two kids. There were no lines to learn as such.

We were filmed going about our daily grind. We talked to each other - these scenes were choreographed - but what we were saying couldn't be clearly heard behind the commentary. Various scenes showed us milking cows and goats, collecting firewood, eating frugally at table, mucking out our living quarters, herding animals and praying to 'the Good Lord'. It wasn't acting exactly but it was exposure, with close-ups and opportunities to show whatever emotions were appropriate, always good practice.

It wasn't much of a drama: just dressing up each day in a hair shirt and leathers, wearing a wig (I'd grown a beard) and walking about the outdoor set with buckets and crude pitchforks - that sort of thing.

The programme-makers had built a smallholding and a group of wattle-and-daub dwellings in a forest clearing outside Chester, the site patrolled by a security firm - well, two fat uniformed blokes working alternate shifts and chain-smoking. We read our 'scripts', booked into a motel and began work almost immediately - within a fortnight of leaving Harold. There were few rehearsals, the number dependent on whether or not the director and the historians doing the commentary changed their minds about something.

All went swimmingly until the fourth day, when I had to enter a pig sty, ostensibly to stun its occupant before killing it. I was filmed lifting a blunt instrument and bringing it down on the pig's head (actually on a sack of rubbish, out of shot, at pig-head height), the squeals and squelching noises being added in the studio. The pig was real enough though, a mucky sow with long eyelashes and an annoying habit of refusing to get up and move around, despite the goading of its handler. Though the stunning and killing (long knife, wooden pails of steaming water) were simulated before the pig was brought in, I was to be filmed entering the sty with the animal visible in front of me. After the uncooperative beast had been persuaded against its will to get up and trot about, I entered the gate with my heavy bludgeon. The animal rushed me and almost took a chunk out of my thigh. The wound required twenty stitches.

I thought that would be it, the job over almost before it had begun, but I was told to take a couple of days off while the attack was taken out of the narrative. I had to have a tetanus injection. The bite had been painful and I was obliged to hobble around. So a different 'accident' was created to justify my slight – but painful - limp.

When I returned to the set, I was astonished to learn that the pig had really been stunned with a bolt gun and, after its throat had been slit, disembowelled by a professional slaughterman dressed up like us. The grisly detail had been filmed, including the collection of the pig's thick, dark-red blood in a bucket and the scrubbing of its slit carcass. I remember looking at the rushes and admiring the way everything had been realistically pieced together. Most of all, I remember the close-up of the dead pig's face, its eyes closed but their long, innocent lashes making the beast look like its comic transformation into something wise and intelligent, and therefore something abused.

There was some off-set discussion with the handler about whether or not the animal should have been sedated before I entered the sty. I didn't discover the outcome. It had had six litters and was fit to be slaughtered. That's what happens.

Perhaps the most remarkable related thing was how clean and pinky-peach the animal looked on the slab after it had been scrubbed with hot water out of doors, the steam rising gently off its surface, the mud removed from its twin-pronged trotters. Anyway, the pig-bite scar would, I thought, stand me in good stead as a talking-point on the beach, at the pool, or in the gym and the bedroom.

We were well into the second day of filming before I came across Mona Strange. She was one of the milkmaids. She and I were then rarely in contact. She was wearing a costume, one of two anonymous extras in the distance, practising the carrying of pails filled, for the purposes of illusion, with a solution of cornflour. It's not easy. During a break while the director coached my 'wife' on how he wanted her to respond carelessly to one of my 'tantrums', I could see there was a knack to transporting milk without its splashing everywhere. I didn't recognise Mona at all; but afterwards, when she was queuing behind me at the catering truck and said coyly, 'Hello, Francis,' I turned and recognised her straightaway, despite the rouged bucolic cheeks, which I thought looked slightly comic. It was the sort of instant recognition that revealed something about our former relationship and made us both regret the time that had passed until our happy re-acquaintance. It might just as well have been no time at all. We kissed - a cheek-to-cheek 'air' kiss, luvvie-style. It's hardly ever thus.

We'd first met at drama college. In the first few seconds it took me to order lunch with my back to her, I first wondered what she was doing playing a bit part after fifteen years as a member of Equity and then realised it was no surprise. Mona was not so much untalented as not pushy enough. She had an undying ambition that was never to be fulfilled. In one way, her story was tragic. She'd trained as a singer but had to give it up because of some problem with growths on her vocal cords. Her finest musical moment on stage had been with some touring opera company, playing the part of Kate Pinkerton in Puccini's *Madam Butterfly*. It's almost a walk-on at the end, albeit one that arrives as the action reaches the point where the audience's eyes are fixed on her character, the woman whose existence finally skews what had looked like being a happy ending. She had just a few lines. After an operation, she was told that she'd never sing again, at least not in the opera house or on the concert platform. She did a stint at drama college, refining the techniques she'd already gone through at music school.

'What's a swarthy country lad like you doing on a film set like this?' she asked.

'Well, we all have to work.' The queue was shuffling forwards. 'It's lovely to see you. What have you been up to?'

She was staying overnight at a different place, so we decided to have dinner together just outside the town. Our relationship had been brief but intense. Mona was one of those women who remind a man that he doesn't deserve her. I mean that in every sense. She always made me aware of how lucky I was to be the object of her attention which I knew was genuine. Her father was still alive but her mother had died from some chronic illness. She took her family responsibility seriously, often excusing herself on the grounds that she needed to be at her father's side. I couldn't believe that she didn't have other close admirers, closer than me even. Though plump, she had striking good looks. It was never an arrangement I could get used to. It's something to do with levels of emotional energy, one of a pair bleeding the opposite dry but reciprocating over a wider area with others they love and who love them. 'Love' is probably the wrong word in this context and I don't think Mona necessarily associated it with man-woman arrangements. She cherished more than loved, though cherishing implies long-term commitment and ever-present concern and I don't believe that applied to her attitude towards me. When we parted undramatically, I therefore felt uncherished more than unloved and I'd never been sure which was worse. 'Unloved' and 'uncherished' are no doubt corollaries of friendship, depending, of course, on what one would be prepared to do for a friend. But a friend is not a lover. One does for a lover what both lovers want and what cannot be denied.

Towards the end of the meal, her mobile went off in her handbag - Tchaikovsky's *1812 Overture*. Heads turned.

'Sorry,' she said, leaning towards me. 'I always forget to turn it off.'

I didn't know any other actor whose mobile was turned off. She looked at the message anyway, close up, her face silvered by the phone's glow, but it didn't require an immediate reply. Before killing it, she said: 'Have you seen this? It's amazing.'

My mobile was always ringing, but I never used it as an unsociable window on the weirdness of life, to be stared at every second in company. She handed me hers after silently thumb-tapping it with a rapidity I'd never mastered.

She'd started rolling a YouTube video clip called *In Mourning for Her Mate,* about an elephant and a goat in some African compound. It lasted about three minutes and showed the elephant scraping the ground, flapping its ears and making pathetic noises where a goat had been tethered before it was stolen. After the clip, a caption came up explaining what had been happening and saying that the elephant, an ancient animal saved from attacks by poachers, was inconsolable after the goat disappeared; it refused to eat and was wasting away. The final shot (the whole thing was amateurish and probably taken with a mobile) zoomed in on the elephant, which was staring at the camera and in distress, its little eyes red-rimmed. It looked as if it were crying.

'It is amazing,' I said, more to reassure her in her enthusiasm than to express my true feelings, which were for animals as defenceless objects of our curiosity, however benign. For some reason I stopped myself telling her about our film of Harold's foxes, perhaps because I realised it might have come within the same category of prurience. It probably did though there'd been no mention by Julie of hurling our video into cyberspace for everyone to watch.

Mona took back the phone and searched for something else.

'This one's dirty,' she said with that odd cry of approval I remembered from when we were together: halfway between a squeal and an expression of disbelief, the sound you might make if someone suddenly pinches you painfully on your inside thigh from behind.

She handed me the phone again. It wasn't another video but a distorted 'hall-of-mirrors' image of her, specifically her boobs, which looked like something gross being offered on a platter. There were other women, smudged and smiling alongside and in the background, hen-night fashion.

'These things can do anything, can they not?' she said.

'Then don't lose it,' I replied, picturing the sickly-thin device slipping through a drain cover.

Recalling all this later, I wondered why a lively woman with such a sense of humour and pathos should have been lacking ambition. I asked her what she'd been doing since we'd last met and was given an actor's life-story not much different from mine. To set against my Hampstead *Rosencrantz and Guildenstern Are Dead*, she offered Ibsen's *Ghosts* at some provincial theatre space near Tewkesbury in which she'd played Regina Engstrand; one week only but an extension in the offing. There were leads in repertory, TV work, voice-overs and some average reviews. But, like me, she'd stuck at it. Perhaps the realisation that we were each one of a blindly determined kind made us call a truce to any attempt at making us look better or more successful than one another. The abandon induced by this accord, coupled with a mutual desire to bury any desperation, made our lovemaking later that night more violent than I'd ever remembered it. It was as if we were punishing each other for our failures and our present humility or putting completely out of mind that poor elephant and its huge and overshadowing grief.

The medieval shoot lasted just over a month. The part of the family's life which took place in the autumn was real enough, but the winter scenes had to be shot as well, with artificial snow. It also happened to be dry so rainy periods were also manufactured. Mona was only around for a week, off and on, and her scenes were later cut. We saw a lot of each other in the seven days when filming had finished. In fact, we spent more nights at each other's place than we did at our own alone. I told her about Harold. She didn't appear to show much interest. I'd forgotten that she'd nursed a parent through terminal illness. People like that must belong to a sort of world-weary club. As I gave her the details, her eyes glazed. I supposed she was waiting for her experience to be trumped, an unlikely event considering that her sick parent died on Christmas Day. I always remembered that. Her father couldn't cope and might as well not have been around. Mona gazed at me when I told her about Harold's timetable for treatment. I think she was wondering if it would be cruel or a waste of time to suggest that he was probably doomed. I didn't mention Julie because it would have complicated matters; not that there was any immediate prospect of Mona and me doing anything serious together. She was on social media and was my 'friend' in the far-flung territories of cyberspace. No wonder she went for long periods without being offered much serious work. At a low point, with one to be plumbed again soon, she did theatre-in-education, touring schools. On the second night we slept together, there was no thrashing around, no abandon. Throughout the night, we explored each other at leisure, rousing ourselves at intervals with the exuberance of a couple who had discovered each other's hiding-places and needed to prolong and intensify the thrill of finding out and of being found out. Phoning Julie during the time Mona was so close and not saying anything about her made me feel guilty. I told her to look up the YouTube clip of the doleful elephant, not letting on how I'd come across it. Grief, like guilt, can be assuaged; but grieving cannot be helped, whereas feeling guilty has to be kept packaged and hidden in lieu of being discharged.

Just before Christmas, Mona phoned to tell me she'd landed a part in a British Council production of *She*

Stoops to Conquer and that she'd be away for two months on tour abroad. The results of the audition had come as a complete surprise. They were certainly a surprise to me. But since our time together on the Chester film set, she'd become more positive. She paid me a compliment by suggesting that I'd been like the healing fish in that Seamus Heaney poem, already mentioned. Whenever sick fish brushed against the tench, they were miraculously revived. I knew from my father, an angler, that tench were found in the depths. They were covered in slime and were dark with an emerald tinge visible only in certain positions, like the tail of a magpie. (Only once did I ever go fishing with my father, a stolid and uncommunicative man. While casting, my line caught in the upper branches of a tree. By the time we'd unravelled it, he'd decided without rancour that we should pack up and go home.)

I enjoyed meeting Mona again and hoped we might see each other sooner rather than later. To say she wanted more from me is not to suggest that I was unwilling or reluctant to give it. On the last night before she left Chester to look for more work, we ate out at a restaurant recommended by one of the cameramen. I still didn't mention Julie. Was I keeping my options open in case Julie decided, however irrationally, to go her own way while I went mine? Or was not telling Mona about her part of an absurd male posturing to do with electrifying one's romantic life with uncertainty and adventure and possibly disaster - the errant lover as mad, bad and only temporarily disappointed?

*

I'd decided after we left Harold that I should phone him each week. He didn't seem to mind. Two close relatives of his were in touch with him but we rarely talked about them. Twice I rang him from the motel while on location and a couple of other times from my place on the weekends when we weren't filming and I'd travelled home. Julie thought it was too frequent and it was true that several times Harold appeared reticent out of a sense of little to report. So I then rang him every fortnight. Apart from the old tiredness in his voice sometimes, he seemed chirpy enough. I asked him if he'd like to come and stay for a few days. I'd got a job as a temporary stage manager at the Royal Exchange in Manchester and had wangled a long weekend off. Julie, furiously writing at the time, said she could do with a change of scenery and a break from keyboard-bashing. 'Why not?' he said. 'I'll check to see if it's OK.'

A few hours later, he phoned to say he'd come, anticipating what would have been my slightly ridiculous suggestion of going down for him in the car and driving back together. You had to encourage in a sick man an ability to tease his illness with little victories of remission. I didn't even ask: 'Are you sure?' He would catch the train and didn't mind making the two connections involved. I agreed to meet him at the end of the line. It was Julie who posed the question. 'What did he mean by checking to see if it was OK?' she asked. 'God knows,' I replied. 'His GP?'

We looked at each other but said nothing.

Confessions

In the days before Harold's arrival, I had a chance to go over some things that had troubled me.

I find inconsistencies depressing. I mean clinically so. Like that business with Norm the budgerigar; the idea that you can't see, or others can't, the gap between your selfishness in 'wanting' a pet and your failure to recognise neither your vanity nor the servitude it has imposed on the animal against its will - or not its will as much as its natural tendency.

The same with the acting business. Mona's family problems placed acting, or more specifically *not* acting, in proper perspective. Whereas with me, despite any breeziness I may display concerning the inevitability of having to perform as a non-speaking cypher in some drama intended only to illustrate for TV audiences a historical proposition, being out of work or having to accept the demeaning sort, always sees the black dog trundling up to keep me company and make sure I don't go out. This was the reason for Julie once saying, close to the end, that I was as mad as she was. Two nutters acting together can be outwardly as well as mutually destructive.

The worst inconsistency, or the inconsistency that dare not speak its name, is the difference between people based on intelligence and education. The class thing again. There's a telling episode in another novel Julie recommended to me, Kazuo Ishiguro's *The Remains of the*

Day, in which the butler Stevens is called upon by a right-wing cabal enjoying post-dinner brandy and cigars to play the typical democrat. There's a film of it now. Stevens, a blinkered cove whose life is devoted to ensuring that the cutlery and other objects on his master's dining table are the right distance apart, is asked a series of difficult questions about the economy and fails to make sense of a single one, thus proving to the anti-democrats that giving such a person the vote would be criminally irresponsible. If the well-being of society depends on the population's knowledge of political issues and what one believes is the correct response to them, ignorance of either would mean that expressing one's opinion at the ballot-box would be a matter of chance. You would hope you'd made the right choice rather than be able to justify it through knowledge and argument. Allowing such lack of authority to be acknowledged - letting Stevens vote despite his comprehensive ignorance - is, of course, the penalty one pays for democracy. Right means, wrong end.

When I first made contact with Harold, I was immediately aware of the differences between us. It wasn't a case of me being an actor and him being a retired coalminer; it was the way our different backgrounds made it seem likely that there'd be positions we would not occupy together and interests we could never share. For a start, he didn't say much - he never did - but that reticence could only have meant one of two things: that there was nothing to say or that he had no means of saying it. There were moments early on when his apparent lack of response led me to consider abandoning my researches. In a debate about which is the more useful, coalmining or acting, coalmining would have to triumph. Perhaps knowing this offered him immediate superiority, so that it was I who would have to explain myself, not he. But what

I disliked was the idea that his silence represented to him a lack of interest in who I was, what I did, and what I thought and felt, not just about our newly-discovered family connection but about other things beyond our immediate reach yet accessible to both of us if we made an effort. Some make the effort, others don't.

In the early days, too, I completely forgot about him, not because I was absorbed with other matters and could not give him my full attention but because the world was making one of its regular departures from my doorstep with the same speed as the gambolling hound coming my way, whom it had roused from slumber and sent towards me in the opposite direction. Departing with the rest was any notion of looking on the bright side. I love that expression; it's the optimist's mantra. If I'm honest, tea with Ethel wasn't as grim as I've portrayed it. I've simply selected the bits that illustrate how I felt about her. It's funny but a lighter description of that afternoon belonged to an optimistic feeling that admitted another view I had of Harold - that he should do more to protect himself and deserved my contempt for allowing himself to appear vulnerable. Ambivalence is the depressive's handmaid. The depressive has mixed views about almost everything and too often errs on the dark side. It explains a lot, now I come to reflect. One tries to fight against it.

Finally, I need to admit having been mildly interested in the occult. Once, while staying at an Elizabethan inn near Warwick, I saw a ghost. No doubt about it. I'd been learning lines in bed - always a bad practice, but I was strapped for time - and couldn't get to sleep. In that curious night-time gloaming which the eyes get used to, a woman in a long dress walked rapidly from left to right across the room at the bottom of the bed, evidently bent on an errand (I think she was holding something in front of her, a dish or jug maybe). The remarkable thing about so-called 'ghosts' is that they are not interested in you and are therefore no threat. They are ministering beyond you in another world. It's like watching a film clip. I call it 'the occult' in my desperate moments; in more objective mood, it's 'the paranormal'. We know little of how the mind works, not just in the sense of an apparition being an extension of thought but also in the idea that we can, at full painful stretch, perceive glimpses of a reality outside ourselves.

Ambivalence, however, can make us destructive of what we decide to reject of two conflicting proposals, as well as of ourselves for the contortions of not being able to choose. If we believe none of this applies to our closest kin and our lovers, we are in denial.

What I couldn't deny was that Harold's predicament in relation to Ethel Chrimes was drawing Julie closer to me.

News from Worthing

It's rarely possible to do now, that trick of stepping out of a railway carriage on to the platform, invisible in a cloud of steam, and standing there while it slowly clears to reveal you all alone and mysterious with your suitcase. I know what they mean by 'the romance of rail travel'. I always remember that scene in the film of *The Railway Children*, when the father, fresh out of jail, is reunited with his insufferable kids.

But it was a bit like that. The train Harold arrived on was almost empty. And he did step down, though he probably paused to get his drug-skewed bearings rather than allowed himself to materialise out of a wafting nebula he'd imagined. Each time I saw him in those days, however short the span between meetings, he seemed visibly poorer, just that much farther along the line of no reversal, a traveller in clearer sight of his unwanted destiny.

It turned out that the Goring Book Club had now obtained copies of Julie's first novel which were being read at that very moment. Harold had finished his, the copy Julie had given him. Despite the further decline, he said he was looking forward to his weekend with us. More than ever, that final journey to the South Coast needed explaining; it had to be more than a deliberate break with the past, a means of leaving everything behind, especially personal sadness. But we weren't ready for the reason he was about to give.

My flat was on the tacky fringes of Manchester. It was an area barely worth exploring but it was close to the main roads into town and therefore convenient for me. Julie had arrived early and helped me get lunch ready. We might have gone out to eat but she thought it a good idea for Harold to get settled in a place where we would all be under the same roof for a couple of days. As with other suggestions from her at that time, there was a moment when I tried to grasp the logic of what she'd said. If it existed at all, it was only ever tenuous and always begged questions. At the same time, I knew that any adverse comment of mine would have to be withheld. I was already conscious of not wishing to upset her unnecessarily. The short temper I was inclined to put down to an artistic temperament, whatever that was, had begun to offer other explanations and I was not ready to entertain them. In any case, it began to rain after lunch so we were obliged to stay indoors, enveloped by a peculiar Mancunian gloom. It was almost as if Julie had willed it.

The first thing Harold did was give me a revised family-tree on a scrap of paper, almost as a peace offering for having been previously unforthcoming. In addition to what I said earlier, I'd never taken his lack of verbal response to be bad manners, simply the normal state of someone to whom idle chatter was something you'd have liked to engage in if a lifetime of ten hours a day at the coalface hadn't made you virtually dumb with fatigue at the end of it. His folded map confirmed the existence of relationships beyond his status as my father's long-forgotten cousin. It was at least an entry into speculation of why branches of the family had lost contact with each other; not that fracture should come as a surprise to anyone who knew or read about other families. A family is a group and members of every group differ and cast themselves off.

Julie wasted no time in seeking answers.

'So you got clearance from the doctor,' she said.

He looked confused. 'Doctor?'

'You said you had to check to see if coming up here for the weekend was all right.'

'Oh, that. Not a doctor exactly.'

'Who then?' As if she didn't suspect.

'Well, Ethel was worried. She always worries.'

I said: 'It's good to have someone to worry about you, who cares about you.'

Julie didn't like that, although I was only trying to be diplomatic. She threw me a look that simmered before an unpredictable outcome. Unseen by Harold, I just shrugged and raised my eyebrows to indicate to her that I was being honest and helpful. In the same way that I often tried to locate the rationality of some of the things she said, she weighed up my statement and gave me the benefit of whatever doubt she entertained.

'Aye,' he said, then, making himself more comfortable in an armchair, 'd'you know, I sometimes think it was Ethel who was calling me that time?'

Julie moved in front of him, looking puzzled. 'Calling you?'

There was a tone to her voice that alerted me to the possibility of some reaction out of all proportion to the way the conversation was proceeding. She sounded as though she were about to berate him, depending on what more he had to say. I thought it amusing but Harold seemed to bridle slightly at what was turning into an interrogation. He belonged to a generation too proud to be patronised.

'Aye, calling,' he repeated, firmly. 'Calling me down to the South. She's asked me why I went and to be honest, I could never tell her. I had no real idea why I went down there unless it was because of the ozone – you know, the seaside where we all used to go on holiday; I mean the mining community. Well, it was a change from being underground. Bournemouth, places like that.'

The mining community - it sounded like something from which he'd been banished or no longer existed. When I came to think about it, there really was no longer any such thing anywhere in Britain.

Julie's anger dissipated into smiles which belied her persistence. 'What, through the ether? Calling you through the ether?'

She made a flickering motion with outstretched hands, the wings of a bird in flight or the visual disturbances of a migraine.

He looked up at her, a man possibly being made fun of, so I intervened.

'Let's take a look at this new family tree,' I said and invited him to sit at the table. Julie, pacified for the moment, joined us but showed little interest. As he named names unknown to me and established connections, he seemed to be aware that Julie required answers to something different.

'Sounds daft, doesn't it,' he said, not looking at her. 'But we don't know how everything works. Perhaps I was meant to go down there, meant to meet someone new who'd take an interest in me, an old widower on his last legs.'

'You met us,' Julie said, presumably meaning that, if anything had been pre-ordained, his contact with us, with me, had to be included.

'Aye, I did,' he said, as if he meant, 'you too.'

After a couple of hours, I'd learned a lot more about my family, or one remote part of it. But the significance of what was new paled beside Harold and his immediate needs and prospects. Now and then, his face would betray some inner contortion and he'd turn to each of us to see if we'd noticed.

Then he said: 'They want to try something new.'

'What?' Julie enquired. It wasn't clear if she were being specific or was expressing exasperation. Harold took it as a genuine enquiry.

'A new drug,' he said. 'Nothing to do with that thing Ethel was talking about. Not that Metaferon thing.'

I half expected Julie to mutter, 'Thank god for that!' under her breath. But she took hold of his hand. It was a fibrous thing still, but now enmeshed in veins like the exposed roots of a tree, and she pressed them with her thumbs, causing them to shift off course, then spring back.

'What do you mean by 'new'?' I asked him.

'The oncologist thinks it might work,' he said. 'She thinks I should give it a go.'

'Oncologist' was a word I knew he'd learned. As I said, even I didn't know what it was until I'd met him and picked up a bit about cancer. Use of the definite article - *the* oncologist - suggested he hadn't succumbed to a fatal embrace. *My* oncologist would make things more personal but also bring the inevitable closer. It would soon enough be *my*, I thought, possession by more than he'd want to be possessed by.

'I suppose those things can happen,' Julie said. 'Communicating with those we can't see or are unaware of, even. It would be lovely to think it could happen, wouldn't it?' She didn't sound very convincing.

Harold turned to her, confused by where she was located but then understanding the reference to Ethel's fanciful 'call'. To me, she was simply showing signs of how her mind was working on its own uncharted pathways. In anyone else, it would be called deviousness.

But for Julie at that time, I now know such a thing as dishonesty had become innocent. Hers was not to reason why.

On the face of it, there shouldn't have been a problem with Ethel. Anyone in my position, having discovered late in the day a relative with a life-threatening condition, might have been re-assured by the presence of someone who had already stepped forward to help, especially a matronly figure like Ethel Chrimes.

As Harold sat there at the table, talking about his relatives and pointing to their names on the map, I felt it were somehow my fault that a sick family member, however distant, should have been unknown to me. I reflected on how that had come about. Maybe it was connected with our rush to privacy as a result of becoming relatively well off - better off than Harold's generation anyway. Freedom of movement and a sense of adventure are made possible by prosperity. My grandfathers used to tell me about the General Strike when they were young and how people came together to help one another, but the riposte to this celebration of community - that the co-operating group was an illusion created by the simultaneous actions of desperate individuals - I kept to myself. It was what my father might have said.

Harold seemed the kind of person who'd have been prepared to discuss these issues or who might appear to be the embodiment of the contradictions they illustrated. The pitman-artist, one minute tunnelling with his comrades in the half-light, the next alone with his half-formed visions, must surely be someone pulled in two different directions at once.

As we broke for tea, I asked Harold what he thought of Julie's book.

'Aye, it was good,' he said. 'I liked the bit about the explosion at the pit. That were clever.'

I supposed he meant it was clever of Julie, a woman who'd never been underground in her life, not even at one of those mining museums, to have imagined the horror of a pit disaster. Actually, she was always keen on research.

'But then it drifts off a bit, like.'

He was referring to the final threequarters of the book, in which the relationship between the newspaper editor and his put-upon business colleague and partner changes to the latter's advantage as tables are turned. Harold wasn't aware that he was being critical or that, by mentioning it, Julie might be mildly offended. For people like Harold, I'd already gathered, honesty had no predicates. You didn't moderate your language or your viewpoint in order to avoid giving offence. He certainly didn't seek in Julie's face any reaction to what he'd said.

But Julie's response shocked me.

'What do you mean, 'drifts off'?' she enquired.

Her voice sounded menacing, and her lower lip began to tremble. I don't think Harold noticed that either - at least, to judge by his answer, he didn't. In these moods, one always felt that she was playacting and that her sense of injury would dissipate. But, although Harold may not have known it then, Julie was always serious, however misplaced her reaction. The first thing to be eroded with people like Julie was their sense of humour.

'Well, you know: the way the editor gets his come-uppance after telling a lie about the disaster in court all those years before.'

'What's wrong with that?'

Harold looked at me for support but I cocked my head, urging him to say what he had to say.

'It didn't seem true to life,' he said.

'Is that what one of your reading group said or what he's told you?'

By 'he', she was referring to me and she pointed in my direction with a thumb levered stiffly upwards from a white-knuckled fist.

He was now aware of Julie's anger.

'It wasn't Ethel,' he said. 'She's only halfway through. She hasn't said anything about it. Not a thing.' He sounded like someone who was being reprimanded.

She didn't relent. 'I should think it's pretty obvious that I'm trying to show how newspapers lie, how their attitude to the miners was the same as the mine owners. The editor's partner is not a journalist; he used to be a poet, a famous minor poet.'

Harold smiled, probably at the use of the word 'minor'.

'I realise that,' he said. 'He's the one who ran the business side of the paper. But what would he be doing at the pithead - and just before there was an almighty blast below ground?'

It was the same point I'd made myself when Julie had thrown a saucepan at me that time. I'm sure she thought we were in cahoots. Or that even Harold, an unlettered manual worker, had seen through the book's conceit.

'So what's this new treatment?' I asked, just to change the subject.

He reached in his pocket and pulled out a letter from the specialist who was treating him - the oncologist. The new drug was called Prodaxel. It had become recently available and was being used by some NHS trusts on suitable patients. It appeared to be an inhibitor, which meant that the enemy could be kept at bay. For how long depended on the patient and how his particular cancer cells were behaving. The letter was seeking Harold's permission to try it, after an appointment booked for a week ahead.

While I was reading the letter and Julie was simmering in a neutral corner, I noticed Harold retrieving something else from his pocket. It was a newspaper cutting, which he began to unfold. Julie saw it and moved towards the table. Harold looked up and handed it to her.

Before I could say anything about the letter's contents, Julie spun round to face us. Her expression was a mixture of disbelief and pleasure, her broad grin subverted by growing annoyance. She held out the cutting in her left hand and back-slapped it with her right. 'Why should this surprise me?' she asked. 'Why should this bloody well surprise me?'

Harold looked at me for support. It was the first real occasion on which I felt Julie's behaviour might have sent him packing. Before too long, the loss of a sense of fun would take with it circumspection. It was the gradual falling off of virtues which keep the rest of us complicated and therefore sane. I thought it would be too much for Harold to put up with, considering the growing weight of his own malignant burden. Then I realised that he desired anger and action and flailing response as the means of dealing with something implacable that resisted opposition, even to the chemicals that cared not a hoot what they did to innocent parts of his body on their way to the testing-grounds. To be useful, resentment had to be in the air.

The cutting was from the *Worthing Herald.* It noted how 'a local woman', Mrs Ethel Chrimes, of the West Sussex Convention of Soul Travel Experiences, was to feature the following day in the *Sunday Telegraph* magazine as someone who claimed to have been given proof of the existence of God (it used the capital G). It must have been a subject too abstruse for the *Herald* itself, which in any case wouldn't have been allowed by the *Telegraph* to steal a march, though the latter was presumably happy to gain some extra readers in Goring and district from what was basically a free advert. That Ethel herself leaked the story to the *Herald* was probably beyond dispute. I assumed the surprise Julie expressed was at the idea of Ethel's confessing that she had access to a higher state. Harold, as usual, was his non-committal self.

'We'll have to remember to buy it,' he said, smiling at both of us in turn. 'I knew she was one of them, the travelling soul lot, but I haven't mentioned it.'

He meant that he hadn't mentioned it to us. We didn't tell him we knew or suspected that the Reading Club members were fellow travellers. Maybe he knew that too.

It appeared for a few seconds as though the three of us were in agreement over Ethel Chrimes's unlikely experience of the ineffable. Either that, or Harold was convinced that Julie and I would have to change our opinion of her.

Forty-a-Day Rabbits

Scanning the TV schedules for that night, I noticed details of a programme about the use of animals in medical research. I asked Harold and Julie if they fancied watching it. 'Yes,' Harold said. 'Why not? said Julie, rhetorically. 'There's nothing much else on.' Well, there was but not the sort of programme Julie liked, and Harold always left the choice of programme to me, even in his own home. In the circumstances, and without wishing to remind him of something he lived with every hour of every day, a programme on medical research seemed like something we ought to watch.

At that stage of his illness, Harold displayed various forms of bravery. Taking in a TV feature that would probably deal with terminal illness and make statements about how, some time in the future, the force about to overcome him would be consigned to history, was pretty brave. I thought the animal angle, if it were to be an issue, as seemed likely, might deflect his obsession, take him outside himself to mount another form of attack on it. I took out a pen and circled the programme in the What's On, a surgeon marking the point of incision with a blue dye.

While Harold was taking a nap late in the afternoon, my mobile phone buzzed. It was Mona Strange. *Hello fellow extra,* she texted. *Give me a ring.* I put the phone back in my pocket without answering. I assumed she was referring to the documentary; I was hardly an extra.

'Who was that?' Julie asked from behind the magazine she was reading.

'Oh, someone wanting to compensate me for injuries in a car crash I never had.'

This was well before the time when she might have grabbed the phone to check that I was telling the truth. The pilot light on, as it were, but no firing, no flare-up. Not yet.

I never expected Mona to contact me so soon after the filming at Chester. The programme hadn't been screened and I'd almost forgotten about it. But she'd been paid; I hadn't - I knew what that meant: that she probably wouldn't appear. They'd tell us about broadcast dates in good time. The series would be interesting to watch just for the amusement of seeing how much of us they'd edited out, if anything. I'd feel sorry for Mona if she didn't make the final cut. All that slopping of pretend milk as she learned to shoulder the pail and all that learning gone to waste, like the slopped milk itself if it had been real.

Late in the afternoon, the weather improved. Julie announced that she was going out for some fresh air. Harold came in and for a moment, didn't appear to notice that she was missing and, when he did, was concerned about her ability to find her way around. Before I could tell him that she'd stayed with me often and therefore knew the area, he'd restored himself to present reality with an almost physical jolt, realising that he was visiting us, not we visiting him. Was that his age or his illness?

I said: 'You know what she's like.' It was an attempt to minimise her odd behaviour; well, it must have appeared odd to him and it was certainly odd to me, though I'd got used to it. 'Aye,' he said. 'I had noticed.' Any kind of conspiratorial closeness in circumstances like that was welcome.

I spent an hour showing him more of the websites which helped me discover our family history. I even let him have a go at using the laptop. He did it without expression, as if any joy or excitement to be derived from it would never be sustained or had been pre-empted by the knowledge that he would not live long enough to take advantage of it. Everything Julie and I did to make him feel better and take his mind off his preoccupations must have seemed to him like therapy, which is what it was. Therapy is fine when it results in a condition that no longer requires its benumbing power. When I showed him how to call up an ancient census and pointed out the names of his forebears, he appeared to take them for the dead they had become rather than the still-living they suggested to me. He thanked me for showing him and then picked up the newspaper cutting, reading it as if for the first time and, having read, subjecting it to some kind of aimless scrutiny.

'It's a difficult one,' he said, 'pumping animals with chemicals and things so that we can end suffering in ourselves.' He turned to me, the cutting still in his hand. For a second, I thought that what he was saying was a result of something he'd not hitherto noticed in the report about Ethel's imminent appearance in a national newspaper, or that the issue of vivisection was already one that he'd discussed with her at her instigation and the report had reminded him of it. Vegetarianism and animal rights were obviously related.

But it wasn't that. It was about the TV programme I'd ringed. He'd made a connection, only to repeat something we'd already discussed.

'We had to have horses to pull the trams across some of the levels,' he continued. 'No horses, no coal. Most of us tried to do our best by them. It was the least we could do for them down there, not in their proper world. Did I ever tell you that some of them bolted? They could kill a man with a kick. Mind you, it was as bad for us as it was for them. We were in it together.' Harold repeating himself was to become a joke.

An hour later, out of the window, I could see Julie returning from her walk. In her shiny blue waterproof, its hood down, and with her spikey blonde hair, she looked like a beacon. In Harold's company or the company of anyone belonging to an older generation, one saw natural behaviour as the other possibly saw it – unnatural and eccentric. It was doubly the case with Julie, as what she did became ever more curious and inexplicable. I could tell Harold thought it strange that she should get up and go out on her own. He asked me when she would be back, like someone who thought it might not happen. 'Here she comes,' I said, nodding towards the window. I wasn't going to defend what Julie did or said or apologise for the differences between us. But I didn't want him to worry. He had enough to worry about.

He ate well that evening, if a little frugally. We knew he liked parsnips and potatoes mashed together so we prepared some especially, the steam rising as I lifted the lid off the tureen. He asked Julie about her next book, 'the next Julie Redmayne', as he referred to it, and she told him more about it than she'd divulged to me. He wanted to know what writers did every day and how they came up with ideas. He said he'd never been to a theatre to see a play, 'only a panto', so we promised to take him. He told us he'd begun drawing again, his paintings having been started and finished without any preparatory sketches. At Ethel's suggestion, he'd embarked on a large detailed drawing of *Didymopanay morototoni.* Julie looked at me and frowned. I don't think he noticed. An hour before the programme on animal experiments, he dozed off in the armchair. When it was time, I asked if we should wake him but Julie thought not.

As he slept on, his head thrown back and his mouth wide open, we watched the programme with the sound turned down so as not to disturb him. It began with a history of the subject: old black-and-white footage of monkeys with wires strapped to their heads, and rats painfully discouraged by electric shock from entering specified routes of a maze. There was the famous shot of smoking rabbits, their heads sticking out of incubator-like contraptions and kept stock-still as masks were fitted and cigarettes inserted, the rabbits' breathing causing the cigarettes to burn slowly to a stub, at which point newly-lit replacements were fitted. A frightened young chimp, teeth bared, was strapped into a rocket and launched into space; mice were injected with increasingly high levels of insulin until they died, on their backs and panting, while the unaffected ones were taken away suspended from their tails and bred with fellow survivors which were themselves eventually given even higher doses; hamsters were run to exhaustion on a perpetually moving wheel. We could pick up most of the commentary but not all of it, so that the effect was of the triumph of evidence over justification. We turned the TV off before the end and let Harold sleep till the nine o' clock news, when he began to stir anyway. We didn't mention the programme he'd missed and neither did he. He was sleeping a lot but when not sleeping was lively enough. Julie made him a milky drink out of some fortifying powder he'd brought with him in a jar. It looked kosher enough, not something Ethel might have made up. As she went to the kitchen, she ran her hand up my arm.

With Harold finally in bed and Julie having turned in before me, I replied to Mona's text: *Busy this weekend. Will ring on Monday. X*

I entered the bedroom and got undressed. Julie made no sound. I slid under the duvet beside her. Still no movement. Now developing my own strategies, I feigned sleep after first yawning heavily. A few minutes later, she half-rolled my way and whispered my name but I didn't reply. After remaining in the same position for a minute or so, she made a fuss of gathering the duvet around her and was soon asleep herself. I lay awake wondering if I was being heartless in not taking re-acquaintance with Mona more seriously. She was always seeking words of encouragement. Why should I not be the one to bring her out of herself? That night, I dreamt that she'd hired me to appear in fancy dress at some all-girl party she'd organised with out-of-work actors. When I arrived, they were all sitting around laughing at something on Mona's mobile - it was a YouTube video of a sloth being goaded with a cattle prod. It was the first time I'd seen a sloth running along a branch. Prod, run; prod, run; prod, run. At the end of the evening, each of us took a *Sunday Telegraph* magazine from a pile at the door of the pub, as you would a free copy of the house magazine at Tesco, but by the time we were outside the building, all copies seemed to have disappeared, as though we'd never collected them in the first place.

The Travelled Soul

'I don't get it,' Harold said, after reading the article about Ethel under the generic headline *Personal Experience*. 'What did she actually see?'

Apart from drawing him closer to us because he was evidently aware that Ethel had not mentioned her 'god' encounter to him, it was a reasonable question and was also slightly mocking. Although apparently not a churchgoer like Harold, Ethel clearly had her own way of accommodating any sense of the transcendental.

The article told of a holiday Ethel had spent in the French countryside with a female friend, not long after their husbands had died. They were both in their late fifties and had known each other since childhood. (At this point, Julie let out a knowing 'Mmm' but it was lost on Harold and didn't seem relevant to me.) One morning, feeling restless and having left a note for her friend, Ethel decided to walk into the nearby village for *croissants*. The walk took fifteen minutes - they'd done it several times together - but on this occasion, Ethel started out early to reach the *boulangerie* just as it opened. Although the sun had risen, its illuminating effect was masked by the wooded area either side of the track. Barely five minutes into her journey, she was startled by a large dog that bounded out of the wood on to the path and stood for a few seconds watching her. It was one of those nondescript French dogs, possibly well-bred but resembling a jumble of different breeds. It was not wearing a collar, and Ethel wondered if it was feral; there appeared to be no handler, no early-morning riser like herself. She brazened it out and strode towards the animal, which began to trot ahead of her before losing interest and returning to the trees, where it sniffed around and took a pee. She kept looking over her shoulder but the dog did not re-emerge. She comments that it was the sort of experience that made one aware of France's immensity and how, in a land of hunters, there could be lots going on in the surrounding greenery that was unseen and largely unheard, apart from the rustle of a bush or the distant crack of a shotgun being fired. Anyway, and she thought this important, the experience with the dog had changed things, changed the morning atmosphere around her, taken it to 'a different level' independent of the increasing light and warmth. In the distance, to left and right and beyond the trees, she could see rows of vines in the open and therefore already catching what there was of the developing brightness, like something others were experiencing but was yet to be revealed to her. Then the world 'slowed' and she was walking at a pace dictated not by her desire to run a practical errand but by something else, something outside time and necessity and over which she had no control, and the amazing thing was that she was not frightened by what was happening; it was not menacing and she was steadily buoyed by a feeling of well-being.

The article was illustrated with two photographs of Ethel: one as she is now, immediately recognisable to us and obviously taken by the *Telegraph*; and another unfocused snapshot of her at the time of the French holiday. She looked much different then, twenty years before, 'almost normal', as Julie commented, not realising that Harold must have taken offence. What with the impromptu stroll and everything else, Harold was fielding

Julie's barbs with a certain amount of tolerance. At the time, I didn't know how long that could last.

Ethel's walk continued. The track left the wood and opened out on to a nondescript area still bristling with the stumps of the previous year's maize crop. It was then that she felt the growing power of the sun, on the rise behind the elevated village. Before her on a steep-ish slope, was the start of the village street. For a moment she could see a multitude of objects as if simultaneously, though her gaze was travelling quickly from one to another. It was a cumulating effect. These objects - a wheelbarrow, a small blue tractor, a coiled water pipe, some buckets hanging from a wooden pole, a zinc bath with its mirror of water soon to reflect the sun, a dozing white cat that might have been ceramic, two rose bushes in full bloom planted incongruously at the corner of the field, and a discarded pre-war tinplate sign for Dubonnet leaning against a thicket of blackberry bushes - looked as though the people responsible for their existence had departed the scene, allowing them to work some effect on her. She rejected everything that might plausibly have accounted for the way she felt. She described herself as being at that time 'a rational person'. She was physically fit (at least, there had been no manifestations later in life of what at that moment might have been early intimations). She and her friend had ended a long period of grieving. Suddenly, she said, these objects or the mysterious entity they represented seemed to gather up their surroundings and 'flow' into her, a movement to which her body responded with an outflowing she could only describe as 'love' and she sensed there were people crowded at the edge of the wood behind her, maybe the villagers who had not yet put in an appearance, though she was not tempted to turn to look and find out; and for what must have been just a few seconds she stood still with her eyes closed as this influx and outpouring occurred out of sync with her breathing which was not rapid - she was neither perspiring nor hyperventilating - but so normal as to be unconscious. She then describes a further altering of her state as the twin and opposite motions 'converged'. It was this convergence, the feeling of being at one with everything - herself, the world, all dead and living things, all memory, all future, present and past - that changed her forever.

After her experience, Ethel walks on to the end of the field, up the slope and into the village. There she discovers routine activities that appear to her as vivid commotion: the post van, yellow 'like out of a child's picture-book'; shopkeepers pulling down their canopies; the café owner setting his pavement tables; the knife-grinder pushing a mounted whetstone in her direction; olive-green shutters being clacked open on the shaded side of the street and shut on the opposite side; and, as she notices particularly, the baker already dealing with a queue of customers, making her wonder exactly how long she had stood transfixed out in the open when it had been her express intention to arrive before the village was up and about. Finally, she sees the dog she had come across in the wood, now resting outside the *charcuterie* and waiting for scraps and snapping at its fleas. Most of all, she was aware that the village at early-morning rest and the village in motion were connected to this inhalation and exhalation, which were still going on as she walked.

The rest of the piece clumsily attempted to explain how she interpreted what had happened to her. Why she'd concluded that God (she, too, gave him a capital G) had spoken to her or that He (capital H) had manifested His presence was none too convincing but that's what she believed. On the way back to the cottage, the world seemed to be 'sharper' and 'more alive' and she felt fearless. She didn't mean that she was no longer afraid but that if something, someone, had appeared on the path in front of her, she wouldn't have been concerned for her safety. 'Quite the opposite,' she said. 'I would have made it so that it was not threatening. I had the power to pacify.'

We each of us read Ethel's testimony in turn and the speed with which we did so must have reflected our prevailing attitude. It was a well-written piece, probably part-ghosted, the result of Ethel's verbal witness being knocked into shape by the journalist. That's what I thought. Harold, who read it first, was more deliberate, perhaps not recognising the woman he knew from her manner of address. Julie stormed through it, tut-tutting as she went, again overstepping the boundary of politeness in Harold's presence.

Harold's 'not getting it' was an invitation for her to offer an explanation.

'It's just run-of-the-mill road to Damascus stuff,' she said. 'The sun's out, the atmosphere's becoming heady, the hormones or however many of them are left are on the boil and the grief is like a deadweight she can't get rid of, making its presence felt when she's down and vulnerable. The menopause as divine revelation.'

Off the cuff, it was an impressive summary, though I thought Ethel would already have survived any 'midlife crisis', as it was called.

Not intending to be provocative, I announced, 'Well, that's one way of looking at it.'

Julie bridled. 'Are you saying that you actually believe her?'

'I think that what she said happened did actually happen. That's all.'

Harold, falling behind as discussion turned to argument, hauled us back.

'So this breathing thing was God,' he said.

'I think that's what she means,' I replied. 'God - the outside world - entering her and she breathing out - I don't know - godliness, understanding, love.'

He was confused. Julie was neither confused nor sympathetic. I believe Harold thought she was saying that Ethel had misinterpreted everything.

Then she raised the stakes. 'That crap about something entering her,' she said. 'It's probably sexual. Freud would have loved it.' She began turning the pages of the magazine, licking her thumb to move backwards, then opening and closing them at random, giving the impression that nothing else published there could be taken seriously. She did the same with the Sunday papers when her first novel came out, while seeking the reviews that never appeared at any length. If she took criticism badly - mine, and Harold's if I'd let that conversation about *Piersfield* drift on - she thought no criticism at all, no recognition, was beneath contempt.

'Well,' said Harold. 'I know what I think.'

Together, our heads turned towards him in expectation.

'I think it's a bit odd that she never told me she would be in the papers,' he said.

I picked up the magazine after Julie had flung it aside. It was open at an article about Magna Carta. I skimmed through it. There were pictures of the only existing copies of the document, each in its glass case and in a row, ready for some kind of exhibition. A paragraph caught my eye. It explained how the original had been written on parchment made from stretched sheep skin. It took me back to the dead pig on that film set, scrubbed up and ready to be used - sow's ears, trotters and all that - and the thought came to me, unbidden and irrational, that I'd had my revenge for the damage it had done to me. I recall feeling any way but that at the time; in fact, I'd felt sorry that the animal should have come to such a sorry end. It's equally silly but I acknowledged connections being made in my mind against my will and all to do with Ethel and her other-worldly experience: a confusing thing to do with eating animal flesh and how that was against god's commandment and how ultimately such a transgression would be revealed to me.

But the significance of a paragraph we'd skimmed, about the dog on the path 'ministering' to her rather than manifesting something inimical, would only be understood much later.

That night, in bed, Julie lay beside me saying nothing for ten minutes - simmering, as I always thought of it. Then she turned on me, rolling over face-to-face and propping herself on her elbow. 'What was all that crud about exhaling godliness, understanding and love?' she snarled under her breath. 'Are we trying to help this poor man or not? How are we going to convince him that she's a crackpot?'

For something to say, I replied, 'Is that what we're going to do?'

She flopped back on to the pillow. I don't know why but I couldn't bring myself to tell her that in her over-excited way she was correct. That's exactly what we were going to do, though it hadn't got as far as sitting down and agreeing a plan. Our joint instinct told us that Ethel was a threat and had to be discouraged. To reduce the temperature, I asked her if she had any ideas how the French experience had led Ethel to vegetarianism and the West Sussex Convention of Soul Travel Experiences but she just sighed, turned over and went to sleep; as did I a few minutes later. For the first time for as long as I could remember, I didn't dream. Before dropping off, I recalled that the *Worthing Herald* had chosen to refer to the West Sussex Convention of Soul Travel Experiences in only the briefest of terms – something about Pythagoras and his belief in metempsychosis, the transfer of the soul from one individual on death to the body of another. The *Telegraph* likewise. I imagined two weary news-editors mouthing the word 'crank'.

The Shell Cracks

Early the next morning, on a day off added to the weekend, I was up first. I laid the table for breakfast and started mine before the others had risen. I turned the radio on for the news, trying to catch its low-volume despatches as I moved around. Standing for coffee and a biscuit, I also began scooping up the dregs of yesterday's newspaper. There was a piece in the non-glossy section about Winston Churchill and how he suffered from depression - 'black dog', he called it. I knew about it from personal experience, of course, but only then did I realise how accurate was the description of something in the room impossible to ignore or get rid of, like a slavering Labrador in the corner, always wanting and waiting to be taken out for a walk and, if you weren't the animal's owner or found black Labradors slightly menacing, a dog that could 'turn', as the saying goes; a dog, in other words, exerting total control. When I heard someone on the move, I promised myself to stash the article and read it later or download it some time.

Harold entered the room, looking unaccountably breezy. I guessed the rogue cells were in abeyance. In revolt or held back: there was no middle way.

'Who did all this?' he chirruped, indicating the laid table, the cereal boxes and pots of jam ready for the taking.

'Me, of course. Who do you think?'

'Well, young Julie. The woman of the house.'

I listened and looked for signs of irony but I don't think there were any. The word 'young' was the giveaway, the paternal, unconscious establishing of hierarchy, though the age difference meant she couldn't be anything but younger; though 'young' was different, father-like, its ultimate authority ever-ready to be invoked.

'We try to share domestic duties,' I offered, lamely.

With a grin, he seemed to accept this and sat down at the table.

'Aye, good thing too.' This said with some resignation, a how-times-have-changed inflexion.

'Tea or coffee?'

'Oh, tea please.' Tea. What else?

He glanced at the ceiling, as if he'd heard Julie walking about or expected to hear her any second and forgetting we were in a flat. The hard-of-hearing still anticipating what was once the audible. But I knew Julie wouldn't be conscious yet. On her own, she was nocturnal. Even when she'd gone to bed before midnight, it would be gone nine o'clock before she was up and about.

'I thought we might go out somewhere today,' I said with my back to him. 'What do you think?'

Transmuted to 'What are you thinking?', it was a question I could have put to him many times in those long, uncertain months, prompted by his tendency to drift off at will.

'That'd be nice,' he replied, before continuing to occupy some imaginary middle-ground. I stared ahead of him too, hoping to join him there. But it was nothing, a discovery I pulled back from because of its imminent gravity. Nothing; oblivion; the gaping, waiting chasm. He was looking downwards now, with a smile rippling his old man's features. He reminded me of an artist's model, someone paid to keep still while someone else tried to make sense of him. He had a rheumy right eye and there were grey hairs growing out of his ears. He often wiped his eyes with a tissue but the hairs had grown out evasively, with no one, least of all himself, to check them. His nose was large and reddened not by drink - I guessed he'd been a lifelong churchgoer, a believer, maybe a teetotaller - but by small pockmarks and some kind of tiny unspecified scar below the bridge, the result of a cut or gouge, maybe work-related. There was a gap between his neck and his stiff shirt collar that once must have been filled with healthy, load-bearing flesh but now betokened fairly serious weight loss or what in a younger person would be the evidence required to prove the extent of a deliberate attempt to slim. I thought of fat people who lost vast quantities of weight, then, for some newspaper photographer, wore their old clothes pulled out to show exactly how much. His cropped hair, steel-grey and glistening, seemed oddly modern; but I was disturbed by a housefly dashing along the nape of his neck, perhaps feeding on some oily extract but evidently making no impression on him. I imagined its being related to the one that had been trying to escape Ethel's sitting-room that time. I wanted to swat it with the magazine containing her Gallic revelation.

'We'll have a think,' I said abruptly to bring him back from wherever he'd drifted.

But he didn't respond instantly and the fly didn't immediately take off; rather, his smile broadened as he turned to face me, saying nothing for a few seconds as my question must have repeated itself or echoed somewhere between the front line he'd ventured to and the place where he realised he was still sitting.

'Are you OK?' I asked.

'I'm fine,' he said.

It was a gentlemanly answer that stood for a desire not to be a worry, not to be a liability to anyone.

Then he said: 'Yes.'

I assumed this was a tacit acknowledgement that Julie and I would come up with something the three of us could do together, that he was in our hands.

'Carry on with breakfast,' I said. 'Don't wait for us.'

Then I heard Julie moving around. He couldn't have heard but again perhaps she was loud enough for something vague to register and he amusingly raised his eyes to the ceiling again. I heard the water running in the bathroom and the toilet being flushed. I heard her in the kitchen. Her elephant's tread used to be a joke. Well, it was funny: the sound and appearance of someone so slight making such a noise when simply moving about without urgency or serious purpose used to make me laugh. Now I knew better. I put up with it; put up with a lot to prevent the rift between us becoming wider; but in doing so, I wondered whether she knew she was being amusing or irritating or had simply forgotten the effect she'd once had. If only Harold hadn't been so deaf, I could have waited for him to comment and see how she responded. His gentleman's discretion, however, wouldn't allow a joke at someone else's expense. So there we were: I hoping a bad day wouldn't make me raise the subject again in jest or anger, and he deprived of the knowledge of at least one of her idiosyncrasies.

All went quiet for five minutes so I got up, walked to the door and called Julie's name. No response. It was a moment that has become engraven on my memory - exactly four minutes to ten o'clock on that particular date - because I looked at my watch, partly to get some idea of how long it was before we could make a move and where that move might take us. I looked into the room where Harold had been sitting but he'd vanished; the sound of tinkling cutlery told me he was in the dining area, helping himself. It's just that I couldn't see him. I'm sure he'd risen earlier only because he could hear - or sense - that one of us was already up. There was something odd about it. Was it the first time he'd done something without deferring to me or Julie? There one minute, then gone, leaving an empty seat. Strange.

What happened next needs to be prefaced with a mention of Norm the family budgerigar. I don't know what age Norm was in human terms, but my parents had had him a long time. I used to wonder if he'd broken some record for long-lived caged birds. Anyway, apart from physical defects that could be dealt with by a vet, he'd developed some human characteristics in his dotage, including unpredictability, aggression, and what I could only describe as manic self-communion. Can pets suffer from dementia as well as ingrowing beaks and claws? On a visit to my parents, I'd came upon a noise I couldn't immediately identify. I tip-toed down the hallway and put my ear to the door of the sitting-room. It was Norm, his intermittent background chatter now raised to a continuous noisy monologue in which, once I'd opened the door and could decipher it as I approached the cage, his entire, normally scattered repertory was rolled up and repeated, including regular squawkings of 'Uck off, Uck off.' My visits usually caused him to stop what he was doing and sidestep towards me along the perch, his head tilting from side to side. But this time, and for the short span left to him, he ignored me - didn't appear to see me, in fact - and carried on conversing without a break, as if to some avian spectre there in the cage with him, and loud enough to make him sound hoarse. A few months later, after I'd taken charge, I found him flat out in his shit-spattered sand and seed, all conversations, all twittering, over. Now, with Harold eating as I walked across the hallway, I reached our bedroom door and listened. Like the suddenly talkative Norm, Julie was having a feverish conversation with someone. Nothing made sense. It was not even uninterrupted and one-sided. There were gaps and questions and answers, sly barbs and acid slanders, the voice raised or lowered beseechingly. There might even have been sobs. Only curiosity stopped me from entering the room. I clung to the only one rational explanation and then, making my heart beat faster and spearing me with what I can only call childlike fright, I heard her mobile phone ringing in the kitchen. It continued to play its clamorous tone – a rock-guitar version of *La Marseillaise.* Disorientated and mixed-up, I entered the kitchen, wondering if I should answer but it stopped ringing. I looked into the sitting-room. Harold was still there. He smiled and he waved, neither the phone's mindless summons nor the unreachable event going on in the bedroom venturing anywhere near him. Only now, long after these happenings involving my long-lost distant relative, do I realise I might have buried a schizophrenic budgerigar.

When Julie appeared, I was sitting with Harold, pretending nothing had happened. He was still at the table, having eaten a bowl of cereal and drunk two cups of tea and was evidently waiting for the toast I told him I'd make but had forgotten about. I could have done a better job of the pretence as I was leaning forward on the easy chair behind him with my arms outstretched between my knees and my fingers intertwined, a picture of anxiety if ever there was one. Plus he and I weren't saying or doing anything. And why would that be? We weren't waiting for her - well, we were, but not with any urgency or anticipation - and she knew that what we were going to do together that day was still undecided. What neither of them knew was that my palms were clammy and my heartbeat was all over the place. A secret had lodged itself inside me, and it was painfully settling itself down before spreading out. I worried what Harold would make of Julie's altered state.

But she wasn't altered. She entered the room as though she, too, had locked away a secret, the secret of her barely-concealed confidences. I wondered how this worked. Did she not think that someone must have overheard? Did she care? Did she know? Was she waiting for one of us to mention it - well, waiting for me, because she was becoming accustomed to Harold's deafness? Maybe it had happened before, had begun after our split, and this was the first time in my presence, within my earshot.

Then I understood or thought I did. Her unaltered self meant that she'd forgotten or was unaware that anything strange had taken place. There'd been no attempt to lower her voice during those weird exchanges. It must have been an 'episode'. If I questioned her about it, would she think, to use an expression, that I'd gone mad? 'You must be mad' - how often had we said that to each other in response to a preposterous or offensive remark, or some wild notion? The *Marseillaise,* or its recent proclamation, threw me a line.

'Your phone rang,' I said. 'While you were in the bedroom.'

I wondered if she'd pick up on the additional information. She might have. It would have been the other side of her, the sharp side, contrasting with the zaniness. When else would it have rung? She did give me a sort of look before turning towards the kitchen, her head the last to go, the half-quizzical gaze leaving a faint trace of itself in the doorway.

'How would you like to go for a drive?' I asked Harold while she was out of the room. 'Into the country. It's not that far. We could have a picnic somewhere.'

I realised he'd never say no to anything. He nodded eagerly and said: 'Aye, that would be nice.'

Julie was on the line. She sounded animated and there was much laughter, so it must have been a conversation to do with writing or publishing. At least the tone was different. Her work must have been going well. I supposed Harold could hear her faintly, could hear something. The way he strained to listen to everything more than twenty feet away must have made him feel uncomfortable, though he never showed it. I didn't want to present him with anything that would make him more discomfited still. The thing you couldn't do with Harold at that time was discuss your own problems. It would have been discourteous of me to bring them up, such as they were, but I wasn't sure about Julie. He'd obviously picked up some of the tension that barnacled to a couple whose relationship had already been fractured and was supposed to be on the mend. Maybe it didn't bother him; maybe he was a closeted man of the world.

I began to think it might be better for Harold to understand that Julie was part of my life that didn't have to be shared intimately with him. The occasions she'd been with me on our visits were fewer than those on which I'd travelled to his place on my own. But I couldn't guarantee anything. The way they'd got on with each other immediately she'd arrived at the railway station in Littlehampton suggested they had something in common, apart from his having worked in an industry that had formed the background to her first novel. I even thought they may have recognised in each other some kind of mutual distress. One thing was certain: whatever my bouts of depression amounted to, they were not in motion; they weren't 'going' anywhere, whereas Harold and probably Julie were on a slide. I had two sufferers to worry about. It was one of the reasons why I thought more and more about Mona Strange, who parried disappointment, had no sense of her capabilities or lack of them, and offered the prospect of uncomplicated enjoyment.

I was thinking about that when an exultant Julie spun into the room and threw herself at me, making Harold lean back in his chair and wonder what was going on.

'*American Smooth*,' she cried. 'They're taking it!'

She might have been speaking a foreign language for all Harold knew what was going on. Seeing him seated there, riveted by bemusement and fright, I wondered if he thought it might have been easier if the stranger at his door, having clambered across from a remote branch of the family tree, had been, well, more 'normal', and his sidekick less impulsive.

As she clung on, her arms around my neck half-throttling me, I spluttered an explanation for his benefit.

'Her third book,' I said. 'They're publishing it.'

She disentangled herself, stepped back and said to us both, 'Not only that. Someone is interested in the film rights.'

Well, from then on, I knew that whatever had happened a few moments before couldn't possibly spoil the rest of the day. High spirits were guaranteed. Harold seemed to pick up on this even though the connection between book publishing, particularly Julie's book, and films were for the time being beyond his ken. He offered his own slightly sarcastic contribution to the gaiety. 'Do you want me to make the toast?' I swear Julie looked around for glasses and bubbly.

'Yes,' I said, acknowledging my negligence.

'Shall I make some for all of us?'

'Why don't I do it? Julie asked.

To Harold, who glanced at me and winked, it was obviously a 'woman of the house' thing, a confirmation of what he had yet to recognise as a prejudice.

We sat at the table, the three of us, and ate and talked.

'What about driving out to Dovestone Reservoir?' I asked. 'We could eat out.'

The two of them nodded, Harold munching loudly and Julie holding a cup in front of her lips about to sip tea and thinking of other, joyous things. Harold couldn't have had a clue where Dovestone Reservoir was; at least, I didn't think so and my question had really been directed at Julie.

Ethel Chrimes, whom we'd read about and talked about and argued over, had departed. In fact, as I began clearing the table, I saw the magazine containing her strange story slip off the coffee table on to the floor. In the kitchen, while filling the dishwasher, I thought of Mona, wondered when I could speak to her, or at least text. It might have to be that evening when we got back and when the other two were in bed. But all the while, I was dreading the night. I would have to join Julie when she was still awake. She'd stay awake purposely to tell me about the book while I waited for her excitement to subside so that I could speak to her urgently about something else.

*

Harold usually sat in the back of the car, like that humunculoid character in *Bonnie and Clyde* (he was shorter than both of us, and Julie was quite small). It was his choice, no doubt deferring to us as hosts. But this time, as I was about to ask him if he'd like to sit in the front for a change in order to take in the view of the countryside around Oldham, specifically the reservoir, and then the folded hills beyond Rochdale, Julie edged in front of us and slipped on to the back seat while Harold, without my having to ask, got into the front with me. I wondered if Julie had forgotten our unspoken protocol or was aware of it but was too bound up with her good news to think it worth following. I don't believe Harold disliked riding in the front; it was just that, on this occasion, he didn't have an option.

Julie, in getting ready to go out, had made herself up as though we were about to do something formal, and her pushy perfume filled the car as soon as she got in. I caught her reflection in the rear-view mirror. I don't know why but the word 'temptress' suggested itself. She was gazing out of the window and in profile, looked surpassingly beautiful in a way I'd never noticed before, a way that seemed to place her beyond me. It were as if a period of indecision had been obliterated by positive thought and she was dressed to do some sort of battle involving the proverbial feminine arts of persuasion. (Then again, in my profession, one often views people amusingly as parts being played by someone else, the person behind the mask.) Not for the first time, I noticed that she and Harold often arrived at an arrangement in which they grew closer to each other. Whereas before, barely visible, he would sit in the back, mainly listening to our conversation and not initiating any himself, apart from answering questions in brief, he now turned awkwardly to speak to her over his shoulder. It annoyed me so that I refrained from asking him if he wanted to join her or swop seats. I soon realised that Julie was getting more out of him concerning his background than I had managed. Was it the writer in her? I let them get on with it. It was, however, chilling to think that the idea of Julie 'got up' as someone I barely recognised now had an added dimension. But what he told her on that occasion was only a repetition of what he'd already confided to me.

They must have been talking beyond my hearing as we were getting ready, because once we were on our way, Julie continued to explain what the new book was about without apparently any inquiry from Harold. I just picked up bits and pieces, thinking instead of the time I'd been in R C Sheriff's *Journey's End* at the Birmingham Rep, a play about the Great War. It had sparked my interest in family history, specifically in my great-grandfather's brother, Matthew, who had been shot dead by that sniper having survived the Battle of Loos. Being a single man, he had made the local newspaper reports of his death the more poignant for having been his parents' first born, which to me seemed just as awful as if he'd left a widow with children. But perhaps that's because I'm single too.

When things went quiet between Julie and Harold - I guessed he now knew as much about her latest book as I did - we were well on the way to the reservoir. The weather was set fair-to-good. Having finished turning around to face her, Harold seemed ready to answer more of my questions. At least I thought it might be a useful opportunity to ask, the car journey making what always threatened to become an unwanted interrogation, with its overtones of impertinence, appear more like a casual chat.

One way of setting him on track was to say something odd but intriguing.

'It occurred to me that our family were a righteous lot,' I said.

'How's that?'

'Well, I was looking at the tree again and noticed how many of the names were religious - you know, Biblical.'

'Oh, aye.'

'There's Matthew, for a start, your grandfather's brother.' It sounded daft to explain who he was. It was the genealogist in me talking.

'Great uncle Matt. Killed in the war.'

I didn't think it necessary for him to remind me who it was. But perhaps he thought I needed reminding.

'Then there was your father, John,' I said. 'Matthew, Ruth, Luke, Mary, Rachel, David, John.'

'There's no Francis in there, is there - in the Bible?' He said it in a way that made me sound like a regrettable and irrevocable departure from this virtuous norm.

Julie chipped in: 'St Francis of Assisi.'

She said it mockingly, not as a contribution to the exchange. I'd never told her much about Norm. Just as well: she'd have played with that. I looked at her in the mirror. She was grinning at me. I felt that what she said was coming from a region one stage removed from where I thought we'd arrived at through Harold's unwitting agency. So I ignored her. I didn't even acknowledge what she'd said by saying something sarcastic, or even critical – that St Francis was not a character in the Bible.

'Ruth was your father's first wife,' I reminded Harold. As if he didn't know. Again, how stupid of me.

'Aye,' he said. His lips were moving, like someone doing mental arithmetic. 'Their kids were Rachel, Mary and . . . David.'

He'd faltered. I didn't know why. It must have been his memory failing him again.

'David,' I said. 'Your half-brother.'

'David.' He repeated the name not so much to retrieve what he had forgotten but to meditate on its sanctity, its Old Testament provenance. I couldn't imagine why he'd forgotten David.

'He died fairly young, didn't he?' A further nudge. David had been a cleric.

Harold was still pondering, now possibly on this tragic predicate of the relative whose name had momentarily slipped his mind. But I knew about David and his siblings. As if in extension of the Biblical theme, he'd trained as a clergyman in the non-Conformist church and become a missionary in India. One day, in the village of Khasari, a rabid dog eyeing him statue-like from the side of the road suddenly bolted his way and bit him once on the ankle. He died in less than 48 hours. There was an interesting though irrelevant paragraph in the newspaper report of the incident: according to an eye-witness, the dog had resumed its catatonic position in the middle of the track whimpering as if it, not David, had been the victim, and had remained in this immoveable and pathetic state until a crowd gathered and someone came forward with a large fence post and battered it to death on the spot. It was also stated that David, while lying on the ground and nursing his wound, tried to intervene in the animal's fate but his protests had been unavailing, his own plight having attracted a crowd intent on carrying him away for medication. I knew about David before that documentary pig had taken a slice out of me. And now, come to that, Ethel's 'ministering' hound in rural France. All of a piece, as they say.

'Father David, they called him,' said Harold, catching up and chuckling. 'Aye. Died from a dog bite out India way. Overseas, at any rate. My half-brother.'

Well, that much he remembered.

All conversation stopped as we climbed on to the high road and the sun moved into position head on. I pulled Harold's visor down, then my own. It was a re-surfaced road, eliminating outside noise or at least magnifying the interior. Julie hadn't said anything. I drove on as the reservoir appeared in the distance like the fragment of a cracked mirror, moving to our left as we approached at an angle in its general direction. It was then that I heard something behind us, a barely-audible sound of paper rustling and then a munching noise. It reminded me of a small animal unknowingly betraying its presence. It was Julie. She'd reached in her bag for a packet of crisps among some nibbles we'd brought and started eating them. I couldn't believe it. Not only had she not asked us if we'd like something, she'd helped herself surreptitiously. Either that, or I'd become as hard of hearing as Harold.

'D'you mind passing those up front?' I asked, a bit sniffily.

Her arm shot forwards between the two front seats with the half-eaten packet in the palm of her hand. Again she passed no comment. Noticing that she'd painted her nails a bright crimson to match her lipstick, I took the bag and offered it to Harold, but he declined. Having understood none of what had happened, he began staring out of his window at the expanse of water below; it was sliding closer to us. A defiant Julie caught my gaze in the mirror and held it as she pulled out a second bag of crisps and began eating them noisily. It was a protest aimed at me. Harold might as well have not been there.

'He nearly didn't go,' Harold said. 'There was a tribunal.' He turned to me. 'Did you know that? They made him go. They sent him to his death.'

What? Well, well - poor David, already a Westmorland chapel minister promoted in jest to a Catholic priest, having fought for his chance to convert the Hindus to Christianity and then having second thoughts for some reason but being forced to stick to his original intent - I didn't know how these things worked - and dying a death as far removed from martyrdom and saintliness as anyone could imagine, a pointless death.

'Blimey,' I said. 'Going through all that and then to be bitten by a mad dog.'

He turned to me, then to Julie, then back to me. 'How's that?'

'David,' I said. 'The trials of a vocation.'

'No, I mean Great Uncle Matt. He was a conshie but his wife nagged him so much he went before a tribunal and asked to be given a military certificate. That tribunal Uncle Matt went before - some of 'em were in bloody uniform. There were lots that got sent, even the sick. There was a deaf man. They said he wasn't all that deaf and they sent him. He was killed too. Probably didn't hear it coming. You know, the whistling shell.'

Bloody uniform. Harold probably didn't see the irony of that. The timid swear word was what registered with me. It was only the second time I'd heard him use what he would have called 'bad language'.

We were descending towards the reservoir and I pulled into a lay-by. At last, Harold was volunteering new, vital information as a corrective. I imagined a jigsaw piece snapping into place, and an important one at that, on which could be seen the parts of an image it would be fairly easy to complete.

I looked across at the water to indicate a reason for stopping.

But Julie said, 'For god's sake. Are we going down there or not?'

I waited a few frustrating seconds before pulling out and continuing the journey, seeking Julie's recognition and maybe an apology. But, as before, she was day-dreaming. I realised there was a lot about Julie that Harold didn't know, and I wondered if someone like him - I don't quite know what I meant by that - would be offended as well as bemused by her inexplicable bad manners: not the behaviour as such but the fact that there was no reason for it.

We sat in the reservoir car park and took in the views. I asked sarcastically if anyone would like something to eat. Harold nodded and I took that as a universal yes.

Julie passed me the picnic bag without comment. On top was her crumpled crisp bag, still opening out like a time-lapse film of a blossoming flower. I suggested that after eating we might motor on to the moors above Rochdale and have afternoon tea in the pretty village of Saddleworth.

I didn't know whether my refusal to be moved by Julie's antics was a good thing or bad, but I had the satisfaction of realising that my response could be read as either a signal that it was considered beneath contempt or an indication that I hadn't noticed. At the moment, Harold's deafness offered him the bliss of ignorance, a condition appearing to be flattered when he got out of the car to stretch his legs and squinting, looked up at the sun, delighting in its warmth like one of his freed pit-ponies.

It was only when we reached Saddleworth, late in the afternoon, that its horrors came fully formed as the place where the Moors Murderers had buried their young victims. Wasn't one of them still unaccounted for? I recalled a picture of a young boy wearing jam-jar specs and a grubby wasp-waist Burberry, with Fate's shadow darkening the background. His mother had appeared on television, seeking 'closure', an expression I guessed she'd learned from somewhere but as good as any for describing the indescribable, an improvised lid slammed on something too horrible to contemplate. What struck me about her was the lack of tears. I supposed the years of unbearable misery had dried her out.

Julie didn't have much to say for herself as the rest of the day went on, though her solicitude towards Harold was touching, as always. I watched them from what she as a writer called 'an objective distance' and it was at such times that I appreciated how lonely her occupation could be. She'd told me as much. My disengagement on that day out, however, was self-imposed. I was juggling the euphoria she must have been experiencing over the news about her book with her simmering dislike and suspicion of Ethel Chrimes. I don't know why but for a few moments I let her and Harold stroll ahead of me. I could see them arm-in-arm and chatting away as they'd done at Littlehampton. I scuffed the gravel path with its tufts of shivering grass and strained to hear what they might be saying. As before, I caught only intermittent laughter, first hers, then his. Perhaps Harold yearned only for the recent past, a woman's intimate company, and saw my interest in him as a reminder of how long gone and incapable of re-living was the distant past, the one I was interested in.

I looked about me at the surrounding hills, watched a lark in song throwing itself against the noiseless wind and thought how complicated everything was, how misleading, not least Julie and Harold now peering into the yonder, he indicating with outstretched arm something he may as a former Northerner have recognised and she listening to what he had to say about it; and certainly not least the ground at our feet concealing the remains of an innocent child as they must have lain when Ian Brady and Myra Hindley walked away from them together without a care, a human care, maybe stopping on the ridge for him to point out the source of that orange glow on the horizon, or something else, something equally fascinating and unearthly and unconcerning.

It's at such times that I recalled the moments when Julie and I seemed certain to be eternally indivisible, a stupid thing to say, I know, considering how we so often collided and bounced off each other. That we tried to embrace, as it were, beyond the world's awfulness and strife, and in spite of our own tendencies to make things difficult for each other, there were moments when our connection resembled a force beyond and separate from us but to which, without needing to consult one another, we willingly submitted. But no sooner had we spun headlong in its maelstrom than it passed on to what I like to think were more deserving cases. Julie, more perceptive if not more patient than I, probably felt something similar long before I'd managed to put the idea, the feeling, into words. Here, then, is the nearest example I could find among her writings of these storms of passion. And could I say that I never knew, I had no idea, despite the flawed chronology. And only now am I shiveringly aware that it is someone talking to herself, or to an imaginary listener.

From Julie's Laptop -2

How long since I've worried that nothing will last, that every gift and everything joyful comes with its renunciation clause? God, that's how a journalist would put it. But it stays, its staying my punishment, my reminder to express myself more memorably. At least before it reneges on me, my love-lust (the double L) for F banishes all others and all other considerations to the periphery. Even sweet little Harold down there in Boring-Goring, waiting to walk into the sunset with his coalminer's arthritic hobble on West Beach. What was that piece of Georgian banality by W H Davies about 'life's river, with its early rush, falling into a mysterious hush as it approaches the eternal sea'? Crossing the Arun at Littlehampton to get to that ocean of pebbles and flint chunks, we see the denial of such mush, coz the river can't wait to get away from the land, feeling at last the warmth and immensity of the brine melting its late bobbing thrust. I see nothing but F, think of nothing but F, want F, knows when he's not with me that he plays the part of the buzzing candystriped selfie stick, my girl's friend, my *flugenheimer*, my little pocket rocket. Want, want, want, want. Even while walking back with Harold from WB that time, shouting at his deafness, I pooled like a freebleed as though I'd pissed myself, all the time clinging to Harold, the poor mutt, while F straggles behind like someone left out. Me Sylvia, he Ted. Who this? Oh, Harold, focusing late in the presence of F, his foreign, megadistant, recently-unearthed relative, when, I suspect, he could either do with someone now that he's gone cancerous or wishes to stroll into the black yonder alone and sod'em all. Poor S O D himself. F says H will have a view about *Piersfield,* one's slow-selling minimus opus, which is about, *inter alia*, a calamitous mining disaster in the Welsh valleys, loosely based on Senghenydd. Well, I researched pretty furrowly, but I'll be interested in H's view of the accuracy of my imaginative flight to the coal face and all who toil there. Everything that interests and consumes F interests and consumes me. As my train pulls into Littlehampton station, they are sitting on the platform - well, F is standing, taking a step forward, while H remains seated and shrunk against whatever Winter harbinger is fingering the South Coast. Looking forward to meeting Ethel whatshername, who is taking an interest in H's welfare. We'll be one big happy family, happy in its own way. Actaw, miner, scribe, and - whatever Ethel is. (Is 'Ethel' coming back; as a name, I mean? Like Maud, Gwendoline, and Nancy? I wonder if the first Cheryl has been etched on a gravestone; or a Jodie, a Scarlett?) On the way to the car, I gather H unto me. We're roughly the same size. It's like marshalling a bundle of firewood (aged man, tattered coat, stick etc, etc), while the Great Hulk follows us, not speaking. A silent type. Of course, I've completed a circle, a revolution. What has it been - two months? Was it something I said? Nothing you said, My Thespian said, with feeling, exiting stage right. And I believed him as he wanted to be believed. So if not words, then what? Exhaustion, the claims of fictitious others (Flora or Bessie or Flora and Bessie in *The Rose Tattoo*; Yvette Pottier in *Mother Courage*; Lucy, Alithea's maid, in *The Country Wife*)? Or factual others, *ingénues* innumerable barred by head-height outstretched arm inside the stage door? Or the 'Actaw's Life', maybe, the constant effacement of self in the interests of the rôle. Perhaps it was me, my plotting of congress, the long long fuck, as exposition (our mutual gnawing), rising action (oh, god, the frolic, the unending frolic), climax (rupture-rapture in the air, a fruit split on a stick), the falling action (comedown from a height, the disengagement, the lava pouring), and then a performance of Dénouement, a one-act two-hander, in which I play Fellatrix to his bashful Pecker (a tacky, withdrawn character, unlike his upright alter ego John Pillicock, and I quote, long & thick & craving a lick). Then again, it was possibly that scene in *Hollyoaks* when he played a probation officer and had to tell a greasy ne'er-do-well who was evasive about allegations of ploughing his way through a youth club's distaff membership to *stop beating about the bush*. I laughed till I fell off the sofa. But his face seized up. Who writes that stuff? There are no laughs in *Hollybollocks*. It was one of his several TV bit parts. I shouldn't have laughed, I should have smiled inwardly, hoping he might see the joke. I felt sorry for him because I loved him and meant no hurt. I don't think he knew how much I loved him, knows how much I love him, will know how much I shall love him. Sensitive men post-1970s don't; they are too concerned about being misread, too aware of lost time having to be made up. Eggshells and all that. It was so good to see him again. I think I said: 'Two months; is it two months?' when we met in the street and went to the arty flix. It was lovely lovely to hear his oh-so-guarded voice again, wondering if I would feel like the victim gone to safe ground but hearing the pursuer's heavy tread and sensing about him the aura of vulpine insistence he always tried to conceal, as though with sheep's clothing. But finally, it may have been something I asked him once viz, did he not think that death was the great romantic adventure? I think I frightened him. But for those eight weeks without F, I was lost on the heath with a severed limb, blasted. I wanted, want life with him to be an escapade. Romance, adventure, odyssey. But for both of us entwined. He Odysseus, me Penelope. But no stay-at-home waiting. Faithful by his side. Homer re-cast.

Mention of wolves reminds me of foxes. They're living in H's garden. I lied to him about still owning a video camera, forcing myself to beg, borrow or buy one just to show willing. I'm overlooking everything: my past and present state, those that dog me, my barring them ingress, their silently breaking and entering while I sleep and my hosting of their importunate voices in my temple until they too slumber, leaving me at peace until something, some bug in the bed, nips them and they wake to the microscopic gnawing of their flesh, the pinhead bubble of blood. They complain to me so loudly as I traipse the aisles of Asda, watching, and all those others coming at me with their filling trolleys who know not that I am an awoken walking chorus they can neither see nor hear.

(In 1878, the English nature poet and weirdie Charles Lovell Darling, having many times watched his dachshund Bess quiver and whimper in her sleep, suggested in *The Unkempt House* that if a dog's brain could prompt imaginings while the animal was unconscious - as opposed to quickening at a constant myriad impulses while it was awake and alert - then there might reside there also some 'soul essence' that behaved exactly like its human counterpart.)

Here's me à la Jim Joyce – Francis oh Francis I dreamed a field of white stallions emerging from the mist at dawn droplets on their lashes and snorting to a halt the steam stoking off their flanks like a bush fire tails a'swishing oh Francis how beautiful they looked those superhorses a pride of stallions a blizzard of stallions and how they each stopped to graze their flanks rippling and twitching and their hooves toying with the ground but look they are full of play one canters off they all follow galloping ears back as though they remember battles fought by their blood ancestors at Airdsville and Samothrace the wild-eyed teeth-bared charge of the white brigade mounted by generals as befits equine aristocracy round and round they go and I see them see me and come to the fence the gnawed fence keeping their distance and I witness thoughts of a white mare empty their smooth pink pockets of members so long the wind catches them and they dribble their incipient seed pulled by the breeze to a sheet to a sail a part soap bubble made by a fairground soap bubble maker and I alone am privy to this and I see I see they are herding a female she of the high tail and dressage-ish trotting on the spot and the wet quivering apparatus puckered wet from sheer yearning with thoughts of her mysterious coming ecstasy like a unicorn or the winged messenger pure white daughter of Poseidon dripping diamonds of seawater in the air on her flight to the clouds or a courtesan her snow-white glow-white bright mantle lifted like the wild-eyed Messalina's on a priapic prowl of the Forum for patrician or plebeian meat it mattered not as long as it held up for once twice oh ambitious lascivious empress watched by Catonius Jutus from behind the temple of Vesta the temple of Antoninus and Faustina quick quick into shadow beside the temple of Castor and Pollux swish

swish through the arch of Titus witness to her damp longing three at a time and to die for his trouble by her pork-pounding hands and now Francis I see yes I see the superhorses defer to the super-superhorse as the sun goldmedals into the silver-skied horizon but she is not ready or she plays not ready so he goes forward bumping against her before she stops and grazes as though nothing were happening but the smell of her oh her smell the perfume of her desire oh how her proffered mechanism reaches out and froths like an insect's ovipositor and how finally he comes shimmering to it his gift to her so long it bends and bows and he rises how he rises like a circus performer out of Lautrec or the Spanish Riding School finding an awkward purchase before a shuffle forwards on his hind legs and the upwards swing into her and her impassivity at this rear happening and its gracelessness so quickly done and Francis I dreamed this but I saw it once in a sluiced farmyard in summer and how I a little girl visiting the farm watched and the hands smirking as the old cob shuffled up to the mud-caked mare and they went forwards at the precise moment of mounting and held it Francis gripped it two-handed and found the place for him and home he pushed and after it seemed like only seconds led out to the box to be taken to some other place requiring his essence. Oh, Francis, I ache.

Mona

When we got back from our jaunt to the moors, I suggested cooking an early-evening meal on the off chance that I could pop to the supermarket for a few things and take the opportunity to phone Mona. It worked out just right: Harold was hungry and not a bit tired and Julie needed no persuading to stay with him and lay the table. It would be fish fingers, his favourite.

Before shopping, I spent fifteen minutes in the car park making my surreptitious call.

'What are you up to?'

'Nothing,' Mona said. 'At home waiting for someone to ring.'

'Well, here I am.'

'No, not you. Someone with a job offer.'

She laughed. I loved her laugh; it was her way of never taking anything seriously, including herself. But she could be serious, in her own way. Laughing at yourself was a serious matter, I once told her. 'I know,' she'd said. 'Tell me about it.' I do recall that that was *precisely* what she'd said. It was so Mona. I'd resisted the temptation to ask her why she would want me to explain something she already knew. I know she hadn't meant that but some of the things she said encouraged you to be pedantic, as a joke.

'I've been trying to find out when that medieval thing is coming out.'

Ah, the angry sow's tale.

'And?'

'In May. But I expect I've been cut. I'm always being cut.' (I was sure she had been.)

'Ridiculous. Don't be so pessimistic.'

'It is ridiculous. I'm not really a pessimist.'

But she was probably right. The worst always happened to Mona whenever she suspected it. Not for the first time, I stopped myself telling her to look on the bright side, because you could bet the reverse would never happen. I wanted the best for her. She was so uncomplaining. Uncomplaining and uncomplicated. I retained this image of her struggling in the mud, weighed down on one side by her milk-pail harness and never being rewarded with an appearance for the effort. How nice it would be if she could show her friends the briefest clip of that instead of some web-post weepie about a bereaved elephant or a speeded-up sloth. That she thought the latter funny was the flip side of being uncomplicated. I didn't laugh at the sloth video. When I told her why, she no longer found it amusing. For a man, a woman like Mona was easy to get on with. Too easy. Express a contrary opinion and she would straightaway question her own. In short, Mona and I were an item waiting to be re-activated - again.

I told her where we were and what we'd been doing. I mentioned Julie. I had to remind her about Harold, though she remembered my telling her about him when we were in the catering tent at Chester. She asked how he was and I told her he was coping. That prompted me to ask after her father. She'd never told me much about her late mother's lingering illness. I had the impression that she'd performed her fair share of daughterly duties.

'He's fine. My father's fine.'

This was said almost wistfully, with a hint of exasperation suggesting that I may have asked only out of politeness. Maybe reporting on her father reminded her of her mother and all the suffering. It must have blighted her acting career. I wished I didn't have to admit to myself that, had I been properly interested, I would already have known about Mona's family situation.

It must be obvious from what I've said about Julie so far that she and Mona were far apart in every respect. The smallest thing would set Julie off, either in a good way or a disruptive one; whereas Mona never took offence, and barely knew when it was being given. The thought of Mona ever throwing a tantrum was ridiculous, but with Julie, there was often no hint of storms to come. In physical appearance, they might have been case histories of what happened when you ate too little or too much, Julie being the stick-insect one, at least when things were getting her down. Mona was fleshy and voluptuous, ruddily happy even when things were going awry at home or in her career. Uncomplaining.

For no detectable reason, I said casually: 'I'd like to meet your father.'

'Whatever for?'

'I don't know. Why not? Perhaps to make up for never seeing him while we were going out.'

I don't know where 'going out' came from, but she didn't pick me up on it. Things had once become serious between us insofar as the length of our relationship seemed to be reflected in the idea of its destination, which began emerging up ahead with its promises of comfort and security - just the kind of things actors want without sacrificing their chances of bigger and better parts. But there was a drift about it, a feeling that it wasn't what we wanted if only we could get round to discussing the matter. Mona made a great drifter, just bobbing along on her own or at someone else's bidding, never taking the initiative. This was true of sex between us which she readily admitted. In fact, she made a virtue of passivity, lying there with a knowing smile, her eyes closed, slowly but surely bringing herself to a damp and wriggling state of readiness and then rejoicing in the thrill of having things done to her. The second time we had sex, however, she reached up and grabbed my shoulders before pushing me aside, rolling over, rising on all fours and simply staying in that position, like an artist's model, but animal-like, and cooing when I made contact from behind, like someone under her control. It was a feeling I've never forgotten, a feeling of tacit sanction, unencumbered by qualms. It applied to other things we did together and the realisation that it all might have to do with Mona's refusal to judge or to interpret my actions unfavourably, without revealing her own thoughts and feelings, that made me take up with Julie, who I mistakenly thought did all that and more and was a creative type to boot, with what I assumed would be a limitless lack of inhibition. When I made that call to her before going to see Harold again, all that still applied; but since we'd got bound up in the Ethel Chrimes business, everything had changed. I didn't know where it was leading. I remember thinking at the wheel of the car while approaching the reservoir that I wished it might be Mona in the back seat and not Julie bathed in that rampant perfume.

'It's time you were going,' Mona said.

'What do you mean?'

'You know what I mean.'

She giggled, as if at a naughty boy caught in some childish act. Mona was innocent only in certain respects.

Quickly I told her how the concern for Harold's well-being had eclipsed my research into our family ties. I told her about our day out. I thanked her for letting me know the transmission date of our documentary, in which we were condemned to be mute players, she almost certainly destined to make no appearance at all. Anyway, I was about to make my own inquiry and to tell Harold. She suggested we meet soon and I assumed she meant just me, not Julie too. It was at that moment, in a Tesco car park under the false pretences she'd seen through, that my sympathy for Mona and her probable departure from the film we'd been in together first began to outweigh my concern for Julie. I recalled, while being filmed, seeing her way off on the perimeter of the set, practising with that heavy wooden shackle and falling time and again in the specially churned-up mud.

It was not, however, her predicament that moved me, she labouring to her feet unaided and looking around in embarrassment and me being unable to help, but her true rustic comeliness and spirit, her strength of character, and the memory of those subsequent times when she climbed out of my embrace and presented herself to me in that crude upright position with her backside in the air, revelling in her own enjoyment as well as mine and deriving pleasure from what seemed like resistance to my movements but which was really her equal and opposite response masquerading as something wicked, something wilful. Julie, I hardly need to say, stayed resolutely on her back, eyes wide open, staring at me as if I were compelled to discover if she were enjoying herself or rejoicing in my inability to do so. Her face and her luscious nether regions always seemed separate components.

Returning to the car after shopping, I wondered if my remark about wanting to meet Mona's father had anything to do with Harold's predicament, with two widowers running down and nothing retrievable bar memories; but two of a sort, possibly coming together in my mind at least.

And I knew, if I hadn't considered it before, that I was going to have to choose between Julie and Mona in any matter of settling down.

*

Having finished before the others as usual, I watched Harold eating. I'd picked up a lot from Julie, from her books as well as what she told me about writers and writing and the observations necessary to construct a view of anything or to derive possible meanings from it. Harold leaned forwards when eating a meal so that his elbows were forced outwards. Coupled with his small stature and the seemingly awkward way he gripped a knife and fork, partly in his fists, he reminded me of a whole line of Harolds similarly positioned and eating in unison and in silence, and that in turn presented me with a picture of a workhouse or some other institution, with no one speaking and the only sound the clatter of utensils on plates from row upon row of impoverished diners.

I also saw how sometimes he ate like a starved cat, at other times like someone forced to down a second cooked meal only minutes after demolishing a calorie-laden four-course one and pushing the food around on the plate with his fork while looking apologetically at us. When I was little, my mother used to put my huge appetite down to 'worms', her inference being that I was feeding the parasites inside me as well as myself; obviously they never got the upper hand. I knew something similar was happening inside Harold, some busy malevolent organism needing constant supplies of sustenance so that its outriders might be sent on their lethal journeys.

We drank our tea away from the table. Unprompted, Harold mentioned that I wanted more information about his early years and he began to talk about his journey to South Wales.

'Everyone was after higher wages and we all knew what that meant,' he said. 'We had to get up and go somewhere else. But no one was prepared to do it. I'd heard there was work down south, more money in the mines and steelworks, so I mulled it over and finally told my parents I was going to leave home. I was about eighteen. I was scared, mind. Though my mother and father didn't object. Far from it. They probably thought I would soon be sending money home to them, to help out. I might have been short but I was stocky, well-muscled from working the land. A lot of the parents wouldn't stand up for themselves when their boys were powerful and strong. It wasn't difficult to do what you intended. I knew boys that had beaten their fathers, I mean physically beaten them, like young lions growing up to take on their parents once they'd grown older too. I suppose they were getting their own back at last for having been leather-belted. Some of the old men, my father included, went downhill fast after a certain age.'

While he spoke, I had my eye on Julie. She was only half-listening and evidently growing impatient. As he continued with his story, she kept sighing and fidgeting in her chair. Finally she got up, excusing herself, and left the room. If Harold thought her behaviour peculiar, he didn't show it but just continued with his story.

I took him up on his reference to lions, saying it was a pity we weren't like elephants which, as Mona's YouTube clip demonstrated, appeared to be almost solicitous and capable of grief. He absorbed my observation but made no comment.

'Once I arrived down there, it wasn't long before I'd forgotten what I'd left behind,' he explained. 'I was never homesick. They all told me I would be. But I wasn't. Perhaps it was the work. It was tiring but I didn't mind because I was well paid - or better paid than I had been.

It felt good to be sending some money home. Not much, but I think it helped. My mother and father were grateful, anyway.'

He paused then and looked towards the open door, obviously wondering what had happened to Julie.

'Excuse me a minute,' I said, and left the room.

Julie was standing in the kitchen, leaning against the worktop with her arms folded.

'What's up?' I asked. 'Anything wrong?'

'You know exactly what's wrong.'

I quietly closed the door behind me.

'No, I don't actually.'

'Actually, you don't.'

I wasn't sure whether she was making fun of what I'd said, mocking my tone of mild irritation and sort of re-arranging my words, or stating a peremptory fact, which was to be followed by an explanation of what my ignorance hadn't allowed me to see.

'He just sits there, telling his boring life story, when she's down there plotting his early death,' she said. 'Didn't he read that thing in the paper, didn't he understand what it tells you about her?'

'What do you mean, plotting his death? I thought she wanted to make him well.'

She ignored this and pushed herself into a standing position. Then she stared straight at me and cocked her head, her forehead lined.

'What does he know about novels anyway? Just because he was once a miner and now attends a book club full of culture vultures, he thinks he knows where I went wrong.'

It took me a few seconds to realise what she was referring to: *Piersfield*, her flawed first novel.

'Let's discuss this later,' I said. 'Come on. He'll be wondering what's happening.'

'Tell him I've got a headache. I'll be there in a minute.'

Before turning to go, I guessed that, deaf though he was, he must have heard something of our conversation, agitated voices in the distant at least. While I'd tried to whisper my words, she'd spoken in a normal voice and not because she knew he couldn't hear much and wouldn't have picked up details.

'Go on,' she said. 'What are you waiting for?'

I returned to the room. Harold was sitting back with his elbow on the arm of the chair, resting his chin in the palm of his hand.

'Is she all right?' he asked.

It was a loaded question - for me, anyway.

'Bit of a headache. Can't find the paracetamols. She gets a lot of them - headaches.'

'Aye. So she's told me.'

I didn't know that. Once more, I wondered what else she'd told him.

Almost right behind me, Julie entered the room as if nothing had happened.

'Sorry about that, Harold,' she said, flopping into her chair like a breezy teenager and picking up the magazine. 'Too much fresh air.'

He didn't see the joke but nodded his head limply and half smiled, not at her but at the wall in front of him, as if an explanation was to be sought in the distance beyond the street and the suburbs outside. He could have been seeking help in the past, trying to draw on experience for explanations of things that now baffled him.

I kept looking at Julie, not that she noticed. She resembled an adolescent when she behaved like one or adopted the mannerisms, like now, with one leg across the arm of her chair and flicking with spittled thumb through a magazine in danger of having its pages torn out one by one. She really was thin and short, often 'poorly-looking', as Harold might have called it. I had two sickly people on my hands. I suppressed a grin at that and at Harold's forgetfulness. We once talked about memory loss in relation to his role as my guide to our common background and when I reminded him, he'd forgotten what he'd said about it. Another joke was lost on him. I wondered how that worked: forgetting you'd forgotten. It sounded like another drop downwards.

It was time to concentrate on Julie, to make her the centre of our attention.

But that night, all was to change.

How do you raise the subject of hearing voices with a person who appears to be doing so but hasn't discussed it with anyone?

Julie and I were together in bed. We were twin effigies, like Larkin's stone couple, staring at the ceiling. I placed my right hand on the duvet above her left thigh and gently delved. She didn't resist.

'We should tell him about duvets,' she said. 'Buy him a couple.'

I wondered if she'd forgotten where we were or - perish all thoughts - she was in two places at once. She'd never mentioned Harold's bed linen while we were down there, just his horse-hair bath towels.

'Why not?'

'I don't know. I almost expected blankets, a bedspread.'

'And you got them.'

'No, but - oh, forget it. He's our parents' generation.'

I was careful not to ask if her parents didn't have duvets. In her present mood, it might have sounded belittling. I told her my parents did, though not before me.

'Mine too,' she said. 'I had to persuade them.'

Her voice was distracted, contrite even. Had she now realised how objectionable she'd been on our day out and was preparing to apologise?

Courage had to be summoned, diversionary paths resisted.

'Are you OK?' I said.

'You're always asking me that. You're always asking Harold that.'

It was true. Perhaps she detected something more than usually worrying in my voice. But she turned her head towards me and smiled. She wasn't so much poorly-looking as slender - thinner than she needed to be. The leg I was holding moved towards mine with mock discretion and with a tremor she raised her knee. My mother told me thin people were 'all nerves' and their 'nerviness' ate up all their fat and that something called their 'metabolism' took the place of exercise. Worms and nerves, the twin interlopers. Thin people were always thin, whether they took exercise or not. Ditto smokers; I was trying to give up.

We lay still for a while, working through the preliminary movements and gestures that confirmed we were of one mind about what was happening and which required no comment - indeed, was enhanced by lack of it. From the next room came the faint sound of Harold's snoring: the long, deep-breathed and uninterrupted sighs and rumbles telling of peace on the surface and turmoil below.

'Could I ask you something else?'

'What?'

'Well, today you seemed a bit on edge. Then, just now, your headache.'

She uttered a barely-audible moan, a private response, as she shifted on to her side and engaged with a narrative running parallel to my enquiries but willing to put up with them for a moment. As her right leg travelled across my torso, she left a damp marker on my hip. I didn't know if this was a good time to ask the leading question or a bad one. Before I could decide, she surprised me, shocked me, with a query of her own.

'Are we being too hard on Ethel?'

I took my time answering, having not yet made up my mind about our southern Soul Traveller. By calling her that, I obviously still saw her as an odd figure, if not one of fun, then of the menacing-clown variety.

'Maybe. But I have Harold's interests at heart. Blood ties and all that.'

'So does she. So do I.'

'You said his recollections were boring, that she was a plotter.'

'Did I?'

With that, she rolled on to her back and we began.

The deed accomplished, as some of my male friends say, with Julie as usual staring at me all the while wide-eyed and with an ecstatic grin, I knew I'd missed my opportunity. For behind those eyes, I fancied I saw others, abettors possibly, with whom she'd come to an accommodation. I found this more distressing than the thought that she was their unwilling captive and capable of being rescued. I didn't know what to do. I knew I might be losing her, and in her going from me, I unconsciously yearned for Mona Strange, the Mona in distress with her milk pail and her faint prospects of advancement, but also with her brute lack of embarrassment; her plumpness, her triumph over metabolism. I just had to keep a check on everything; that was all. Though, to be honest, Julie's writing was better than my acting. There's always a way of making that sort of comparison. It was even possible - but what do I know? - that our disagreements were caused by unacknowledged jealousy on my part. When you've begun to identify the existence of demons, the unconscious becomes a populous place, whose clamour is far off and for the most part inaudible.

'You know that programme I did, the documentary?'

'Mmm.' This sleepily.

'It's being broadcast in May.'

No answer. I looked across. She was gone. She along with the others, to judge by that ineradicable simper and the meeting of minds behind it.

Outlook Express

A month before he was due to start his first chemo, I returned to phoning Harold once a week - after lunch on a Sunday. We'd agreed to do it, my polite insistence overcoming his feeling that I should do so only if I really wanted to, though he said he appreciated my interest in his welfare and that it was thoughtful and considerate of me to think of him. During one of these calls, he told me that he'd bought a laptop. He said it was how Book Club members communicated between meetings – emailing, I assumed.

I could never picture Harold typing out screeds of observation and analysis, especially on a newly-acquired computer screen. Like all wise old men, his wisdom was dispensed with throwaway brevity. The last refuge of such people is the redoubt, unless they have plenty more to say in support of their opinions. But Harold never struck me as being one of those. Did he feel obliged to back up what he said but knew that his respectful companions, though disagreeing with him, would not require it? Ethel had taken him to Curry's, where he'd bought a PC. She too. They'd also both bought mobiles.

'We're messaging as well,' he told me. 'Ethel is teaching me. I'll let you have a message when we've finished.'

There were ten core members of the Goring Book Club. Each had bought a copy of Julie's first novel and discussed it. I got the impression that Harold had been appointed guide to its background and authenticity, though he could have had little knowledge of how a small weekly newspaper operated years before or even what it would have been like to experience and survive an underground explosion. But, as for the latter, he'd at least worked in a place where death and disruption could have been easily imagined and communicated. He was full of surprising facts about coalmining. For example, I never realised that caged canaries were still being used underground to detect methane or so-called fire-damp. The ponies, too, though in declining numbers. What happened was, in the presence of gas, the canaries would start singing and then keel over dead, the signal for the miners to scarper in the opposite direction, presumably chased by a wraith-like but invisible cloud. It reminded me of the morning I discovered Norm on the floor of his cage behind that pelmet made by my mother. Except that Norm had died from old age or boredom or endless repetition of the incomprehensible sounds my father had taught him.

An hour after that phone call, my mobile pinged with a message. It was from Harold. He'd obviously meant when we'd finished talking, not when he'd finished learning to transmit. It read oddly with no mention of the phone conversation we'd just had. He'd tried to let me know what would happen on the day but he'd evidently typed out something from the hospital's letter to him, down to recording that the 'infusion' would be over at '18:00 hours'. Ethel would take him and bring him home, he said. I knew that. So did Julie. I would be working with no chance of time off. That Harold's well-being, actually his fight for life, was close to the centre of my own existence and to Julie's after a fashion was becoming obvious. It was just as well that he'd agreed to keep in touch in two ways. We or I would get down there as often as we could. It was a vague, if well-meant, promise.

The next morning, I had a text from Julie saying that she too had received an email from Harold. Not the same one evidently, because they'd discussed the possibility of her going down to see him if I couldn't manage it. I thought this was worth more than a truncated text message with its infantile abbreviations. *URN4A sprize*, she'd tapped. *H has learned to email.* It might have been a Mona text. By now, this feeling I had of me and Julie running on different but parallel tracks was becoming common, though it was obviously not as she saw it. It was like being with someone suffering from amnesia except that the sufferer had no awareness of her forgetfulness. I simply waited until our tracks converged and things became normal again. I had no power over such convergence; in fact, I received no notice of when it was about to happen. I feared that it might be only a matter of time before she was whisked off in a different direction or became derailed.

For example, I thought her desire to protect Harold from Ethel Chrimes's natural remedies would be a question of argument and rational persuasion when the time came. It clearly exercised her. So I put her animated concern down to enthusiasm. But I was always doing that when I should have assumed an element of the irrational. I took the following extract from the welter of items in her laptop Documents folder. When I re-read it, I'm sometimes tempted to berate myself for not thinking equally seriously about Harold's well-being and the threat to it posed by Ethel and maybe her fellow Soul Travellers. Then again, and the idea of the writer as researcher aside, Julie seems to me to go way beyond what would be required to raise an objection to it, in seeming almost manically engrossed in an aspect of the issue that didn't really matter. The comments in bold type and/or in parentheses are hers.

From Julie's Laptop - 3

The first known example of so-called 'double parasitism' was recorded in 1967. A Chilean botanist, Dr Jorge Vergara, and a Brazilian entomologist, Professor Raissa Branco, were working respectively on the life-histories of a parasitic plant and a parasitic insect.

Dr Vergara was an expert on the group of mistletoe-like plants belonging to the family *Santalaceae* which attach themselves to trees and live off them. It might take decades but the tree will eventually weaken through the parasite's debilitating activities. In July 1966 he'd been informed of the discovery of *Santalum variegatum*, a mutation of *Santalum album*. It was found growing on a specimen of *Didymopanay morototoni* (**the Chrimes tree!!!!**) in the Amazon basin.

While examining cuttings of the mutant plant in the laboratory, Dr Vergara noticed the remains of a dried animal exoskeleton stuck to the underside of a leaf. He recognised it as that of a sawfly, believing it to be *Shizolena terpsichorii*, a parasitic insect specifically named because of the apparently co-ordinated 'dancing' movements of its red-and-blue larvae when feeding, but hitherto unknown as a parasite of the genus *Santalum*. He contacted Professor Branco, an old colleague, who confirmed his identification.

Not long after, Dr Vergara and Professor Branco began a joint research project to find out if the double dependency had any ramifications. Their first published paper, *Di-morphic Parasitism: Physiological Inter-relationships of Santalum variegatum, Shizolena terpsichorii and Didymopanay morototoni*, was the first in a series of investigations which proved that the insect appeared to neutralise the deleterious effects of the parasitic plant. Moreover, the many specimens of *Didymopanay morototoni* to which *Santalum variegatum* had become attached, itself having first been colonised by the ravenous 'chorus lines' of *Shizolena terpsichorii* larvae, dramatically reduced the potency in the tree's leaves of a milky substance called Beta-dioxymetasalicilate - **'Metaferon' (!!!!!)** - or halted production altogether.

Amazonian tribes had long used plant extract as medicines, including Beta-etc etc etc from *Didymopanay morototoni.* But the strength and amount from this source continued to vary. It was a mystery until Vergara and Branco ascribed the variation to increased double infection by the two parasites. Uninfected trees had become fewer and fewer as the parasites went about their work (**Double Whammy!!**). The quest for rare, uninfected Metaferon-producing specimens became part of native lore and minor jungle wars were fought over them. (**This was in the 1970s and 1980s – must have been before logging gave the jungle-dwellers something else to think about.**) Metaferon had been used by the natives to cure a range of ailments, including snake and dog bites, boils and **TUMOURS**, and, combined with additives, to induce what Vergara, Branco and their co-researchers describe as 'celestial states', which were the culmination of ritual ceremonies.

Nothing more on Metaferon, except this from 2007:

(**??????**) The holistic use by Americans to treat cancers (**!!!!!!**)

NB: Maybe write a story from all this, viz. Vergara and Branco are lovers. The utter pointlessness and indifference of Nature (what's a parasite FOR FFS!!). Science equiv to knowledge for its own sake. The dancing larvae (god with a sense of humour, wanton boys and flies, etcetera). The search for Nirvana through drugs, an ever-fruitless quest. Get E Chrimes in as crazy figure, making contact with jungle witch doctor at séance ??????!!!!!!!

Better still, use names of Vergara and Branco in some other science-related story, set in a zoo. A failing zoo. In Sweden (why not?), with old delinquent primate.

Chemo 1

Theatre duties meant I couldn't get down to Harold's place to be there for his first treatment. The stage manager was at an arts conference and I had a deputy but he reported sick on the day. Not that 'being there' could have been anything other than as his chauffeur and a possibly irksome presence. Ethel was driving him to the hospital and waiting there to take him home. It was Ethel's driving that worried me first, more than any undermining of me as a kinsman or of me and Julie as his double-act friends and supporters. Harold had told me, and I later found out, that she drove like a Kamikaze pilot, not fast but with an urgency that seemed to reflect some reluctance on the vehicle's part to join her in self-destruction as she needlessly shifted gears and grappled with the steering-wheel. A bit like Jean Grimaldi.

I hadn't even got from Harold any detailed idea of what chemo treatment entailed in terms of being hitched up to a tube, being filled up with a chemical and feeling sick every day for weeks.

'It's poison, you know,' he told me in case I hadn't realised. 'It gets to the root of the problem but threatens the rest of the plant as well.'

He seemed surprised and impressed by his metaphor; it was in the way he looked at me, as if seeking approval for it. Later on, Julie would have groaned, beyond caring what Harold thought. That's the way her illness went. She would have complained that he'd read it somewhere. She would lose all awareness of others except as confusing presences and eventually lose all awareness of herself, or so it appeared: there was something else she was concentrating on, something out of sight, possibly coming in and out of focus and sometimes disappearing altogether. It was on those occasions that I felt most wanted, most helpful.

In fairness to Ethel, she did phone while Harold was hooked up to the sick-making liquids meant to cure his sickness. It was a brief call as though she'd been rudely interrupted; but I suspected that she'd been sitting at his bedside or in a side-room with nothing much to do except wait. A grudging call, Julie said. Maybe it was. But at least she'd made contact. I asked her how Harold was coping. There was a pause. I imagined her looking up at him from her chair to check or glancing at him through a window but more likely standing in a corridor next to a public phone, though she now had a mobile.

'As well as can be expected,' she said. 'It won't register for a bit. Later, I expect, when we get home. But I'll make him something.'

Another pause. I'd got used to Ethel's either-or style of conversation: either she lectured you, or you prised information from her. I guessed she wanted me to ask her what she was cooking. Then I remembered from looking it up on the internet how chemo patients could eat nothing immediately before treatment and not much after.

'What's on the menu?' I asked.

'Well, not sausages, that's for sure.'

Another pause while she let me work that one out. But I didn't need to.

'I'll try and get down there as soon as possible,' I said.

'Just you?'

'Not sure.'

I didn't want her to divide and rule.

Then the phone went dead. I waited a few moments to see if she'd ring back but nothing happened.

That day I was two weeks into a new job as assistant stage manager at The Edge, a theatre and arts centre. The play we'd been rehearsing was Strindberg's *Miss Julie*. It was the third night of a week's run. I had a few hours off and went to the cinema to watch *American Sniper*. My Julie never had much of a sense of humour and when I told her I'd got the job with the Strindberg, saying something to the effect that we were 'about to direct *Miss Julie*', she just congratulated me, not saying anything even acerbic, such as to suggest that she hoped I'd have more success with the stage Julie than I'd ever have with her - which is what I might have expected and which she might in a certain mood have thought or uttered. If the play had been called *Miss Mona*, the response from Mona Strange would have been something titillating, like 'You can direct Miss Mona anywhere you like.' I was always needing, as an ideal position, to be somewhere between the two, between Julie's rigidity and Mona's ever-collapsing defences. Considering *American Sniper* took viewers to a place they could barely imagine, and then with difficulty, I found it disappointing, its depiction of the protagonist as 'a killing-machine with a heart of gold', as someone later described it, avoiding what the Iraq war was about and why it was so unnecessary. The *Manchester Evening News* would say that the production of *Miss Julie* was 'a minor triumph'. Words made anaemic by over-use, Julie would have said, ignoring the strange use of 'minor' and suspecting that, in real terms, sniping was more complicated than Hollywood could ever understand and that the production of *Miss Julie* had been anything other than a moderate success. Moderate, minor - they both took something away from the appraisal.

While I sat there in the thinly-populated dark watching Bradley Cooper on the screen decide whether or not to take out a child who'd just picked up a loaded rocket-launcher and was aiming it at his fellow infantrymen, I kept thinking of how distance neutralised pain and the thought of it. I don't believe it ever happened for Julie. I knew she was at home on Harold's first day of being attached to his particular killing-machine and I suspected that at times she was on the settee in a foetal position, her imagination livid, visualising the toxins running wild through Harold's veins and attempting to 'take out' his little fortress of agony and every peaceable place besides.

I knew how long the first treatment would last and when Harold and Ethel would have returned to his house. I didn't want to phone straightaway. I hoped Ethel or Harold himself might contact me first. But they didn't. I gave them an hour, which allowed me time to get home and have something to eat. Then my mobile rumbled. It was Julie.

'Have you heard?' she asked. 'He feels terrible. I think we should go down.'

'Well, I didn't expect he'd want to go out on the town.'

This, as I suspected it would, must have sounded callous, a dismissal of her concern and a denial of mine. It was also a further example of the return of her bluntness, the bypassing of pleasantry, the absence of both a context for anything she was about to say and a preamble. It was as if I were simply a marker to be tiresomely acknowledged en route. The expression 'out on the town' wouldn't have appealed to her either. (What? A cliché as the response to a serious matter?) Such things had been the reason for our separation. Two people too often out of sync. When we got together again through Harold, the pleasantries returned and were evidence, I thought, of a change of heart, a re-consideration. But I was probably wrong; I thought they represented nothing more than the temporary decorations of a solid core, her true self, or the self she had become. I felt sad – for her and for us.

'Go down? What - immediately?'

She knew I was needed at The Edge.

'I could go,' she replied, meaning without me.

'He's got Ethel.'

It sounded like reproof, or even a reason for her not going, and was received in silence.

Then she said: 'Ring him yourself. Now. And make sure you speak to him, not her.'

'I will. I was going to. Don't let's fight - not over this.'

'We're not fighting. Just ring him before he goes to bed.'

She sounded like my mother whenever she thought my responses were short of the desired urgency. There was a pause which I hoped might be followed by tender feeling but there was nothing. She just said: 'See you,' with not even an inflexion that might have made it mean more than it seemed.

I did ring. Ethel answered.

'He's very tired,' she said.

But I was irritated to hear her say, as if censuring me, that Julie had already rung.

Anyway, I had a few words with Harold. He said he felt OK but was 'bushwhacked'.

I left it at that, telling him to take care and that I - we - would be down to see him as soon as possible.

That night, after the performance, I was sitting in front of the television with the sound turned down. As I placed the phone on the table beside me, wondering whether to phone Julie, something about the pictures on the screen transfixed me. It was a news programme about the IRA attack in Regent's Park, which had resulted in the deaths of eighteen military personnel and their horses - seven horses, in fact, belonging to the Blues and Grays. And I wondered whether I were alone in being shocked at the time, and again in that later documentary, not by the bodies of soldiers, which anyway had been swiftly removed, but by the horses lying in the road awaiting collection. I kept looking at the old footage, then at various people being interviewed, survivors perhaps, and thought it must be like that after an explosion, your disorientation and deafness suddenly making the world skewed and silent. Perhaps that's how Harold felt though I had no wish to go into details with him.

The next day when Julie hadn't contacted me - not even an email - I rang to tell her that I'd spoken to Ethel and Harold the previous night. She didn't remind me that she'd phoned him before I had. She didn't say anything much.

But to go back. I returned to the theatre through the park opposite. I knew it well. I often slip over there, especially in summer, and fetch up on one of the seats surrounding its central oak tree, just to look or read or think - cogitate as my mother used to say. It was dusk but it wasn't cold. The seats, like the whole park, seemed to be surviving against the odds. They were covered in marker-pen graffiti and lewd proclamations of love: 'Lois fucks Shane'. Despite poop-scoop signs, there was dog shit everywhere. This was not poop-scooping territory. In Autumn and Winter the scurrying squirrels reminded me of rats; vermin, as Harold had reminded me. But survive it does: Spring brings a sort of victory, a floral celebration; Summer a burial of malign intent. It reminds me of Harold in his present state, a man contemplating ups and downs but fortified by occupation against further hard knocks. Even though the grass was permanently worn at the edges to caked mud, the council still took a trimmer to it, filling with tarmac the gravelly gap that as a consequence opened up between path and greensward. I saw a man sit down on one of the seats after he'd attached a leather sling to one of the oak's lower branches. He then encouraged his 'Staffy' terrier to take a few leaps before attaching itself to the end, after which it swung there, biting and growling, until it hung stock still like something pre-flayed in an abattoir, its biting instinct enduring long after the spasms of excitement it had triggered. A model of tenacity. Needless to say, dogs in the park have to be kept on a lead. Tenacity and anarchy then. While suspended and still, the dog had shat hard black bullets of uncollected poop.

It's funny but I felt closer to Harold, a distant relative lately discovered, than I had to almost anyone else in my family. Perhaps I mean that my closeness to others was taken as read and never expressed because there was no need. There is probably a need and I suspect that I come from a family in which a lot that remains unspoken should not and is so because of some deficiency of emotion and manners that no one will admit.

I got to thinking too about that blog mention of Julie's, the one describing her visit backstage with her friend Bronwen at *Equus* and meeting me and the Short-Arse Dogsbody of an AD; also, its reference to a phone call I was making with my horse-suit half rolled down. Actually I was taking a call and it was from Mona. She'd later seen the name in caps on the screen. Mona was in one of her smothering phases and they were sometimes becoming too much for me. I'd told her so and had asked calmly enough for a respite. It was granted and for a while we met as de-fused lovers over coffee or lunch (never dinner), with no post-prandial acrobatics at my place or hers (or, in the case of a mid-morning Costa, her car or mine). Then we floated apart, eventually to the point of rarely making contact, and the next time we met was on the documentary film set, queueing for hot dogs.

Knowing all that, Julie could easily have linked the mutual casting-off of me and Mona with her sighting of me outside my dressing-room. This, by the way, is not a case of reporting something about someone that she is no longer in a position to confirm or deny - Mona is, though the same applies - but to offer it as an example of her belief in inter-relatedness, which she said in some interview or other was the source of her creativity. This was not the same as fate, which, as I've always understood it, means one cannot intervene or regard any happening as being due to chance. But Julie's idea of the hidden relationships between things was all that made sense of the world and explained how her imagination worked. In one of her stories, the start of an affair might easily be sparked by the end of another, unwittingly observed. Julie always seemed to be making mental notes of everything to see how this idea checked out.

Although my function in the run of *Miss Julie* was peripheral and non-creative, my regular patrols beyond the auditorium during a performance or in their ghostly aftermaths found me lingering in the wings or below stage from whose musty confined spaces sprang such sights as a disturbed teenager riding a horse played by a man in costume or, as then, the cat-and-mouse manoeuvring of an aristocrat and her upstart menial.

That night, when just about everyone else had left, I was climbing the short flight of steps to the stage from the dressing-room corridor when the threatened sow made another lunge, as I like to describe it. The shooting pain was almost as bad as the initial bite. She was out to get me. And she would, lying in wait as Harold's treatment ran its course.

Recuperation

At the end of a few other theatre productions, I was driving to Goring with Julie. She'd attended one of the *Miss Julie* performances. Previous arrangements having been scrapped, I'd been phoning Harold at various times after his treatment; and so had she, I discovered. Unlike her, I'd also been in touch with Ethel. I didn't dare mention it and hoped that Ethel wouldn't say anything in Julie's presence that gave me away. As far as I was concerned, Ethel Chrimes was no longer a threat but an oddball, though not yet a harmless one. Harold told me that she'd arranged for a nurse to call in every couple of days or be available at short notice. Now that Harold's prostate had been needled and zapped and poisoned, I assumed that Metaferon had been demoted to last resort or was off the scale of considerations altogether.

The journey down included a couple of pit stops. Since learning of Harold's 'trouble down below', I'd been conscious of my own susceptibilities in the nether region. One of my grandfathers had died of prostate cancer. Or was it 'with' prostate cancer, as Joe or Phyllis had commented? I'd been bookmarking a lot of internet stuff on the subject, especially concerning the impatience of cancer cells to be buggering off to create havoc elsewhere. Maybe that was what was meant by dying 'with' prostate cancer; a bit like being bitten by a mosquito, suffering from malaria that weakens the heart, and dying much, much later from a cardiac arrest after the offending gnat had spawned a million zillion generations. In the loo, I looked down at what the medics called my 'flow'. It seemed strong enough to put out a fire. Above each bowl at eye level was one of those discreet posters urging young men to make regular examinations of their testicles, the diagrammatic anonymity embodying the discretion. At one time there was a late-night ad campaign on the TV, gingerly recommending the same thing. I was with Mona then; she told me she'd have no qualms about conducting my examination herself. Julie would never have said that even when, for a while at least, we were beyond the prospect of confrontation. It seemed that cancer was choosey about where in the male reproductive zone it organised its insurrections; but young whirligigs or superannuated glands, it was heading in the same direction.

Returning to our table, I saw that Julie had moved. For a second or two, her absence unnerved me: my rucksack was still on the floor beside my seat but all her paraphernalia had gone. I imagined she'd been spirited away. It was no idle thought, considering how she oscillated about my greater stability. We were in one of those inhabited bridges that straddle the carriageways, and she'd moved to a seat overlooking the whooshing traffic. I halted for a moment to watch her staring out of the window. I never came to terms with her delicate elfin beauty. Like everything else about her, it seemed untouchable. Maybe I did too much thinking about her and not enough proactivity of the sort she'd described (but, frankly, I'd done very little about). Maybe it was always from a distance that I appreciated how lovely she looked, that appearance of peace and quiet self-possession that hid so much turmoil. A Renaissance artist would have painted her, which reminded me that the beauty and inscrutability of a portrait are inaccessible. Was being with Julie an always-doomed process of sabotaging these qualities in order to gain access? Did she think that life with me would lessen her in some way? It would account for our uncertain and frequently bad-tempered relationship, its tendency to fracture, and the way compromise would hover at the fringes like a guest dying to be invited to dinner.

I recalled the zoo-bound family I'd come across on the M40 that time. Because I'm tall and Julie was below average size, she always looked much smaller beside me and we could have been taken for father and daughter at first glance, the few years between us exaggerated by the dissimilarity in height and her liking for what I always thought of as student attire, though I never referred to it and never complained. More and more I found myself invoking tacit fatherly concern, something that always drew me close to that aura of detachment as a fingertip hovers near a dull hotplate.

I didn't ask her why she'd moved. Without inquiring, she'd bought me an espresso, a coffee I liked but not exclusively. She was watching the cars and lorries streaking silently towards us, then disappearing with a faint roar beneath; in thought, distracted, as she often was. I'd learned, but not very well, to take pre-emptive tacks. I would never have said: 'A penny for them?', as I would have to Mona. In any case, she would always tell me herself. In one way, I supposed this deference was a mark of my attitude to our relationship, in that I was always sort of willing it to go on; continuously goading her would have been the quickest way to end it unless anything I did in the way of reparation and encouragement was doomed to failure by her wilfulness.

What she said, while still staring at the traffic as though its motion were feeding her argument, was surprising. It referred to something already suggested but that she'd probably forgotten.

'Maybe we've been too hard on Ethel.' (She didn't say 'we have', with emphasis on the 'have'.)

As she continued to avert her gaze, it sounded as though she were communing with herself, thinking out loud.

I asked her why she'd changed her mind but not that I agreed with her.

'I don't know.' She was facing me now, her expression suggesting that she'd made a huge mistake. 'Ethel Chrimes is mysterious. That's all.'

Her tone was disapproving; it seemed to suggest that it was I who had first raised concern about Ethel. I didn't object. It was a relief to know that she'd jettisoned what would surely have become an obsession.

'We'll just have to keep an eye on things,' I said by way of timid agreement.

I hoped my statement would find favour. Sure enough, and gratifying from my standpoint, she slid a hand across the table and covered mine. Hers was dainty but cold and red-raw with fingernails nibbled to the quick. It was another of those moments illustrating what any permanent life we planned together would be like: compromise on her terms. That's not a judgement but an observation. I often thought I might be able to live with it.

We were soon cruising through the Surrey Hills on the way south. After a while, I could see the traffic ahead slowing down. Julie sighed. The sound of distant sirens reached us, and we came to a halt.

The sun on her window was making her sleepy. I asked her if she wanted to lie down in the back. Without answering, she opened her door and changed seats, immediately curling up and resuming the conversation rather than going to sleep. Foetus-like, as often, she seemed to have reduced in bulk even more.

Then I let her lie quietly for about fifteen minutes as we stuttered forwards. The road ahead curved to the left. In the distance the traffic was still creeping along. I thought of what it must be like for an estranged husband, after an access weekend, trying to return a sick daughter home to her mother before the condition worsened and recrimination ensued over lateness and lack of communication. Cocooned in the back, Julie appeared also to have reduced in age: no longer the eternal student in multicoloured woollens and Doc Martens but a pre-pubescent sucking her thumb. That was one of her habits. I mention it only now because, in the car that time, I expected to turn around and find her doing just that.

There was a noisy estate in front of us that wobbled like a mobile disco. The three occupants were gesticulating with their arms and clutching the roof. A football fan's scarf trailed from a back window. As we moved forward a few yards once again, its front passenger tossed an empty beer can on to the verge. I wondered what kind of person would do that; what they were like in other situations, always in can-chucking mood. Stalling at one point, their wagon represented chaos barely contained. I half expected its driver's patience to wither and the vehicle to be swung on to the verge and driven ahead at a crazy angle as if through a jungle, its natural environment. 'Beasts of the field,' I muttered.

Julie heard me. I used to forget that she was always in observation mode, eyes peeled, ears pricked.

'This mob in front,' I said. 'Scumbags.'

She said nothing. I looked around. She was still lying on her side, her eyes wide open.

'You're too quick to judge,' she said.

'Am I?'

I tried to say it as though I'd been found out, an innocent, and would never repeat the offence. Other inflexions were possible: that I didn't agree; that I didn't agree and couldn't care less; that I was insulted by the accusation and expected an apology. With Julie, I used to think which one would best please her. It was really no basis for a life together; or it was but it would be ever lived on the cusp.

'What will happen to Harold?' she asked.

'Nothing too painful, I hope.'

'I think he's going to die.'

'We're all going to die.'

She recognised no sarcasm in that and said: 'Death expectancy of the human race is currently running at one hundred per cent.' (Well, sometimes she had a sense of humour.)

We laughed together. That was good. I sighed whenever I heard her say something funny, especially when I shared the laughter. I don't think it ever denoted joy. Being joyful with one another, sharing the sort of happiness that little could corrupt, was an aim with us, not a continual state or even a normal one. In a magazine interview, she'd confessed that completing three thousand words in a day represented ecstasy.

'We should contact Ethel,' she said. 'Maybe take her out for a meal or visit some place.'

'Don't order meat.'

I'd told her about lunching with Ethel and Harold.

'Right,' she said, as if she'd forgotten and was a child again, receiving an instruction that brooked no demand for explanation.

'Can I ask you something?' No answer. 'Why have you changed your mind about Ethel?'

'I've already told you.'

I recognised that as a prelude to further explanation and knew it would soon follow.

'So you have,' I said.

'She's an elderly woman on her own, doing what her god has told her is right. We godless types should have no difficulty with that. Our godlessness will prevail, Harold will do well by the NHS, and Metaferon will return to its place in the realm of the travelling souls. Why else would we be non-believers?'

'Metaferon!' I uttered the word with a half-chuckle, confirming the whole Ethel business as a joke soon to be revealed as such.

With that, the traffic began to move.

*

When we pulled up outside Harold's house, Ethel's car was on the drive.

Julie was first out, trotting to the front door with the ends of her long scarf, one of Bronwen's creations, almost touching the ground despite being a couple of twists around her neck.

By the time I'd got out and retrieved our luggage from the boot, Harold had answered the door and Julie had her arms around his neck. In the background, I could see the still presence of Ethel, blocking the light from the kitchen. In the upstairs window next door, Phyllis had parted the blinds and was looking our way. About to make herself scarce but seeing that I'd noticed her, she waved, then disappeared.

Harold, in his own word, was 'tip-top'. He looked better, more - well, upright. An odd thing to say about a man no taller than five-foot-five. But when such a man has been ill, and the sickness seems to have weighed on him like the heavy tarp on his car, any reversal is almost startling. He'd contributed to the image - haircut, shirt, tie, loose tank top, a new pair of shoes. Not that he'd ever been slovenly, as I knew from our attendance at church and his visit to us. For people like him, I supposed, battling illness was as much a matter of outward appearance as inner resolve, a generational thing.

Julie made what I thought was an over-enthusiastic act of greeting Ethel, who was taken aback but with half a smile that denoted - well, I wasn't sure what. Did she think we'd been won over? That said, most of our objections to her alternative medicine had been in the form of discussions in her absence. There'd been no direct opposition, unless when in her company she'd picked up a mocking attitude, a dismissive tone, which she felt had to be resisted. The word 'resistance' cropped up a few times in the West Sussex Convention of Soul Travel Experiences newsletter. It's all online, a bit amateurish and half-hearted. Resistance probably referred to the unwillingness of an opponent to come round to your way of thinking, rather than the refusal of someone with a counter-argument to see its flaws. It's the difference between self-righteousness and obstinacy. For a moment, and if Ethel's smile was one of surprise, I realised we were alike in our reaction to Julie's change of heart. I still didn't understand it but that didn't mean much.

After these brief pleasantries and seeing Harold in more-than-reasonable shape, I caught his eye and performed a cup-tipping gesture with my right hand. 'Aye,' he said. 'Everyone for tea?'

I went straight to the kitchen and put the kettle on. Ethel didn't follow me in as someone whose authority was being subverted. It was comforting to know that I had as much relaxed authority in the house as she.

Julie in her interrogator pose asked the questions.

'So how do you *really* feel?' she asked.

I might have winced at this if I hadn't known that Harold wouldn't take it the wrong way and Ethel wasn't certain that his recovery was genuine.

'Marvellous,' he said, sitting up. 'Really good.' He slapped his bony knees. 'I've got myself a mobile. She's got one too.'

I knew that, of course. This reference to Ethel as 'she' amused me, and I stifled a smile as Julie looked up, presumably expecting to see some slowly twisting sculpture suspended from the ceiling.

Before she could enquire about its location, Harold delved into the cushions between them and, like a magician, pulled out a wafer-thin Nokia.

If I weren't always trying to anticipate Julie's responses, I might not have interpreted her sour expression and silence as the opposite of delight, her embarrassment at having made a silly mistake.

She held out her hand for the phone in the way a parent does whose child has been caught with a banned implement - a catapult or a bullet of lipstick.

It was here that Ethel uttered her first words: 'Everyone seems to have them these days. I don't honestly see the point.'

Julie held the phone as if she hadn't seen one before. More importantly, she didn't react to Ethel's opinion. It was Harold who did that.

'They come in useful,' he said, staring at the phone as though he weren't going to get it back. 'It takes pictures.'

I recalled the difference between Julie's mobile, mine and Mona's. Julie's stored a dozen photographs at most; mine and Mona's too many to count. I'd yet to show Julie the photographs I'd taken of the Strindberg run and subsequent ones, including the final party which she'd declined to attend, telling me it was 'your show'. (Actually, she was right: hardly anyone brought spouses or partners.) At one point, Mona seemed to be attending a party every weekend and taking about fifty selfies at each. The very thought of Julie taking a selfie was laughable.

Then, escaping her reverie and handing me Harold's mobile, she said: 'Take one of us all.'

It was difficult to get everyone in. Because Harold was so short and Ethel so large, the best I could do was to crouch with the three of them at my back, Ethel standing in the middle and Harold and Julie leaning inwards. I told Ethel she'd have to put an arm around each of them.

'Do I have to?' she asked, not, I guessed, because such intimacy was foreign to her but because in not seeing the point of a mobile phone, she saw little to be gained by having her picture taken with one. Hers was the same Nokia model as Harold's. Twins.

Anyway, it worked despite the result looking like the innards of a barmy rugby scrum. I said 'Smile' before I thumbed the button, and we all did. A group selfie.

When I checked the picture on the phone's Gallery, I noticed two others there.

'What's this, Harold?' I asked.

He took the phone from me, looked at the pictures, and said, 'Oh, that's next door. The other day. The kids told me about it, and Aurora came out and asked if I had a camera. Well, I did - after a fashion.'

The picture was of a perfectly-formed skeleton of what I assumed was a cat.

'Wesley found it,' Harold explained. 'He was digging for some reason and the skull came up. He must have spent an hour, you know, scraping around for the rest. The kids helped him. I wondered what was going on when I saw them out of the window, all coopied down like a gang of scouts dib-dibbing and looking at the ground. Funny, isn't it? Wesley the archaeologist.'

Julie took a look before handing it to Ethel.

'I had to go back in and learn how to take a photo,' Harold said. 'All I've got to do now is email it to them.'

'I'll teach you,' said Julie, with a swift glance at Ethel. 'Doesn't anyone next door have a mobile? Everyone has a mobile.'

Actually, this was a short while before everyone did.

Harold & Me

The intimacy of any relationship is confounded and even thwarted in groups of more than two, despite the bohemian argument, the mutually-communing hippy ethos. Julie was hippy-ish, if only in appearance. Even allowing that Harold and I were always moving towards whatever would pass for close familiarity but never really got there, I thought the nearest he'd ever come to it was comradeship underground. But what do we know, especially about those states that seem safe from late contradiction? Miners were the supreme emblems of unity and singleness of purpose, weren't they? One for all and all for one, they marched together under banners with common intent and clarity of outcome. Didn't they? Harold had left the pit to work somewhere else before the British coalfield erupted in a national strike. He described it as 'an explosion on the surface'. When I saw the Orgreave film footage again in a TV documentary, I knew he was right. It looked like a movement of common purpose being viciously broken up.

The afternoon when we'd walked back from Chanctonbury Ring, Harold had told me something about his wife. We were moving downhill. It was when he was in front; when I was again struck by how much he resembled the stereotype of the miner: short and compact (I forgot to mention that his dapper, almost arty, appearance was kind of slapped in its face by the flat Welsh 'Dai' cap he was wearing.) He had his back to me. I suppose it's the sort of position a man about to confide in another male prefers to assume; or rather, finding such conditions propitious, they begin opening out.

'I miss her, Francis,' he said. 'I miss her a lot.'

I quickened my step to get closer, but still at his back, and raised even higher above him by the slope. 'Oh yes?'

I guessed he was talking about Marjorie.

'A lot.'

'You mean Marjorie.'

He didn't hear me. I had to repeat it. Then he heard.

'Mmm. Yes.'

We'd never discussed her much before. Her name had only been mentioned a couple of times. Wanting to know more about him, I expected her to come into the picture early. But he'd been telling me things haphazardly and we hadn't gone into detail about his marriage or his married life. It were as if my knowing that he was a widower had relegated her to a doubly removed, almost irretrievable past. Up until that afternoon walk, I didn't know how she'd died. He hadn't told me but I could have found out from a death certificate. In one of her awkward moods, Julie accused me of prying into Harold's life, no sooner having done so than taking an excessive interest in his well-being. At one time, she didn't like the idea of being able to 'find out about people' on the internet which I thought an odd opinion for a writer. But at other times, we looked up details of her family together, she clinging to my arm and nuzzling against me while almost lost in an oversize woolly jumper. I had the impression, though, that she was uninterested or not taking a real interest and that her face aglow in front of the laptop screen was that of someone having stumbled upon something wondrous but not yet revealed and nothing to do with what I thought was a joint quest.

Harold was now taking more rapid steps because the path had grown steeper. I drew alongside him, walking on the grass and leaving him to tread the well-worn trail.

But instead of learning about Marjorie, I was told more about life underground.

'You took things down with you,' he said. 'Your life on top. All of it.'

'How do you mean?'

'A man is no different just because he's dropped in a cage into the dark. You had to look out for yourself. A cage, it was. We were shut in.'

I thought he was talking about the whole experience of mining: that it was de-humanising, brutal. He'd already told me the word 'dropped' was meant literally; that they just let the cage fall through the shaft before applying the brakes. Like kittens being drowned in a sack, he'd said.

'The black made a beast of you, Francis.'

This remark came across loudly, as something I needed to remember. I had to stop grinning when he looked at me because I was amused at the way he sometimes shouted as the hard-of-hearing often do.

'One time, I was attacked. I was walking from the pony stalls and was punched in the head from behind. While I was on the ground, the chap who did it spouted something I didn't properly hear. It turned out to be a misunderstanding. He thought I'd said something about him and I got a half-apology. He was obviously a man who couldn't accept he'd made a mistake and done something wrong. There were some fights. Fistfights. I always thought we had enough to worry about down there without taking our other problems with us.'

I formed an impression of Harold the outsider, an artist, forced to work alongside men with whom he had little in common, the surface riff-raff. But that wouldn't do.

'What I'm saying is that we were a mixed lot down there, just like we all are above ground. Except that in the gloom the bad was at home, it grew bigger. It was more than gloom; it was black when the lights went out. That's when you were aware of the bad 'uns.'

I couldn't imagine Harold Taylor in a fight, even in places where those subterranean tunnels expanded until it was possible to rise to your full belligerent height. But I did see him in boxing terms - a bantamweight. Maybe he held his own against men of the same build and size.

'But there was more to that life than hewing away a mile down,' he said. 'In the beam of your lamp, the air was thick with the dust. We all breathed that in, whether we'd been mistaken for someone else or no. And when we stepped out at the end of a shift, we all felt we'd been rescued. All the men said that. One voice, like.'

He always referred to it as 'the dust', the definite article giving it a threatening aspect.

Once more, his accent betrayed his origins and the places where he'd spent most of his working life - Old Westmorland and Wales. Wish I could indicate it better here.

I said nothing, hoping he'd tell me more about Marjorie before going on to say that, despite the colourful life below ground, actually being below ground and the privations it involved transcended everything; so that men were bound more strongly by the things they shared than those, like vindictiveness or a short temper or a hatred of foreigners, that divided them. He never did; and I've never been sure. Although Equity did its best for actors, it would always be a motley membership. But I suppose it was the same: actors are in the dark till the lights go up.

Then he came out with it. 'Marje - I wasn't much of a catch, Francis. I was irresponsible, whereas she was straight, always sensible, always did the right thing, had the right idea.'

Use of the description 'straight' as now meaning something else didn't register with him. Live in the past and you employ its language.

This was all I was left with. He didn't elaborate. We were approaching the car. As we passed through a gate, the path dipped where it had eroded. He gripped my upper arm but not to steady himself because we had negotiated the lower level, and he lightly squeezed my arm before he let go.

That evening, I recall now, he came out of the shower and, girded by a towel, stood at the bathroom door as I was passing to go downstairs. He was framed by a backdrop of steam.

'Look at this, Francis,' he said, turning to show me his back. It was flecked with scars and more of those blue veins, scattered like trapped worms under the skin.

If I'd touched them to grasp the significance of what they represented, I don't think he'd have minded. I can't recall what I said. 'Good god,' probably. He did tell me later that he'd thought the decision to go on strike had been unwise. He also told me again how Marjorie had died, this time in more detail: of a stroke in bed at night, while he and she were fast asleep. The detail was in how he'd dealt with it, the practicalities. Strange, but I thought the information might come in useful.

Relapse

Harold's improvement was short-lived. He began to suffer what the hospital called 'delayed symptoms of recovery', by which they meant, apart from anything else, that the expected side-effects of treatment had kicked in. Maybe some inner strength, retained from his time as a miner, had held them back for a while. Stomach cramps and sickness were the worst. He hadn't much hair to lose but almost overnight, it was gone. He texted me a picture of his comb: it was thick with it. He'd taken a selfie in which the laden comb was in close-up and he himself balding and out of focus. Even more vague but nonetheless unmistakable was the figure of Ethel Chrimes sitting forward ghost-like on the settee behind him. It was his fingers that caught my attention: also sharp and fore-shortened in all their horny-handed detail. I was already wondering what would happen about his second course of treatment. Although I couldn't make out her features in the photograph, Ethel seemed to be looking straight at me and asking the same question or with a self-satisfied stare of vindication that I couldn't make out. A medical check had ruled out Prodaxel as a treatment.

The Edge theatre must have liked what I'd done on the *Miss Julie* run and on other productions because I received an email asking if I'd like a permanent job there, doing the same thing. There were some interesting productions on the way. I declined; as an actor, I needed to be available for roles. Then there was a follow-up phone call. The manager wanted to know if I'd consider continuing with the position for the time being. Again I refused. Julie was furious, her rage tempered by some good news on her third book: plans to make a film of *American Smooth* were progressing. Either way, I felt that no one was taking me seriously as an actor. But, partly out of frustration and the need to eat, I rang the theatre and accepted the offer.

'You would have been crazy to refuse,' she said.

I gave her a 'that makes two of us' look which, because she really was disturbed, was obviously lost on her. I never felt that my depression was ever anything to be raised as a means of identifying with her and leading to mutual understanding and support. She was not a hospital case - yet. But all hospital cases must have enjoyed, if that's the right word, some pre-diagnosis state of freedom. Compared with Julie, I was just sometimes miserable. And sometimes when feeling down, I thought she was fully aware of her boorish and erratic behaviour and could remedy it.

'Anyway, I've had some bad news from Worthing,' I said. 'Well, not good.'

'About Harold.'

She said it as though she already knew what it was, which she well may have and was waiting for me to find out for myself.

'He's in a lot of pain.'

I told her what had happened. Did she know? By this time, she was making as many calls to Harold independently as I was, sometimes telling me, sometimes not.

'He must have a second course of drugs,' she said.

She was emphatic, like a medic answering a question that hadn't been put.

'Should we find out what he wants to do?' I asked.

It was a stupid question, and Julie looked at me, seeming to revel in my stupidity but in a forgiving way, as though ignorance were part of my charm.

'I'll ring him now,' I said.

She pulled out her own phone and began scrolling, turning her back on me.

I rang Harold, but it was Ethel who answered.

'He's not too good,' she said. 'When are you coming down?'

'Can I speak to him?'

'He's asleep upstairs. Are you coming down?'

It was an odd query, with the accent on the *Are*. I didn't know what she meant. Bizarrely I somehow took it to mean that we had decided without their knowledge that we'd never visit again.

'Well, of course. He will obviously need another dose of chemo.'

Julie must have known Ethel had picked up Harold's phone. She secreted hers, stepped forward and grabbed mine.

'Hello, Ethel,' she said. 'Julie here. How are you?'

She walked away from me, turning her back again, seeming to indicate that this was something I couldn't deal with. Without further prompting from her, Ethel was obviously chatting away, about what I couldn't imagine, until Julie said, 'It's what we talked about, isn't it?'

I let her continue until the conversation ended and she handed back my phone.

'What was all that about?'

'Ethel agrees but doesn't think Harold is prepared to go through all that again.'

'Agrees what?'

'That a further course of chemotherapy may be necessary.'

'What do you think?'

'I think she's right. But the decision should be Harold's.'

'You've changed tack.'

'What?'

Her brow creased and she began to colour.

'I mean you're agreeing with Ethel Chrimes the Soul Traveller.'

'We've discussed that,' she said.

'Have we? Did she say anything about the word that cannot be mentioned - Metaferon?'

'As it happens, she did.'

'What, just now?'

I knew that hadn't been the case.

'I've spoken to her about it on another occasion.'

'Were you going to tell me?'

'If it became necessary.'

'Either we're against quack remedies or we're not. Which is it?'

She bridled.

'We need to go down, Francis. Soon.'

She'd brought a proof copy of *American Smooth* for me to read but picked it up as she made to leave.

'I thought you wanted me to take a look at that,' I said.

She ignored me, blew me 'a thespian kiss', as she called it and left. It was the way she sometimes did things, forgoing the usual intimacies of greeting and leave-taking. As I often did the same, we'd tacitly hit on a mutual way of avoiding what we used to call 'sticky sentiment'. The test of that, of course, was our willingness to stay together despite it. Which for a long while and genuinely, we did.

Noises Off

Two days before we were due to travel to Goring, the phone rang.

I didn't recognise the voices at first, any of them.

'Hiya, Frank. Is that Frankie?'

It was Wes. If he hadn't told me, I could have guessed from the shouting in the background: the Crazy Gang, going crazy.

'Shut it, you lot!' he bawled. 'I'm talking to someone.'

I could hear him even through the hand he'd obviously placed over the phone.

'Sorry about that, Frank. The boys are playing up.'

It struck me that the boys were always playing up.

'What can I do for you, Wes? Is everything all right?'

I didn't bother to disabuse him of his notion that I was Frank or Frankie, not Francis. I did know that any call from him or Aurora - this was the first - would be about Harold. He had rung my mobile. Not thirty seconds into his call, the landline started purring. I let it drift into answerphone mode.

'There's been a lot of kerfuffle from next door, from Harold's,' Wes explained.

A pause. I wondered if he expected me to say, OK, I'll be there in a tick. I wasn't sure if he remembered I was in Manchester.

'What do you mean, 'a lot of kerfuffle'?' It was a serious question. I didn't know what exactly 'kerfuffle' meant; nor, I suspected, did Wesley.

'You know. Shouting. Singing. Loud voices. Women's voices. And men's. Humming, like.'

Humming?

'Did you investigate?'

Silence.

'Did you go around?'

'Nah. Aury said not to bother. It didn't last long. But it was loud. The singing and shouting, I mean. Not the humming. I was outside, fixing the car. She said I ought to ring you.'

'What do you mean by 'singing' and 'humming'? What sort of singing? What's happening now?'

'They're watching *X Factor*.'

He meant the gang.

'No. At Harold's.'

'Dunno. A couple of cars went. Just singing and humming. The others are still there, including the fat woman's.'

'What fat woman?'

'The one as is always there. The one who looks like Jo Brand's older sister.'

I smiled at this spot-on description of Ethel.

'What do you mean by 'cars'?'

'It's regular. Well, now and again. They all come.'

The Goring Book Club, aka the Soul Travellers - possibly.

I thanked him and rang off. Then I picked up the cordless, thumbed 1471, and dialled a number with the same code as Harold's. It was Joe's and Phyllis's.

Phyllis answered but swiftly handed me over to Joe.

'Thought we'd ring because there was a lot of noise from next door about half hour ago,' he said. 'It's the reading group. They're usually quiet, as if they're up to something. There was an argument, loud. It lasted about ten minutes, off and on. Then the front door slammed and two of them left. Man and woman. We could hear it through the wall, you see. Oh, hang on - the others are leaving now. There was humming too; well, like a humming noise, a motor.'

I pictured him looking through a chevronned chink in the blinds, over his shoulder the eyes of Phyllis, and over hers, the Monarch of the Glen, spotlit, lord of all it eternally surveyed.

'Yeah. Just the one car there now. The one that's often there.'

'A black Nissan Micra, muddy?'

'That'd be it.'

'Oh, by the way,' I said. 'It might sound like a daft question, but did you hear singing?'

'Funny you should say that. It was not so much singing as - well, I don't know.'

Nor did I.

I thanked him as I'd thanked Wesley - for his vigilance - and assured him on no particular authority that things would be OK.

I tried to imagine what the commotion had sounded like to them, particularly in the case of Wesley, forever surrounded by the Crazy Gang's din. Maybe in people bound up with themselves, any departure from the norm is disturbing. I thought of domestic acts of violence and the stillness that must follow them as the perpetrators stand there wondering what they've done, and what the consequences might be - say, the arrival of the police after a call from the neighbours.

I put the best gloss on it: that Wes and Aurora and Joe and Phyllis were taking their jobs seriously; that noise coming from the house of a man who kept to himself so much was unusual and worth noting and reporting. It was twenty past nine. I thought of phoning Joe again to tell me when the Nissan had departed, but it sounded too much like subterfuge. I'd wait till ten, then call Harold on a pretext.

But I never did. I just sat there thinking how much was going on without my knowing. For instance, that the Book Club was meeting or had begun meeting at Harold's place and that Joe and Phyllis knew what the regular gathering was, the frequent transformation of Harold's brick forecourt into a parking lot. It couldn't have been going on long or Harold would have told me. But then Harold was ever keeping things close to his chest. There was no reason why the book-lovers shouldn't hold their meetings in each other's houses. Maybe they did.

Nor did I ring Julie, though for a few minutes I was tempted. Harold's condition was our shared concern by then, not that we'd come to any arrangement about that. Didn't I already have examples of her acting independently where Harold was concerned? I remembered the walk from West Beach with the two of them linking arms and Julie whispering and shouting in his ear and laughing, and me trailing behind. Within half an hour, I was to have another example when Julie rang. She sounded agitated.

'Francis - you have to wake up. It's obvious: they're one and the same.'

'What are?'

'What do you think? The book club and the soul travel group. With her directing operations, if you'll forgive the expression.'

I stopped myself from telling her that that was ridiculous. But it was always possible, though not as sinister as she was making out. Then I realised: she'd just rung Harold or he'd rung her. It was still the time when there were reasons for the irrational.

'Have you spoken to Harold?'

'Five minutes ago.'

I waited for the further explanation that I knew would be critical, a shove downwards into the boggy depths of whatever was going on. It turned out that Harold hadn't bypassed me: he hadn't phoned her; she'd phoned him. But why? She took it as a criticism.

'Why not?' she snapped.

'Well, it's just that there's been some incident.'

I told her about the calls from Wesley and Joe.

'Oh, that,' she said, wearily. It sounded as though she regarded it as history, something I hadn't yet grasped. It was becoming a feature of our slippage from each other; she ahead of me or behind or in a different zone from me altogether. 'Harold told me Joe had gone round to see if he was all right because he and Phyllis had heard something going on - shouting.'

'And singing?'

'That too.'

While I wondered what kind of sixth sense had led Julie to ask after Harold at that precise moment, she consolidated her thesis.

'Don't you see, for fuck's sake? He's their pet monkey, a dumb creature with an ailment. There he is discussing books while all the time they're soul travelling about his head. Francis, we have to do something.'

And with that, she rang off.

I wondered if her attitude squared with the conversation she'd had with Ethel a couple of days earlier. Perhaps she was reacting to strange events as they happened. Or had her view of Ethel changed again? I couldn't keep up with her. Only her concern for Harold which was also mine allowed me to ignore her switches of mood. I wondered whether we were on the same side in relation to Ethel's influence over Harold and if so, where events were taking us.

I phoned the man himself. No response. On his landline, the answering machine clicked on and an American voice told me there was no one to take my call. It probably wouldn't be long before this appearance of an interloper having taken over Harold's house and personality and speaking oddly on his behalf would be for Julie the real thing. I left no message when invited. Harold would be asleep. He wouldn't know I'd tried to contact him.

In the middle of the night, my mobile juddered. It was Harold.

'Hello. What's up? What time is it?'

'Can you come down?' he said.

I was only half awake.

'What - now?'

'No,' he said. jaded. 'Some time. Soon.'

'But we're coming down on Saturday. Remember? Are you OK, Harold?'

'Aye,' he said. 'So so. Not really.'

First Post

On Saturdays, my mail arrived early. I was about to get into the car to pick up Julie and set out for Harold's place when the postman handed me a letter. The address was handwritten. Most of the letters I receive these days are official and typewritten. Because of that, and because I am always reading properly-written texts in the form of playscripts, a rare handwritten letter will ping its barbarisms at me like insults. There's enough of it on social media: *OMG!!!!! its u I didn recognz u!!!! Wow!* That was one of Mona's, after I'd texted her a picture of me dressed as Fabian backstage and pre-curtain at the Burrell Theatre, Truro. ('A workmanlike *Twelfth Night,'* the *Falmouth Packet* reviewer wrote unhelpfully.) We'd known each other a long while, phoning now and then in acts of mutual commiseration. She took the initiative more than I which reflected the greater number of times she'd failed an audition or hadn't been called to one. Neither of us had much of a CV.

Not even the seriousness of what she had to say in the letter encouraged her to desert entirely the illiterate mode of a posting. Whenever she contacted me, no mention was made of Julie though she knew we were an on-off item. I don't think this was deliberate; just naïve.

Anyway, her father had died. She'd been his carer for the best part of a year. *I'm an orphan!* she shrieked. *A 44-year-old orphan fur Chrissakes!!!!*

She could have emailed or texted the news but I think her failure to do so indicated the depth of our relationship: I needed to know but not immediately. As it was, she'd written before the funeral, the date, time and place of which she included. So I took the letter and its length - four sizeable pages - to establish that depth in a different way, a more lasting one. It was a chronicle of almost ten years as carer, first devoted to her mother in the presence of a 'useless' father (a term I assumed had been simply standard usage by a woman about a hapless man), and then to the 'old man' himself, about whom she had not much to say, all her grief having been expended on her mother. But her final paragraph was intriguing, almost an invitation to discover more: *He's finally gone, Francis. The dirty bugger's finally gone and left me. I'm free!!!!!!!!* He reminded me of my own father whom I saw again teaching Norm to cuss like a trooper while my mother and I were out.

I have a friend, an old school pal. We meet regularly but not often. It's one of those friendships about which one says that, even though time flies and we now see its passing written on our faces, there is no falling away of what I suppose you'd call intimacy, albeit that blokes never use such a term when referring to themselves. His name's Geoff. We can tell each other anything, discuss most subjects; we can confess without embarrassment. He was with me and a few others when I met Julie at the pub, that time she was again with Bronwen. I had a sudden need to phone Geoff - though we rarely have cause to do that and not because emailing has taken over from it - about what was happening. I didn't mean just Mona's re-appearance which simply jolted me into considering other events: the threat she would pose not to me and Julie as an item but to Julie herself; Harold's mortal predicament; Ethel Chrimes's true intent - and

Julie's intentions towards her. Just telling Geoff all that, unburdening it, would have helped in some odd way even knowing that, at the other end of the line, he probably would have been walking about, dealing with some other matter, drinking coffee, winking at some mutual acquaintance in the room to whom, with hand over his mobile, he would have mouthed my name. I would have shared something just as I felt Mona was sharing with me not just the news of her father's death but how it had removed the one obstacle to our firmer attachment. But, as in most cases with friends like Geoff, I never did, partly because events had begun to move rapidly. Maybe it was because our closeness, impregnable against even that winking eye ('Oh my god, Francis is in deep emotional shit again'), would always be there when I was more desperate for the reassurance it guaranteed. So I put Mona's letter in a drawer and drove to Julie's place.

As I pulled up at her house, I could see her waiting for me outside the front door. This was another of the things about her that irritated me: the assumption that I would turn up exactly on time. It wasn't the punctuality or her being ready that annoyed me but the performance there'd be if I were late; then I would ring the bell, notice that the door was off the latch, push it, and find her standing and all ready to depart in the hallway, arms folded. But I was wrong to be annoyed because I was more often late than on time and it must have begun to irk her, along with my inability to get myself ready when she was calling for me. Compared with her homes - she'd lived in three places during the time I knew her - mine was a dump, an immoveable reproof, as she saw it, to her sense of order and tidiness. When I mention my exasperation, it is only a feeble attempt to make it the equal of hers; it never was. I make no case for my superiority of arms in the gender wars: what arguments ensued were always, on my part anyway, the gush of instinct. My problem was that her frustrations were not intended to show me how impossible it would be for us to make a go of things; so when I saw her waiting for me that Saturday, I knew, insofar as Julie was ever predictable (and when she wasn't, I was convinced in my upbeat moments it was nothing to do with her), that she would breeze down the path, shut the gate, dump her big sports bag on the back seat, slide in beside me, give me a peck on the cheek and say: 'To southern climes, my man!'

On the way down, the phone conversation we'd had about the incident, if that's what it was, at Harold's house was repeated. This time, Julie was less impatient, less insistent that I was oblivious to what was going on. I could guess as well as she what was happening. She reverted to her former apology for how she'd felt about Ethel. Joining the M40, we moved on to a new subject. We were close to that place where I'd seen the young girl and her grandparents on their way to the Wildlife Park.

She told me about her plan. I could see out of the corner of my eye that it was neatly written down in a new notebook on its first page. I smiled. She sometimes reminded me of a schoolgirl. Men with women enjoy an ever-changing relationship; they become protective, and seeing their partner as vulnerable, even childlike, is not helpful, is not encouraging of a sensible rapport, though the protective instinct may well be genuine. Thank god Julie was not always guileless, otherwise that instinct might have become overweening. I was familiar with the turning of tables.

The plan involved going along with Ethel's suggestion, giving Metaferon a try.

I was again astonished but said nothing. I didn't want to repeat the argument we'd already had. There was a sequence: we try not to be 'sarcastic' with Ethel, especially in Harold's presence; we introduce the subject of Harold's future treatments; we mention Metaferon to Ethel as though we had forgotten its details, even, perhaps, the name; we get Harold's unbiased opinion: if he wants to try Metaferon, we discuss how we should go about it in terms of approaching his oncologist and raising the subject (Metaferon was a pill, which you simply swallowed with water, like aspirin). And if he agreed, we supported him.

Julie didn't ask me what I thought. She rarely did. I once raised this and she said we understood each other so well that we thought alike and didn't need to enquire. That was true sometimes. It was amazing how an idea that one of us came up with had been fermenting in the mind of the other. It gave us a sense of the rightness of our partnership; we felt something clicking into place, locking us together. It gave us - me anyway; I can only report my feeling - hope.

Since my doubts about Julie's initial attitude towards Ethel had been badly received, I continued to make no comment. Well, I did – just: 'Sounds good.'

I half-expected her to say that I'd changed my tune but not knowing what she'd say reflected what was incalculable about her. Again, that's not a criticism but an impression. I just said the first thing that came to me, allowing for a nominal second of what was to become pointless consideration. She went through other steps dictated by her plan, then closed the notebook tightly with both hands.

The sun had come out and was lasering her side of the car. She wound the window down a smidgen and pushed the seat back so that she could stretch out. She'd placed a raffia bag between her knees on setting out and as her legs straightened and her eyes closed, she shoved it forwards with her feet. I could see a rough-cast book in there, a proof copy. It would be *American Smooth*; I didn't have to ask. Alongside it was a bound copy of *Piersfield*.

As Julie dozed, I wondered about Mona's letter. It gave me the weirdest feeling - her dozing and my thoughts, I mean, as if she and Mona were coming in and out of focus before me. What Mona said about her old man was curious. I'd have to reply. I decided to text her first to say that I'd received the letter and that it had intrigued me. I was trying to work out what would happen between Mona and me. I never expected a letter like that. A series of texts, maybe, and a few phone calls - she'd contacted me a couple of times at home on my landline - but now she'd been released from her duties as carer, did it mean that she was headed my way? We already had something in common - the broadcast of the documentary film - and I thought it right that I should go to her father's funeral (otherwise, why the details?). I decided that I would go.

It was just then, at the point where these few matters had been half-decided to the accompaniment of the car's steady drone, that Julie, her eyes still closed, began a monologue whose nature I could not determine even though the words were clear enough. I thought first that she was addressing me. I dropped speed to listen more closely. She was talking about some unspecified incident and what should be done about it. It meant nothing to me. The chatter stopped and I assumed she'd been dreaming, talking in her sleep. Maybe I should have woken her up. But nothing seemed to be troubling her.

After a minute, she began again, chuckling now and then, and I realised that she was having a conversation. It was like sitting beside someone on the phone. Again, I couldn't bring myself to wake her. Harold and his problems, indeed the very reason why we were driving south to see him, had been consumed by this other unfathomable happening.

The sun was still shining but I felt that it had grown cold. I leaned across and pressed the button to close Julie's window. She slept on, her discussion over. It must have been a friendly one because a permanent smile was printed on her lips. I slowed the car even more so that she shouldn't wake too soon. I couldn't think properly; nor could I control the movement of the figures lodged in my mind, all jockeying for prominence, each with a purpose of its own: Harold, Ethel, Julie, Mona, Wes, Aurora, Joe, Phyllis, and the Crazy Gang, the last not demented or being a nuisance at all but slouching, grim-faced, wondering with me about what's going on.

Not Being Sarcastic

Julie had brought a copy of *Piersfield* with her because, unknown to me, she was to address the Goring Book Club.

When I say I didn't know, I mean she hadn't given me any details, a date. As our next visit to Harold coincided with the club's monthly meeting, there'd been just a vague understanding that we would both go along. She and Harold had agreed on that between them. By then, I was used to finding out that she'd been in contact with him; I'd also become used to her not telling me the outcome.

Considering Harold's precarious health, I wondered if she were placing an emphasis on her book and the club appearance that might have been a tad selfish and out of order. Then again, she may have thought it would take his mind off things. Harold never said anything about having spoken to her. Why should he have? Harold was innocent of our complexities, probably assuming that what he'd discussed with her was automatically communicated to me. We did present ourselves as indivisible and non-controversial, with the usual shades of pretence.

That said, I hadn't known him long enough to judge him as anything other than a welcome addition to the family. Like us all, he probably had secrets and pockets of guilt stashed away. What sort of marriage had it been for him and Marjorie, I wondered?

When we arrived, Harold was on his own. We could hear the TV before he'd answered the door. It was loud at first, and then the sound was turned down as his Amplicall chimes cut through the noise. He loved the name and often repeated it. We'd bought 'them' online when he was staying with us. He liked the idea of ordering something in cyberspace and having it delivered, possibly when he wasn't in. He told us the postman was used to shoving bulkier packages through the redundant catflap on the outer porch door; he'd never bothered to remove it. Now and then, a neighbour's cat would step through it but leave once it saw its further progress barred by another door. In summer, though, the interloper would stay put, snoozing in its little sun trap.

You get used to the initially off-putting whiff of other people's houses I mentioned before. It's always different. Harold's widower, carbolic-tinged version was a miasma trapped by unopened windows and suffused with the remnant smells of cooking, of the last meal. But it also had a comforting weight, settling you into the accommodating furniture in front of the telly. Though he'd lowered the volume, it was still at normal pitch for anyone else, so that we talked above its annoying music and chatter. Harold had eaten lunch: there was a tray on the floor with the remains of something substantial crusted on a plate. For Harold, it would have been 'dinner'.

'I'll put the kettle on,' Julie said, reaching for the tray.

'Aye,' Harold commented. 'I'll take your stuff up.'

I raised my hand to object and did it myself.

At the bottom of the stairs, I saw Julie in the kitchen. She was singing.

As I made my way to 'our' room, I couldn't get her out of my mind. There was something wrong; at the same time, she seemed perfectly normal, give or take some strange habits. It created that odd feeling of helplessness in me again, the idea that she could cope with whatever troubled her, jousting with the imperative that I should take responsibility for doing something about it. Refusing to act was justified by the shaky belief that she wasn't troubled at all and that what we might call her 'demons' were, in fact, benign companions. She once called me 'Francis No Mates' so I appreciated the irony of this circle of made-up friends, if that's what they were. But I had to raise the subject again, a subject I knew nothing about. Madness is always seen as threatening to the mad themselves as much as to those confronting or dealing with them. 'Confrontation' is probably the wrong word. But what's the right one? As a kid, I used to cross the street when the local nutter was walking towards me in that jumpity way of his, an obedient hound trotting behind, but all I was doing was helping myself to the pity due to him.

We were slumped before the telly supping mugs of Julie's strong tea when Harold announced that Ethel was coming round. In another of those little slips prompted by words and expressions, I giggled, hoping to explain my amusement by saying that I didn't know she'd lost consciousness. But Julie, ever alert, and clearly attuned to words as much as I, jumped in before me.

'That's good!' she enthused, levering herself upright on the edge of her chair. 'We haven't spoken to her for ages.'

In fact, we'd been talking about Ethel endlessly and to the point where I'd begun to see her as non-threatening as one of Julie's 'voices'. (Is that what they were - voices - and not some imagined auditors compelled to sit in silence and listen to her speaking, their responses as imaginary as their ghostly beings?) Over the weeks, I'd begun to wonder if her changes of opinion about Ethel Chrimes were presented as dramatic simply to avoid the possibility of appearing to agree with what, up till then, had been my minor objections to them. Only now do I think she might have forgotten them altogether, minor or not. I couldn't tell. That had become the problem: one could never tell. I just wish she were still here for me to raise the subject with her, as one of those contentious things that couples can only resolve by talking them through: but beside my periods of depression, occasional and tiring and mostly grand headaches, her mental condition resembled a state positively to be desired. An odd way to put it but it explains why some say the sane are mad and the mad sane, though not 'the lunatics are in charge of the asylum' which means a situation not to be wished.

'I've brought something for you,' Julie said, leaving the room.

Harold looked my way to check if she were addressing me.

I gestured ignorance and curiosity.

Julie returned with her raffia bag containing the rough copy of *American Smooth* and *Piersfield*. She took the first out and handed it to Harold as if it were a box of chocolates. For a second, she shivered with excitement and anticipation, raising her heels and grasping her knees with outstretched arms like a flapper, as her smiling face sought his response. She was wearing new Doc Martens in purple glitter, with red-hooped white socks.

I remember feeling put out, one of those instinctive reactions she prompted in me before I began to make allowances, though that never really happened. She'd forgotten having brought *American Smooth* for me to read and leaving with it before I'd done so, another act I couldn't explain as either deliberate or accidental or thoughtless. Maybe with Julie, the normal sequence of events lost connecting links so that they made no sense or offended me but had no meaning or significance for her at all. As she sat there in childlike anticipation, I realised, as I should have done before then, that she might be a danger to herself. Is that how things worked? I wanted to know how they did. My need to know about that had almost overtaken my keenness to find out more about Harold and about the rest of my family. There was this chain of links and before she'd hauled it in via what we call thought processes, the links were dropping down at random just after she'd reached them; but it didn't bother her and she kept hauling in, unreasonably making her way forwards in what she thought was a straight line but to me was a stuttering progress in which she was ever on the verge of falling, in attitudes of having lost her footing.

As Harold stared at the front cover of a package he'd probably never seen the like of before - it was about 300 A4 pages in a soft-cardboard clip folder - a car engine revved and I looked up to see Ethel's car turn into the driveway. Harold didn't hear and Julie's mind was on something else.

'I think she's arrived,' I said.

Harold let go of the manuscript, which dropped on to the carpet with a thud. He got up to open the front door. Before he reached it, the chimes on full volume rang out. I turned the TV down. Julie almost collided with me as she stepped forward to pick up *American Smooth* and clasp it to her chest, a mother whose child had been unforgivably mis-treated. She even stroked it with her chin, seeking no sympathy from me, no eye contact. Again I felt invisible to her. I was learning not to take offence: if I were invisible, it meant that others, more threatening than I, would be ever out of sight. It was somehow a satisfying experience because it was enlightening. Smug? I think not.

Almost before Ethel sat down, Julie had returned *American Smooth* to her bag and announced, 'I think we have things to talk about.'

'We have!' Ethel confirmed with a schoolma'am emphasis from which Julie might have recoiled.

But she didn't. Nor did she bridle when Ethel said something about Harold's being 'my patient', or make a comment like, 'What do you suggest, Nurse Chrimes?'

Julie was as good as her word.

The other word, 'patient', uttered before the three of us turned to face Harold with varying degrees of solicitude, saw the man himself begin timidly to raise his right hand as if to ask a question or raise an issue, then lower it, perhaps submitting to what he thought might be wise counsel in the offing. As he did so, a football bounced off the roof of Ethel's car, bounced again to window height, then settled out of sight before one of the Crazy Gang retrieved it, looking in on us with a scowl that seemed to be not so much an expression of a trespasser's bravado but all youth's contempt of adult knowingness and conspiracy.

Charles Lovell Darling

What Harold had been about to ask before we heard the ball bouncing and looked through the window - he wouldn't have noticed at first - was whether or not Ethel had remembered to bring 'that book'.

Julie looked at me, presumably thinking his question had something to do with the club. Ethel drew from her handbag not one of the Goring Book Club's chosen titles but a small monograph, hardly a book, which Harold indicated should be passed to Julie who held it before her with a beaming mixture of joy and surprise I hadn't seen for ages.

'Harold here mentioned that you were interested and I told him I'd picked this up in the Lanes,' Ethel explained. I could never get used to her abrupt way of speaking, intended, it seemed, to pre-empt contradiction even where none would have been expected.

Julie held the cover up for me to see but didn't explain what it was. I couldn't read the title; the picture on the front was of a man resembling the elderly Charles Darwin. We'd been to the Lanes in Brighton a few times. She didn't so much dive into the second-hand bookshops there as allow herself to be sucked in.

Harold took the book and passed it to me. It was called *Parameters of Sense: A Short Life of C. L. Darling.* I recalled the time when Julie had shouted the name of Lovell Darling in Harold's ear. She'd also included a paragraph about Darling in her laptop entries, the only other time I'd come across him or she'd referred to him again, except for our trip to Dieppe, where he'd lived – more about that later. We are all to some extent 'in our own worlds', Julie at that time more than most. Charles Lovell Darling: also the author of *The Unkempt House* (as Julie mentioned in her notes).

Flicking through the book to a background conversation about Harold's state of health, I noticed that Darling, apart from anything else, had been an early and amateur taxidermist - well, later than the Egyptians obviously but early in the modern sense, a bit of a dabbler as pioneers often are. I wondered if Byron's Otter was his work; it had looked a bit grotty. One of the illustrations was of a stuffed Harris Hawk with outstretched wings, and it would have reminded me of another Hitchcock film if the bird hadn't looked somehow inert - in fact, theatrically dead, a prop and a bit moth-eaten and pathetic. I wondered if there was such a thing as a bad taxidermist. I tried to imagine the procedures that led to the precise act of stuffing (with sawdust?): the bird laid out on a zinc dissecting table like an eagle on a flag; the de-gutting after Darling, wearing perched *pince-nez,* had made the first incisions and, satisfied with them, contemplated a messy removal of the innards. I saw Mrs Darling seated beside the fire in the room below, carrying on with her knitting as their dachshund on the floor next to her thrashed intermittently in its doggie-dreamscape, lightly whimpering with teeth bared. Typical, Julie would have said, that I should have assumed the wife's role to be subservient. She would have meant typical of a man, specifically of a man who had failed to consider other possibilities. She would have been right, of course. That Mrs Darling, if there had been such a woman, would not have merited being written up like her husband would be vindication of the picture I'd concocted as well as an indictment of its truth, something Julie, and not I and men like me, would not have considered without being prodded.

When I closed the 'book' and looked up, resolving to examine it later in more detail, a new wall fixture caught my eye. It was a painting, a street scene, but the street was a grey cone and on its tip was balanced a mountain below ominous clouds. In the middle of the street and walking away from the viewer between two rows of terraced houses rendered impossibly vertiginous was a group of blackened figures, obviously coalminers. I was torn from this double distraction of lives, Lovell Darling's and Harold's (or Harold's former one), by Julie's raised voice.

'Francis!'

I saw Harold in tears and staring at me with the others. The three of them seemed to be waiting for an answer to some query but with distraught expressions indicating my inability or reluctance to supply it.

Julie: 'Haven't you been listening?'

I began a tentative shaking of the head.

Ethel chipped in. 'He's not going through with it. More chemo. Not another lot.'

I had the curious feeling that Harold was weeping for me, for my inattention or my lack of sympathy or even my want of understanding.

'It's too much, Francis,' he said, drying his eyes and blowing his nose with a Kleenex Ethel had handed him. 'You can't imagine the pain, the sickness.'

He uttered the last sentence in a tone that sounded almost hateful, a victim whose suffering had been not so much bypassed as deliberately ignored by the person he was speaking to.

I attempted that 'new man' thing of dropping to my knees in front of him and reaching out to place a hand on his shoulders; or perhaps I'm imagining that's what happened. I do remember moving closer to him anyway, because when I was near enough to have offered physical comfort, he lowered his head as if in shame at our joint lack of manliness.

'We never knew,' I told him in a half-whisper. 'You should have let us know how bad it's been.'

But Julie corrected me. 'He did tell us. Of course we knew.'

She had moved behind Ethel's chair in an act of alliance. At least, Ethel didn't contradict her and had presumably been ministering to him during the worst times, when we weren't there. Not for the first time did I wonder how much contact he was having with his sisters or other relatives. For sure, they and we were not acting in consort. When Harold lifted his head and gave me an apologetic look, it was obvious that he now realised his exchanges with Julie were not always shared with me. Ever self-centred, I thought fleetingly how useful it might have been for Julie and me to have swopped roles. She probably knew more about him as a man in mortal danger than I had gleaned of him as a blood relative. The blood, of course, had been added to by my great uncle's second marriage. Perhaps that was it. His early reticence had been not guarded but a recognition of the distance between us and the years of separation in which each other's existence had meant nothing, if we ever thought about it at all. His mobile phone and laptop lay together next to the TV. At that point, I no more wished to find out from them how often he and Julie communicated than to consider raising with her the subject of sharing information. But I would - just once.

Almost before the word entered my head, Harold had used it. 'We're going to try it. You know, that Metaferon.'

I sensed Ethel moving forward to the edge of her seat and Julie following to be at her side. This is where we are, I thought; there's little point in objecting. Getting him to re-consider would have been like condemning him to more distress. But I wasn't sure. At the same time, what did I know about chemotherapy and whether or not it was guaranteed to work? I felt that Ethel and Julie were ready to pounce on any reservations I had. Might Metaferon, if it were endorsed by his consultant, his oncologist, not cause worse symptoms? I opted for the easy way out, believing it was probably the right way too. It was Harold's life. He was in charge of it because he was still capable of being in charge. I wouldn't interfere; I'd let - we'd let - Metaferon interfere, hopefully with the result we wanted.

Nevertheless, Harold looked at me guiltily, a man imprisoned in his default position. I wasn't sure what mine was or even if I had one. All I could think of was how much had been decided without my knowing and if it were permissible to ignore the sight of a woman whose voices could talk to her while she slept, and talk as friends talk, amicably. Was it something I had to get used to, as she seemed to have? Or was it something that might soon have to be certified?

Readers All

I'd never been to a book club before. Nor had Julie. It was a bit low down on her publisher's albeit modest ways of meeting her readers and promoting her work. But she'd been in the papers and she was doing it for Harold. We'd convinced ourselves that the Goring club and the West Sussex Soul Travellers were one and the same, or had members in common, though since Julie had begun warming to Ethel instead of vilifying her, the link now seemed laughable or irrelevant and hadn't been mentioned for a few weeks. I don't know why we hadn't asked. Ethel was making her own way to the meeting - at the club chairman's flat overlooking the sea - so I expected on arrival to be faced by a horseshoe of grim literary types seated at a table, with copies of *Piersfield* emphatically closed in front of them. Harold had briefed us: 'The chairman says something about the book we've all been reading, then we sort of all have a go, have a say. There's tea and biscuits, sometimes cake. And chat.'

The eats and drinks seemed more attractive to him than the talk.

On the way there, I mentioned the new picture hanging on his sitting-room wall, assuming it was one of his.

'Oh, aye,' he said. 'Ethel's been getting them out. There's quite a lot upstairs. I never bother with them these days. She says they should all be where we can see them.'

Although he didn't sound convinced, Julie voiced approval, snapping her changed attitude to Ethel more firmly into place. 'Quite right too!'

She was in the front passenger seat, not simmering in the back as she was on our trip to Dovestone Reservoir. Now it was Harold in the rear, his dapper features and form again reminding me of that manikin character in *Bonnie and Clyde* – C. W. Moss, I now recall. But I couldn't help reminding myself that he was a very sick man, more so now that he'd declined further NHS help. I smiled at him in the rear-view mirror but he was staring out of the window. He had a lot to think about. I wanted these small details about Julie to mark big improvements, despite her unpredictable ways. Her voices appeared to have abandoned her for a while. I wished they'd disappear for good, move on, like a bothersome gang bored with the victim they'd been bullying. I still hadn't talked to her about them. But I would; it was just a matter of choosing the right moment, the only problem being that in retrospect it might be re-interpreted as having been the wrong one.

Just as we were in sight of the sea and approaching the left turn into the street Harold indicated, a dollop of flying seagull shit splashed across the windscreen. Hitchcock again. We all shuddered and then laughed. I wondered if it were a portent.

I'd been feeling a bit apprehensive about the meeting in view of Harold's previous remarks about *Piersfield* and my historical reservations about some aspects of it; not to mention Julie's earlier view that some club members might be, were, spooky masqueraders. Harold's comments about the book had been throwaway and mine offered unthinkingly before I'd convinced myself that I'd done so in a spirit of constructive criticism. OK, Julie's responses had seemed a bit extreme. I was still learning and into the habit of not repeating certain things or the way they'd been expressed. But I couldn't anticipate what the Goring readers would think.

The meeting was in the chairman's front room on the second floor and its course would prove to be not much like Harold had indicated. The sun was in and out and when shining was so bright that you had to shield your eyes if you wanted to take in the view. The window, itself having received a gull's attention in one corner, was partly gritted with sand and needed cleaning. There were blinds which I hoped would be at least partly lowered. There was, however, no frosty welcome; far from it. The cake and biscuits were on two plates covered in Clingfilm and set low on a coffee table, and the members - four women, two men, and the male chairman - walked towards us with faces alight when we appeared in the doorway. A warm welcome indeed. The only odd thing about it was that all seven held to their chests a copy of the book in imitation to my mind, and of course unknown to them, of how Julie had hugged the abandoned manuscript of her latest. The scene looked rehearsed and somehow, for that reason, false; unless it were the first time they'd had a published author attend one of their sessions. We should have asked Harold; he hadn't said anything. Julie might have been in the papers but she wasn't a best-seller. On the sideboard was a small beechwood urn with an inscription on a brass plate; it said: *Tiger, who Showed us So much Affection, 1980-1995.* You wouldn't put a child's ashes on display. For the home of a book club member, there weren't many books.

After introductions and some polite conversation, we all sat around in easy chairs. Tea was served. The chairman half-closed the blinds, which made the room darker than it needed to have been. I forget his name but he wasn't the chairman for that meeting, the rôle obviously being rotated. He was just the host. The woman whose turn it was coughed to bring the meeting to order. She was wren-like but confident and well-spoken, possibly a retired academic or schoolteacher. I wondered why the women in the group outnumbered the men; even more so than was evident that morning, according to the apologies for absence which were all female.

The chairwoman's opening remarks alarmed me slightly. 'Can I begin by saying that we've heard the good news, Harold, and we wish you the best. As always, we shall be following the treatment with interest and moral support.'

Harold nodded and glanced at me, placing his personal copy of *Piersfield* on the table, his action appearing to be linked to what had just been said.

Julie was turning the pages of her copy, evidently looking for something. Had she not heard? Had she heard and rejected its possible significance? Were her old theories waking up and restless in some suppressed corner of her mind?

Just as the chairwoman was about to continue, Julie muttered, almost under her breath, 'Hear, hear!'

Everyone looked at Ethel in silence which was broken only when one of the members began to applaud softly.

I was then amazed to see everyone, including Julie, though belatedly in her case, bow their heads. There must have been some signal I hadn't noticed. I couldn't tell if Julie hadn't seen it either and was just copying the others. The chairman - not the woman whose turn it was to take charge that morning - said a few words; in fact, a prayer:

'We give thanks, O Lord, for the opportunity to see Thy spirit move through all, but especially through our devoted dumb friends to therein reside; and through the tongues of others in praise of Thy bountiful works. We also ask Thee to abide by Harold Taylor, in his coming hours of need, and to help us help him.'

Naturally, they're my capital letters. Most literary types I know are probably heathen. But devoted dumb friends? Therein reside? Did she mean Tiger and his ilk? Why the prayer to start?

At least seven Amens were said softly and *ad lib*, like confessions made by a gang of plotters subdued by hours of deprivation and questioning. I couldn't tell if Julie said one as well or just half-mouthed it. There wasn't much evidence of divine bounty in *Piersfield*. I tried to catch her eye but she was smiling at Harold. A man described as being in need somehow begins to look more like one. I didn't notice either if Harold had responded to the prayer or if he had closed his eyes. Harold's closed eyes at that point in his life could have signified anything.

But an assumption had been made about me, about me and Julie, of the sort that always brought me, us, to the edge of raising an objection; and, as always, I just seethed. I had so much to discuss with her. (I say 'us' but with Julie, I was now often referring to expectation and guesswork rather than evidence; I think she would have seethed, had something not got to her.)

After reminding everyone who Julie Redmayne was, something I found amusing because I felt the need to be reminded too, the chairwoman went on: 'I wondered if Julie would like to say something first, as it's her book. Perhaps say what she thinks *Piersfield* is about. Like Harold had at first, she slightly mispronounced it.

I winced. Julie never said what her books were about. (That's telling. I can also 'tell' that she almost invariably corrected a mispronunciation.) But she spoke anyway.

'*Piersfield* is about truth and lies, friendship and alliances, obscurity and fame - and life on a small weekly newspaper in Wales called the *Herald of the Hills*,' she intoned, still looking for a page in the book. She sounded impatient, like a teacher giving an easy answer to a question that had stumped her dumb pupils. That she didn't look up from the book when she was speaking reinforced the image. She was wearing another pair of glasses - bright red. It was the first time I'd seen them. She found the place she'd been looking for and bookmarked it. Only then did she face her audience.

I thought of her second book. She'd never said much about it. What attention it attracted was lukewarm. It had taken a while to arrange the meeting we were at. There'd been other books on the club's list. But *Piersfield* had to do with coalmining, Harold's background. In view of my criticism and Harold's - hardly criticism, more difference of opinion - it might have been a bad choice. As if to ensure that we knew exactly what *Piersfield's* story was about, in her view anyway, she re-capped, again making her appear weary and us slow-witted.

'As you'll recall,' she continued hopefully, 'at the Piersfield Home for Retired Journalists, the embittered newspaper editor Henry Wickham is fading fast. He is visited regularly by his former associate, the *Herald*'s commercial manager Arthur Honeywell, who, decades before, had been a moderately celebrated poet - a minor poet.'

There was an emphasis this time on 'minor', making me think it a deliberate play on words, considering the book's subject-matter and Harold's presence. He was sitting in an armchair opposite me with two women either side; one had placed her hand on his arm, a bronzed but gnarled hand with its wedding-ring loose on a thin finger.

'But deeper currents move beneath the surface of their relationship,' Julie went on. 'Honeywell had been with Wickham at the scene of the Blackstone Face mining disaster and at subsequent hillside meetings at which riots had broken out among the miners. Wickham's dubious testimony did for the miners' leaders in court.

'Would someone like to continue?'

The Goring Book Club looked ruffled. Perhaps they, too, expecting an address and some enlightening author comment, felt they were being treated like children. Ethel Chrimes rescued them from whatever it was - their discomfiture or shyness.

'Well,' she said. 'Much later, Mr Honeywell was put in charge of the Piersfield newsletter, much to Wickham's distress. Wickham, always envious of his colleague's literary reputation and now stuck in a nursing home, felt humiliated. As a modest editor himself now, Mr Honey-well uses the newsletter to tell the truth about those riots - that the incriminating things allegedly said about the miners in court were based on Wickham's false testimony.'

She was holding her copy of *Piersfield* in front of her and appeared to be reading from it, or from some typed insert, possibly one of the book's reviews.

Emboldened by Ethel's initiative, the woman with her hand on Harold's arm took over, speaking unaided.

'On his way to visit Mr Wickham at the home,' she relates, 'he sees a fire in the distance. It is Piersfield burning, the building I mean. Up in flames. Mr Honeywell helps to rescue people but his friend Mr Wickham perishes with many others.'

There was a moment of silence in which Julie, half-smiling, might have been about to contemplate not the description of an end to life - the Goring Book Club members, average age about seventy-three, didn't have an unlimited number of volumes to read and consider - as much as the way Harold's comforter had referred to Wickham as 'Mr' Wickham, thereby in some embedded desire to avoid conflict, making him Mr Honeywell's equal.

That was something the book had obviously wished to avoid, if it weren't obvious to everyone.

Julie raised her eyebrows and cast about for someone to continue. Harold piped up.

'This Mr Honeywell gets into the papers,' he explains. 'Big time. Honeywell the hero.' (I thought that was good; it wasn't in the book.)

'Then they discover he was this 'ere poet back in between the wars. What I want to know is, why was he up there when the explosion occurred and at the riots? He should have been in the office. He was an accountant or something, wasn't he?'

As I've already noted, this had been one of my reservations too. Actually, Honeywell had simply been walking near the pithead when the explosion happened. He was at the protest as an interested observer. Harold had previously confined remarks to the description of the Blackstone explosion and the casualties, something which Julie had researched, obviously without direct experience of her own. Maybe Mr Honeywell had been a frustrated journalist. Meeting Harold wouldn't have made her regret that she hadn't done so before putting pen to paper: Harold's life underground was as uneventful as mine was turning out to be on the boards. He hadn't taken issue with the incidents described in the book; but Julie, in the early days at least, had thought it a criticism veiled by tiresome good manners and the reluctance to offend a woman or be seen to be doing so. If she had hated that - the very idea of withholding one's views in case they might hurt - then I would have agreed with her.

Ethel took over again. Did she sense that Julie was under attack because she was vulnerable? Did she know about and understand Julie's vulnerability as well as I did? Had Julie, her estimate of Ethel modified to the good if not completely revised, been confiding in her? Hearing voices - wasn't that Soul Travel stuff?

Such questions made me distracted and I looked around the flat, the flat with a view. Out of the window, I could see a row of bathing-huts in different colours; beyond them a band of pebbles, like West Beach, enclosed either side by a seabound platoon of groynes; then a flat grey Channel, its horizon misted. There must have been a draught at the window, because a spider's web in the top left corner rippled, its custodian unmoved by what must have been common hourly occurrences. In the angle between walls and ceiling, barely visible, looped its old dust-covered spinnings like decorations, the means of access to an undisturbed domain. I followed them round and thought of how much events often went unnoticed by those grown beyond the claims of anything other than just remaining alive in the face of what would soon be reached, its path unfairly strewn with late obstacles, the slippage of the flesh that made a gold band begin to work itself loose of the ties that had bound. In Piersfield, the place and the book, Mr Honeywell, having had his moment of long-deferred recognition, is in Florida on a cruise and is caught up in a race riot. He receives injuries from which he doesn't recover. That's also what I took exception to in the book: the contrivance of mirroring disaster (the Piersfield fire) and public disorder (Honeywell's Florida nemesis). I don't think Julie ever forgave me.

I still find that book club meeting odd: how Julie seemed to have forced club members to prove that they'd read the book - like a comprehension test - and how they had enjoyed convincing her that they had. Afterwards, she gave them what they wanted from a real live author, including why and how a book gets written, where its inspiration comes from and what, if anything, was coming next. She told them things she'd never told me. Not that I'd asked. Maybe if I had asked, shown some interest more often, we'd have got on better. I think we'd reached the stage where she accepted that I was someone who could not so much look after her but had her interest and well-being at heart. Questions were asked and answers given. At the end, when the chairman disappeared to make more tea and everyone gathered at the window to take in the view, I reached over and opened Ethel's copy of *Piersfield*; the insert was indeed a review, about four paragraphs photocopied from somewhere. On the title page, the name of Julie Redmayne was struck through and Julie's signature appended below a written message which said, *To Ethel. With affection and the best of wishes. I hope you enjoy it.*

By then I really didn't know what was going on.

We raised the 'religious' element of the reading session with Harold as well as the 'soul travel' stuff but all he said was, 'Aye, I know. It's something Ethel believes in. And the others.'

'Do you?' we asked. Almost in unison.

'Not really.'

Other Effigies

The whirr of late buses to Brighton and Chichester. A joyrider's Monza roar. Police sirens and flashing blue lights. Gull cries ripping up the night. And in between them, the lamplit peace and silence of Goring-on-Sea at 1:30am.

Me: 'You OK?'

Julie: 'Mmm.'

I was already in bed. We'd stayed up late with Harold, talking about Metaferon. Julie had Googled some more info and downloaded. It seemed simple, hardly meriting the term 'treatment'. The packet of pills looked innocent on screen; there'd be the usual small-print disclaimers with explanations and warnings on thin folded paper. The course of treatment cost a fortune. What could go wrong? Or what could go right? In twelve days, Harold had an appointment with the specialist. We couldn't be there for it. Ethel would see to things. 'Ethel and the others,' Harold had said. Julie'd made no comment on that. I don't think he'd meant his half-sisters.

I watched her undress. Her beret, denim jacket and anaconda scarf were already hanging on the back of the door, her red glasses folded on the bedside table. She lifted an outsize Fair Isle sweater and then undid the mini-skirt and removed it, like a piece of knight's armour. She rolled down her woolly blue tights (the blue a joke, I assumed), leaving a T-shirt and pants. She halted for a few seconds, sideways on and holding her hands together as if in prayer but not long enough to be praying. After that, she turned away from me and pulled off the T-shirt, making her spine and its knuckle-white vertebrae stand out, the back of her ribcage too. Then she pushed down her pants, bending over until they were around her ankles, when she slowly regained height and daintily stepped out of them, leaning over again to pick them up. It was like the early days, when such manoeuvres represented the slow choreography of bliss and expectancy. She'd lost weight again. It was happening all the time: weight on, then weight off, both connected with her moods. Whenever I drew her attention to it, she'd told me not to worry; it was hormonal, or related to the way her book was going, if it were going at all. At our second or third meeting, before we first slept together, she'd looked up at me and said, 'I've got no tits,' her face amusingly steeled against the possibility of my rejecting her because of it. I'd laughed while she feigned a hurt expression and beat me furiously on the chest with her fists. But it was true: smooth mounds rather than boobs; and the assault was fake. Back then, on that first night, it was just one of the things whose absence turned mourning and regret into unconditional love, for most, I suppose, a fitful state. Not remembering whether it was the second or third meeting is simply a late recall of a condition awaiting its cue.

She had no pyjamas. I don't know what had happened to the Winceyettes.

She got into bed and lay on her back, saying nothing but not, as she usually did by then, turning away from me after a minute or two on her side and going straight to sleep - re-assured, I supposed. We could hear Harold coughing in his bedroom.

Stillness. A car alarm, farther away than next door, quickly cancelled. Silence again. I had this vision of the

Crazy Gang all asleep, mouths agape, in the same superwide bed, and Wes and Aurora, zonked out downstairs watching some late documentary about women driving huge lorries in Alaska at speed along ice-covered roads.

'Me earl, you countess,' I said.

She nodded her head and re-arranged herself, a smile surfacing. 'Mmm.'

This tight-lipped affirmative was a start. I was referring to the medieval sculptures we'd seen at Chichester Cathedral, just thirty minutes up the road: a knight and his wife, Richard FitzAlan and Eleanor of Lancaster, immortalised for a second time 500 years later by Philip Larkin in his poem, *An Arundel Tomb*. I'd read it once at a poetry festival whose organisers had had the good sense to hire actors to speak the verse. Unlike most other tomb effigies, the earl and his wife are depicted with her hand in his, not gripped but lightly touching after he had removed his gauntlet. A wag at the festival asked me if I'd seen the recumbent stone pair. I hadn't at that time. He then asked if, when I did see them, I would think that the hands did not depict a touching marital scene at all but the wife re-paying a groat she'd owed her old skinflint of a hubby. That was before I met Julie but I'd told her about it, probably when I was boasting of my accomplishments in a pub somewhere. We'd gone to the cathedral that time with Harold on the day he'd taken us to St Barts to lay a few more Toblerone traps. He hadn't heard of Larkin, which surprised me; nor had we told him that I'd once read *An Arundel Tomb* in public.

Anyway, Julie had been first to reach the earl and his countess. Turning to me, she'd said: 'That's nonsense about her owing him money. They are being intimate, as if all their pomp and formality were as nothing compared with a small token of love. Larkin was right. I sometimes wonder about your friends.'

I'd wanted to assure her that the actor colleague who'd been so irreverent was not my friend, in fact had been a complete stranger until we shared the dais, but she'd hooked her arm in Harold's and was explaining Larkin to him as they'd wandered ahead of me. (Had Harold not been with us, she would probably have said the actor's comment had been 'bollocks'.) Or were they talking about catching ecclesiastical rodents? I was amazed that she'd remembered the anecdote. Were there others, disparaging ones, queueing to be disproved or acorn-buried and ever condemned to rot? I knew Larkin had nailed it; suspected too that my colleague had also known.

It was time to speak.

'Can I ask you something, Jule?'

She turned her head to face me, always believing that 'Jule' was a pacifier, a path-smoother, which it was. Men rarely know that women know too; about most things. But at least she didn't mind.

'Are you OK? I mean, are you really OK?'

She levered herself by the elbow and rested her chin in her hand. With the fingers of her free hand, she twirled my hair.

Then she shocked me. 'Are you referring to my friends?'

I tried not to appear startled.

'Friends?'

'Yes. Friends. Are you going deaf?'

She assumed that I knew what she was talking about, because her head hit the pillow again and she continued.

'I've seen someone about it, about them.'

(Why didn't I know that?)

'Do they bother you? Why didn't you tell me?'

'Why? Are you going to sort them out?'

She chortled so noisily that Harold must have heard if he'd been awake and not been deaf. However much I extricated myself from the male herd and was prepared to leave it behind for her, she would send me back to my maleness.

I thought again how difficult it was, despite medical opinion, to treat the mentally disturbed as though they were normal. In my experience, treating Julie normally and not with kid gloves only made things worse. I can't really describe it except to say that, if two people regarded as normal are behaving normally and one loses their temper so badly that they scream like someone deranged, then, all things considered, they *are* deranged but not in the sense that we really know it, the clinical sense. I still ask myself what the difference is, apart from the obvious fact that, in cases like Julie's, something had taken permanent hold. Julie was often mad with me. Later I rarely responded in case it was something beyond her control. I believe Harold used to wonder why she was sometimes badly behaved and why I didn't react like a 'normal' person. I didn't wish to confuse or frighten him by saying I was sometimes not my normal self either. He did say once, about something unrelated, that we were a pair, meaning, I assumed, that he hadn't met a couple like us before but wasn't intending to regard getting to know us as anything other than a delight.

'On the way down,' I said, 'when you'd nodded off to sleep.'

'Yes.'

I couldn't tell from the inflection if it were a question requiring me to explain or a statement confirming what I was about to say. She showed a hint of a smile, probably because the way men went into detail about roads, routes and places when describing where they'd been or where they were going amused her.

The headlights of late passing vehicles swept across the far wall.

'You seemed to be having a conversation.'

'Did I? Then I probably was.'

She turned to me again, waiting for the next question. At least she was receptive. I wished I were not so tired. I needed to be wide awake.

'Are they friendly? Who are they? What do they want?'

She surprised me.

'I've heard you talking in your sleep. We were like we are now. Me propped on my pillow, listening, you rabbiting on.'

I was going to say I didn't believe her but I stopped myself. It might have meant that, even if I did talk in my sleep, it wasn't her kind of chatter, detailed nutty chatter.

'What was I saying?' she asked.

'I can't remember. Wait a minute; yes, I can. Someone wanted you to do something and you were refusing.'

'It was probably my mother. I was always answering her back, mainly about the way she never stood up to my father. Her just letting him have his way all the time annoyed me.'

I'd told her about how my father had taught our budgerigar foul language. She'd thought it was hilarious. Sometimes, when we were having a row, she'd tell me to 'uck off'.

As she was waiting for me to continue, we heard Harold flushing the toilet. It happened several times in the night. Sometimes we heard it, sometimes not. It had become like a tolling bell in the distance. I was too young to be making nocturnal visits to the loo. Not until I met Harold and read up on prostatitis - I could never pronounce it - did I understand why my great-grand-parents had piss-pots under the bed. I assumed it was my great-grandfathers who needed it but I was probably wrong. Bladder trouble, it was called, the need for a pee at awkward times. Before they moved to sheltered accommodation, my maternal great-grand-parents didn't even have an inside loo. My father told me, as a joke, about the piss-pot sticking out from under the bottom of the bed when my aged great-grandmother was mortally ill. I wished I'd asked more questions about the family before I discovered Harold. Concentrating on him meant that I'd not yet found out what my grandparents died of, let alone *their* parents. I had a vague memory of being told that one of my great-grandfathers had expired 'on the operating table'. It was how I knew you could die with prostate cancer, not of it. I still don't know why my great-grandfather was being operated on in the first place.

We waited for Harold to go back to bed and heard the cistern filling in the loft above us. Silence.

'You have to share more, Jule,' I said, expecting her to round on me.

But she didn't.

'I know,' she said, meaning either that she knew but wouldn't, or knew but felt unable. 'I'll keep taking the pills.'

This glib reference to her medication, for which she'd allow me little shared responsibility but was keeping her on the rails, almost ended the conversation. Except for the following.

'You and Harold are right about the book,' she said. 'Thank you for not bringing it up this morning.'

'Harold did.'

'Only his misgivings.'

'True. Local knowledge.'

I remembered Harold's queries about *Piersfield* as, on the contrary, having had nothing to do with his experience of coalmining. He'd still wanted to know how and why a newspaper's commercial manager, Julie's Mr

Honeywell, would have been witness to the explosion and the riots. So did I. When you are asked for your opinion, you usually develop the courage to answer honestly in the hope that your questioner will appreciate candour. I'd loved the way the other reading club members had neither agreed with Harold nor defended Julie, of whom they appeared slightly in awe. Ethel had said something about artistic licence and everyone seemed happy. It didn't sound like a phrase she'd used much. I still don't know when and in what circumstances Julie had signed her book. Not at that morning's meeting certainly: she'd never left my sight. I'd seen her sign Harold's - or I'd heard Harold asking her to sign; that had been a while back. The toilet flushed again; the 'toll-et'.

'Poor Harold,' Julie said.

She rested her head on my chest, held me around the waist and went straight to sleep. I looked down and picked gently at her cropped blonde hair. The roots were growing out, as they did every few weeks. I'd forgotten what her natural colour was. It was like something inimical coming to the surface, out of her brain, and every so often needing to be suppressed. The comparison with her mental state amused me. Harold asked me more than once if she were 'all right'. I think he was referring to her sometimes ashen colour. I always re-assured him. I never said, 'Why don't you ask her yourself?' For all I know, he may well have. I never knew what picture Harold had of me; I did suspect that Julie had supplied more than a few details. I don't know what picture anyone has of me, and that, I hope, applies to all of us.

Before I too nodded off, and in a half-dream, I saw Harold, the long-lost Harold I wanted to know, drifting away from my centre of attention accompanied by two anonymous figures who had convinced him that I was someone he'd never get to know or be able to depend on which, considering how long we'd cared not a jot about each other's existence, was true. And then some sudden gust of wind or other whipped him away and the two figures began arguing with each other as to which one's fault it was that their charge had escaped them. I remember that one looked back - I must have been following behind, thinking myself invisible - and that it was Ethel or someone who looked like her. But events I've not reached yet may have distorted my memory. One thing that always intrigued me: despite her troubled mind, Julie could remember everything. A meal she'd eaten at a restaurant with me on some specific date three years before could be described as though it had been the previous day. She saw past incidents as clearly as she could invent images - believe me, the pit-head rescue scenes after *Piersfield*'s explosion are gripping - and would no doubt dismiss anything banal, such as the explanation that the squall that took Harold away from his minders was nothing more mysterious than - well, it's obvious.

I can't remember when Julie told me about her diagnosis. I thought social anxiety syndrome wasn't connected with schizophrenia, the condition we all associate with madness. I read a lot about it – schizophrenia, I mean - and came across the case of the writer Charles Lamb and his sister, Mary. Charles took care of Mary after she'd stabbed their mother to death during an episode of mental breakdown. And like all of us who see the mentally ill as a physical threat, I admit having been several times fearful in Julie's presence, especially when she was staying with me or I was sleeping at her place. But, like our apprehensiveness about ghosts - the spectres that never actually appear (well, I have to doubt that) - any trepidation quickly proved irrational and I slept soundly, as did she. In any case, my infrequent gloom, though never qualifying me to join the Batty Club as a full member, always gave me a source of sympathy. Julie told me Lamb wrote a poem called *Epitaph for a Dog* and I looked it up ('Cheap monument of no ungrudging hand'). I recalled that there were two stone dogs at the feet of Larkin's earl and countess.

Bogoff

The next morning, after we'd laid the table for breakfast and were waiting for Julie to come down, Harold and I were wondering where to hang another of his pictures. Ethel had found it upstairs, like the first. He had about twenty of them stacked in the bottom of a cupboard. This time, she'd chosen a still life of yellow chrysanthemums in a vase, with one detached flower head and a leaf lying crumpled beside it in a trickle of water. I don't know why she'd started rummaging through his collection- to cheer him up presumably. I had a vague memory that 'chrysanths', as my father used to call them, were associated with death. I couldn't imagine she'd chosen it for that reason, as something over which she exerted some kind of soul-travelling power.

Julie entered the room and we showed her the picture.

'Nice,' she said. 'One of yours, Harold?'

'Oh, aye. Ethel chose it.'

'She has good taste. Tea or coffee, everyone?'

This was the pattern when we were at Harold's: he and I were up first to get breakfast ready. Julie was always last, deliberately, I think. She always boiled the kettle and brewed, so we would wait. Even then, I believe Harold knew that indulging her was somehow the right thing to do, even if he wasn't sure why.

Harold's flower picture was an oil painting on canvas about the size and shape of his *Daily Express*. It was very good. There was a lot of detail, close work, which must have taken him ages.

Julie shouted from the kitchen. 'We're out of blue top. I'll go and get some.'

There was a corner-shop supermarket nearby. Before Harold could finish saying that it was OK and he'd make do with the cartons of milk he always had in reserve, and while I shouted in vain that I'd go, she was through the door. When I got there, I could see her running down the road. It worried me but I didn't want to scare Harold. In a few seconds, she was crossing over and walking down the opposite pavement.

Harold and I knew we'd have to wait for her to return but he gave me a strange look. I think that was the point at which he realised something was seriously wrong. We carried on discussing where to hang the picture, finally deciding on a place opposite the painting of the two miners walking down the hill; it looked like a hill from the crazy angle. While I held the new canvas in place against the wall, Harold wandered over to the window, fingered the blind, and looked out. Even I wasn't sure what was happening. I told him she wouldn't be long.

He switched on the TV. The early morning news had finished and a programme about bogus charity collectors had begun. I caught a snatch of a young woman with a pixelated face and clutching a tub of coins. She was being led away by the police and the sub-title read: 'Where did your friend go?' I assumed it was the policeman talking. Maybe the woman and her missing accomplice had been collecting for prostate cancer and the other had run off. Harold kept TV sub-titles on permanently.

'She's not OK, is she, Francis?'

'Who - Julie?'

It was a stupid, matter-of-fact response and the look he gave me showed that he thought so too. It was the look of an older, wiser person, a family member no less, speaking *in loco parentis*.

'She said something to me, you see.'

While telling me this, he was zapping from one channel to another, giving me time to answer.

There was little point in asking him when and where. The cathedral possibly? That time before at West Beach? More than one place and one time, no doubt. On the phone? Apart from the odd weekend, it was difficult for us to get down there.

So I told him about social anxiety syndrome, making it sound like something you grew out of and minimising its effects. I didn't mention the voices. I still had the chrysanths picture in my hand. He pointed to it and said: 'Do you want to choose one? I was planning to give one to you and Julie at some time, anyway. Come on.'

He led the way upstairs to that other room. Just inside the door was the cupboard with the paintings. He opened it, coopied down and handed them out to me. With his head and shoulders in the cupboard dark, he looked like a corny reminder of a collier at the face.

Most of the pictures were of mining-area scenes in earthy colours: cloudy skies, rollercoasting terraces, grim winding-gear. There was one drawing in charcoal of a donkey.

'I like this one,' I said. 'Well, I like them all. I thought you might have done some of the pit ponies.'

'Donkeys stay still,' he said.

I told him that I remembered as a kid on holiday riding a donkey at Weston-super-Mare: the slow plod, the head for ever lowered, the cute fluffy ears sticking through a sombrero, and its mates all tethered and in a line, ready to canter off. But they always went at the same slow plod. For some reason, their minder didn't allow parents to walk alongside. As we started moving away from them (I didn't tell him this), my mother and father grew smaller and waved and I imagined it was for good and that I'd never see them again. All the donkeys had names written on jolly bandana things strapped across their foreheads. At Weston, the tide goes out so far that the sea disappears, leaving a battlefield of mud. My father complained that as well as paying for a short, out-and-back ride for his son, he was being invited to contribute to some home for old donkeys, probably the sort of place pit-ponies went to on their summer lease.

Harold looked at his watch, probably trying to work out when Julie ought to be back. Then he turned to me. I could tell he wanted further explanation.

Back in the sitting-room, I told him that social anxiety disorder sufferers didn't hate crowds as such; only when someone criticised or questioned them, which at its worst, Julie had explained, was like someone from the crowd getting too close. The crowd was this grey moving mass which suddenly focused into a head or heads that seemed to say: 'Hang on. I didn't get that'; or 'I don't agree with you. How can you say such a thing?' He looked confused and not fully satisfied. I used to wonder if people like Harold, working-class people, lived such uncomplicated lives that they were never bothered by anything self-tortuous; or, if they were, they had the strength of character to keep the feelings at bay. Maybe that's what Harold was thinking then, that a lifetime of pick-axing a black wall, shovelling the results, and scabbing your bare spine on a granite tunnel roof made you too tired to doubt yourself or see others as a threat you never understood. Had he received some inkling of that other life with its self-consciousness, when he had started painting, and had had it confirmed when Julie and I appeared? Was his initial reluctance to talk about the family, our family, not shyness at all but a late re-appearance of people representing a life he had relegated to a pastime and who years before had receded into the crowd, the same crowd from which Julie feared the poke of an interrogating head? Basically I was as working-class as he was, more so in fact if piecemeal availability of work rather than full employment, however draining, were considered. It's an odd world.

He seemed to be taking in what I'd said.

'She told me about the tree, and them two scientists. Something to do with insects.'

'The Metaferon tree.'

'Aye. That was it. I've been drawing it.'

He stared at me as a child does who's said something faintly controversial that might be taken one of two ways. Then he retrieved from me words I was about to speak, a question I was about to ask. It was spooky, in an Ethel Chrimes kind of way.

'Julie's told me a lot of things.'

She certainly has, I thought.

'It's her curiosity,' I said.

I wasn't sure if he meant me to wonder what precisely she'd told him; if, that is, it were something that reflected badly on me. My attitude to Ethel, for example, which had been a matter between me and Julie.

He examined his watch again. Julie had been gone twenty minutes.

'I hope it doesn't rain,' he said. 'Otherwise she'll get wet.'

'If it does, she'll ring me to fetch her.'

He then gave a little chuckle of disbelief and went to the window again. He must have seen her mobile still on the TV table where she'd left it when she came downstairs and guessed her quirky ways might include a willingness to get a soaking out of bloody-mindedness or for whatever other reason had popped into her brain like a head out of a crowd.

I watched him staring through the blind. I wanted to ask him not about our family ties but about Ethel and the soul-travellers, whether or not he'd been won over. He still went to church on Sundays. Were soul-travel and churchgoing opposing concepts? It didn't seem like it. Perhaps Ethel also worshipped on Sundays, but not at St Bartholomew's anyway. I would take him and pick him up but not join him in the pews, except for those first couple of times.

'Oops, what's up?' he said. He was still at the window.

I thought there must be some incident involving the Crazy Gang but sidling up to him I saw the police car in the drive and its two officers in the front getting out. From the back seat, crouched down in her beret and giant pullover as if trying to hide, Julie observed us as if that's why the police had brought her there: to identify us as the cause of whatever bother she was in. But they had been called when she'd stopped in the mini-market aisle and began talking and shouting at someone - no one that any of the other shoppers could see. And, apart from me explaining to the coppers that she'd be OK and explaining to Harold that she was exhausted with work and a bit stressed, she came in and went upstairs to sleep. Harold opened a carton of the long-life.

While we drank coffee, I told him I'd buy one of his paintings.

'Well, I'll still give you one for nothing.'

'Buy one, get one free,' I joked. 'Bogoff.'

I don't think the term registered with him, but he nodded assent anyway.

From Julie's laptop - 4

'We came in Sight of a Noble Pile of building, which diverted us from our former Discourse, and gave my Friend the Occasion of asking me my Thoughts of this Magnificent Edifice: I told him, I conceiv'd it to be my Lord Mayor's Palace, for I could not imagine so stately a Structure had been design'd for any Quality inferior; he smiled at my Innocent Conjecture, and inform'd me this was Bedlam, an Hospital for Mad-folks.

'The Protagonist's response: I think THEY were Mad that Built so costly a Colledge for such a Crack-brain'd Society!

'And I counter'd, that were not this Bedlam the very place where Unfortunates could be viewed as Mimicking creatures of the wild, such as at play, and in Violent Conflict - their teeth bared; - and in lapidary Sojourn on One Legge, or Two, or Four, this last such as the Doleful and Unmoving Ass, for the delectation of Spectators?

'The Protagonist: It is the same.'

Edward Ward, *The London Spy, 1698*

*

'We called on my dear Friend R---, for I had heard she was low of Spirit & in Need of sust'nance Diverting as well as Physic; and, indeed, did we find her in Accommodation (to wit, her own Bedchamber) curtain'd 'gainst Bright sunshine, that did Radiate, it seemed, all Souls in the Capital's tho'oughfares below her window, such Souls being long animated with Discourse & Laughter. Fain would she be Encouraged to leave her Shadow'd Abode; till, a visit to Bethlehem were mention'd, at which she Leapt up in great excitement, & reached for her Bonnet & Cape, and turned to us who were so Transfix'd by her sudden Alacrity – incorporating a Miraculous recovery of Demeanour – that it had been the same as though WE had been banish'ed to the limits of Melancholia & SHE our Saviours!

'So to Bedlam we hasten'd, called by Master Severini 'Our Zoological Garden of Beastly Human'kind', and by my good friend Ned Ward 'The Lord Mayor's Palace', according to his new periodical, such as occasion'd surprise from his Acquaintance, who knew it as a 'Lunatickes Colledge' and on par with the Lions of the Tower & the fireworks of the Artillery Gardens & the Averies of Birdcage Walk as Destinations wherewith to fritter an Idle Hour.'

From the private diary of Miss Catherine Dowd, Stamford Hill, London.

*

You up there. What do you see? Me but not my world, I'll bargain. Always wondered what that meant: I'll bargain. Or warrant. I'll warrant. You see me, I'll warrant, blinking up at you from down here with the others. If I fiddle with my eyelashes, flicker them, they cage you like, like, the teeth of *Dionaea muscipola*, flytrap de Venus. Nothing worse, I'll bargain, than the imprisoned who know not that they are so, are imprisoned. Incarceration, a word only a miteless mite less beautiful than pavement or insouciance. You titter, I'll warrant, behind your bars, behind bars. Behind bars in your bonnets, your crinolines, your Bethlehem best. Look! My friend (not my friend) has been like that for TWO HOURS!!! On one leg; viz, a *Uniped.* Tired by now, I'll warrant. Not blinking, arms folded, a 'turn' as they say, a huwoman sculptchewer. Catherine - Great Catatonic Cath. Yeeeeeeesssss!!! I can see you pointing at her, pointing her out to those who have been amused and are now bored, I'll warrant, by Mr William Bill Lovelace, superannuated hotel porter, in the DUNCE'S CORNER again, back to us but, I'll bargain, bargain again, doing that thing he does every five seconds, like, looking over his shoulder with quick twist (wonder his head doesn't spin off) and downturned gob to see if he cares; OR a ready-or-not-I'm-coming 'It' cheating as the others hide themselves inside an oak. Like. WTF is it with 'like', you teenage lunatics in the gods, you gallery barstewards coming and going talking of, like, Michelangelo. Up there on your mobiles. Let the others come to the front FFS and grab a gander at Lucie who happens FOR ONCE to be on cue for the one-woman *Saturnalia* matinée in her white nightgown, white-night gown. ITEM: the dirty bare foot wiggled through the door ajar. ITEM: the showahairyleg. ITEM: the leap into the open, lunge into the light. I'll warrant they won't, like, let Cuthbert join us, for he Satyr, she Nymph O'Mania, the Oirish fuck machine. (Lucie, Lucia di Lammermoor, Lucia mad issue of Nora and James, Jimmy Joyce, who it is said, like, visited her EVERY FUCKING DAY). There now, you three who've come to the front, and you two hopping up and, like, down while she in the middle appeareth so SICK. Well, you're just in time, I'll bargain, for - here he is – Mr Charles Lovell Sweetheart, who, like, shall recite AT RANDOM from *In* like *Memoriam* till the lunar rise and they have to take him away still spouting non-Tennysonian *ad libitum.* FFS don't let him loose on Walt *Whitman* and his Shards of Glass. Lucia watches shadows flow like, like, slicks. Is that applause from up there? Titters and plaudits? Why, like, I'll bargain it's Cuthbert a propos of nowt starting his spittle stick, his dribble dip. Record two feet one inch, like, till it leaveth him as a gobfroth on the floor and his lower lip doth glister red 'n' like full and sluglike, like, and delivered of its mouth cataract and in that position, like, do await the Guinness Boke of Rekords, as hath been promis'd but never appeareth. But this crevice in the brick wall captures me and a Lunatick captured is NOT value for entertainment. Do I hear them a'booing up there, a'messaging and a'texting images of us? A flying fuck, like, I couldn't care; for, I see OMG an inch from my nose a fist of ladybirds in the brick, maybe two hundred, a thousand million, a peeled pomegranate of ladybirds, and all clasped together for warmth, like, in the gap out of all weathers and at peace in their companionship; and one alights on my thumb joint and my watching it is rewarded with a flasher's polkadot flash and a show of thin black taffeta before it flies off to the watchers up there, like, watching, and a'downloading. And now they have others to be gawked at: silly little Harold from Hades and the horrible Ethell who hath SEEN GOD and been sent to the soft room to bite on leather and the unfaithful Francis, poorhorse, whinnying for a MOANER. But they don't do, like, anything, so the watchers shuffle away and I am left with these three: Harold, Ethel, and Francis, and a zillion ladybirds which hide from Cuthbert who is 'It' and findeth them not and heareth not, like me, their tiny myriad scrapes, crackles and hisses but the worst of these is ETHELL.

Edward Walter Strange, Deceased

Driving to the crematorium for the funeral of Mona's father, I passed a stable. It reminded me of *Equus*, or of how that play came about. I could see from a roadside sign that it was some kind of racehorse establishment but the house and its ancillary wooden stalls were a distance away. They therefore floated by as they would have in a film's tracking shot intended to dwell on something significant or sinister. I could just about see a few horses' heads above the stable doors.

The play centres on an act of unspeakable horror: a group of cossetted horses are blinded by a youth with a metal spike. It's not seen on stage but is an historic fact which the audience knows about before the play begins. For the production I was in, we used the published paperback version of the play, in which an experience similar to mine is recalled: the playwright is driving with a companion through 'bleak' countryside when a stable they were passing reminded the companion of 'an alarming crime' he'd heard recounted at a dinner party but about which he could remember only one detail (the hideous blindings). The playwright chose not to divulge this detail in his play and since the companion had since died, was not to be revealed to him unless he looked into it himself. But the playwright decides that the story as told to him on that drive was enough for him to re-imagine the nature and consequences of a 'dreadful' act.

Bob Berridge, in awe of 'gee-gees' after seeing, as a kid, that albino carthorse 'alight' in its impossible space, hadn't heard of *Equus* when I mentioned it on being asked what parts I'd played as an actor on stage. Nor was he impressed when I explained it, though he joined me in silent conjecture of what those ill-fated horses thought as their ears pricked at the squeaking door in the middle of the night. Or perhaps he was thinking of what Shergar made of the commotion in the yard and the gang tip-toeing towards him with their pockets full of sugar cubes and the air about them clouded with their effing-and-blinding whispers and their breath perfumed by strong drink.

By this time, I'd returned home and read Mona's letter in full. I wish I'd got back to her immediately. It appeared that for years she'd been abused by her father, before her mother died. I only had her word for it. It hadn't stopped her looking after *him* when the time came. In her letter, she said it was a chance for her to abuse him. Mona joked about everything. She was the opposite of Julie. Mona wouldn't even have ticked me off for not replying to her immediately about something so shocking. She always thought too well of people. But I never found out why she hadn't told me before. Maybe she thought it was just something that happened, like possibly ending up on the cutting-room floor as a make-believe milkmaid. Or maybe we hadn't known each other long enough. Such disclosures often come late in the day.

There weren't many at the funeral. As our tiny procession entered the chapel, it divided into family and others, separated by three or four empty pews. An organ wheezed fitfully like someone on a life-support machine. Two hymns were sung, mainly by the man conducting the obsequies. It was a Christian service so he was obviously a non-denominational 'man of god'. Mona was in the front pew with a barely-consolable person I took to be an aunt, and a few people of her own age, brothers and sisters or in-laws. I knew a couple of them. There were a sizeable lot. We odds and sods at the back glanced at each other, wondering who we were and why we were there. I mostly mouthed the hymn verses like the rest. I was unacc-ountably more inhibited than I'd been with Harold at St Bart's that time though no less a stranger in the midst. At one point, Mona, wedged in, turned and smiled at me, kind of dislodging the equally tubby individuals beside her.

Outside among the tributes ('family flowers only'), I was the centre of attention as Mona introduced me to everyone. Relatives were introduced and the ones I didn't know shook my hand; also the ones that did know. After these formalities, everyone stood around facing me and I wondered if they were waiting for me to say something, to address them in actorly fashion. Despite what she'd told me, I felt they knew about the shadow cast by beastly Edward Walter Strange and saw me as some kind of saviour. Mona exaggerated my soap opera appearances; no one questioned me about them so I didn't mind. She claims they never knew about her dastardly father, or if they did, they kept it to themselves.

Mona hadn't said a lot about the abuse. We never had much discussion about anything, I supposed on the grounds that eventually it would lead to a difference of opinion and the polarisation of views and positions: such as the position of herself and her father as the bedroom door shut quietly behind him so as not to disturb his wife who may for a long time have been covering her ears with a pillow and closing her eyes tight. I could only guess at how many others she'd told. Had she even confided in her mother? Each time I tried to raise the subject, she'd sigh and stare into the middle-distance, where the detail, the precise narrative, of her father's molestation was taking place as if in a film clip. In her case, (she was a devoted *Trekky*), it would have been a neon-glowing, miniaturised scene transported from the past to the ground in front of her. Mona was always too ready to minimise the grotesque with inanity or a full-bodied legover. 'I don't wish to talk about it; I want to interfere with you,' she'd say. As she went about her work, I'd ponder the nature of consent or the nature of a lack of it, the lack of approval; and the subtle way in which she may have been getting her own back on someone who thought he was enjoying the experience rather than being assaulted. Her obsession took strange forms. One of the viral YouTube selections she sent showed two dogs mating in the middle of the road while traffic stopped in both directions and drove around them. Were these simply manifestations of horror subdued out of all recognition to the point where the world laughed?

Anyway, like all events rising above the predicates that threatened to make them anything other than what they really were, the afterglow of Edward Walter Strange's cremation saw us sitting around talking and drinking - and eating competitively cucumber and egg sandwiches before they curled up and dried.

I looked across at Mona who appeared sexually provocative in the tight black dress she'd chosen to see off her father and it struck me that if ever there were people of whom you could say you always knew where you were with them, it was people like Mona Strange. But you couldn't and it wasn't. For just a few minutes, she seemed alone and abandoned by the guests who'd been supporting her. I caught her eye and she smiled. I still don't know what that smile meant or what secrets it was doing a poor job of keeping under wraps.

Julie Makes a Move

Literally. I received a message from her to say she'd found the rental flat she'd been looking for and hoped to move to in three weeks. It was equidistant between Ethel in Rustington and Harold in Goring.

I didn't even know she was thinking of moving down there, let alone that she'd done anything about it. Normally I'd have been dumbfounded but where Julie was concerned, shock registered simultaneously as surprise, even incredulity. I'm almost 100 per cent sure of that - her thinking of it, I mean. It wouldn't have been something she'd have mentioned just in passing and we'd never discussed it.

I was already aware of how her independence had begun disrupting our relationship as well as running parallel with it, the latter being something I'd become used to.

But there's independence and independence: the one you accept as part of the need to maintain some sort of integrity in case anything goes wrong (I assume that's why you do it) while acknowledging the same desire in the other, the same right; the second is one you exercise at the other's expense or in spite of the right to know, to share. In our case, this was too rational a distinction. The collision is in the discovery or the announcement. If Julie had found out that Mona and I were growing closer, it would have de-railed her as surely as a confession would have. Leading some kind of double life, with both of them thinking that neither would object, was akin to Julie telling me she was about to move from Manchester to West Sussex as though my knowing or having an opinion about it didn't matter and never would.

I'd begun wondering if I could have lived with that: the unpredictable morphing ever more frequently into the unthinking and insensitive. Separation and divorce are always the result of some version or other of this change of personality. My friend Geoff believes any domestic arrangement between a couple lasting more than three years must have turned into a sham. Geoff's a cynic.

Just before Julie signalled her intention of moving, I'd started to limp more or less permanently. It had been happening a lot after the latest prognosis. For months following the sow's attack, I was in pain. It was pretty bad, but not enough to make me try to alleviate it by taking the weight off my foot. When the limping began in earnest, as it were, it reminded me of some resistance being overcome - I mean unconsciously. Part of my body was fraught and looking to the rest of it for help. I didn't need to limp but I just did. It was weird. My immediate reaction was to wonder if there were any theatrical roles requiring visible evidence of infirmity; or if I would now be classified as a disabled actor having to lobby for equal rights. (The Edge at the time was being urged to host a short-run production of *Othello* in which the Moor was a wheelchair-bound white actor prepared to 'black up'; it was one sort of inclusivity over-riding another. The board's dithering over a decision - it was postponed - was meant to hold out the prospect of something happening, while avoiding an outright negative.)

'J makes a move' or 'J is making a move' is what I told Mona a few days after her father's funeral. Unlike Julie, but probably for genuine reasons to do with Julie's temperament (I hesitated to tell Mona it was a condition),

Mona was always interested in other people and their tribulation, never in her own. Considering she'd had enough of it herself, I thought it a commendable trait, a selfless quality. So she knew about Harold and Julie and Ethel but not much about the dynamics among them and the connections that posed problems constantly demanding solutions, which would have interested her more. Problems were usually enough for Mona to consider; her answers involved the expenditure of emotional energy and were often comic. That said, I often wondered if Mona's interest was genuine or just a polite expression of an ingrained sense of duty, however undermined. I hadn't told her about Julie's mental state but she knew about Harold's cancer. Mona was more comfortable with one lot of trouble at a time:

> *Hiya Francis Exxon How U Thankx agin for coming to the funeral. Didn't xpect so many. U didnt tell me about H. Izzy better? Looking 4wards 2 the doc. Had my cheque (!!!!). Did I tell U? Will fone soon. AML XXX*

I'd had my cheque too, but after hers.

There were indeed a lot paying respects (sorry, Julie) to her old man, the filthy octopus. You couldn't tell if their grim faces denoted sadness or disgust. His unwanted attentions, or rather their late disclosure, indeed remained within the family.

Then two days later:

> *Hi sweetie XXX Just had great idea. We shd watch the doc 2gether. Dyad say? Snuggles in front of the box with a BIG 2blerone? LMK. Lurv U XXXX PS Get this*

She'd attached a GIF repeat clip of a baby in a one-piece pyjama suit falling over, asleep, on a settee, while the family's Rottweiler follows its left-to-right headlong tumble time and again. It looked a bit sinister to me, what with the dog looking on with its back to the camera and its ears flapping alternately up and down: the prelude to some horrific TV news item maybe, about an infant savaged to death in the home.

A week later:

> *F hun : - (U nevR keep me UTD about H. Wot abt Ethel 2?? Remembr UZ she was odd. Looking forward to Sat XXXX ; -)*

I hadn't told her much about Ethel, except to say that she was a retired Domsky teacher and an embattled vegetarian. I never mentioned the occult. The Saturday she was enthusing over was the first time since I met Julie that we were to be together without Julie's knowledge; in fact, to Julie, Mona was just the name of a complaining fellow actor, ('Moaning Mona'), though I'd told her I was going to the funeral. She'd shown no interest. She didn't know that Mona had been sexually abused.

On that date, Mona and I watched a DVD of *No Country for Old Men*. Just before the film ended, we lay half-undressed on the settee in 'fumbling mode', as Julie used to call it. Although Mona had told me not to treat her with 'kid gloves', I always felt that, in her animal abandon, she was suppressing the temptation to call an abrupt halt in the midst of a blizzard of traumatic memories. It was also the time when whatever cement fixed me and Julie together was crumbling and Harold's welfare was becoming her focus; a time when it became obvious to me that Julie saw individuals but not their connectivity. All these issues were pleading for guidance and moral summation, and at that moment they seemed to arrive in the tone if not the actual words of Tommy Lee Jones's world-weary sheriff in the film. Like him, I didn't know what was going on either.

After that, I phoned Mona as often as I texted or emailed Julie. It was one form of communication giving way to another. There was a shift of allegiance. Whatever damage had been done to Mona Strange was easier to deal with and I felt that she believed I could do no wrong; it was therefore a case of moving with her, physically at first, in a region with no barriers. We had our depths: to do with ambition (or lack of it); our limitations, and our prospects. With Julie, obstacles were everywhere. Mona limped with me; Julie had slipped anchor and I feared for her.

Quackery

Metaferon came in tablet form as an American import. It cost a lot. As a former coalminer, Harold couldn't have earned that much. We'd never got round to talking a lot about Marjorie, I supposed because she had died before her Biblical span (or before she was seventy, as Julie would have preferred it), and death had become for Harold not so much a solemn inevitability shared with the rest of us but more like a message delivered early by one of the Crazy Gang, who'd rung the doorbell and from behind a hedge was smiling at his discomfiture. Marje must have had money. The house in Worthing, according to Ethel, was worth almost 'half a million'. I don't remember how that had come up in conversation. It was on the main road to Brighton and Arundel and therefore commuter territory for London.

'Then there's the question of his will,' Julie reminded me. It wasn't a reminder because the subject had never arisen.

'Well, I don't want to feature in it,' I said.

'I didn't mean that, stupid. We both know who will feature in it.'

The word 'feature' left a bad taste. She grimaced.

'So, who would?'

'Don't be sarcastic.'

It was a mistake to ask Julie a question to which you both thought you knew the answer.

'I understood you'd made your peace with Ethel Chrimes.'

'What made you think that?'

While Harold still had faith in conventional treatment, Julie encouraged him; but as soon as he'd refused another course of chemo and Metaferon, or something similar, became the only alternative, she took against Ethel again. I originally thought that hostility towards her had subsided for shame's sake. Then I discovered this note on her personal laptop (she never used passwords): *EC as domineering matriarch,* mutatis mutandis, *having influence on all around her. Beneficiaries and casualties. Details, viz, tweed coat + big black buttons like saucers. And girding belt. Tent-like black flower-pattern dress. Buxom. Two chins. Severity of feature. Mannish. Nil sense of humour.* Based on other entries, I recognised this as one of her fictional characters lining up to come into being. Julie's changed attitude towards Ethel was just a writerly thing: the personal temporarily ditched in favour of the objective. Ethel had worn a similar coat at the restaurant that time. Taking it off had seemed like an act of defiance or rolled-sleeve intent.

Although adverts for Metaferon in America had come close to offering a cure, they'd been muted before its passage across the Atlantic. Claims to cure cancer are illegal over here. Metaferon had become an innocent homeopathic treatment whose effect was vague or non-existent. Its advocates, people like Ethel, read only American testimonies of the miraculous. But I sometimes wonder if Ethel knew the situation was hopeless and was simply jollying Harold along. I'd discussed the possibility with Julie who'd come with me and Harold to discuss further prognosis with his oncologist (Ethel had been in bed with a cold). The medical view was that Metaferon would probably do no harm - meaning that any harm it did couldn't be any worse than galloping cancer - and that if Harold wished to try it, he should not be dissuaded.

As we sat in her consulting-room, the oncologist smiled at me and Julie and may have winked at us, though it could have been a tic. She never mentioned it aloud but I guessed she meant that Metaferon's effect could be incidental and that there was nothing essentially wrong with that. But she wouldn't go on record as having prescribed, advocated or directed any course of treatment other than the one Harold had refused to continue. The smile concealed a disclaimer. My reading about cancer since discovering Harold told me that the end could be rendered virtually painless: 'peace in the arms of Morpheus', as Julie, possibly with tongue in cheek, was to describe Harold's final days. The oncologist said she'd look into Metaferon and we arranged a further meeting. We told her our trio would probably be a quartet next time.

The box containing Harold's tablets bore the trademark Metafix. They were small white things dated and looking innocuous in the usual foil strip. Among the list of ingredients was Metaferon (Beta-dioxymetasalicilate extract of *Didymopanay morototoni*) and other basic substances re-named to sound scientific: such as ascorbic acid, lactose monohydrate, and microcrystalline cellulose, each in impressively declining percentages. The expected leaflet of thin paper inside unfolded to an A4 sheet covered on both sides in almost illegible small print. There were diagrams of the aforementioned tree, *Didymopanay*, giver of life and hope; bleached-out, black-and-white photographs of Dr Vergara and his entomologist colleague, Prof Branco; the mutant mistletoe-type plant *Santalum variegatum;* and the 'dancing' insect parasite *Shizolena terpsichorii.* (Julie's laptop notes must have been the result of her own researches. She was diligent on that score.) There was a cartoon panel in which Vergara could be seen working in his laboratory and Branco in hers, both looking down microscopes. *Didymopanay* was shown being attacked - if that's the word - by the double parasitism of mistletoe and insect, and another of a line of Amazonian Indians depopulated by the lack of what they never knew was called Metaferon. Finally, there was a panel showing Vergara and Branco behind a tray of saplings. Vergara, the botanist, had succeeded in growing from seed what he hoped would be specimens of *Didymopanay* resistant to attacks by first the 'mistletoe' plant and then, as a piggy-back parasite, the dancing-larvae insects of *Shizolena terpsichorii.*

It appeared that Beta-dioxymetasalicilate (Metaferon) could be extracted from the tree at an early age and certainly when it could be protected from infection by *Santalum variegatum*, such infection mostly introduced by the dispersal and depositing of seeds by birds or tree-climbing animals. The extract derived from these younger trees was five times more potent than that from mature specimens and obviated the need to penetrate deep-forested territory for them; in any case, the adult *Didimopanay* was comparatively rare.

The story read like an example of the gods engaging in their disinterested sport: the dancing-larvae insect harmlessly parasitic on the already parasitic 'mistletoe' but enabling the tree to survive while halting or reducing its production of Metaferon. If it could be believed that Metaferon was indeed a cure for cancer, as it had been for the ailments of face-painted natives on the forest floor, its disappearance would seem even more divinely callous. I couldn't help thinking that the kick-step-kick larvae of

Shizolena terpsichorii might have been deliberately chosen for this celestial rolling of the dice.

Only later did I discover where Julie had led Branco and Vergara by the hand to their immortality in fiction (that idea for a story she mentioned about a failing zoo and a misbehaving primate). I also wondered why a rainforest pigmy, as it may have been, should be denied a cure for a scorpion bite and a source of ritual ecstasy and escape, any more than an ex-miner should not be allowed to subdue a body in revolt.

The final quarter of the sheet was devoted to testimonials. Half-anonymous advocates, such as 'RL, Wyoming' and 'DBH Jr, NY City', told briefly how their cancers had been stalled or banished by Metafix.

Julie, Ethel and I accompanied Harold to his next, and last, interview with the oncologist. She had asked that he re-consider his decision to discontinue chemo, the course she'd recommended but not with much enthusiasm, it has to be said. I recalled seeing on her desk a framed photograph of herself with a small dog - well, I could just about make it out if I leaned forward when she left the room for a few minutes. The dog was licking her face with a long purple tongue and she was smiling with her eyes closed. I wondered if the dog had died, like Tiger, and this was her reminder of the bond she'd shared with it, or if the photo was a source of reverie while she was at work and the dog was sitting in the window at home, awaiting her return and barking at passers-by or other dogs. I don't know why she'd left us on our own. She returned and sat upright at her desk to deliver a statement for which she appeared to have sought sanction or bravado somewhere else in the building. It was one she must have made no end of times. She flattened the Metafix leaflet on the desk with an outstretched palm – we'd already shown her the tablets - and slid it slowly towards us, speaking as she did so, her head lowered.

'I cannot stop you taking these tablets. All I can tell you is that I am not recommending them as something that will make your cancer go away and that no one else in my profession would. Although there appears to be nothing harmful here, I cannot guarantee that there will be no side-effects. The claims for them, as you know, are illegal.'

She looked at me, Julie and Ethel in turn, as if defying us to contradict her. We didn't have to. It struck me that chemo was extremely harmful and, in the case of cancer cells, lethal. Maybe she was telling us in a roundabout way that the tablets would be useless. Harold had made his decision. There was a lot we already knew, especially about side-effects. That Metaferon would be Harold's last chance wasn't doubted. Nor was the possibility that it might not work. She wouldn't have seen any disagreements in the accord suggested by the way we were all leaning towards him.

But what was the reality? Had Ethel become less bossy because she knew it was the means of winning our support for Metaferon, in which she believed devoutly? Was Julie's ambivalence towards Ethel the same process flawed by a temperament outside her control? Was I helpless and hopeless because what Harold wanted was the only factor to be considered, about which it was then pointless to argue?

If only these notes were not a true if sketchy account of what happened but one of Julie's fictions, or someone else's, able to explain motives and resolve outcomes, supported by evidence and testimony and offering conclusions of a sort. Then our forlorn foursome on one side of the desk and the consultant on the other might be rendered not so much complex and debatable as detailed, rounded and beyond argument, if not censure. I can only report what I remember of what I heard and saw, such as an oncologist - a young woman maybe unaware of turmoil in some faraway, Lilliput-sized part of her lower right breast - casting a glance at the photo of herself and the dog (a large, wide-eyed mongrel) as we stood and helped Harold on with his coat. She must have known how even the charlatan has a place in our eternal clutching at straws and how she would be confident in her explanation of a miracle, should it occur. Like the events noted here, miracles can only ever be reported, not proved.

After that meeting, we called in somewhere for tea. My mobile rang while we were waiting to be served. It was my father's cousin, Mary, Harold's half-sibling. I'd told almost everyone in the family I could contact about Harold, commenting that we were an odd family when it came to keeping in touch. 'Inexcusable,' Mary's sister, Rachel, had said, including herself in the criticism. Their late brother, David, seemed so distant a memory as to have virtually never existed. We aren't a big family, a fact which validated Rachel's comment. My mother had one brother, a proverbial 'black sheep' with two children who only ever appear as head and shoulders on the horizon and then vanish for ages, like part of an unherded flock. That Harold, the issue of my great-uncle John's re-marriage to Kath (both now dead, though Kath lived to be almost 95) should have been known to me only by reputation and from vaguely-recalled sightings again made me reflect on families generally. I realised how typical we'd become, even as a small unit with no tendency to maintain closer contacts. Unless I marry and have children, something in the family line will die out, like an animal or plant species becoming extinct. When the others heard that I'd tracked down Harold, they were less than excited because basically I'd re-discovered them as well; or maybe shamed them into admitting that they couldn't tell me more about him than I'd already discovered. My news of his illness seemed to encourage in them and all the others - not many - a kind of vested torpor, an understanding of my willingness to be the family's messenger and chronicler. That was never my intention.

I repeat: some unemployed actors write books, some make snow globes, others keep their memories sharpened; I joined a family-history website. Julie once said my interest in family history was a means of assembling the cast I rarely had access to, a comment on my status as an actor who began his career playing a non-speaking horse. I don't recall what stage she was at in her wobbling from one persona to another, so I might have suggested she did the same when short of ideas for a new novel. But I may have said nothing.

Mary wanted to know the latest, so I'd got up from the table and spent five minutes telling her. When I returned and apologised for taking the call, Julie and Ethel were arranging for us to take Harold on a bracing day out to the coast.

'Your tea'll be cold,' he said.

And it was. Again there was a hint of reproach in his voice, exaggerated by his place in the Julie-Harold-Ethel trio which again seemed to be operating independently of me.

I sat down and sipped my tea anyway and began to laugh.

What was I laughing at exactly? I wasn't sure. But Metafix began to be a joke, irrespective of whether or not it might turn out to be the supreme example of a placebo and cure Harold by default. Was I laughing at the possible vindication of Ethel Chrimes as she proclaimed her miracle, refusing to believe that it just reflected the human body duped into going to work on its destroyers?

'What's so funny?' Julie asked me.

But I couldn't give her a sensible answer. I knew what I wanted to say: 'Quackery - what a funny word!'

Ethel Makes a Move

When I arrived at Julie's new furnished flat, Ethel was there.

'Hello, Francis,' she said. 'What do you think of it?'

'Very nice.'

Julie's voice shrieked from another room. 'I bet he said it was very nice!'

Ethel looked at me and raised her eyebrows, her lips venturing a half-smile.

'Yes, he did!' she shouted back, without taking her eyes off me.

Julie pirouetted into the room.

'I'll make some tea,' Ethel said and left us in a tight embrace from which I extricated myself to nod in her direction. Offering to make tea was invariably a decelerator. We drank a lot of it.

'She wanted to come,' Julie whispered, giving no explanation.

I'd not asked her why she'd taken the flat. By that time, I wasn't questioning Julie's actions or ideas any more than was necessary so long as they were not a threat unacknowledged by her. I'd gone straight there after phoning Harold.

'I'm OK,' he'd said, with a lift of incredulity in his voice. He was into his fourth week of Metaferon. 'They seem to be doing something. You know - the tablets.'

Yes; I did know. I imagined his invaders bemused by some unconfirmed report of a counter-offensive against the odds. Cancer had become for me a miniaturised version of *Lord of the Rings*: all darkness except for a slender gold band of hope, wearing away or tending to become irretrievably lost.

I'd agreed with Julie that we should discuss at-home nursing for Harold when the time came. The discussion would involve Ethel, who'd already made provisional arrangements. Relatives were on the margins, awaiting reports with not much anxiety or interest. '*If* the time comes,' she'd corrected, with no hint of mockery. Her face hadn't registered any indication of what she'd meant. In the interests of a quiet life, as they say, I'd lost the will to reconcile Julie's contradictory positions and statements. One minute I believed she had more in common with Ethel than there were differences between them, the next that she was still on my side and with the sense to make sure Harold didn't suffer. It depended on what day of the week it was or what hour of the day. I'd ceased to care because, where Harold was concerned, it no longer mattered. I cared more about how many people with problems had few close kin to depend on. Possibly she did too. It wasn't dependence in the abstract; there were things to be done, practicalities. I knew only too well that Julie herself was dependent and that I was failing her because her weakness often seemed like petulance and her unreasonableness like eccentricity; human frailties, my response to them included. But she was, in the clinical sense, unhinged.

Ethel returned with the tea. 'So shall we talk about it?'

I wasn't sure what she meant but with Ethel, it was easy to threaten belligerence. 'About what exactly?'

'Whether Harold will need the people I've contacted to come in.'

Julie, who was cooped up in the crook of the settee as usual - a slightly grubby one, I noticed - definitely sniggered, though I don't think Ethel heard. Was Julie thinking what I was thinking: that Ethel was referring to the foxes - they were still there - and the need to get rid of them? She meant, of course, palliative care nurses. On the other hand, she may have been laughing at Ethel's choice of words.

'Isn't it a question of when rather than if?' I asked.

'You lack faith,' Ethel said.

'I certainly do.'

'You certainly do,' Julie said, bounding over to sit on the arm of Ethel's chair.

It was time to tell them that I'd also contacted one of the nursing companies recommended to us by the oncologist at an earlier visit, as a 'precaution'.

'We'll leave it to you then,' Julie said. 'Capable hands, and all that.'

Ethel remained silent.

It was also time to say something I'd been rehearsing for a while in order to placate Ethel - and Julie at a moment like this when they were in cahoots.

'Look,' I explained. 'I don't object to Metaferon but we have to prepare for the possibility that in Harold's case it won't work. That doesn't mean it never works.'

Julie had her hand around Ethel's shoulders. As Ethel perked up and raised her head, Julie withdrew and reversed into her former position on the settee.

'Yes,' Ethel said and, shifting to the edge of her seat, 'Yes. Of course!'

She sounded as though this was something she should have thought of herself as a fall-back and would use in future Soul Travel arguments. I guessed that for people like Ethel Chrimes, the obvious was sometimes blindingly prophetic.

Julie showed me around the furnished flat. She hadn't properly moved in: her 'stuff' was on its way. I knew from her place in Manchester that she required little. I mean, I'd lived there with her off and on. Here there was one bedroom, a narrow galley kitchen, and an office no bigger than Harold's box-room but in which there was already a small writing-desk and a beckoning laptop.

Ethel came up behind us. She was in a more cheery mood.

'Well, let's talk about it then.'

I wondered for a moment if she'd discounted Julie's view that I should deal with Harold's final needs and wished to revert to combined action. But no; she'd planned our day out to the cliff tops near Saltdean, east of Brighton.

We had another mug of tea and some 'shop cake' Ethel had bought and sat together on the settee. She suggested that the four of us should go in her car but I said I was happy to drive. She'd worked out how to get as close as possible to the cliff without Harold's having to undergo anything like a strenuous walk. In any case, she said, Harold had 'the constitution of an ox'. Julie glanced at me and grinned, probably at the cliché and its inability to derive from the comparison it made not a tithe of the strength it needed to make an impression, especially in Harold's case.

'It must be the top,' she said. 'Harold insisted.'

Julie explained. 'He's quite into Charles Lovell Darling and wants to look across at Dieppe, where Darling lived for the last part of his life.'

That was something else I didn't know. Harold's interest, I mean. I knew about Darling's French domicile; I imagined it packed darkly with badly-stuffed birds and stoats - and otters - behind glass.

I did know, however, that, though one might on a clear day see Calais from Dover, the likelihood of catching sight of Dieppe from Saltdean or Brighton was remote, even with binoculars.

Still, it reminded me of my wish to take Julie to Dieppe as a surprise one day. Had it not been for Harold's condition, we might already have done so. But with Harold's condition at their centre, events were spinning outwards.

Ethel had walked over to the window. 'Sadly, you'll have to get rid of these.'

She was barely audible, her head lowered as if she were praying.

We joined her in solemnity, looking down at a ball of ladybirds; scores of them, huddling in a corner, barely moving. We watched them in silence.

Toblerone

In the Middle Ages, warriors from Berne were often depicted as ferocious bears. Valerius Anshelm, a writer, told in 1513 how Bernese soldiers captured a live bear after the Battle of Novara and brought it back to the city. The bear was kept alive in the city's moat. It was Berne's first makeshift bear pit.

In 1857, twelve bears were kept in a pit, the Bärenplatz, which can still be seen today with live bears inside. Since then, Berne's bears have also been able to move out of their drab pits through a tunnel to the nearby Bear Park along the banks of the river Aare. It was built to offer the animals a more natural life.

Today, 'bear flags' fly from the city's buildings. The bear is the main character in its famous carnival. There's little chance of seeing the animal in the wild, though the city rejoiced a few years ago when, for the first time in nearly two centuries, a wild bear was seen wandering through the canton. The last time that had happened was in 1823.

But as I told Mona before we'd snuggled down in front of the TV that night and while David Attenborough was silently recalling some ancient zoo quest in the background, there was the case of Sophie Schneider.

'Why is there a picture of a mountain on a Toblerone packet?' Mona asked me.

'Look at it carefully.'

She picked up the giant chocolate bar she'd bought for our evening in front of the TV. Neither of us had seen a preview of the film but the fact, already noted, that she'd been paid earlier than me probably meant her scenes had been dropped. I knew much more about that kind of work than she did. Whenever you invited Mona to do something, she always adopted an exaggerated manner, like then, as she examined the Toblerone logo at close range. She turned to me, her face screwed up in bewilderment.

'There's a bear hidden in it, hidden in the mountain,' I explained.

She peered again.

I had to point it out.

After she'd sent me the email suggesting we gorged on Toblerone while watching ourselves – or me - on the screen, I bought a bar on the way to a matinée. 'Assistant stage manager' sounds important, but like many other job descriptions that don't involve the possibility of getting your hands dirty, it obscures a heft of boredom. I spent a lot of time in my 'broom-cupboard' drinking coffee, reading *The Stage*, eating chocolate - and surfing, a word which entered the OED in 2000 with 'bungy' (as in 'jumping'), 'cool' (as in 'OK by me'), and 'text' (as in 'to send a digital message').

I'd forgotten that Toblerone was so sickly-sweet. Mona would have no trouble putting a bar of it away. She was a relisher; her watchwords were 'appetite' and 'enthusiasm' - and presumably 'endurance'. I had to guess what it had meant to care for someone who had abused her. She never told me much about it, so much so that I wondered if she really had made it up. I saw her as an eager recipient of the benefit of a doubt. Had there been just one incident, remembered in detail by her and the source of undying shame for him?

The theatre was closed each Monday, but I used to go in and show willing, checking on items that needed no checking. Other arty things went on at The Edge every day of the week. I liked to think that the theatre needed someone on hand to represent it, even on dormant Mondays, when there was no prospect of ticket sales, especially for the sort of shows we put on. Mona was completing a stint with a theatre-in-education group, something to do with life in the Manchester slums. I picked her up at a junior school, where a few of the kids had been given non-speaking parts, as the adults, in professional costume, moaned and groaned about tough times in the 19th century. (The kids' parents had made their rudimentary historic garb.) She'd rung me earlier: 'Fiona's in overnight.' Fiona was the old Ford Fiesta she drove around in, then being repaired. I was parked outside. As she walked my way and waved, I could see she was carrying something that turned out to be a cut-out cat made of plywood. The company's van was being loaded with props by two of her colleagues.

'Shouldn't that thing be going in with the other stuff?' I asked, as she fed her ample form through the front passenger door and tossed the cat and her rucksack on to the back seat.

'I'm borrowing him for a while. He needs looking after - like you.' I looked over my shoulder: the cat was black with a white ruff and was designed to be stood upright, like a tea-cosy. She pecked me on the cheek. I breathed in *GHOSTbond* hair glue mixed with the whiff of honest actorly perspiration. Junior schools don't have showers.

We'd agreed to view the film at my place. I'd phoned Harold a few days before to tell him it was on and I rang again as we ate. 'It's after the David Attenborough programme.' Mona started to laugh and shouted towards the phone, 'Not to worry, Harold, we don't say anything!'

I'd told him about Mona and having to go to her father's funeral; I'd also told him about other people in my life but the worsening of his illness seemed to limit the amount of new intelligence he could take in. She knew more about him than he did about her. 'That was Mona Strange,' I said and waited for him to ask where Julie was. But he didn't - because Julie was with him. She knew about the broadcast and that I was working. Harold said, 'Ethel's at a meeting. Mona who?' I told him I'd ring to find out what they'd thought.

'Sophie whatshername?' Mona asked, echoing Harold's query.

The Schneiders were from a small village near Delémon, capital of the Jura canton in Switzerland. There was Lukas and his wife Emma, and the two children, Rafael and his sister, Sophie.

Lukas Schneider worked in the Swiss Patent Office for the young and then unknown Albert Einstein. One morning in 1908, Einstein sent Schneider to the factory of the Fabrique de Chocolat Berne, Tobler & Cie, in response to an application from Theodor Tobler, its joint owner, for a patent. Tobler had invented a triangular chocolate bar incorporating honey and crushed almonds. 'Bring me a piece,' Einstein had said, staring distractedly in his customary manner on tiptoe across the city's rooftops as the sun streamed through the open window of his office. Colleagues called him *Le rêveur Einstein* – Einstein the Dreamer.

Schneider brought more than a piece: Tobler gave him a huge box of samples to be distributed among the office staff. He had to apologise to Einstein for being late back, for, in his excitement, Tobler had regaled him with coffee and *solothurner tort* and wanted to know all about the young patents examiner and his family. After the award of the patent, Tobler wrote a letter of gratitude to Einstein in which he praised Schneider's interest and professional manner; he'd especially liked the suggestions Schneider had made about Tobler's idea of including trading cards with the company's products, to be redeemed by customers once a set of them had been collected.

Scarcely eight months after Tobler had received his patent, Schneider's fifteen-year-old daughter, Sophie, was involved in a bizarre riding accident. While on a family holiday in the mountains, she'd gone hacking along a familiar forest trail with her brother Rafael. They were both experienced riders. At some point, according to Rafael, his sister's horse, which was in front by four lengths, was startled by an animal that scuttled across the path in front of it. Rafael said it was a bear though he couldn't be sure (bears were rare in the mountains at that time, though not absent altogether; Lukas Schneider had simply asked his children to take care). Local hunters thought it might have been a wolf or a lynx but Rafael's mimicking of the animal's distinctive movement on all fours, in particular its detail of the upturned fingers to represent claws, convinced investigators. Whatever, Sophie was thrown to the ground, receiving head and spinal injuries from which she never fully recovered; she spent the rest of her days in a bathchair until her death thirty years later. The accident was reported in all the Swiss newspapers, in some cases graphically. One account quoted the mother, Emma Schneider, as having heard Sophie's horse 'galloping madly, its shoes sparking on stones' and then seeing it flash past the family's log-cabin 'like a wild thing, its green teeth bared, its mane swept back'. Rafael had returned alone, screaming for help.

One report suggested that Rafael may have worsened Sophie's injuries by first attempting to lift her on to his horse. Who should intervene at that point, describing the story as 'a calumny, a distortion', but Theodor Tobler himself, then fending off criticism that his trading-card scheme, which offered a cash redemption of ten Swiss francs in exchange for a full set of cards, was encouraging schoolchildren to spend money unwisely. His publicity on the Schneiders' behalf did Tobler no harm and the Schneiders and Toblers became close, Tobler himself paying for Sophie's various spa treatments. But as the Tobler business expanded and the family's wealth increased, the Schneiders' fortunes declined, symbolically presided over by Sophie's emaciated and immobile figure. Seven years after awarding the chocolate-bar patent, Einstein published his Theory of General Relativity. Reporters visited the Patent Office for quotes from the employees about their distinguished former colleague. Lukas Schneider sat with a journalist for thirty minutes, praising Einstein as well as relating the story of the triangular chocolate bar, but nothing of his testimony was published. Schneider, always a pessimist, became dejected, more so as Rafael, despite Tobler's rebuttal of the statements made against him, was badly affected by suggestions that he may have done the wrong thing by his injured sister and afterwards led a life of idleness and debauchery. It has even been suggested that Rafael actually did try to move his sister as she lay helpless and in great pain.

The Village: How Our Ancestors Lived lasted over an hour. A wailing, new-born child was heard first, as the titles segued into our Chester abode. Less a village, more a rude settlement and bulwark against the elements, the fictitious East Elkinwick was where we were born, struggled, survived and died. In fact, the crying infant accompanied the burial of an old man, and I became the village elder, his successor. I was not long for the world either, though, in TV doc terms, I last over forty-five minutes. My skill at ploughing and animal husbandry was being passed on to my son, the one heard mewling at the start, and my wife and daughters washed and cleaned and prepared meals when they weren't helping us menfolk in the fields. The seasons came and went (rain machines turned the set into a quagmire and we all stood back and marvelled at the snowblowers as they covered the ground and the rooftops in a white mantle before manufacturing a blizzard into which we all had to lean). The cameras were almost entirely on me and my family. A scene in which I was shown making love to my wife was shot later in a Midlands studio - easy money, including travelling expenses. My growing son and I were seen killing geese and chickens (we just picked up the animals; the killing was done separately too). A pig's ceremonial appearance was attended by the whole village. As everyone gathered round, I looked for Mona but she said she'd been stood down for that scene with another of the extras. The moment for despatch came. I was filmed entering the sty with a bludgeon, which I raised above my head with two hands and brought down on that sack of rubbish (not shown). There was much squealing (pre-recorded). My injury, but not my 'real' time off, was considered for inclusion but rejected because it involved too much re-scripting. While we were shown hanging the butchered meat joints (plastic) after the pig's corpse was scrubbed (real), the camera panned to a window and closed in on the distant milking parlour. Two milkmaids entered, each carrying a four-legged stool. Beyond them, from the parlour's other door, Mona should have exited with her wooden yoke and pails, but the film cut to the milk being churned to butter (more imported clips).

'They've really bloody well lost me,' Mona said. She knew they had. 'Mind you, I was covered in mud after the fall. I suppose a bit of dust and dirt on the hem looks natural but not a whole splurge of muck. On my face too. That first milkmaid was Chrissie Pipe. She was in *Corrie* once, coming out of a shop.'

Mona Strange: ever-philosophical.

My death was quite an event. I was taken to the burial grounds like a god entering Valhalla. It was just as well I was lying down with my eyes shut: I'd eaten a dodgy burger from the canteen on wheels and had the most frightful gut's-ache. As the camera was placed on my chest and wobbled at the approach of the grave, I'd let go a loud rolling fart. Everybody had fallen about except the weary director who really did shout 'Cut!' I thought that only happened in Hollywood films of Hollywood films being made. *The Village: How Our Ancestors Lived* finally bore no resemblance to what we'd gone through.

We watched the credits roll at the end. The film-makers hadn't missed a trick. The names of Christine Pipe and the other milkmaid were listed but not Mona's: no appearance, no mention. At the end, it said no animals had been harmed in the making of the documentary. Actors had, though; well, one.

Mona zapped the TV off and leant towards me.

'I want to feel your wound,' she said.

And she did, going about her work with relish, appetite, and enthusiasm. Mona regarded the descriptions 'plump', 'chubby' and 'sizeable' as sexy terms of endearment. She once texted me a pic of her and her friends on another night out. The message was *Porkies on parade!!!!!* Mona was buxom but not fat.

For a long time, I was reluctant to make the running during these intimacies. I assumed she was working out her attitudes to men, whether or not her father had been typical of what they were capable of. I smoothed her hair as someone would smooth a resting, comforting pet and let her do what she wanted. To that end, I allowed myself to be distracted though not disengaged. I stared at the empty Toblerone carton and wondered what happened when a mouse entered one of Harold's traps at St Barts. What had he said: that they went away, their gut full of Mousedoom crystals or whatever they were – oh yes, Crystalkil - to die somewhere else? It seemed a bit messy. There was this image of the verger with an outstretched arm, carrying away mice corpses by their tails and dumping them in the graveyard's bunker for dead flowers and wreaths. It would be better to have them expire conveniently inside so that they could be slid out.

I was trying to anticipate a question from Mona about the Toblerone logo, as to why old Tobler should have hidden a bear in it. I'd told her the story. But it was something I'd wondered myself. Did he incorporate it as a reminder of what had led to the life-changing injuries sustained by his friend's daughter and as a symbol of the unseen threats to life and to the success of commerce and prosperity despite them?

Mona fell asleep. I got up, laid a blanket over her and phoned Harold from my bedroom. Julie answered.

The Walk to Windlass Hill

'You were very good,' Julie said. 'Impressive, albeit a man of few words.'

Harold began to laugh. He must have been sitting next to her in front of the TV, with his hearing-aid in. By then, we'd persuaded him to get one; it was a gift arriving too late. She didn't mention Mona or her absence but knew we'd watched the documentary together. Julie was now Harold's neighbour, more or less. She handed him the phone.

'I thought you were bitten by a pig,' he said.

'I was. But they didn't show it.'

Then Julie laughed. She could hear what I was saying.

'You two are in a good mood.'

'Aye,' he said. 'I'm feeling all right.'

Then Julie came on again. She must have grabbed the phone.

'The trip's next Friday,' she said. 'We'll go in Ethel's car.'

'Nothing like living dangerously,' I said, not mentioning the suggestion that I should drive.

*

I'm not sure precisely when we realised that the spirits embraced by the West Sussex Convention of Soul Travel Experiences belonged to animal wildlife and family pets, not so much to their owners or anyone else; early on, I believe, after we thought it was just an inclusive 'all God's creatures' thing. You tend not to go into detail with crank stuff. It explained a lot, though, especially Charles Lovell Darling the ham-fisted taxidermist. Things grew hazy towards the end. We'd made lots of assumptions after examining the website and reading up on it as best we could. But the written literature is scant: Soul Travellers embody exclusivity in word-of-mouth correspondence. The West Sussex website refers to 'blessed entities' or 'obedient companions' or 'devoted friends', hardly ever to human beings by name so the 'souls' we may have assumed were human were the opposite. Mutts, cats, hamsters - and presumably Bob Berridge's albino carthorse, standing like a giant sculpture in its shed, and the mighty but spirited-away Shergar, though I'd have betted a cert on Bob not being a Soul Traveller.

Soul Traveller beliefs originated in religious philosophy, ethnicity and social movement, as an offshoot of Christianity but not a rejection of it. Travellers, their name also embodying the nomadic 'missionary' tendencies as a means of disseminating their creed, were known in the 18th century but may have been around in the 17th, even the 16th. The Travellers themselves are now thinly spread, in decline, difficult to locate and regarded as odd but harmless. While the Bible is the source of their faith, they believe it is not enough to reach divine revelation and that doctrinal conflicts and human capacity for harm and guilt interfere with their devotion.

Their goal therefore is to internalise the living spirit of God in creatures with none of these tendencies and then to preserve it so that, through the perfection of extra-sensory powers (holding hands, and the frequent mantra-like humming repetition of the word 'Herm'), God's spirit will be revealed within each sickly human like a rosebud opening and will perform the miracle of a cure, helped by natural remedies. Individual humans recognised as having played a part in developing such remedies were revered or placed beyond the criticism aimed at those who would attack the stricken human body - say, with chemicals and X-rays - wherein resided the Holy Spirit, like some sleeping comforter, and destroy it. This emphasis on sentient creatures meant that vegetarianism or veganism were pre-requisites for Soul Travellers.

I relate all this while barely able to staunch a titter. It turned out that Ellen G. Darling, wife of Charles Lovell Darling – yes, she did exist - had founded something called the Good Book Christian Church in 1810. Through the ages, Soul Travellers were encouraged to adopt their own approaches to the basic doctrine and Ellen's variation, further elaborated by her brother, was popular in West Sussex. Apparently.

I realised, too, that the Darlings, Charles Lovell first, became better known to Julie after she was given the book bought in Brighton. That time when I heard her shouting Darling's name into Harold's ear, she might have been repeating something he'd already told her or introducing him to someone who interested her. Ethel must have told Harold about the Darlings and Harold had told Julie, though she obviously knew about Darling before she and Ethel had met. But it's all mixed up. I wished I'd kept a proper diary. Maybe Harold had been embarrassed to mention anything about what Ethel really represented.

Anyway, when Ethel arrived to pick us up, she stepped out of the car and stood for a moment, looking to the skies. It reminded me of the ladybirds incident at Julie's new flat. She appeared to be communing. Then again, she may just have been giving thanks to no one in particular for the fine weather.

I sat in the front. Julie gave me a 'you're brave' look as she got into the back with Harold, who was looking better than I'd seen him for weeks.

Ethel's driving was still harum-scarum, hard on the brakes and gears. Consideration for other road-users was not in her gift. She still leant forwards on the steering-wheel, like someone making her way through a hostile crowd. On arrival at the car park, we skidded to a powdery halt.

Perhaps jolted into thinking about other matters, I became conscious of never having discussed with her that article in the *Observer*. We'd mentioned it, of course, in a congratulatory way straight after its appearance. But knowing that talking about it and the experience in the French countryside it described would probably have led to heated exchanges about 'belief', we kept quiet. She may well have interpreted our congratulations as the endorsement of the truth of her story, even of its significance as revelation. What the four of us knew about anything at any given time during those months - the 'Harold months', as I now refer to them, almost twenty-two - is never to be established.

We weren't far from the highest summit of the cliffs. Like the visit to Chanctonbury Ring, our arrival there had saved us a strenuous hike. They were the proverbial white cliffs of the South Coast, their bright chalkiness, though unseen at that point, appearing to beam out in illumination towards the grey-blue Channel.

Ours was the second car to arrive. No one else was around.

We set off up the slope - barely such - to the first peak on a path that eventually kept about twenty feet from the cliff edge. There was a warning notice where the car park gave on to the path at a gap in its wooden fence, and others planted in the turf at intervals as we reached the top. Once there, we were mildly breeze-blown.

'Where's Dieppe?' Julie asked.

I pointed in the general direction but the French coast couldn't be seen.

I asked Harold if he still felt OK.

'I'm fine,' he answered. 'I've always wanted to do this.'

Ethel smiled at him. After we'd gazed out to sea and reflected for a few moments, shielding our eyes from the glare, she turned to the left and continued walking. We followed. Ahead, the path rose and fell with the gentle wave-like motion of the clifftops. We could see the cliff faces now, and smaller and smaller warning notices beside the path. A couple of other strollers were vanishing over the hill in the far distance. Danger up there was a matter of common-sense. As the notices explained, you ventured towards the edge at your peril.

'Remember Chanctonbury?' I asked Harold who was walking in front of me. We were still in a group.

'Aye,' he laughed, scuffing the grass. 'It's all chalk here.'

It may have been the comment of a man who'd spent his life digging things out of the ground.

Harold stopped again and searched for France with a pessimist's blank stare of resignation. I waited for him. Ethel and Julie were walking slowly in front down a steeper but still gentle slope and chatting.

'She tells me you're off to the Darling home over there,' Harold said. 'You know, on the ferry.'

'She?'

'Your Julie. Should be interesting. The Darlings started it all, according to Ethel. Metaferon et cetera.'

I had to fight my way out of this unintelligible thicket. 'My' Julie?

'Did she? Are we?'

'Didn't you know? It must be a surprise. Don't tell her I told you.'

He turned to me then in slow motion, held back maybe by a nervous system weakened by months of treatment and the need of his cancer to open up a new front against what might turn out to be a sham, its volleys of solidified white powder no more effective than the million tons of it compressed under our feet. I wasn't sure what kind of look it was: pitying, confused, unbelieving? Or all of those? He had enough personal problems of his own without having to work out what was going on between me and Julie. Even I wasn't sure. Mona could have explained it all in a Facebook message with an attached GIF of six Labradors barking *The Star-Spangled Banner.*

Harold was standing just off the path in the direction of the sea; I was on the path, with one foot on the other side of it from him. As he turned his head away to gaze in the direction of France again, I looked left and judged Ethel and Julie to be less than a cricket pitch's length in front. Ethel was off the path on the 'dangerous' side but still within the distance separating path from warning sign. We'd really gone for the view and didn't intend to walk far. In fact, if we'd walked beyond the next dip, it would have meant a fair old climb to the next summit for Harold and presumably Ethel. So downhill was fine. The path wound slightly inland, still following the cliff contours, and would connect with another, then out of sight, to take us back to the car on a roughly circular route.

Harold and I continued walking, heads down in conversation. I knew about the Darlings and their antecedents so could bluff my way through, admitting to taking a trip with Julie that I knew nothing about. I said I was looking forward to a day out in France, even inviting him to join us.

'Oh, I thought you were spending a weekend there. Or was it a week?'

'We'll see. We haven't worked out the details yet.'

What happened next is still a muddle in my mind. All I had was approximate concepts of distance.

'What the heck!' Harold exclaimed.

He'd stopped and had grabbed me by the elbow. I thought he was having some kind of seizure. He was looking straight ahead; my whole attention was on him and what was happening to him. He raised his right arm slowly and pointed. Ethel was half-crawling, half-rolling downhill towards the edge of the cliff; each time she tried to get up, she fell forwards again, heading at an angle from the path as it began turning away from the sea. Julie was crawling after her, trying to get to her feet. But whereas Ethel's stumbling could not be helped, Julie's was almost all the result of trying to stop herself from following Ethel. Even before I'd begun running towards them, Julie had stood up and was frozen to the spot. She let go an almighty scream at the point Ethel disappeared. The scream, I recalled later, had become instantly lost in the vastness of the place. But the most vivid recollection for me is, and always will be, the split-second between Ethel being there and not being there. Because continuity was broken in an instant.

Just before the path began its left curve parallel to the inward sweep of the clifftop, at the point where Ethel must have fallen and begun her descent, the distance between the path and the edge was four feet less than it was where we'd stopped to look for France. Other places along the cliffs were three feet less, though not at downward locations where a fall could be especially dangerous. Since then, the whole path has been marked out to make it safer. I remembered the measurements; they were part of the enquiry, the inquest. The facts were important. We'd had to go up there, you see, with the police and the men with tape measures, and other officials with doubt written on their faces. Broken continuity; it wasn't like that when Harold died.

The accident was featured on local and national TV and in the daily papers. The three of us were approached for quotes but the police kept reporters away. Or maybe the Press didn't after all feel it right to bother us. In any case, the incident soon gave way to follow-ups about clifftop dangers. There was even a BBC Sussex TV 'special'; I remember the signature sounds of gulls crying. Apt, I thought, though I knew they were just hungry.

*

It was Harold who told us that Ethel wanted to be buried in a basket.

We were in his company almost all the time after her death, especially when the official coming and going had ended and we seemed to be waiting for something to be said, something that would explain things.

As you do when a person you know has passed on, we got to talking about her. That was when we raised the subject of Soul Travel at length for the first time. Having discovered the West Sussex lot and Ethel's place among them, Julie and I never mentioned it to anyone else, not even Harold. Why? We wanted to see if their connection with it would manifest itself. I suppose Julie's initial objection to taking Metaferon as a stupid, even irresponsible, exercise was a reaction against Soul Travel hocus-pocus, short of censuring it out in the open. But I had to tell her that one didn't have to be a Soul Traveller or anything else extraordinary to believe in homoeopathic medicine.

Harold was either evasive or semi-ignorant of what Julie surprisingly and mistakenly called 'the occult'. She knew about the Soul Travel's Christian connection through the Darlings. But things had happened too fast for us to set aside issues for discussion. And I'd passed the stage of querying a possible solecism. Ethel's family, none of whom we knew except from passing mention once or twice, were looming. A few were staying at her house, the ones we'd met after the accident. Funeral arrangements hadn't been discussed because of the autopsy and everything. Until Harold did.

'Wicker,' he said while in a bit of a daze soon after the initial shock had passed. 'She was adamant. It had to be a wicker basket. In a field.'

'A field?' I said. 'A basket?'

'Aye. She wants to be buried with Mother Nature, in a special plot out Lancing way. They all know about it.'

By 'they', he could have meant Ethel's family or the Soul Travel lot (aka the Readers). Then he clarified.

'It's this group she belongs to. The Convention.'

I laughed out loud. Julie looked at me crossly. Harold leant forwards and must have been about to ask if I were all right.

'It sounds like some rock band: Ethel Chrimes and The Soul Travellers.'

If it did, neither of them saw or appreciated the joke. By that time, events were pulling me down - Harold's cancer, Julie's mental state, Ethel's death - and in such circumstances, I would do or say something off the track.

It turned out that the family did indeed know about Ethel's funerary wishes.

*

Far Horizon Green Burials had erected a small canopy in the corner of its field near the Old Shoreham Road. It was an idyllic spot. The deep blue sky was sewn with vapour trails. Across the field in rows, it looked as if a small orchard was establishing itself in one corner and spreading outwards. Everything about Far Horizon was green. The emerald vehicle we followed from Ethel's house (the body had been returned after investigations) was a cross between a traditional hearse and a van. We watched her dark green basket-coffin lifted on to a green trap drawn by a pony and followed it on foot down a dreamy, leafy lane flanked by an avenue of youngish trees in long grass. It reminded me of a fantasy world populated by midgets, hobbits. The grass in the field itself was cropped to make it look wild but not overgrown. In the distance was a rectangular pit and beside it, a mound of earth covered in an Astroturf blanket. You knew it was a grave but it looked out of place, covert almost, as if what was about to be done there was forbidden.

The committal was non-committal and read by an indeterminately religious person whom I half-recognised as one of those present at the Reading Group's seaside meeting. The travelling soul but not Soul Travel as such was mentioned twice. Then the basket was lowered into the ground before we were ushered towards the little green marquee for tea and sandwiches. I guessed that the provision of all these extras was weather-dependent.

As we were talking and deftly balancing green paper cups and plates, I spotted a figure walking down the far side of the field with what looked like long paper scrolls under his arm. A surveyor? When he saw us, he turned about and re-traced his steps. Musing for a few minutes, my cheeks filled hamster-like with strange cress-and-pickle sarnies, I turned and looked in vain above Ethel's grave for her soul, some large foggy cloudlet (she was a big lady) rising and hovering with difficulty before it started off, not so much travelling quickly as making slow-ish progress towards infinity, towards Worthing and then south to the Continent, before dashing around noisily and out of control like a deflating balloon and its squirt of raspberries: a human soul chasing whatever animal had nurtured the spirit of God in readiness to make her better if she were seriously ill. But the end had been unexpected and quick. I never really understood how Soul Travel worked.

Only when Julie, Harold and I were walking away with some of the others did we notice a group of four or five wandering back into the field again. Stopping short of Ethel's grave, they formed a circle and held hands. If you'd listened closely, you would have heard words spoken and then an almost inaudible humming, drowned by the noise from a plane taking off at Brighton City Airport. For every human not requiring intercession of the spirit being incubated in wildlife, there were countless others, like Harold, who needed it to be kept alive. Or so I assumed. For a second, I imagined every animal in the area, high or low, stopping to listen, open-mouthed and humanised, as if in a Walt Disney tableau. The ground beneath my feet began teeming with life beyond human vision. I should have known that there'd be no ham sandwiches.

A week or so later, when the earth had settled on Ethel's grave, real turf laid and her grave-marker tree planted - a sapling ash - I realised that they'd been not paper scrolls I'd seen but polythene tubes to protect the young trees from gnawing animals; rabbits mostly, but goodness knows what else. A few of the trees had succumbed; others were rockets, primed for flight in their cylinders. The holy spirit in their gnawing enemies must have been having a rough ride.

Burial in the wild. What next? Or, rather, who? Poor Harold himself, I'm afraid. But not in a field.

So Long, Old Chap

It was a vigil, more like; not one second here and the next gone, over the edge. Towards the end, the bedroom curtains were drawn and the death scene was bathed in low electric light. I'm sure the Reading Club members, aka the Soul Travellers, saw it as some kind of ritual observance, miracles having failed. Not many family to speak of either. The Travellers travelled up and down stairs to make gallons of tea. I wondered if their doleful expressions were due to the slow passing of a friend (if not a convert: I never really found out), the failure of Ethel's wonder drug, or the absence of Ethel herself, their leader, another of their friends. The only exception to the standing around and the ethereal coming and going was the care nurse from the company I'd suggested and hired. She was well rehearsed - knew that Harold, surviving on whatever mechanism of his late desperate remedy was at work in keeping him alive and alert, would without much warning sink further and die, like a sick animal and, again like a sick animal, do so without complaining. He made odd whimpering sounds whenever anyone spoke to him. I had to smile at one point, imagining that his soul wanted to be up and travelling and was trying to make him let go and that he was holding on to it like a miner straining to hold in place a fully-laden coal trolley threatening a runaway. Now and then, he would clench his fists, then return his hands obediently to their formal repose. Pain and the dissipation of pain, I assumed.

For most of the time, he was silenced by the nurse's opiates. She obviously knew how much he needed to maintain his almost beatific state. Using the upstairs loo a couple of days before he died, I opened the vanity cupboard on the wall above the wash basin. Inside was his latest box of Metafix and its last remaining foil sheet with just three of its blisters lanced and their contents downed. On the window sill was a small beaker with water still in it; around the basin itself, some shaved stubble a few days old. He'd obviously given up on the Metaferon when his body told him all was lost but had kept shaving to keep up an appearance. At the beginning of the end, the nurse had offered him an electric razor, which he'd declined. Sometimes you have to wait for the end well before it begins. Even Ethel, I thought, might have realised that a Metaferon tablet was just a microscopic portion of Beta-dioxymetasalicilate buried in a lump of chalk and as irretrievable as old Tobler's bear was, hidden in his Alpine logo.

Julie had organised the visiting arrangements. We'd told those relatives we knew of that Harold had a few weeks left, maybe less. Two or three came, others sent their excuses by letter, their handwritten notes in an envelope a reflection of all forms of distance. Wesley came round, then Aurora (someone had to supervise the Crazy Gang). Joe and Phyllis arrived together, the first time walking away because they didn't want to ring the bell and make a noise - so they said. The only ones there on the last two days were me, Mary, Julie and one delegated member of the Reading Club, possibly on Soul Travel duty as well and looking for a sign. Oh, and I almost forgot: the vicar of St Bartholomew's, who put in several appearances during the Metaferon period as though called upon by some invisible directive to counter the forces of heresy, that's if he knew about the involvement of the West Sussex Convention at all or indeed if it were heretical. You can never tell these days. One of the remote family members who contacted us was from Marje's side - just one. He was unforthcoming and twirled his hat a lot by the rim. I got the impression that he'd come too late to impart something that might have been useful but which he'd forgotten on his long journey. There's so much about which we get intimations but nothing detailed and firm. And without it, we are left with supposition or surmise or no inclination to speculate at all. Certainly not much to write about.

Mona came to the funeral at St Barts but kept away from the last dim days in Harold's bedroom. It was a fairly long journey for her. I didn't ask Julie if she could put her up. It would have been too complicated. By that time, I don't think Julie would have been suspicious. I could have explained that Mona had been cut from the TV documentary. Julie would probably have just accepted it. She was so bound up with Harold's problems in those late days and cultivating a relationship with Ethel - or not. I couldn't work out the details of the latter. Then again, she might have been jealous of Mona and wanting to know if there was any romantic connection between us and threatening to walk away again or cite it as proof that our renewal was a sham obscured by our joint concern for Harold.

Wesley and Aurora turned up at St Barts like a comic turn, Wesley in a Teddy Boy outfit and Aurora bound in what looked like clothes made from multicoloured rags.

The morning after Harold died and the funeral director had left, Wesley was in the garden surrounded by the Gang who were looking our way dumbfounded while Wesley, the father of at least three of them so Harold reckoned, was pointing to the bedroom window, now with its curtains open, as in the scene from *Raleigh's Boyhood.*

Maybe he was using the example of the cat skeleton to explain what had happened to Harold. How you explain cremation to kids I'll never know. Harold was cremated. Nothing to be disinterred, no miracle-working spirit to be chastised for not doing its job.

Did it say something about the members of his family who turned up for the funeral that they acceded without reservation to his wish for me to scatter his ashes at his old place of work?

The Lesser Ouse

What is life like where a river meets the sea - where, beside West Beach in Littlehampton, the Arun begins its eager rush to the English Channel and the Ouse its more hesitant flow to meet it farther along the coast at Newhaven? What would we do without the pathetic fallacy of rivers rushing or flowing with human eagerness and hesitancy? (Julie had alerted me to the 'pathetic fallacy'. You could do English at Lancaster without knowing for sure what it meant. 'Google it,' she said.)

Bass and mullet can be caught in the tidal reaches of the Ouse at Piddinghoe. Sea trout run up the river as far as Barcombe Mills, north of Lewes. Eels and flounders are also present, especially at low water. Tactics are needed to catch these inhabitants of brackish reaches. Lures will attract the bass in low light on a flooding tide.

The groynes at West Beach and other places restrict the eastward transportation of sediment. Chalk dominates the coastal geology and forms the prominent ridgeline of the South Downs visible from the sea. Unique underwater chalk cliffs stretch from Brighton to Worthing, the Sussex coast being the only location in Britain at which chalk strata exist as both reefs and cliffs. Dunes have formed at Climping beach at the mouth of the Arun, a spit exists across the estuary at Shoreham on the river Adur and there are sedimentary deposits at Newhaven harbour. This is where Dover sole spawns and sea trout and elvers follow migratory routes.

How do I know all this, all this dull recitation of facts?

After Ethel and Harold died in quick succession, it read like a balm, sentences following each other in orderly succession, without the jolts and disruptions of controversy; read, too, like quiet observations of what might be interesting or useful, not just to fishermen but to those fascinated by the world outside themselves and their concerns: facts about chalk that did not involve a woman falling off a cliff but reminded one of an awesome albino carthorse impossibly occupying a stable; and about Worthing that would no longer see a sick ex-coalminer chugging along the front in a toy train.

Julie and I were having an early pub lunch before catching the Newhaven ferry to Dieppe. While she was in the loo, I was reading all this stuff in a wall display below a criss-cross of fishing rods and beside a cutting from the *Sussex Express.* Under the headline, 'Superfit Sea Trout Return Annually to the Ouse' was a letter from Dr Keith Corbett of Newhaven:

> The sea trout of the Ouse catchment attain larger sizes than do most other UK stocks, and unlike their salmon relatives which only survive but one spawning after returning from the sea to the river to breed then die, our superfit species can successfully return annually up to five times over their life span.
>
> I once worked in the Ministry of Fisheries' freshwater research laboratory. Perhaps more importantly I'd already been captivated by the angling on the Sussex Ouse, which I had started back in the 1950s. (My grammar school teachers often wondered where I was off playing truant - now they know!)
>
> However, that happy period of my life was spoilt by those summers when many sea trout were trapped in the warming water of their main

> fishing pool at Barcombe Mills, with slow deaths then following via the ulcerating disease furunculosis. This lamentable situation arose via a negligent combination of the Ouse Preservation Society and local farmers demanding that water be held back uncompromisingly for upstream agricultural benefits.
> All that was needed was a temporary overnight opening of the sluice gate in and out the main pool. But would they? No, and the needless loss of these splendid fish continued unabated over each hot summer. Shame on them!

Fitness, happy summers, negligence, slow deaths, furunculosis. It was a wonder I hadn't found Harold suffering from the delayed effects of dust on the lungs: pneumoconiosis. He'd told me about it and I'd Googled it too. Our happiness is rarely spoiled by thoughts of others toiling on our behalf underground, where they are as good as trapped.

From that display, I also learned about the famous people associated with the place. They included Ho Chi Minh, who worked there as a pastry cook in 1913 and was an enthusiastic rat-catcher; and Charles Lovell Darling, author of *The Unkempt House* and 'noted' taxidermist. On our way out, I showed Julie the Darling reference. 'Ah,' she said, but it did not detain her.

Beyond the breakwater, the Channel was rough. Our French ferry was tethered at the mouth of the river in quiet water. Having stowed the car and gone up on deck, I looked down, wondering if Dr Corbett's super-fit sea trout were so agile that, like dolphins, they broke the water's surface in their riverrun urge to proliferate. (Julie had told me about 'riverrun'; I loved it; I'm sure she said it was a word coined by her beloved James Joyce). Once boarded, I assumed we'd put to sea despite the conditions. I overheard another passenger saying that French ferries sailed in all weathers. Ours did; and it was on time.

Harold had been dead for two months. I'd been back at the theatre but still spending time with Julie at her new place when I could; it was a long journey down. A remote next-of-kin had taken on the sale of Harold's house. With Ethel out of the way, as it were, the Reading Club members had departed the scene, as well as whatever dual role they'd had as Soul Travellers. Maybe in their latter guise, they preferred to be invisible. I'd popped in to see Wesley and Aurora, and then Joe and Phyllis. The Crazy Gang had encircled me on Harold's driveway, asking me about their former neighbour and explaining to me how he'd been 'burned' and how his 'ash was in a pot'. I'd thought of extending my family searches with Harold as my starting point but I'd always thought, despite his hospitality and friendliness, that whatever we were seeking had long gone. I'd be an interloper chasing people who didn't want to know. It's a cynical and suspicious world.

We sat in the caféteria area at the back of the boat. A rolling swell made crockery and cutlery slide, like objects moved by an unseen hand. Two passengers rushed to the loo, hands covering their mouths.

'Harold would have enjoyed this trip,' I said. Julie nodded as if dumb. She was reading a magazine. 'He told me you'd organised it.'

I meant that I knew she had – obviously – but that he'd told me before she'd announced it.

'How did he know?'

I thought of what that question signified, the extent of her curiosity, the state of her memory for events that had happened in a straight line. I wanted to say, 'You told him,' but I just shrugged.

I had to take time off work at The Edge, citing some family crisis, which in a sense is what it was. I'd let her tell me things about Charles Lovell Darling and his wife that I'd told her myself. What was it about him that interested her? *The Unkempt House* was the middling chronicle of a semi-bohemian life in London at the end of the 19th-century. It might have been autobiographical. There were name-dropped mentions of celebrities he might have seen and conversed with - Robert Ross, Richard Middleton, Arthur Machen - but no evidence of deep friendships or involvements with them. These were minor writers which suggested he was a lesser figure than they. Perhaps he was their kin as much as Harold was mine: a man wishing to connect but with no real prospect of doing so and with skills that didn't really come up to the line. I never thought Harold's talent for art was any less than mine for acting; neither was much to write home about. The thought had been wobbling around in my mind, refusing to be stilled, until I saw the pictures of Darling's stuffed animals. Even for an amateur, they were third-rate with an amateur's blind ignorance of the monstrosities that over-enthusiasm and lack of self-criticism can create: an impossibly bloated jackdaw, a cross-eyed owl, an unevenly-packed vixen made to sit in a chair like something out of Beatrix Potter, its tongue a flat leather substitute for the real thing. Perhaps the wall of The White Lion, Newhaven, was the most prominent reference to him, sitting improbably beside the founder of the Indo-Chinese Communist Party.

It was a short journey. We went aloft to watch the ferry dock. As we slowed almost to a standstill, with Dieppe moving closer and for a few minutes enveloping us, Julie put her arms around my waist. I responded by putting my arm across her shoulders and pulling her towards me.

She was so frail. What was she feeling? My reaction, as so often, was protective.

'We'll look up the others too,' she said.

I didn't know what she meant but I went along with it. As far as I knew, we were having a few days of rest in a different place after all we'd been through and looking up Charles Lovell Darling, or what remained of him. Did the French have the equivalent of our Blue Plaques? Maybe there was one attached to the house in Newhaven where he'd lived. We should have got there early and found out or looked it up beforehand.

'Who shall we call on first?' she asked.

'I don't know. You choose.'

'What about Oscar Wilde?'

'Why not? And then?'

'Whistler or Sickert, the painters?'

'Sounds good.' (I knew who Whistler and Sickert were.)

'Calling on' these characters suggested that they were still alive, which is how I imagined Julie saw them - presences without voices or perhaps that as well.

I never knew these people had a Dieppe connection until I Googled the place after Harold had told me that Julie planned to take me there. Wilde had gone straight to Dieppe after his release from Reading Jail; it was also where he handed the manuscript of *De Profundis* to Robert Ross. (I once auditioned for Lord Caversham in *An Ideal Husband.* Leaving the room, I looked back at the three auditioners at their trestle table and saw one shaking his head. I never discovered what it was about my reading that had made them reject me.) Wilde had been shunned in Dieppe. Only fellow decadents such as Ernest Dowson and some Parisian poets wanted to be seen with him. Dowson introduced him to the local brothel. Aubrey Beardsley also lived in Dieppe for a while. But there was no mention of Charles Lovell Darling.

This state Julie had wandered into, of a reality whose details and features she assumed I knew about, was one I could never get used to. Indeed, it was the final stage of my denial that she needed help. It was a stage of irresponsibility on my part, the conniving at something I knew was not in her interest. At times my complicity, intended to avoid a disruption of what to her passed for normal, must have bordered on criminal neglect. But it was easy for me to comply: I'd spent most of my working life in conditions of make-believe; so had she. We were made for each other. Only hers had an extra dimension. When she snapped out of her imagined life, it was often into another in which there was sometimes a cast of characters, some with speaking parts. It goes without saying, though I think I've already said it, that she was on permanent medication. I always tried to act my way into what she believed to be real - like admitting knowledge of things she'd done and organised without telling me, or believing she'd told me, and getting mad at me for not remembering (that's when I forgot to pretend that I remembered). That trip to France, for example, that used to take an hour on the Newhaven-Dieppe packet and often ended in a cloud of fog at the centre of town.

On the first night we slept like Darby and Joan, a couple who'd done with sex and never regretted it and no longer thought it important. The following day, we walked down a street named after Wilde and had a drink at his favourite brasserie, Le Café Tribunaux. We could find no memorials to Wilde and the other luminaries. That night though, after discovering a Madame Brodeur whose house had an upper room devoted to Charles Lovell Darling, our lovemaking was mutually consuming. I'd never known Julie be so tender. We touched each other like connoisseurs fondling Meissen figurines. As in the early days, we gave ourselves to each other as innocents unaware of what among our future discoveries might make us wary or inhibited but certain that we were in the presence of something, call it truth, as fragile as porcelain. Only after we slumped on our backs and heard a distant foghorn did I think of Mona and realise that I preferred the struggle to find Julie's essence to the ease with which I could reach Mona Strange's uncomplicated core. I promised myself to persevere, even if it meant looking after Julie when she denied needing help and fought against its approach.

The next morning Madame Brodeur was waiting for us. Someone had told her father about Darling years before and a UK trust now sent money to keep his upper room - then a garret - presentable to visitors. Admission was five euros. She took our money and handed us each a well-thumbed laminated sheet of information. Much of it was about his taxidermy, of which there were a dozen examples in the room as well as a writing desk, a cabinet of books and a hat-stand with a green bowler and an Inverness cape. There was also a large, framed photograph of Darling above the mantelpiece. Soul Travel and Darling's place in its development were treated at length. A lot of information was provided about Mrs Darling, and about the link between taxidermy and Soul Travel theory. The most eerie exhibit was a recording by Darling and friends on cassette tape of the 'Herm' mantra. I'd just clicked 'Start' on the recorder when I heard the most frightful crash. Madame Brodeur had left us to it but was obviously not far away and entered the room in seconds. I looked around to find Julie standing before the picture with a hefty book in her hand. She'd smashed the glass. Poor old Darling, as though his philosophy were not obscure enough, now stared at us through a shattered mosaic as the chant continued. I apologised and handed Madame Brodeur an excessive wad of euros to pay for the damage. Perhaps a mother herself, or a woman who had known stress and its wild perimeters, she took the money and laid a hand on my shoulder as I escorted Julie away.

Misadventure & Disturbed Minds

One Thursday, Julie was travelling by coach to the Lake District. At Knutsford services on the M6, the coach made a scheduled stop. None of the other passengers, who had disembarked to revive themselves in the overhead café straddling the carriageways, saw her wandering about aimlessly before heading for the petrol station and the slipway exit. At 1:15pm she ran through a hedge on to the hard shoulder beneath the café and threw herself under a lorry. Passengers queuing for food and drink or already seated on the south-facing side saw scores of vehicles piling into each other for about a quarter of a mile as the lorry braked. It had been raining. The accident site took twelve hours to clear. Amazingly, there were no other fatalities. The weird thing was, she'd bought a double Twix at the garage shop.

I was at the theatre, superintending a matinée, when my phone rang at 3pm. It was the police. They had found Julie's mobile; it had been knocked out of her jacket on impact and had slid beyond the accident site.

There weren't many names on her contacts page. They'd tried ringing a couple in the alphabetical list before mine without success. I was in there with her parents, Mack and Dorothy Williams, but she'd listed them as M and Dot, so the names didn't mean anything. They'd rung Bronwen, among the first on the list, and she'd told them to look for me, Francis. The caller asked me if I were a friend of Julie Williams, knowing that I was. I smiled because it sounded like a test of my allegiance. I said yes. I always thought of Julie as Williams rather than Redmayne. The caller then asked me to prepare for some bad news. Funnily enough, my immediate reaction on hearing about the accident was to feel sorry for the woman on the other end of the line who had to tell me about it and whether or not a female police-officer had been chosen because the 'deceased', as Julie was later referred to at the inquest, was female too. But the oddest thing was that, as soon as I was told how Julie had died, the photo she kept of Ringo, her cat, shot up before me like one of those fairground rifle targets zinging pock-marked to an upright position for more punishment. Ringo, a soul travelling back to his mistress, and joining her in whatever passed for the abode of the eternally disembodied.

After confirming that Julie indeed was, had been, my friend, I didn't know what to say. Bronwen had told the police about Mack and Dorothy but the officer had rung me because Bronwen had said that Julie and I were 'an item'. She asked me if I were OK, then told me that Mack and Dorothy had been informed. In an odd way, I always saw myself as Julie's next-of-kin, thinking of what might have been had we not bounced off each other so often instead of coming together for good or ill.

My office door was open - hardly an office, as I think I've said, more a tarted-up store cupboard - and shuffling past, ready to go on stage, were the characters of Pozzo with his slave Lucky at the end of a tether. The play was Beckett's *Waiting for Godot.* I'd once understudied for it at a different time and in a different place. It was as if it were coming back to give me another chance. Lucky was short, about five-four; it had been an inspired piece of casting for an actor whose range was probably restricted by his height. Lucky was making the most of it, already grimacing and salivating on to the filthy rags he was wearing - 'getting into character', as amateur thespians say. Pozzo looked like Laurence Olivier in *The Entertainer.* For the ridiculous Pozzo, Lucky is little more than a craven beast. Then they were gone, leaving a space, a Beckett-type desolate void that reflected my own. I wanted to re-call the policewoman, just to speak, to hear her tell me the kind of things I probably wouldn't want to hear, to have a chat about our mutual feelings of horror and helplessness; I wouldn't want to be a police-officer, always clearing up various sorts of mess. I wanted to know where Julie, Julie's body, was. I wanted to ask her how Mack and Dot had taken the news and if someone had called on them rather than phoned. I needed to contact them and commiserate. We hadn't had a lot of contact, though Julie and I visited them fairly often. I believe I made more sense to them than she did, despite her modest fame. Sometimes Mack would stare at me as though I were the son-in-law he would never have. But I probably delude myself. Maybe he was willing me to disappear from her life for whatever reason a parent might have, in the case of Mack and Dot one to do with a daughter with problems they felt obliged to deal with, preferably on a one-to-one, or two-to-one, basis. I'll never know. Dot, who'd been in amateur musicals, was in awe of us both. That's not my opinion; it's what she told us as Mack stoked clouds of smoke from his pipe to obliterate embarrassment. Possibly.

Ethel's inquest made the national newspapers. There'd been a few paragraphs about the accident itself but not many. The inquest raised an issue: the safety of the UK's clifftop walks. Beachy Head was cited as a place that would have to be barred to visitors if its high suicide rate were to be reduced to zero. But Ethel's was not a suicide and the repercussions were greater. The National Trust and the Ramblers Association were called to give evidence. The coroner, recording a verdict of death by misadventure, grabbed his fourpenn'orth by asking all coastal landowners to ensure greater safety of their high paths. They still walk above Seaford but on routes farther in from the cliff edge.

Julie's was my second inquest. That was in the papers too: *M-way Horror: Writer threw Herself in Front of Lorry.* I gave testimony at both, in Ethel's case as an observer who only saw what happened when it was too late, and in Julie's as, well, her live-out lover. It was pointless denying that Julie suffered from social anxiety syndrome; her doctor said so. I didn't say anything about the voices but said I was often concerned that she lived too much 'in her own world'. Everyone else - Bronwen, her parents, for instance - seemed not to know the extent of her disability; but why should they have? She disguised it so well. What was idiosyncrasy to them was something more serious to me, which she could nevertheless contain. Her publisher painted a picture of her that I didn't recognise, praising her talent and promise. She left no note. In Julie's case, the coroner took the opportunity to highlight her gifts as a writer. Had he read her books? I doubt it.

After the Dieppe incident and when we'd returned to her place near Harold's, I'd told her she had to get help. She promised to, and just like other times, I left her feeling that she suddenly knew what she might be capable of. When I asked her why she'd smashed Darling's picture, she said: 'It was for Harold.' I only interpreted that one way. The coroner decided she'd taken her own life while the balance of her mind was disturbed. I never knew why she was heading for The Lakes on the M6. She hadn't told me. But I knew that where she'd killed herself was like the place we'd stopped at on the

M40 on the way south. I've never read anything into that. Maybe I should. But there'd be no point.

Pretty soon, the after-shocks of that angry sow's bite persuaded me, like poor old Harold, to seek different work in a far-off place. Not long after, I responded to an advert for a post of carer here at Oakwood Lodge, wanting perhaps to help people rage against the dying light, albeit the dying of the Gloucestershire light, which is the same as the dying of the light everywhere else except that it has a name that makes it in theory at least peculiar, elusive, out of the ordinary, as the name *Anax imperator* lifts the Blue Emperor above the undifferentiated mass of dragonflies and the anonymity of the end that awaits them after - what, eight weeks max? An illusion, of course, like the part played by an actor or the ability of a pill called Metafix to see off cancer. (I got that entomological stuff from another donated volume, *The Observer's Book of Pond Life* (1974), inscribed 'Edward Petroc White, Glendower House, Monmouth School for Boys, 1981'. Wonder what happened to him.)

Big Pit

That afternoon, the end of the world had come to Blaenavon. Not nigh but accomplished. All Harold's 'black gold' had been torn and funnelled from the depths and the skies were dark and thunderous and skewed with slanting acid rain. That was it. There was no going back, no longer any hope or optimism. Humanity had mostly fled. The trees were scorched and bare, the cattle in the fields lay 'dead' or were stuck in mud like sculptures, the old mine - Harold's mine - a museum piece that had become a real museum.

There were three others in the waiting-room: a foreign group of two adults and a young girl about eight years old. I couldn't place the language. Polish? Romanian? Russian, possibly? Sitting in pews salvaged from a disused Baptist chapel (it said), we watched a video of the mine's history: time re-cycled on a loop, a pack of postcards being dealt, including several of grim contestants in a moustache competition, and many smeared torsos hewing their way out of a tunnel in which they'd been confined. Sitting in front, the adults were explaining the video's story to the child in a low unintelligible tongue but she showed only fleeting interest and spent most of the time staring at me, paying my respects behind them and clutching a shoe box. I wondered if she'd ever shared a cage at a wildlife park with marmosets.

Through an authentic dirty window, we saw the winding-wheel start to spin. After ten minutes, a door opened and the guides, former miners, stood there as if daring us to enter before we were invited. Behind them, the previous group were climbing out of their orange work suits and removing their miners' helmets. Then they were gone. Dilwyn beckoned us forward. We knew it was Dilwyn because he told us and it was written on his lapel badge. I'd already informed the management of my wish to scatter ashes below ground and they'd obviously told Dilwyn. He didn't remember anyone called Harold Taylor. His mates looked the four of us up and down and decided on our overall and helmet sizes. We were in the wings. Dimly lit, the place was running with damp, its walls decorated with pipes and valves, naked conduits and motors. We put our costumes on and followed Dilwyn to the open cage. The other miners started laughing. They were all looking our way. Maybe Dilwyn had pulled a short straw of some kind and they were sharing a joke at his expense. The previous group had played its part; we were on next, Dilwyn our Chorus of information. We huddled together as he clanged the cage door shut. Up there in the fly tower of this abandoned playhouse, we were about to descend to the stage.

Harold, I recalled, had told me about life underground, how it wasn't about fraternity at all, but often about enmity; the removal below of whatever animosities governed life on the surface, but played out against a different background. He also told me they let the cage drop freely and put the brakes on at the last minute. I watched Dilwyn's hands and wondered whether or not they would operate the brake mechanism, wherever it was. But the walls of the shaft slid past fairly slowly until they couldn't be seen. 'Falling freely' didn't mean at the end of four hundred feet of slack cable which had to be fed out until we stopped with a jolt that would have killed us. The brake must have been applied by the winding-gear operator outside. I don't know. I turned to see the child looking up at me in her comical child's coalminer outfit. She was staring at me again while talking in Polish or Romanian or Russian to her adult minders, her parents, communicating to them exactly what I was doing in case they had to intervene. Or she may have been having a conversation with me or asking me a question about whether there were ponies and canaries to be seen once we began our subterranean tour; they'd both appeared on the video among the pre-film era stills. The way Dilwyn winked at me suggested that he could understand what the child was saying but wasn't going to let on. Depositing human ashes or not, what was a single bloke doing on the Big Pit visit anyway, in that weather - one who'd obviously never laboured for wages? If only he'd known. I smiled back at the child and thought of her as someone going to work with the adult miners. I knew a bit about that; it was on the video too but probably lost on the youngster. Like most other kids, explanations of adult ways involving her weren't sought. Afterwards maybe, as Dilwyn explained and they translated about ponies hauling coal and canaries dropping dead in their cages at the first sign of gas, she would sit down and listen intently, perplexed by the inexplicable cruelties of the world.

It was at that point down below when Dilwyn got us to turn off our helmet lamps and we stood there in the supreme example of darkness, of black nothingness, that I performed my *coup de théâtre*. Dilwyn had agreed to give me two minutes while he talked, mainly to the child, in a disembodied voice. I opened the urn containing Harold's grey ashes and let them fall. Even they turned to invisible blackness, there being no light to make them stand out. Without illumination, there can be nothing. It was death's dominion, a place to which others were already leading me.

Re-emerging after our tour, I noticed that some of the ashes had stuck to my orange suit. I flicked them off. It was just as we entered the final area of the tour where miners would return whatever it was they had to take underground - some tab or other - that I saw the cages. There were four of them, two piled upon two, and in each one a canary; not stuffed like a Charles Lovell Darling exercise in preserving the former domicile of the Holy Spirit but as lively as Norm, their more colourful (and talented) cousin. Beside the cages was a newspaper clipping with a picture of a blackened miner holding one of the cages, as if he'd collected its occupant from a pet shop as a replacement for one whose death had spared a hundred lives. The headline was: *Saved by the Bird.*

Flock

One morning, after a round with the pill trolley, (Bob Berridge had called it my 'Zonk Bus'), I was in the kitchen, doodling Harold's life travels on a piece of paper: south from Old Westmorland to the Welsh coalfields, back to Cumbria, and south again to Sussex, his wife jettisoning herself en route. He might have been trying to escape from something; a travelling soul in flight.

Harold was a coalminer and an artist. A miner would surely have wanted to avoid a life underground, not go looking for it, as he did at Blaenavon. Did the artist's life raise a late possibility of exit? Did the modesty of recognition in the book about collier-painters signal the existence of a barrier as yielding but as impenetrable as the seam of coal he hacked and churned at, day in day out? I'd never got round to those kinds of personal enquiry. Not that I would have received any useful answer. At the end of his days, I guess I represented a possible expansion of his horizons when all he saw was everything contracting. There may have been an element of cruelty to that, under-scored by those sunset panoramas on the South Coast.

He must have viewed me and Julie as people who cared about him, though the rupture of concern represented by our difference of opinion with Ethel over Metaferon must have confused him or made him despair. I'd discounted the possibility that, as a lost relative found by me, virtually a stranger, he did not wish to be discovered for any number of reasons; I think he would have told me if that had been the case. The subject of pitworker unity had never arisen - it was in the queue - although a clip of Arthur Scargill had popped up on the TV for some reason, eliciting from Harold the remark: 'Poor old Arthur.' I knew that Harold had left the mines to take some labouring job in a foundry before retirement.

I thought more of his family might have attended the funeral. Then again, I recalled a few family ones of mine where I'd intended to be present but at the last minute had decided to forgo. Not turning up at a family funeral is a measure of one's connectedness or lack of it. In the end, no one cares, having accepted the distances between family members and all they signify. I have not been able to bring myself to write about Julie's funeral: too much death, too many leave-takings, some things too personally harrowing to share. It was a simple, straightforward business, the circumstances of her death not mentioned.

Mona withdrew as well, I guess for the same reason that I was attracted to her: the entertaining shallowness that came across as innocence which would have required me, with her enthusiasm, to take control of our relationship. Julie had needed someone else's guiding hand for a totally different reason. We'd ended up estranged even when we were together, my concern matched by her lack of awareness of it. We could probably have survived post-Harold in our own complicated way, knowing that what we valued and had in common was almost always unspoken. One little trait I loved and miss: meeting after a short gap, she'd secrete into my pocket without comment a bag of Revels which I would later share with her. If asked, in the desperate days, what had bound us, I might have said 'confectionary'. Depending on her mood, she would either have giggled or frowned at that. I miss her terribly, I miss the tensions we shared, because they always held out hope of relief and placed us both in an atmosphere of lively awareness of each other, my frequent moments of despair notwithstanding. We were both, after all, involved in the wonders of the creative imagination, me in the third division.

There may also have been strains between Julie and her friend, Bronwen. At the pub that first time, I detected some unspoken anxiety in her features: for example, the half-smile expressed by the solicitous when everyone else is doubled-up with laughter at some joke or recollection at your friend's expense - a curiously knowing half-smile. But we never got to know each other. After we'd left, I told Julie that I liked Bronwen. 'She's all right,' was her response. I didn't try hard enough to find out if Bronwen deserved better. If she'd said the same thing to someone else about Julie, it would account for why she never got to know us - me, anyway. Bronwen strolled in and out of my circle somewhere close to its perimeter but she may well have remained in contact with Julie. How could I know? Julie was secretive, and not willing to be interrogated.

Out there, wandering the high hinterlands of my existence, Bronwen would have passed my father, who I imagine might have been engaged in crude banter with Mona's dad, each hiding the extent of his dissipation. My father never talked to me about anything. He was like a lot of fathers at the time: sons of men who'd lived through a war and may have fought in it too. Teaching a budgerigar to squawk obscenities in his wife's presence was possibly the remnant of some unexamined male tendency to assert superiority over women, in the sense that it wasn't something women were likely to do. My father sometimes came home tipsy on a Saturday night. As far as I knew, he was never violent towards my mother and I never heard them arguing at the tops of their voices. They were of a generation for which education had offered sight of a Promised Land, but for reasons I've never discovered they landed on its shores, fit only for menial service. Was there a flaw, a dented gene, which would account for my flunking at Lancaster? If so, we had not the wit to acknowledge it or find a way around it. My father said he hated school because many of his teachers had seen war service and remained embattled, with him and his chums as the new enemy. I often heard him sharing memories of these flailing ex-warriors with his mates. And my mother, mentioned here only as a victim, so far removed in character from Julie that, whenever they met, there seemed not the slightest prospect of their ever understanding each other. Then Geoff, the friend I hardly ever see but my friend nonetheless. It's worth me repeating that we all have them, pretending that when we see each other rarely, it's as though we'd never been apart. It's an illusion; just a feeling, never to be tested.

Then Mona again, up there on the slopes, thinner now with all the others, befriending anyone who'd stop and listen to her. How did she get there? As a permanent refuge from Julie in that late lost phase, she was ready to consume me and I was willing to be devoured. But after Julie had gone, (pathetic description, she would have said), the Mona I expected seemed deflated overnight, shrunk to the reality of what the future with her might be like: industrial sex leavened by GIFs, Stickers, Emojis and YouTube clips of piano-playing cats. I can see Joe and Phyllis, sheltering themselves from anything that might require too much commitment; and Aurora and Wes, leaning on a rock and smoking something sweet and vaporous while their Crazy Gang leap about beyond their control.

But I do Mona and all these others the disservice I mention at the beginning. We tear and grasp at knowledge, accruing bit by bit, keeping our gains at the centre, attempting to ensure that none of it strays through forgetfulness or failure to know more than there is to be known. We often come late to understanding. My pursuit of Harold is the perfect example. I sought what I should have known; it was my late and desperate shepherding.

We are at the core of our own circles, not the centre of the universe as some detractors might comment to discredit us, but in a place of our own defining from where we try to make sense of all that goes on around us. And usually failing.

Have I included everyone involved in this story, even the ones like Bronwen who just impinge on it - the ones about whom it is difficult to learn anything? And if anyone is not included ('excluded' suggests hostility aforethought), is it not impossible to tell anything about them? Telling and showing: I can tell you the way to Cinderford from here but I can't show what awaits you when you get there (there's a statue of a coalminer wielding a pick-axe; I know that). It's the unknown rather than the unknowable. Maybe the unknowable includes what attracted me to Julie and why Julie, despite my many shortcomings, was always there beside me. Item: we were inexplicably attracted to each other. Item: yes, we were an item, a planetary pair momentarily in conjunction but each of us always on the move.

So many lives unimagined, so many people half-known, so many of the known unknowable. And is not a budgerigar taught to be foul-tongued the supreme example of both - neither knowing why it speaks nor ever able to understand what it says? And Julie's brother, whom I met only twice, both times fleetingly, and whose name - Malcolm - I had never uttered: is he still on his Catering or Food Technology course, whatever it's called? Then, beyond, these elusive people, all the happenings buried in an incomprehensible past such as the involvement of a weekly newspaper accountant in an event his journal was reporting - did they do things differently then?

Merryvale Community House (formerly Oakwood Lodge) Forest of Dean

Molly and Millie

The management's Zero Pets rule here has always been a bit wobbly. Actually, it's a new management, as we've been taken over and given a new name. It happens a lot in order that bad or indifferent reputations should be scrubbed from the record. In a place like ours not far from here, some undercover TV reporter with a hidden camera recorded incidents of abuse and the place was closed; when our former bosses knew the item was being broadcast, they feigned a transmission breakdown so that our residents shouldn't witness it, but they made sure the staff here did. It was the usual jerky footage, with raised voices, unacknowledged cries for help, blotted out faces as if viewed through a cataract (appropriate, I thought), a pile of submissive, screaming flesh on the floor. All in all, a case of the truth being too awful to confront.

Anyway, in theory most of the old rules have been retained, including the one concerning pets. Residents were once allowed them but, before my time, the place came to resemble a menagerie, with smells inside and comprehensive fouling outside, especially in the rose borders, where it was painful for gardeners to scoop the poop. Now they're more or less banned. Of course, when someone here died, as Mrs Grimaldi did not long ago, followed by Bob Berridge a few weeks later, there always used to be a problem about what to do with the pets if the deceased had left one behind. I've had to imagine next-of-kin getting into their cars clutching a cat transporter as though its occupant were destined for the local canal: it's the insouciant swing, the careless crash against the car door that tell all, possibly as much about attitudes to the person 'no longer with us' - sorry, Julie! - as the unwanted animal itself. All that said, keeping pets at Merryvale were rare events.

The version of the rule operating when Bob arrived was that an existing pet could stay until it or its owner died, whichever was the sooner, but new residents, those moving into a recently-vacated apartment, were not allowed to own them. It worked for a short while until Bob came here with two pet mice. Did he know the rule? He hadn't asked permission and they arrived with his other belongings. Bob was almost manically devoted to his pink-eyed rodents, Molly and Millie, so the management decided that all future requests should be judged on their merits, knowing that most of them – if there were any at all – would be refused. Bob set up the cage and its squeaking wheel in his bay window. Sometimes when you entered his rooms, he was half asleep and the mice were clambering all over him. It was an eerie sight, more disturbing than touching. I had to pick them off him and return them to the cage. What he couldn't do was rid the place of smelly mouse piss, however often the cage was cleaned and the room sprayed with Lavender Mist; though one wag asked how we could tell the difference between the results of Bob's incontinence and the determined peeing into fresh sawdust of Molly and Millie, their secretions boosted presumably by some pungent female hormone.

At least he and other pet-owners allowed me to suggest that the programme of talks here could be expanded by each pet-owner explaining what their animals meant to them, or had meant to them, with stories of some of their stranger exploits. Bob's talk was about mouse husbandry, which sent most of his audience to sleep, because it was aimed at those, hardly any, who might be persuaded to keep mice themselves – 'I'd like to move on now to treadmills and other means of exercise' - an event unlikely to find favour with the management on grounds of possible infestation alone. Early on, I discovered that Bob had been a bookie. All the Bs. His knowledge of horses was truly encyclopaedic. It was he who slipped me some rambling notes about Shergar, hoping that I might 'knock them into shape' for the purposes of a talk. The talk never materialised, but the Shergar notes are enshrined at the opening of this story, and dedicated to the memory of their author, Julie's possible caveats notwithstanding.

I never thought I'd write this, but those last months with first Harold and then Julie were horrendous. Friends tell me I did my best. But my best was self-centred, as I believe it must always be. I looked after them because it did me good. Not 'did me good' in the sense that serving their best interests, often a messy business (I say no more), did them good too, although in the short-term, physical sense it must have; not that either of them could have been aware of it. Some would say the ultimate act of kindness stems from knowing that those receiving your kindnesses are ignorant of it. Rather like doting pet-owners and the dull recipients of their love. What I did is called 'selfless', meaning my own interests didn't count. But it was the opposite of selfless: it was selfish. I didn't even feel as if I were doing the right thing, whatever 'right' means in this sense. It was right, meaning it was my duty, something one picks up unconsciously from upbringing, and that if you don't do your duty, you tumble in people's estimation – but, again, that's about you, about your status in the eyes of others. Failure to carry out your obligations can lead to punishment, but then it's not only your duty but whether or not you're law-abiding.

On my afternoons off, I think about all this in relation to my job as a professional carer. Did I sit with Bob because I was paid to, or because I felt sorry for him (I did), or because his smile and the limp raising of his hand whenever I left his room made me feel good (it did)? And if it made me feel good, was the good feeling any different from the one enjoyed (it wasn't)?

Anyway, after Bob's body had been taken to the undertaker's Chapel of Rest, I entered his room for a PMA (post-mortem assessment), something that has to be done before the relatives arrive and take everything away. We make a sort of inventory, in case there are accusations of items going missing, though in Bob's case, and like all bereaved pets, I knew that Millie and Molly were a priority; I'd seen him feeding and watering them the day before, rather furtively I thought. Most of the valuable stuff, such as signet rings, silverware, heirloom crockery and odd amounts of cash, will have already been placed in the safe or removed immediately *peri-mortem* by the family. In Bob's room, this had included a pewter rose bowl presented to him by the National Association of Turf Accountants as a retirement gift; on its side was embedded a brass medallion bearing an inscribed racehorse with front legs sticking out together and back ones doing the same in the opposite direction – anatomically incorrect, as Bob pointed out to me in his own way, but possibly an easier job for the engraver. There were never any roses in it. I guessed that pewter rather than anything more expensive said something about his status; perhaps the NATA had a stash of them, ready to be doled out to its members at expiring time. While making my list, I heard squeaking and rustling coming from Millie's and Molly's cage (both were technically white but Millie had black markings resembling a brinded cow's).

On investigating, I was amazed to discover three mice.

As well as the girls huddled in a corner, there was a brown one, which, I swear, stopped what it was doing and, twitching its pale pink snout, looked up at me with what I can only describe as a proprietorial bearing. How to explain this? Bob had always been open with me. But this third character had clearly been smuggled in. No one else in the place had pet mice – perish the thought – so the interloper hadn't been passed along. God knows when the duo had become a trio. A month before maybe. I'd had no cause to check. Bob had once introduced me to a mischievous and dapper younger brother, with ruddy cheeks and drink always on the breath, and a line in bad jokes and innuendo. After a while, one forgot the pets were there. I fed the mice, filled their water dispenser and reported that I'd do something about them the next day.

I could see from the doorway the following morning that something was up. The straw which Bob added to supplement the sawdust had been gathered into one corner, and padding furiously on the exercise wheel was the stranger (I'd long sprayed the wheel with WD40 to stop it whimpering). I walked towards the cage, a clear-plastic construction with a metal base, still in the bay window where Bob had first placed it. Beyond, I could see low grey cloud stretching to the horizon in all directions, heavily laden with the rain which was sprinkling everywhere, signalling a dull prospect. 'In for the day', as Mrs Grimaldi used to put it, gazing forlorn through her own window at yet another reminder of finality and the loss of hope, another day with an empty visitors' car park. I often feel that Oakwood Lodge, or Merryvale, our outposts of 'eldercare' (I wonder if that's been picked up by the OED) satisfied my own glum tendencies. If we're feeling blue, we need the Blues, for confirmation that we are not alone and as an expression of the bleak port where we've suddenly docked without reason. When I told Mrs Grimaldi on one of our supermarket jaunts that we needed to return in time for a visit by the Musical Moments group, she just went on continuously browsing the shelves and said, 'I don't need cheering up.' She meant that the *Skaters' Waltz* would only interrupt her thoughts and, if they were nostalgic, never assuage any longing they might encourage. That's not speculation: I actually put it to her and she looked at me tearfully and nodded, like a long-interrogated crime suspect deciding it was time to confess.

Then I came upon a miracle.

Nestled in the straw ball she had prepared and unnoticed by me the day before was Millie, the Friesian one, suckling eight naked baby mice as their father, obviously their father, treadmilled his endless victory laps. There would be variety, I noticed. Three of the young had a brownish rash beneath the skin, two had Millie's dark patches, and the remainder were pure pink. All were suckling. What is mouse milk, for god's sake? I'd never gone back this far before. I mean in the history of anything, to the very beginning (the male's unseen nano-second of congress a few weeks before included). I noticed that Molly, slightly bloated, was to one side and breathing heavily. There was no chance that she, too, hadn't been got at by – what did I decide to call him? - Chester. A hairless gang of eight by Chester out of Millie. It's perhaps not unexpected that the miraculous should occlude everything, even the menial duties of a care home assistant. What had Bob been thinking of? I could just see him and his brother conspiring. To do what? And then the brother smuggling Chester in, and producing him from his jacket pocket gently, in the middle of a half-clenched fist. As they scrambled topsy-turvy for sustenance, the young looked to me like those plastic figurines one used to find in boxes of cornflakes, in this case the pawns of some extra-terrestrial at the bottom of a pecking order surmounted by flamboyant dinosaur-like creatures, half humanoid, half rasping animal, and breathing fire; cannon-fodder swarming at ground level in some inter-galactic conflict. As if to consolidate my imaginings, Molly then delivered herself of six slightly smaller progeny, each as far as I could make out in its own tiny plastic bag. This seemed to spur Chester on to more agitated locomotion inside the wheel.

Well, they had to go. The caretaker put them in a canvas bag and drowned them in a stream. It was just further confirmation of a sad world, and our slow receding from its sadnesses.

Remains

After Julie's death, her family arrived to take away her things.

She had a couple of laptops. I'd looked through them. What I called the professional one, with her notes and researches and her writings, copied before I handed over; the other, with its personal stuff including the extracts I've included here, I kept, intending after perusal and selection, to send it on as something I'd found after the event. If it's any sort of mitigation, I also kept some of her pens and the Stanley knife she used to sharpen her pencils and which I once thought of taking from her, as a person primitively fearful of the mentally sick and what they might do with a sharp object when prone to 'episodes'. Oh, and I 'retrieved' that book on Egypt I loaned her after finding it on our donation shelves.

At the time, I felt bad for being dishonest; but I don't feel so awful now when I think how unfriendly her people were when they came around, how unfriendly and short on feeling. I was Julie's partner after all; well, as good as. Had she told them something bad about me? Did they see us both as arty types, encouraging each other in the uncertainty and insecurity they had spent their lives avoiding? Her brother, the trainee chef, wasn't among them.

I suppose that when people do away with themselves, as my father used to describe it, there's always the suspicion that the cause of the disturbed mind referred to formally by the coroner lies somewhere else, with *someone* else.

I'd put most of her belongings on the table in neat piles and laid her clothes across the back of the settee; it wasn't much of a wardrobe but it was colourful and its items small. Emissaries for her parents, the relatives picked over them as though checking that everything was in order or deciding what could be usefully taken away and what left. (I repeat: I liked Mack and Dorothy; they were kind and amazingly tolerant of our unconventional lifestyle - well, it was unorthodox to them. We never discussed Julie's condition; I just assumed that they knew about it and confident that we could both cope. I wonder now if they were not ignorant of it altogether.) The silence of the emissaries, their deliberate movements, irked me. I felt that their attitude reflected what they thought of their dead relative as much as what might have been their low opinion of me. A last belated sense of belonging to Julie rippled through me because of that. They seemed polite, not commiserating; businesslike, not apologetic.

After Harold died, we'd accompanied Mary and Rachel and their spouses to Harold's house. They thanked us for visiting him during his illness and seemed a tad embarrassed. I never asked Harold how many times they'd been to see him. They were aware of his declining health. I think they'd been once. He never said anything.

A month later Joe rang me to say Harold's house was being advertised as a let. After a few weeks he said some-one had moved in: 'a nice young couple'. He also said the foxes had gone; they'd 'just vanished'.

I don't know what happened to Harold's stash of pictures. I did ask Mary and Rachel if they'd come across a possibly half-completed drawing of a tree; a tree shaped a bit like a giant umbrella. They didn't answer. Maybe they didn't get my letter. I didn't pester them. I would, though, like to have had one of Harold's paintings - not the chrysanthemums, but a coal-mining one. On the wall of my Manchester flat it might have become a talking-point, to go with the photos on the shelf of me and Harold; me, Harold and Julie; and Julie on her own, alone with her demons which she might have insisted were nothing of the sort. I wanted to get that group selfie of us printed from my mobile's Gallery, but it has vanished, along with Harold's foxes. The thought of those foxes sparked the hunter instinct encouraged in me by my *Ancestry* surfing, and far off in my imagination, as a spectre coming and going on the horizon, I spied David again, Harold's fugitive half-brother, martyr to a missionary spirit, and wondered after all if it were worth chasing him *post-mortem* as I'd pursued Harold in life. Perhaps not. But I decided to keep in touch with Mary and Rachel; that's if they wanted me to.

There are others in the Taylor family tree, of course, not mentioned in these notes. I imagine them perched silently on branches I haven't shaken yet, some low down and some at a great height but all sitting still and apprehensive, hoping I won't start clambering towards them.

*

One of the other things I copied from Julie's laptop was the following story, never published, and possibly a first draft. Julie always marked her unpublished work-in-progress with a WIP. I've removed it. She'd got it written, after all.

From Julie's Laptop – 5

Old Viktor

By Julie Redmayne

Dusk at the Ornskoldsvik Zoological Garden is accompanied not by exotic birdsong, the trumpeting of elephants or the baboon's high-pitched warning cry, but by silence.

If Raissa Branco was not the first to notice this, she was certainly the only one to think it worth mentioning. Young and eccentric, Vergara calls her. Raissa Branco and Jorge Vergara, two Brazilians adrift in Sweden. At six o'clock, Raissa is responsible for closing the two gates when the last visitors have gone and before the guards have made a final check.

She is walking now, at twilight, around the outdoor section of the aviary. Detention and freedom are matters often cited by Raissa at break times. Vergara, who looks after the seals and smells of fish, even when he deputises at the turnstiles for the cashier, Mrs Karin Beckstrand, has advised Raissa to lower her voice when mentioning such issues. Vergara has mixed feelings about Raissa's eccentricity. In many ways, she is the perfect companion he craves; in others, he feels he could not match her eagerness. But he admits that she has a relationship with the primates that none of the others can match. She talks to Viktor, the old gorilla, and he seems to listen. But Viktor's days are numbered: he has been throwing stones and other small objects at visitors and his fence has had to be raised.

As she strolls past a bamboo break, its leafy canes gently swaying, she can see Viktor imprisoned fifty yards to her left, sitting alone in that awkward way he has developed with age. In the gloaming, he is following her progress to the gates. He now has a stoop which makes his arms and knuckles and their use as walking aids look clumsy. Raissa has noticed that he sits and stares at the ground more and more. She thinks he is meditating. About what? Vergara asked, immediately regretting the slight contempt that edged his question.

As she starts up the incline beside a flamingo pool littered with the day's discarded drink cans and wrappers, Raissa can see Mrs Beckstrand in her booth of light up ahead. She wonders if the resentful Mrs Beckstrand alone epitomises the flaws of the Ornskoldsvik Zoological Garden more than old Viktor or the hush and stillness that settles on the place at nightfall like a curfew. The source of the cashier's bitterness is not known. Mrs Beckstrand continues her oblivious accounting, a cigarette between her teeth, its smoke stinging her eyes. She turns tearfully to acknowledge Raissa's arrival.

Mrs Beckstrand wears a stippled rubber cap on her right thumb as an aid to counting banknotes. A week ago, when the turnstiles had quietened for a while, she called to Raissa and waved her over. In place of her clipped pleasantries, she said: 'Raissa, I want to ask you something.'

Raissa planted her elbows outside the Perspex screen with its talk-through disc and propped her chin on her hands.

Mrs Beckstrand continued: 'Do you have any family, Raissa, anyone close?'

It was a strange question, Raissa thought, uttered as someone might who wanted to borrow something. 'Why do you ask?'

Mrs Beckstrand did not like her inquiries answered with a further question and said: 'Well, it's just that...oh, nothing. It doesn't matter.'

'No, I meant...'

'Honestly, it doesn't matter.' This said with peevish emphasis.

Mrs Beckstrand waved her hand rapidly in front of her face to delete the exchange, just as a crowd of schoolchildren were approaching the entrance. Raissa noticed that she also placed her hand over her mouth as someone would who was stifling a rare and embarrassing sob.

This time, Mrs Beckstrand is mouthing silently as she counts, so Raissa goes ahead and locks up. Mrs Beckstrand leaves at the bottom gate each night. Raissa closes that gate too before everything is double-locked by Security. Mrs Beckstrand doesn't see Raissa hold out her arms and look around her, smiling knowingly at the absence of roars and cries.

Suddenly, Vergara appears from behind a hedge.

'I thought you'd gone,' Raissa says, startled.

He jerks his thumb towards the ticket-office and says: 'I'm waiting to see Mrs B. Spot of bother with her fancy man. She told me about it on the bus last night.'

Raissa cannot resist an image of Vergara waiting - 'skulking' presents itself - across the road in Fabriksgaten for Mrs

Beckstrand to emerge after work. Vergara likes the movies and Raissa is half-expecting him to ask her out. Without looking at him, she says, 'Fancy man? What do you mean, "fancy man"?'

Vergara says, 'Good god, Rais. Don't you know anything? She's been with him for years. Smart fella, something to do with shipping. Works all hours and travels abroad. Anyway, he's gone - walked out, just like that.'

'Perhaps that's what she wanted to tell me the other day,' Raissa muses out loud. 'She took me by surprise. Inside her booth. I was wary.'

Vergara looks confused.

'You know,' she adds. 'Like something in a cage, changing its tack, trying to deceive you.'

Vergara continues on his way, waving without looking at her.

Sometimes on her evening circuit in winter, the silence, or her perception of it, has for Raissa a minatory character, as though the animals are ganging up. In this eerie atmosphere, she wonders if Mrs Beckstrand has contributed to her estrangement, has done something to cause it (or not done something that would have prevented it). Poor Mrs Beckstrand: her lover has flown.

Raissa looks back and sees Vergara standing in silhouette ten yards from Mrs Beckstrand's booth. He does not move. His gaze is fixed on the woman wrapping cylinders of notes in elastic bands (not many these days, to be sure), blinded in one eye by cigarette smoke. He knows Mrs Beckstrand cannot see him while she is drowned in her pool of light. Then he is inside the booth and they are arguing: at least, their faces are close together and Vergara's arms are outspread. Raissa wonders if Vergara is telling Mrs Beckstrand to pull herself together or if he has made an ill-judged attempt to replace the 'fancy man' in her affections.

Minutes later, Raissa is standing by a bench, watching old Viktor. Then she hears footsteps. It is Mrs Beckstrand on her way home.

'So Jorge has told you,' the cashier says, coming to a stop.

Mrs Beckstrand is always dressed smartly. Raissa is reminded of someone who can be easily transformed into a beauty, despite age. Under Mrs Beckstrand's arm is a scuffed leather briefcase.

'I'm sorry, Mrs Beckstrand. I really am.'

'Ah, well. These things happen.' She is clutching the briefcase to her breast as possession, comfort, shield. 'Raissa, do you mind if I say something?'

Raissa senses what is coming.

'Don't discourage him,' Mrs Beckstrand says. 'Jorge. He's a shy one really. Give him hope. You two are of a mind when it comes to animals. And he is a looker, you know.'

The advice-seeker offers advice! Raissa understands. Vergara's arm-waving was despair (*Can't you have a word with her, Karin?* he probably said. *I think she'll refuse me. I don't want her to worry herself about having to say no.*)

'I'll see,' Raissa says, mystified, with a non-committal look sideways.

Mrs Beckstrand sniffs heavily, an act of relief, finality. If she has shed tears, there will be no more. 'Goodnight, Raissa,' she says. 'Remember what I said.'

Raissa watches Mrs Beckstrand step elegantly through the door built into the heavy main gate. She imagines her at the kerb, waiting to cross busy Fabriksgaten. For some reason, she also thinks of a man on the deck of a ship pulling away from shore in the moonlight, a man with a new destination, the wind in his hair.

Old Viktor displaces her interest in these human foibles. She walks slowly towards his compound in the half-light. She treads softly and seats herself on another bench, half in shadow, and watches him. Something he does makes her slide further along the bench, out of sight beneath a willow's overhang. There is a sudden pounding in her chest. She thinks Viktor must hear it and detect her presence. But Viktor is absorbed in something new, something she has never seen before. He is picking up objects as he often does and after sniffing them and discarding what he doesn't need, he is holding them in his hand. Each time he does so, he looks over his shoulder, as if to make sure he is not being watched. She then realises that what he throws away is edible. He is smelling to reject the tasty and soft-centred. She sits forward, intrigued, for she believes that what Viktor is grasping in his hand, retaining, might be missiles, the bits and bobs that land on the path in daytime to the amusement of onlookers, some of whom toss them back, a practice abhorred by the Ornskoldsvik management. And he is seeking not reproachful interlopers but victims, the act a reflex of another one that has taken him, taken his brain, by surprise and confounded its usual implication. *He's collecting!*

Viktor begins moving about in his painful way, the objects still in his hand.

Raissa hears someone knocking at the side door. The security man on his rounds hears it too. Raissa watches. Mrs Beckstrand has returned. She has her back to Raissa. She sounds hysterical.

As Raissa strains to hear what Mrs Beckstrand is saying, she is surprised by a voice behind her. It is Vergara again.

'Rais,' he says, half-whispering.

'Jorge! What on earth are you playing at?'

He steps forward and sits down, nervously looking towards the bottom exit.

'I need to speak to you,' he says. 'Isn't that Mrs Beckstrand...what is she doing?...I thought...'

'I thought you'd gone too.'

'I stayed behind, to speak...Oh God, she's coming this way...to look for me...'

'Look for you? Why would she want to do that?'

'She's suddenly taken against me for some reason. I don't know. I was supposed to meet her in Fabriksgaten...at the Florestan...'

Raissa smiles at these odd subterfuges. Vergara excuses himself, explaining that he is returning to their hut. Mrs Beckstrand begins making her way towards them, up a gentle slope. Seconds later, she passes in front of Raissa about ten yards away, with stomp-like tread, head lowered. She is breathless yet resolute. Thinking everything is to do with Mrs Beckstrand's truncated love life, Raissa focuses once more on old Viktor, who is moving around intermittently, like a levered boulder.

Viktor now appears to have two fistfuls of small objects. He squats and examines them. He wipes his nose with the back of his wrist. He lumbers forward again towards his play-place, an area laid with bark chips and overhung with tyres attached to ropes. Walking with difficulty and pain, he suddenly stops before a large stone and drops the objects he is holding in his left hand. One hand thus freed, he lifts the stone and secretes beneath it the contents of his right hand, followed by the rest of his collection, allowing the stone to fall carefully - there is no other word - into place. Raissa jumps to her feet and strides into the open. Her heart, her imprisoned heart, is banging about inside her ribcage. She looks about her, seeking the perpetrator of this illusion, this trick played on a lone, unsuspecting woman. *He is saving them up!* she says to herself. *He is storing his ammunition for tomorrow!*

But other voices displace her phantom exclamations. Old Viktor hears them too. They belong to Vergara and Mrs Beckstrand, the lovers, who are coming towards her along the path. She makes no effort to hide again.

'You promised me you'd be there,' Mrs Beckstrand is saying.

'I had to speak...'

'Jorge Vergara, you are a coward. I waited. What were you thinking of?

They pass Raissa, almost without noticing her. Raissa can see the security man fanning out the contents of his key-ring like a card sharp and wonders if she has it all wrong and that it is Mrs Beckstrand who desires the embraces of Vergara but is tempered by her recent loss into believing her instincts eternally ill-fated. It would explain a lot of things: Vergara's solicitude towards her (to make Mrs Beckstrand jealous enough to declare herself openly); Mrs Beckstrand's anger (at her divided self); the *contretemps* in the booth (Vergara imploring Mrs Beckstrand to make up her mind); Mrs Beckstrand's advice to Raissa to encourage Vergara's designs (an attempt to resolve matters in her distraught and tragic favour); and then Vergara's staying behind to speak (wanting her, Raissa's, advice, another woman's advice, about how to respond to fickle romance). As she thinks about these possible explanations, watching Vergara and Mrs Beckstrand step through the little door on to Fabriksgaten, something lands at her feet, bouncing once. It is a small pebble. She picks it up and squeezes it in her palm. In the distance, Viktor stares at her from millennia past, his eyes blinking.

*

These events took place in the Autumn, just before leaf-fall. By the following Spring, Mrs Beckstrand was dead: cancer of the lung with secondaries. The business with Vergara had been sorted. He'd been taking money from the till over a long period while deputising for her, as she suspected, but her leniency and tact had been extended to the moment of his confession, and he gave in his notice.

The evening Mrs Beckstrand waited in the Café Florestan to confront Vergara after work and talk about his fall from grace was when she knew there was something wrong with her. It wasn't just that she'd been left on her own or that she'd repaid some money herself and buried the other losses in the accounts. The embarrassment of having to cross Fabriksgaten, ring the security bell, grasp the iron knocker in desperation when no one came, and walk past that delinquent old gorilla to have it out with Vergara made her overwhelmingly tired. If only Raissa Branco had not left so soon after Vergara. Raissa - so many questions she even answered you with one; innocent Raissa, as yet without insight or knowledge, but the perfect antidote to Vergara's foolishness and a potential foil to its slide into cupidity. She tried to bring them together but none of her strategies had worked. Raissa left after the stupid gorilla was put down because of old age, its internal agonies and its outer manifestations of the unacceptable. Vergara always said Raissa had a way with Viktor, whatever that had meant. They've all gone; but the Ornskoldsvik Zoological Garden still struggles along without them.

Timely Meditation

Millions upon millions in generation after generation don't know or don't want to know. Others know but wish they didn't and hide their knowledge as a dog buries a bone or a squirrel its acorn. (Actually, I've never seen a dog bury a bone, and a squirrel hiding an acorn only on the telly.) It doesn't matter if the bone is never rediscovered. For the dog and squirrel, though, there must have been a moment of contentment at the prospect of enjoying it and, in burial or hoarding, a confusion of joy deferred. The truth must be like that - a marvellous thing, a discovery, something so precious that the pleasure of it cannot be faced and must be put by for a brighter day. This is how I think about it, at the same time knowing that the comparison is as confused, though not in a bothersome way, as the buzzing brain of a dog and a squirrel, and that the truth can be unpalatable - bitter, as they say - and secreting it, making a secret of it, is a means of not facing up to it, hoping it will be forgotten, never to be found again. The truth is buried because that's a way of getting rid of it: the disposal of the truth; springtime for its own sake, not dependent on finally confronting an experience intended to see you through into the abundant seasons, the seasons of abundance.

To be honest, Harold had been going on a bit that time on the cliff top - about not being able to see Dieppe. And I was growing angry at how Julie's parallel course was running ahead of me, something indicated literally at that point as she sauntered in front with Ethel on her outside. I couldn't really believe what I saw happen, if it did happen, if it was - is - the truth. Even if it didn't actually happen and I imagined it or thought of it as something that might have happened in the circumstances or that my desire to have not wanted it to happen was as much the truth as anything that did, beyond my state of mind, my desire to want everything to turn out for the best - for Julie as much as for Harold. So yes, I saw it, was certain I saw something but I hid the memory in the ground, under the leaves, so that no one at the inquest, no one enquiring, could make anything of what, in a manner of speaking, wasn't there, that didn't belong in the realm of a cold, factual, sensible investigation. There was a death; for most, that's usually more than enough. What I saw or didn't see, having nothing incontestable about it, could make no contribution. The truth uncovered by scrutiny may leave more important, irrelevant truths buried. An act of burial does not guarantee an act of retrieval. If a dog or a squirrel could be said to know anything, they might know that but they know nothing so they don't.

The truth, like a miniature golden hare, an ornament mischievously concealed, may lie undiscovered forever. While Harold was looking in vain for Dieppe, did I see it: from Julie a distinct push, a nudge, and Ethel losing her balance and falling and starting to roll, and rolling and starting to slide and sliding to her death? Did I?

John Webster & the Sacred Necropolis

The last act of Webster's *The Duchess of Malfi* presents a series of deaths: the Cardinal kills his mistress, Ferdinand develops lycanthropy (the mythical transformation of a person into a wolf) and Bosola, struck too late with remorse, vows to avenge the Duchess. Intending to protect Antonio, he accidentally kills him. Bosola stabs the Cardinal and Ferdinand but is wounded and also dies. Of the whole family, only the eldest son of the Duchess and Antonio remains alive. I know; I've been there and heard the boards creak as each falls.

An American critic, Morris F Messager, said *The Duchess of Malfi* was about the aggression and domination of the male. It centred on violence and brutality. If it were not for human cunning and lone female ambition, he said, we could be witnessing 'the encircling manoeuvres' of animals. It wasn't far removed. (I got that from a theatre programme, *the* theatre programme.)

The book on ancient Egypt I pilfered from our donation shelves and gave to Julie, and which I retrieved with her laptops like someone re-united with his lost property, has a section on animal mummification. Animals and birds were mummified and placed in huge catacombs at Saqqara, twenty miles south of Cairo; there were sometimes up to one million mummified animal remains. Such mummies were found in all parts of the country and a wide range of animals was embalmed.

The animal mummies of Egypt, of course, were different in significance from the results of Charles Lovell Darling's amateur taxidermy and those of whoever stuffed Byron's otter (if it really did belong to Byron). But the reasons why the Egyptians preserved animals - to send beloved pets towards an afterlife; to provide food for humans in that same afterlife; to supply votive offerings to a god; *and because some were seen as physical manifestations of a worshipped deity* (my italics) - suggest similarities. There's a spiritual connection. A stuffed polecat would be all Ethel Chrimes's Soul Travellers had to remind them that where there was now packed straw was once the habitation of nothing less than the Holy Ghost; though I never understood why they needed reminding when they were surrounded by living examples all the time. Maybe it was because they declined to speculate on why their God, in the form of said Holy Spirit, chose to reside within not only a budgerigar but also a wasp and a giraffe, and all other creatures not slaves to their bidding and sometimes dangerous when poked.

However much we may think their beliefs absurd, Ethel and all the other members of the West Sussex Convention of Soul Travel Experiences died, or will die, happy in their certainties or 'uncertainties' or even 'delusions' as we who will die sad and not wanting to die are obliged to call them. (I really never knew if Harold the churchgoer was comforted by his faith or if 'convention' was a grandiose term that covered an always small gathering, a cult.) When dressed as Ferdinand, the Duke of Calabria and brother to the Duchess, I am as certain of being he and the words he speaks as I am of the period in which he lives, confirmed moment by moment by the fake Jacobean hose that clings to me and makes me itch and sweat, never believing that before long my pretence will be exposed and I will be, for an hour or two, reduced to nothing of consequence. Believe me, I've been there; it's a savage actorly demotion, equivalent to a fall. I don't think I've mentioned till now (Julie did) that the name of the lead horse I played in *Equus* was Nugget; to the boy, Alan Strang, who blinded those horses, Nugget was Equus, the horse god.

*

Every Thursday, the Forest weekly newspapers arrive. They each aspire to being complete seven-day worlds, different only in events from the ones that preceded them and the ones that will follow, but always with beginnings, middles and ends. But they are no more complete than the 'world' of Merryvale Community House - Oakwood - with its arrivals and departures, or the 'worlds' of Robert Berridge, Harold Taylor and Julie Williams (to reduce her to her former self; a minor fall). I read them from cover to cover: livestock markets, gymkhanas, fawning and meaningless reviews of *See How They Run* ('The comic timing was perfect; Arthur Jones was superb as Lance-corporal Winton'), reports of St Briavels WI meetings, unattended damp in council houses - and the following incident, about another self-styled world; a captive world within a captive world, as it were.

Local Rag

Colony of Leaf Cutter Ants in Shocking Demise

(from the *Coleford & Staunton Gazette*)

A FREAK accident at a leading conservation attraction in Gloucestershire has killed off the UK's biggest colony of leaf cutter ants.
Rats are believed to have chewed overnight through wiring in the colony's display room at Bug World, near Coleford in the Forest of Dean. Most of the ants were electrocuted or died when the temperature dropped or when they fought among themselves in a state of shock.
The thriving colony, estimated at 350,000, dwindled to almost zero and the Queen ant was among the casualties. It meant that no more eggs were laid.
'They had no reason for living,' said a tearful Miranda Stinchcomb, Bug World's Press and Marketing officer. 'Now, they are having to be replaced by an ant specialist who has gone to a rainforest in Trinidad to find new ants and another Queen.
'This has never happened before. Obviously, we are going to address this again. We have commissioned Andy Williamson from Zoologica International to find and bring us back a new Queen leaf cutter ant and colony. Andy works

with local farmers and pays them not to kill the ant colonies so he can collect them before the planting season, when they otherwise would be exterminated to make way for crops.'
Ms Stinchcomb added: 'It is a fascinating scheme involving local farming communities, hunting for the Queen through huge underground chambers, extracting the ants' fungus gardens, getting seriously bitten, and transporting around 10,000 ants back on a plane, after which they will hopefully settle and breed and flourish in a new home created for them.'
She said the ants themselves were pretty strong. 'In the rainforests, when the native people sustain a wound, they use leaf cutter ants to tear away the damaged flesh to avoid infection.'
The wildlife trust running Bug World would wait for the new colony to establish itself before deciding on the attraction's future, she added. Power supplies to the whole site had to be investigated and where necessary replaced. Last year there were plans to expand the facility.

FACT CHECKER
* LEAF cutter ants don't eat the leaf pieces they cut and carry. They're taken into underground chambers and mixed with ant poo and saliva. A fungus grows on this mixture and the colony feeds off that.
* IN HIGH season Bug World attracts up to 1,000 visitors a week. The ant colony is its most popular feature.
* LOSSES while Bug World is temporarily closed for complete re-wiring could reach £300,000.
* BUG WORLD's ants could not survive in the UK's outdoor temperatures.
* ZOOLOGICA International was involved in a scheme to allow visitors into cages holding marmosets at a Midlands Zoo but the scheme

was abandoned when a child was bitten, though not seriously.

*

Leaf Cutter Ant Colony Loves New Home

(from the *Coleford & Staunton Gazette*)

A COLONY of leaf cutter ants imported from Trinidad to replace one which perished in ant mayhem at a Gloucestershire conservation attraction has quickly established itself at its new home.

Staff at Bug World near Coleford were devastated when rats chewed through the power cable supplying light and heat to their 'Cuttery', killing the egg-laying Queen and thousands of leaf cutters. With the Queen dead, those remaining ants not electrocuted or expired from lack of warmth had no purpose and attacked each other.

Bug World Press and Marketing officer Miranda Stinchcomb estimated the number of dead ants to have been in the hundreds of thousands. 'It was like a battlefield,' she said. 'One or two survived and kept cutting leaves and transporting them along the ropes we've set up horizontally at a height of seven feet. They struggled for a few days, then went down into their chambers and never came up. The colony was wiped out.'

Ms Stinchcomb said Andy Williamson of Zoologica International had been sent to the West Indies to find a new colony of leaf cutters.

Andy told a *Gazette* reporter that the egg-laying Queen was what made the ants cut leaves and make food.

'It's sort of why they do what they do,' he explained. 'The Queen's a powerful lady. But once the ants become derailed, they lose their direction and see other ants as a threat and attack them, just because they are there and in the way, really - of exactly what, they're not certain. They were designed to cut leaves, transport them to their chambers and use them to create food. They are insect farmers.'
Ms Stinchcomb explained the new colony had taken time to bed in but was now active.
'The old leaf tank is still there but we Hoovered up all the dead ants and replaced the soil tank with new dirt or very fine imported leaf mould. Many of the dead ants were strung out along the ropes connecting the two tanks or had fallen on to the Cuttery floor, a lot of them joined together where they'd seized each other with their incredible jaws in fights to the death. It was as though they'd been frozen in the middle of a game.
'Nothing happened at first but we stayed up late with Andy two days after we'd introduced the new colony and kept an eye on the leaf tank and the ropes above our heads. Work experience trainee Shane Limbrick saw them first, just a pair, like two little ships with green sails setting out on a long sea journey, soon followed by the others.'
A spokesperson for Forest of Dean Council said the electrical wiring at Bug World 'had left a lot to be desired' and had been checked as a health and safety precaution and replaced. Rat infestation had also been dealt with. The attraction, which saw 50,000 punters through its turnstiles last year, plans to open a locust compound.

* ANTidote Andy! Andy Williamson said he was always bitten when looking for a Queen leaf

cutter but now took an antidote drug. 'I try not to disturb them too much,' he admitted. 'But all they see is this black gloved hand poking about in their affairs. It must seem like Armageddon. No wonder they get angry!'

Dear Editor...

In your report about the new colony of leaf-cutter ants which has replaced the one destroyed by electrocution and other causes at Bug World, near Coleford, you quote Andy Williamson of Zoologica International as stating that such ants are 'designed' to be insect 'farmers', and that any disturbance of their colonies in the wild must 'seem like Armageddon'.
Mr Williamson is entitled to his opinion and maybe (despite what I assume is his status as a scientist) he is a religious person who believes in a world created and ordered by a Divine Being, and for him to discover through human curiosity. For such a person, that world no longer appears cruel and haphazard but meaningful, however difficult it is to understand horror and unfairness as anything other than what happens when the dice is carelessly thrown.
That industrious insects who presumably know neither the source of their industry, nor what it is for, nor what any catastrophe ahead of it might be 'like', should have a knowledge of explanations that might indicate otherwise seems so far-fetched as to be ludicrous.
The sight of two leaf-cutter ants setting out again on their time-honoured immemorial trail and observed as resembling two little ships with green sails at the start of a long voyage tells us more about ourselves than about an insect's determination or foresight, which don't consciously exist. For sure, they have no inkling

of the upheaval that preceded them or the dangers ahead. They have no sense of tragedy. Were we not all like them! As the blinded Gloucester says in Shakespeare's *King Lear*, Act 4, Scene 1, merely distinguishing between one kind of god and another:

'I'th'last night's storm I such a fellow saw,
Which made me think a man a worm. My son
Came then into my mind, and yet my mind
Was then scarce friends with him. I have
heard more since.
As flies to wanton boys are we to th'gods;
They kill us for their sport.'

Yours sincerely,
Francis Taylor,
Merryvale Community House,
Nr Staunton, Forest of Dean.

*

My letter was not published.

But, dear editor, for my own benefit, I'll add this to the letter you zapped from your screen, no doubt with a titter: the Believers are sometimes right. St Paul, for example, who said we have only an imperfect vision of what passes before us but at the end of time, all will be made clear. Won't the end of time, though, be not in front of us but behind, as we swoon into a pyramid of Quality Street at Morrison's, or, if a rat, start gnawing innocently at an electrical cable?

Sometimes at night, I cover my head with the mask I liberated from the props department at the end of the *Equus* run, to re-live a time ended by the lunge of a dumb pig. I see even more darkly through the glass. What are these shadows approaching my stable, what the low Irish whispers, the Dutch Courage smoke on the breath? Are these shades the people I never knew, never got to know, couldn't get to know - horse-stealer, lover, friend, religious nut (or not), new-found relative, all with most of their memories squirrelled away? Am I low animal life, wanton in my suppressed wildness, taunted by what I never understood or would never understand? What's that myriad buzzing and biting around my eyes and my arse? I shake my head to lose it but it springs back like a throw of tiny magnets. About my body too. I twitch to swish the tail I don't possess. But I am an actor; I am acting magnificent horse, my magnificence in the knowing minds of others, my own not knowing the thing that kills me for someone else's sport, blinds me and my fellows with a spike; and I hear the drone of bees, the fast-beating wings of souls travelling, the rosy sow abed and grunting for the thing that won't come because it's not there.

I am man and I am horse deity. Equus. Not knowing the end is coming and knowing only too well that it is.

*

My phone rumbles. Out of foreign parts emerges the latest video clip from Mona Strange, who's on tour: a smiling rhinoceros. *Can't you C?* she texts. *It's a smile. In a daydream. A rhino reverie.*

I remove the mask. My head lolls forward. My hair collapses on to my brow a second later and I brush it back, using my left hand fingers as a comb. It always made Julie smile, and a smile from Julie was priceless. Who was it said that a smile – or the memory of a smile – was the great yea-sayer; the cheeky celebration of triumph over misfortune; the light that would forever elude the enveloping dark, the dark of the big pit?

Postscripts

So little cause for carolings
Of such ecstatic sound
Was written on terrestrial things
Afar or nigh around,
That I could think there trembled through
His happy good-night air
Some blessed Hope, whereof he knew
And I was unaware

From *The Darkling Thrush*, by Thomas Hardy

It's easy to make a character move and look differently when it's an animal. But how can you make your character's movements and gestures interesting and unique when they're 'just' a student, businessperson, townsperson, or other generic human being? Use your animal instinct – try thinking of your character as an animal.

Kerry Hishon - actor, stage director and writer, quoted on the *Theatrefolk* website, January 6 2018

Acknowledgements

Thanks to Penny Reeves at Saron Publishers for taking on and skilfully editing this book when it was not a novel in the traditional sense but a story told in a different way. Hers is the sort of brave decision one has come to expect from independent book publishers.

Without the understanding of my wife, Ann, in not minding either the inordinate amount of time I spend at the PC or my daydreaming about what I'm going to write on it, I'd never get anything done. As a historian engaged in family history, she also inspired the starting point of *Notes From the Superhorse Stable.*

My confidence as a writer would be diminished were it not for the editors of both printed and digital journals here and abroad who continue to publish my work.

Julie's *Old Viktor* is a version of *Old Roffe*, a story of mine which appeared first in *The Lonely Crowd* magazine and then in my collection *Who Killed Emil Kreisler?* published by Cultured Llama.

I'd created a draft design for the cover of *Notes From the Superhorse Stable* before handing the task to my talented nephew, Matt Jarrett, who wanted to take a stab at it. His effort outclassed mine in every particular and is the one we chose without hesitation.

Abergavenny, 2022

Printed in Great Britain
by Amazon

80892211R00251